INCA

INCA

THE SCARLET FRINGE

Suzanne Allés Blom

A TOM DOHERTY ASSOCIATES BOOK

NEW YORK

INCA: THE SCARLET FRINGE

Copyright © 2000 by Suzanne Allés Blom

Map copyright © 2000 by Emory L. Churness

A Forge Book
Published by Tom Doherty Associates, LLC
175 Fifth Avenue
New York, NY 10010

www.tor.com

Forge® is a registered trademark of
Tom Doherty Associates, LLC.

Library of Congress Cataloging-in-Publication Data
Blom, Suzanne Allés.
    Inca : the scarlet fringe / Suzanne Allés Blom.— 1st ed.
        p. cm
    "A Tom Doherty Associates book."
    ISBN 0-312-87434-0
    1. Atahualpa, d. 1533—Fiction. 2. Peru—History—Conquest, 1522-1548—Fiction. 3. Incas—Fiction. I. Title.
PS3552.L6362 I53 2000
813'.6—dc21

00-031813

First Edition: October 2000

Printed in the United States of America

0 9 8 7 6 5 4 3 2 1

Dedicated to the hundreds of people who gave me advice when something they said brought forth eager questions. To the sailors, horse lovers, anthropologists, librarians, strategists, chemists, and all the rest: even when I did not follow your advice, your comments made this book better.

PREFACE

This novel is alternate history. The 1998 *World Almanac* has this to say about the conquest of the Inca Empire: "A civil war had weakened the empire when Francisco Pizarro, Spanish conquistador, began raiding Peru for its wealth, 1532. In 1533 he seized the ruling Inca, Atahualpa, filled a room with gold as a ransom, then executed him and enslaved the natives."

I have always been irritated with this sequence of events and its result. This narrative is a thought experiment about what might have happened if one event changed slightly. Until the celebration of Majestic Festival just before the first chapter begins, events in the Inca empire happen as they actually occurred. In chapter headings, I tell how actual history diverges from the events in the novel. As the story progresses, a new world unfolds.

Because this story is told from the viewpoint of the Inca empire's people, all names are given their meanings as their bearers would expect. Atahualpa is Exemplary Fortune.

Named Characters in Their Order of Introduction

Exemplary Fortune, a prince of the Four Quarters
Young Majesty, the Unique Inca, the emperor of the Four Quarters
Flowerbud, Exemplary Fortune's friend, an Inca
Owl Pattern, Exemplary Fortune's mother, a Kitu Dove
Royal Reckoner, Young Majesty's chief advisor
World Reverser, Young Majesty's grandfather, a former emperor
Royal Reckoning Inca, Young Majesty's father, a former emperor
Shrewdness, a commander under Young Majesty, an Inca
Tobacco, Young Majesty's chief of turn-workers, an Inca
Llakun Root, an Inca courtier
Macaw, chief of the Matron tribe in the city of Recognition
Thorniest, a military commander under Young Majesty, a Kitu Dove
Esteemed Egg, one of Exemplary Fortune's wives, an Inca
Qantu Flower, one of Exemplary Fortune's wives, an Inca
Skein Reckoner, one of Exemplary Fortune's wives, a Wind-Moon
Chatterer, Exemplary Fortune's oldest son
Select Seed, captain of the Inca fortress in Recognition, an Inca
Bright Rainbow, Young Majesty's chosen heir
Hummingbird, a Matron youth
Fishscale, Hummingbird's father
Happy Speaker, a prince of the Four Quarters
Molle Tree, Hummingbird's friend, a Matron
Whence Grasping, an Inca courtier
Ginez, a stranger
Tamed Ocelot, a stranger
Majestic Headband, the First Unique Inca

Guanaco, a tampu-keeper, a Lynx Lake
Whence Happiness, Young Majesty's first queen
Cable, a prince of the Four Quarters
Chosen Creator, Young Majesty's second queen
Magnanimous Strength, the governor of Granary Province, an Inca
Young Fox, one of Macaw's advisors, a Matron
Francisco Pizarro, a Spanish commander
Greek, one of Francisco Pizarro's associates
Adobe, a Matron
Seaweed, a Taciturn
Muyushell, a Taciturn
Mother Egg, Young Majesty's third queen
Beautiful Plowridge, a prince of the Four Quarters
Reckoning Sadness, a prince of the Four Quarters
Beseeching Cotton, a prince of the Four Quarters
Whence Reckoning, a prince of the Four Quarters
Exemplary Hawk, a prince of the Four Quarters
Excellent Royalty, an Inca courtier
Inca Fox, a military commander, an Inca
Shrewd Reckoner, the Divine Speaker
Majestic Quinoa, an Inca courtier
Splinter, an Inca military captain
Molle, a Flamingo Lake ten-captain
Grasshopper, one of Exemplary Fortune's wives, a Warm Valley
Coca Neighbor, one of Exemplary Fortune's wives, a Garland
Pure Joy, one of Exemplary Fortune's wives, a Black Loincloth
Puku Dove, one of Exemplary Fortune's wives, a Meadow
Martin, a Taciturn
Diego Almagro, Francisco Pizarro's partner
Anaconda, a Pollen captain
Highest Strength, a governor of Completion Province, an Inca
Black Hawk, a Ten colonist
Beautiful Orchid, a Pollen administrator

Cornstalk, a Pollen ten-captain
Chalomongo, a Pichunche
Cui, son of an Inca father and a Pichunche mother, an Inca
Michalongo, Chalomongo's grandson
Tolacache, a Pichunche
Iwagante, a Pichunche
Potato Flower, an Inca speaker
Ear-Chopper Eagle, a Ten commander
Majestic Reckoner, an Inca commander
King Carlos, the Spanish king
Gonzalo Pizarro, a brother of Francisco Pizarro
Juan Pizarro, a brother of Francisco Pizarro
Hernando Pizarro, a brother of Francisco Pizarro
Mad Queen Juana, the Spanish queen
Oca, a Ten
Red Deer, one of Exemplary Fortune's wives
Shrine Tree, a Pollen captain
Cristobal de Mena, a Spanish captain
Hernando de Aldana, a Spaniard
Sebastian de Benalcazar, a Spanish captain
Diego of Trujillo, a Spaniard
Far-Spear, a Pormoco captain
Siskin, a Ten turn-warrior
Hernando de Soto, a Spanish captain
Vicente de Valverde, a Spanish friar
Inca Garden, an Inca courtier
Fecund Dove, one of Cable's wives, an Inca
Alder Tree, an Inca captain

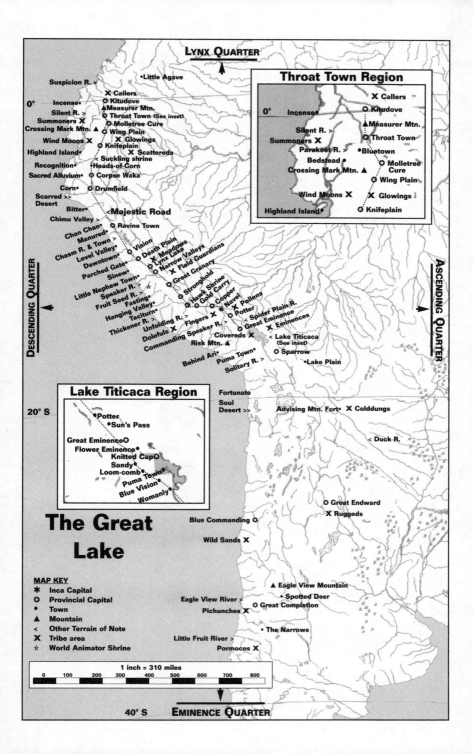

1

THIRTY-FOURTH YEAR OF YOUNG MAJESTY'S REIGN
MAJESTIC FESTIVAL MONTH

In actual history, after the Unique Inca Young Majesty finished
his conquests, he did not leave the city of Kitu Dove again before
he died. He, and Exemplary Fortune with him, stayed in the far
north.

A s Exemplary Fortune stepped out of the Sun temple at Throat
Town, the thatched roofs across the plaza struck his eyes with
a golden light. The thatch mirrored the blazing Sun. When Exemplary Fortune had walked inside, a nourishing rain had been
falling. He had not known the Sun had chosen to confirm the
speaker's foreboding so dramatically. He raised his eyes as high as
he could toward the deity who was shining with such unseasonable
brightness and said a silent prayer for understanding and for the
Unique Inca's well-being.

A llama caravan, framed by dark stone buildings under the
golden roofs, walked into the plaza from the south. Though Exemplary Fortune could not see into the packs they carried, he knew the
convoy brought supplies for the Unique Inca and his scant retinue.
He wanted to believe this procession was an answer to his prayer,
but none of these llamas were a Sun-chosen white. Besides, this row
of placid pack animals was itself a sign of disorder. Always before,
whenever the Unique Inca traveled, everything he could possibly

want had already been redistributed to the provincial capitals and tampus where he would stay. Always before, wherever the Unique Inca went, hundreds of courtiers and thousands of turn-servants stood ready to serve his every need and the every need of the empire.

Always before, the Unique Inca, Exemplary Fortune's father, had spoken his intentions beforehand and set out in a timely and orderly fashion. This time, the Unique Inca, Young Majesty, the embodiment of the empire and the guardian of its health and order, had left the city of Kitu Dove in the middle of Majestic Festival's celebration. His sudden and unexpected departure had torn the fabric of the ceremonies that welcomed the yearly tribute from the provinces and numbered the Four Quarters' people. Those ceremonies should have shown the Sun, the empire's guardian, how well the Four Quarters was ordered, reinforcing people's prayers for rain in the preceding months. It would not be surprising if the Sun had become upset with the Unique Inca, His chosen child. And yet, it seemed that the Sun's own omens had prompted Young Majesty's departure.

Four days ago at noon, the fourth day of Majestic Festival, thousands of people had been gathered in Kitu Dove's plaza to hear the Divine Speaker's assessment of the coming year. After the Divine Speaker had sacrificed the chosen llama on the ceremonial platform in the plaza's center, he had stiffened noticeably and said, "This llama does not presage a fruitful year. We will sacrifice another." The crowd, as always awaiting a favorable omen, had stirred a little but stayed confident until the second and third llamas' auguries were as ominous as the first. The Divine Speaker had then said, "The Sun has decreed that this year will bring drought and poor harvests to the Four Quarters." The crowd had begun to wail dolefully, letting the Sun know their sorrow, still hoping He would relent upon hearing their cries.

No one had expected the Unique Inca to rise from his place next to the speakers on the platform, walk through the crowds, and out of the plaza. He had gathered the Fingers tribesmen to carry his golden litter himself. Exemplary Fortune had nodded to his friend Flowerbud, and they, like other nearby courtiers with no festival duties, had followed Young Majesty out of the city south along the Majestic Road. Only Owl Pattern, Exemplary Fortune's

mother, had joined the small group later, after, she told Exemplary
Fortune, she had soothed the Kitu Dove tribespeople. The Kitu
Doves were her own tribe, and she was a persuasive speaker. Doubtless she had convinced them that the Unique Inca's actions were
reasonable. But the monthly llama sacrifices had foretold drought
before, and this time the empire was ready. The Four Quarters'
storehouses held food enough to last through several bad harvests.
Even if Young Majesty believed the Divine Speaker had misunderstood the Sun's warning, there was no separate rumor of rebellion
in any of the provinces; and, on the borders, only the Colddungs
and the Highland Islanders opposed the empire, neither a serious
threat.

Exemplary Fortune knew Owl Pattern worried—as did many
in the court: Young Majesty's other wives, his courtiers, even some
of the people working their turn for the empire. Young Majesty
had grown moody and restless over the past few years. Before the
latest festival, no one, not even the speakers, had heard any danger.
It seemed to many that Young Majesty's fretfulness was the Four
Quarters' only weakness.

Yesterday evening, the Unique Inca and his small retinue had
reached Throat Town. At dawn this morning, Young Majesty had
sent Exemplary Fortune to request a private sacrifice to the Sun to
learn the Four Quarters' fortune in the coming decade. That omen
had confirmed the Unique Inca's disquiet, but Exemplary Fortune
still did not know the source of the threat to the empire. It could
be his father's heart, crippled by worry.

Exemplary Fortune shook himself out of his foreboding and
walked across the plaza to its east side, where the governor's compound housed the palace of the visiting Unique Inca. The llama
caravan had already stopped just inside the common entrance to
the compound, and courtiers talked with the caravan's leader. Hastily assembled turn-workers had begun to move among the llamas.

As Exemplary Fortune walked past the men, he thought the
governor could not be happy. The governor had only been able to
gather a thousand or so locals to cheer Young Majesty as he was
carried into Throat Town, not an insult to the Unique Inca given
the short notice, but, if the governor were ambitious or prone to

worry, few enough to make him uneasy. And now he had to rearrange the turn-work schedule for the province's people. Balancing the needs of the various tribes in each province could be delicate, and this was the start of potato-planting season, when people would want to be in their fields. Besides, people would be ready to rest after their own celebration of Majestic Festival. After Exemplary Fortune finished talking with his father, he would find out from Royal Reckoner or one of the other courtiers what reward the governor was being given for his troubles.

The section of the governor's compound reserved for the Unique Inca was busy and bright with people in many tribal headbands coming and going on various errands, conducting the affairs of government or waiting to see the Unique Inca in person. If it were not for his own inner disquiet, Exemplary Fortune would be pleased at the speed with which the court had adjusted to Young Majesty's desires. He looked up at the sky between the buildings. It was blue and cloudless, promising no rain for at least a few hours. He sighed a little, a private plea for rain. This much at least was clear: the stability of the Four Quarters would not be helped if drought traveled with the emperor.

Exemplary Fortune went into the building that served as the Unique Inca's audience room. The chamber was filled with Inca and honorary Inca courtiers in their various earrings of gold, silver, or copper talking quietly among themselves. Kitu Doves and other northern tribespeople serving their turn for the empire, with long hair and no earrings on their hidden ears, bustled about on various errands.

Near the back, the Unique Inca was seated on his golden stool. The fringe of the scarlet headband of his office hung down between his eyes, and he wore a dark blue tunic embroidered around the neck and down the front with squares outlined in black and filled with scarlet and deep orange designs. He was discussing the agricultural production of Endward Province with two courtiers and a man who wore a Rugged's turquoise headband; he was probably that tribe's chief. From what Exemplary Fortune heard, it sounded as though the chief had been trying to introduce corn into an area suited only for potatoes and quinoa. Corn was the better crop, worth working extra for—if it would then produce. Young Majesty sounded skeptical that this would ever happen.

His father looked up as Exemplary Fortune stepped into the open space in front of the Unique Inca's stool. "Come, my son," he said, and then to those he had been talking with, "This is business I had to interrupt earlier."

"I am most happy to await your pleasure," said the chief.

While Exemplary Fortune seated himself on the open scarlet-and-black rug next to the Unique Inca, the chief stood, bowed low, kissing his fingers to his lips, and then walked with the two courtiers toward the doorway.

The Unique Inca looked around at the others in the room, excluding only Exemplary Fortune from his gaze. "We would be alone."

Exemplary Fortune's heart contracted with dismay. This was not proper procedure. He did not want his father to be so ready to disrupt the Four Quarters' administration to learn news of the future. To invite chaos in this manner could only mean that the Unique Inca believed omens of the fluid future more important than the empire's governance in the solid now. Many would call this madness.

Without a word, all those in the room stopped what they were doing and left. Flowerbud gave Exemplary Fortune a questioning look, but Exemplary Fortune could only give a small shrug to signal his own lack of understanding.

When the room was empty of all but the brightly patterned sitting rugs scattered like fallen flowers across the floor, Exemplary Fortune's distressed tenderness found voice. "Father," he said.

"My son," answered the Unique Inca, "my dear son, what have you to tell me?"

The room's silence was loud in Exemplary Fortune's ears. "The omen was mixed," he said, his voice absorbed by the dark stone walls, the stone walls that sat in the earth, where the future lived. The walls surely knew more than he, if he could but interpret their silence. "The Speaker did have to sacrifice three llamas, but only the first predicted utter disaster." That llama had somehow pulled out of the assistants' arms while it was being cut and stood up, but his father would understand that. "When we tried a second time, that sacrifice gave a generally good result." The viscera had come out cleanly and in one piece, but the lungs had not still been pulsing. The speaker had already heard about the ominous sacrifice in Kitu Dove and had been distressed with even this indeterminate sign.

Exemplary Fortune continued, "Since the matter is so important, neither the speaker nor I was satisfied with such an ambiguous outcome, and we sacrificed the third. With the third animal, all went as for an excellent future, but the animal itself was reversed inside. The speaker was very startled, crying, 'What is this?' He told me the Sun had given us a sign such as He is willing to reveal very seldom. 'We have asked Him three times,' he said, 'and He has given us three different answers, but I believe they form a coherent message if we knew the correct interpretion. I cannot speak officially because this waka animal is not an omen I have studied. Still, I believe something very strange and perhaps quite horrible will remake the Four Quarters; but, when the cataclysm is over, the empire will recover and become as strong as before.' He said nothing more, but he was plainly troubled." Exemplary Fortune stopped, waiting for his father to respond. Since the Divine Speaker was still in Kitu Dove, no one here could better the local speaker's interpretation.

Young Majesty did not speak for a time. "I have been having bad dreams," he said finally, "strange dreams that I do not know how to interpret, like an excellent omen from a deformed animal. From one perspective, you say this is good, but you become uneasy, and, the more you think about it, the less sense it makes."

"The llama was not deformed on the outside," said Exemplary Fortune.

"And how can that be?" asked the Unique Inca.

"I do not know."

"I wanted you to ask to learn if the omen in Kitu Dove was only for me, or if the Sun would give another a similar answer."

Young Majesty had wanted to know if Majestic Festival's sacrifice had foretold his death. Looking at his father, Exemplary Fortune saw him clearly, not as he had looked ten or even four years ago, but as he looked now. Under the emperor's scarlet fringe, his eyes were hooded, and his face set in weary lines. He looked tired—

no, more than tired; he looked old. He was only fifty-three. World Reverser had been eighty when he turned the empire over to Royal Reckoning Inca, and he, in his turn, had been seventy-three when he died. "Father, perhaps you could—" Exemplary Fortune began.

Royal Reckoner stepped into the doorway. "Forgive me."

"Speak," said the Unique Inca.

"A relay-messenger has arrived with a quipu from Recognition."

Exemplary Fortune's heart beat faster. Young Majesty had sent Commander Shrewdness to Recognition to subdue the Highland Islanders. He could not imagine how that battle would affect the whole empire, but the timing seemed god sent.

The Unique Inca tilted his head as though listening to more than Royal Reckoner's words. "Show him in."

Royal Reckoner nodded to someone outside the room. The messenger, still breathing heavily, walked into the room, bowed low, and pulled a quipu out of his pouch. Fingering the quipu, he said, "The chief says a strange boat has come to Recognition."

Not a message from Shrewdness then.

"It had three masts with sails and was shaped like a house. Forty strange men with beards and silver clothes were on it. They took gold, silver, and foodstuffs and left animals and birds. They also left two of their men and took three of ours." The relay-messenger held out the quipu uncertainly. There was supposed to be an accountant in the room whose job was to read it.

Bemused, Exemplary Fortune stood up to retrieve the quipu from the young man. He ran the knotted cords through his fingers. The main cord was blue twisted with gray and fawn to indicate Recognition. There were nine cords hanging from it, and the cord for the boat had a subsidiary cord knotted to number the three masts. According to the quipu, there were five birds and three animals; llamas were actually what the color indicated, but the messenger knew that, and so the animals must not be llamas; not meat eaters, either, or the quipu would have indicated that. An unknown grazer then. "We understand your message and will keep the record," Exemplary Fortune said formally.

The Unique Inca nodded to Royal Reckoner, who gestured in his turn to the young man. As they turned to leave, Royal Reckoner's eyes regarded the Unique Inca and his son levelly, as though evaluating their dispositions. Exemplary Fortune wondered if Young Majesty had told his chief advisor about the dreams he heard from the future. He had not spoken of them before to his favorite son or to Owl Pattern.

Exemplary Fortune sat down again. That this message was tied to the question he had asked the Sun he did not doubt, but he did not know how to interpret it. A strange bearded man had been with the Colddungs who had attacked Advising Mountain Fort in Sundried three years earlier, but that fort was one thousand five hundred miles from Recognition, and no mention had been made of silver clothing in those reports.

"So," said Young Majesty.

"Father?" asked Exemplary Fortune, wanting an explanation of that flat word. "We need to know more," said the Unique Inca, almost as though he had not heard. "We need to know, and there may not be much time." He had the look of those who lived in wild places receiving omens and messages no one else could hear. "I will send a relay-message to Recognition to tell the chief and the fortress that the Unique Inca will collect the envoys the strangers have left, but I want you yourself to go, learn what you can about these strangers, and bring the two men to me."

"If we need to prepare for their arrival," said Exemplary Fortune, watching his father closely, "I should stay with you to help ensure that we will be ready both to satisfy their every need and to uncover and meet any threat they or their people might pose." His father knew he had the diplomatic skills necessary. He did not want to leave now when his father's heart seemed so unbalanced.

Young Majesty nodded in seeming agreement. "I would have you with me always. But you know my heart. In this matter, I would not trust anyone else. I will be in Kitu Dove. Go now quickly."

Exemplary Fortune had nothing left to say. Besides, Young Majesty was clearly speaking as Unique Inca rather than as his father. "I hear and obey," Exemplary Fortune affirmed Young Majesty's command. He did not understand his father's heart in this. A few strangers, traders from the sound of it, came to visit the coast, and Young Majesty immediately decided to send his favorite son alone to handle the matter. One would expect him either to send more men or else someone of lower rank. Exemplary Fortune kissed his father on the cheek and left.

Outside, Exemplary Fortune responded to Royal Reckoner's questioning look with a nod that had the chief advisor gather everyone's attention with his eyes and signal them back into the room. If the Unique Inca's audience chamber had been staffed, Royal Reckoner would already have had a courtier get a travel wand and assemble an escort for Exemplary Fortune's journey. Now Exemplary Fortune stopped Tobacco, who was in charge of the Unique Inca's turn-servants, as he moved toward the doorway.

"I need eight strong men who can be gone for a month," Exemplary Fortune said. His task should take only two tendays; but, if this mission was connected with the Sun's omens, he should allow time to untangle complications. "Have them meet me outside my quarters." The Unique Inca had no army units with him. If Exemplary Fortune needed warriors, he would have to take them from Recognition's fortress or Shrewdness's army.

Tobacco bowed and looked to an assistant to relay the order. Exemplary Fortune could see questions in their eyes, but he did not have answers. Young Majesty was hearing something from the future that, even with the hints the Sun had given them, Exemplary Fortune did not understand.

When the other courtiers went back inside, Flowerbud stayed in the passageway; and, after Exemplary Fortune finished talking with Tobacco, he sent his friend to summon both Llakun Root and his father's chief accountant from the Unique Inca's audience room. Exemplary Fortune knew that, in his father's heart, he had already left and so would not be in the Unique Inca's presence again until he had come back from his mission. Flowerbud could still go into the Unique Inca's presence without causing problems. The chief accountant came out of the room first, and Exemplary Fortune gave him the quipu with its accompanying message. The accountant ran the quipu through his fingers the way Exemplary Fortune had, confirming the message through touch and sight.

Llakun Root came into the passageway with Flowerbud while

Exemplary Fortune was talking to the accountant, and so he had to explain little about his mission to them. He told Llakun Root, "Since you are the only one here in Throat Town who has been to Recognition in the past three years, I must ask you to tell me everything you know about Recognition's chief."

Llakun Root looked a little nonplused. He ran errands and went with higher-ranking courtiers on missions, but he was not usually asked to give reports. Exemplary Fortune waited for him to gather himself, and he finally said, "The chief's name is Macaw. He is personable, and the Matrons, the area's tribe, seem to like him." He thought a few more heartbeats, then shook his head. "I did not talk with him directly, nor listen to enough other conversations to know his specific likes and dislikes or his strengths and weaknesses. He has several sons and daughters. One son appeared to be nearly twenty."

Exemplary Fortune repeated Macaw's name once to be sure he had understood it, then thanked Llakun Root for his service. Llakun Root went back into the audience chamber, and Flowerbud walked alongside Exemplary Fortune as he went to the stores to collect a travel wand.

As they walked, Flowerbud said, "The Unique Inca's heart is filled with the future." He had deduced Exemplary Fortune's worried thoughts very well from the bland words he had given Llakun Root and the accountant. It was vital that the emperor hear further than his subjects, and especially that he anticipate the future.

Flowerbud's thought should be comforting, but, given his father's actions, Exemplary Fortune did not receive much solace. "When you return to Kitu Dove," he said, "tell Thorniest that Young Majesty has sent a warrior prince to Recognition."

Flowerbud digested this in silence for a few heartbeats. "I do not understand what you can do alone," he said finally.

"Nor do I."

"I will tell Thorniest," Flowerbud promised.

That was a comfort. Thorniest was the empire's best strategist and Young Majesty's longtime friend. If anyone could decipher the Unique Inca's intentions, it would be he.

When Flowerbud left Exemplary Fortune outside his quarters,

his eyes were still puzzled. He would talk to Thorniest. When Exemplary Fortune returned to Kitu Dove with his news, whatever it was, Thorniest, and therefore the northern army, would be ready.

By the time Exemplary Fortune reached quarters, Esteemed Egg, Qantu Flower, and Skein Reckoner, the three wives who had come with him to Throat Town, had already gathered to help him prepare for his journey and ready themselves as necessary. They had heard he would be continuing south but nothing more. When he had explained what little he knew, Qantu Flower and Skein Reckoner both looked at him with a question he had to answer. He had to decide which wife to take with him on the journey.

Chatterer, his oldest son, who was listening wide-eyed to the discussion, had come with Esteemed Egg. He was only six, too young to travel fast and too young to take into unknown dangers. Esteemed Egg could not come with him. Skein Reckoner was the cleverest of his wives; but, as her black-and-fawn headband proclaimed, she was of the Wind-Moon tribe, and, in the past, the Wind-Moons had had strained relations with the Matrons of Recognition, who lived on their southwest. Qantu Flower was Inca and carried herself with all the nobility and poise of that tribe. If he was to impress the representatives of another people, she must be his choice.

"Qantu Flower will come with me," he voiced his decision.

Without a word, Skein Reckoner handed him a fresh tunic and loincloth of dark green that the three of them had already brought in. Chatterer announced that he would watch for the turn-workers and slipped out the doorway. Skein Reckoner and Esteemed Egg helped Qantu Flower put on a dark green dress that matched the tunic they had gathered for Exemplary Fortune. They fastened her dress with a gold pin that matched her earrings and recombed her hair to lie smoothly down her back. Exemplary Fortune and Qantu Flower were just settling matching green-and-gold cloaks over their shoulders when Chatterer came breathlessly into the room. "They're here," his son announced, "eight couples. They say they are working for you."

Qantu Flower pinned her cloak while Exemplary Fortune bent down to hug his son. "Take care of yourself while I'm gone," he told Chatterer. He looked at Esteemed Egg and Skein Reckoner. "I will be back as soon as I can." He said no more. He was oddly at a loss for words, infected by his father's disquiet.

The turn-workers outside were from the Glowing tribe, men as well as women wearing their hair in a long braid that was coiled atop their heads and fastened with crimson ribbons. A man handed him the small bag Tobacco had given them, dried coca leaves and quinoa ash for the high-altitude journey. Exemplary Fortune distributed a ration to each and said, "We are traveling to Recognition as quickly as possible. I will tell you more in the tampus."

With no more ceremony than that, they jogged out onto the Majestic Road. Exemplary Fortune looked back once at the Sun temple, with its thatched roof still gleaming golden in the noontime light. He pressed his lips tight against the worry in his heart, and ran south with the rest. The group crossed the bridge over the Black River and ran out into the rising farmland on the other side. Soon they were above cropland among bunchgrasses where llamas grazed. Here one could see only snow-crested mountain peaks flanking them on both west and east. Here the chill air whipped the heat away from their bodies. In a while they would come to another warm farming valley with another stream. By the time they started back up into the highlands, they would welcome the cool air's caress. He knew these valleys and highlands well. Since the Glowings lived just two days' run south, his turn-workers knew them too. Only Qantu Flower had not traveled here often, and she would betray no uncertainty.

The eighteen of them made good time running and walking into the afternoon, and then into dusk. As the first stars began to spread across the sky, they reached Molle-tree Cure, the next provincial capital south. Men he had fought with greeted Exemplary Fortune by name as the group ran into the city, and, before they settled themselves, the Inca governor invited Exemplary Fortune and his wife to dine with him. He should have expected this, Exemplary Fortune thought, but he had not. He had never traveled with such a small group before. To turn down the invitation would be impolitic. But he had nothing to tell the governor. He wanted to get to know his assigned men. Qantu Flower and he exchanged a knowing and sympathetic look.

With an inward sigh, Exemplary Fortune told the turn-workers not to wait up. Then he and Qantu Flower bathed, put on fresh clothes from the tampu's stores, and went to the governor's compound. It happened as Exemplary Fortune had expected. The meal was excellent, and Qantu Flower and he became engaged in pleasant conversation with the local officials; but, when the governor hinted that he would like to know Exemplary Fortune's mission, Exemplary Fortune's knowledge was scanty enough to make the governor feel that something was being concealed. He clearly did not believe Young Majesty would send his son out with so little explanation of his mission's purpose. He had to be wondering if or how he had so lost Young Majesty's favor that his son would not share news with him. Qantu Flower's presence was not enough to reassure him. To mollify him, the two of them stayed later than Exemplary Fortune would have liked, listening and asking friendly questions about the province and the governor's family and clan.

When they returned to the tampu, the Glowings were still up. As soon as they walked into the tampu's giant hall, the turn-workers unrolled the bedding the tampu-keepers had gotten from the stores. If Exemplary Fortune asked, they would undoubtedly insist they had not simply been waiting for the two of them.

The group arose again at first light and spent the day running mainly in the highlands above even the tolerance of potatoes. Here were only llamas with their herders and the bunchgrasses that the llamas ate. Around them were the mountains that the road avoided, dipping instead into river valleys terraced up as high as corn would grow. Snowcapped Crossing-Mark's peak loomed ever larger in front of them.

The turn-workers ran and walked happily, racing each other, clearly enjoying the journey. Qantu Flower and Exemplary Fortune both encouraged them, Qantu Flower laughing with the turn-workers at their game. Exemplary Fortune, however, could not laugh convincingly, and, after a pointed look from Qantu Flower, he let her be the one who fostered the play.

Exemplary Fortune's heart was vexed with thoughts of his father's decisions over the past few years. The Unique Inca had lost any interest in extending the Four Quarters. Exemplary Fortune had thought he understood his reasons. The last campaigns north of Kitu Dove had been hard fought and unpopular. It was time to consolidate what they had won, to make their new conquests part of the empire and discover the talents of the Four Quarters' newest tribes before expanding any further. Also, the land to the north was hot sticky jungle inhabited by naked barbarians who seemed hardly worth the effort of incorporation. Now, though, Exemplary Fortune wondered if he understood the Unique Inca's reasoning at all.

That evening the group stopped at a small tampu between provincial capitals. Exemplary Fortune did not want to repeat the misunderstanding of the night before. The old man who staffed the tampu was overwhelmed to see two Incas, one wearing the standard Inca headband of scarlet and yellow and the other the yellow headband of a prince, unannounced at their quiet stop. His wife was not so easily amazed and soon had him hauling out blankets. She did look sideways at Qantu Flower as she gathered dried potatoes from the stores, but Qantu Flower and the Glowing women soon put her at ease. The stew they made together was rich in fat from the cui that bustled underfoot.

"It's what we have," the old woman said, as they set out the food, "though I suppose it's not what you're used to."

"Grandmother," Exemplary Fortune told her, "this reminds me of the stew my mother's turn-cook made for me when I was quite small. I have often wished I could taste that dish again."

She blushed happily. The Glowings relaxed too. They were pleased to be with him, but they did not quite know what to do when they were not moving. After dinner, Exemplary Fortune explained that they were traveling to Recognition to bring back to the Unique Inca two strange men who had been left in the Four Quarters. Qantu Flower then took the women aside to acquaint herself with them, while Exemplary Fortune asked for a gameboard with the colored beans and die to play and-ten with the men. He lost the first game, which bothered the men until he laughed. "This is not my skill," he said. "Let me learn from you." And so they showed him their simple strategies until it was time to sleep.

The eighteen woke again at dawn, ate another rustic stew, and set out. The Sun sent a light drizzle, encouraging for workers in the fields but unpleasantly clammy for an all-day journey. They ran now to keep warm, and Exemplary Fortune wondered what the weather was like in Kitu Dove, where his father would have returned by now. He could not know. When he reached his father's side again, Flowerbud would tell him everything that had happened while he was gone. He pushed the useless wondering from his heart and concentrated on the journey.

If they did not encounter hail or driving rain, he expected to reach Recognition in three more days. His mission in Recognition should take no more than a day, and then he would return with the bearded strangers. The strangers would determine how quickly he reached Kitu Dove. Lowlanders were not used to traveling all day, and he had heard it said that some fishermen who spent all their time on boats could scarcely walk at all. If they had to, the men would carry the strangers. The group moved quickly through the day, rejoicing as much as possible in the drizzle and trying vainly to outwalk it.

The night at another small tampu was uneventful save that Exemplary Fortune won most of the and-ten games, which pleased the men immensely as it proved him a quick-witted leader worthy of their respect. At midmorning the next day, the group paused at the Suckling heightshrine, with its first sight of the Great Lake sixty miles west and two miles down. Exemplary Fortune could not make out Recognition, but he could trace the line where the miserable coastal jungle ended and the desert, which extended all the way down the coast, began. He could almost distinguish the ironically named Highland Island, where the empire's warriors were currently fighting in the hot stickiness. They stopped just long enough to make an offering of a wad of coca each for the vista and then ran on.

In early afternoon they reached Heads-of-Corn, where they turned off the Majestic Road onto the coastal lateral. Though they still made reasonable time, the branch was too steep for a controlled run. Exemplary Fortune fretted at the pace the stepped road forced on them. He had begun to think of reasons why his father might have sent him alone to Recognition. If the bearded strangers came back with an army while Commander Shrewdness was fighting on Highland Island, the empire forces still in Recognition's fortress would need a commander who had enough military experience to counter unexpected strategies and who knew Shrewdness's heart so thoroughly that the two of them could hope to coordinate strategies even when they could not communicate. Select Seed, the fortress's captain, had fought mainly against the Colddungs and did not know Shrewdness or Exemplary Fortune well. Their small band had passed no relay-messengers with wands in Recognition's colors, but the strangers could return at any time. Exemplary Fortune wanted to talk with both Select Seed and Macaw before any armies invaded. Talking with Select Seed, especially, would be a delicate matter if Exemplary Fortune contemplated taking command of his troops later.

The road wound down along cliff faces and rocky terrain. For much of the way, they could see, spread out below them, the yellow-brown sandy desert and past it, the darker green-spotted irrigated fields around Recognition. Beyond the city, the Great Lake stretched bluely until it seemed to merge with the sky at the limit of vision. Sometimes, though, the road turned and narrowed along the cliff faces, and they had to concentrate on the rough-hewn rock or fill beneath their feet. Once, the road ran through a spur of rock in an arch not long enough to be called a tunnel. As they traveled downward, the sky became a brilliant azure untouched by hint of cloud, and the air grew warm, the Sun's heat unrelieved by the upland air's chilliness. At dusk they came upon a huddle of houses clinging to the edge of a terraced hill. The houses were adobe and had the flat-topped roofs so characteristic of the coast. The settlement also had a tiny tampu only large enough to hold ten of them. The couple who tended it told him Recognition was still three thousand feet down and eighteen miles away. Unwilling to risk traveling along unknown rocky ravines and cliff sides in the dark, Exemplary Fortune decided to stop for the night. They set up two small tents in the road for four couples to sleep in.

Everyone else was ready to relax, but Exemplary Fortune had to stop himself from going outside to strain his eyes for strange boats on the Great Lake. He wondered if the Unique Inca had sent a message to tell Bright Rainbow, his designated heir, of his premonitions. Bright Rainbow and many of the other princes were in Navel planning another campaign against the Colddungs. If the bearded strangers planned to invade along the northern coast, it would be most unwise for his brothers to lead their planned army southeast. Exemplary Fortune had no control over what they did, or, here away from the court and his friends, what his father did either.

He kept his feelings from both the turn-workers and their hosts. Qantu Flower clearly knew he was uneasy, but they did not talk about his worries in these quarters, where even a whisper would be public. Instead, while Qantu Flower talked with the women and spun yarn, Exemplary Fortune played interminable games of and-ten with the men and told tales of the Caller campaign. The men enjoyed his tales of adventure, which boded well if Exemplary Fortune's fears materialized. The tampu-keepers were less helpful. As close to Recognition as they were, they had no knowledge of the bearded strangers except such fancies as that they ate silver and carried sticks that made thunder.

Sleep did not come quickly, and such sleep as he did get was uneasy with half-remembered dream bits. His legs cramped, and he was hot. A warrior's necessary campaign discipline seemed to have deserted him. He woke before dawn, and the whole group left the tampu as the Sun, rising over the mountains behind them, sparked the giant water before them with light. But their path was still in darkness. Like so much now, it seemed an ill omen, but he could not stay still any longer. The Glowings, too, were anxious to move, and their wish to face the day was simple pleasure in their assigned task unalloyed by irrelevant worries about other princes and the rest of the empire. Qantu Flower watched Exemplary Fortune and kept her thoughts to herself.

It took them most of the morning to work their way down off the cliff sides, and it was afternoon before they reached the irrigated fields walled off from the road by clay walls to protect the corn. The road was ideal for running, but the Glowings had wilted in the heat, and Exemplary Fortune did not force more than a trot. His turn-workers were, after all, neither Incas nor warriors.

They reached Recognition near sunset, its brightly painted buildings shading the road with welcome coolness even before they reached the city. The whole group was hot and sweaty, and it was already almost too late to visit Chief Macaw. Exemplary Fortune abandoned any hope of starting his mission that day, and instead contemplated the luxury of a tampu that was likely to have facilities for a real bath.

Three elderly couples kept the tampu next to the compound where the Mothers who tended the Sun temple lived. The tampu was of painted adobe like all the buildings in town. Even the Sun temple was adobe rather than stone.

There were indeed bathing facilities, though the bath was large enough for only one at a time. The bath was of a piece with the rest of Recognition. The town, with its Sun temple and Mothers' compound, clearly had pretensions to cityhood, but was not nearly as sophisticated as the tampu-keepers thought. Of course, this was the coast, where water was scarce, but bathwater would be recycled to the gardens and so was not a major luxury.

Exemplary Fortune asked the most garrulous couple to stay with them after dinner to relay the local news. They were obviously delighted, and, at last, they had firsthand information about the two men he sought. "They stayed here the first night," said the woman, "and if we had known what kind of people they were, we would have had Macaw, our chief, give us guards for protection."

"I used to go out with the trading rafts," said the man, "before I banged up my leg, and I could tell right away they weren't the kind of people you'd want to turn your back on, but, like Macaw said, they hadn't any other place to stay. No kinfolk." He snorted. "The way I look at it now, their family probably kicked them out as an alternative to hanging them. It's not good manners, though, foisting your problems on other people that way."

"Not responsible," the woman put in.

"Actually," the man continued, "I think we were all a little overawed by the thundersticks, and that boat was pretty amazing, too."

So the sticks that made thunder were real. Exemplary Fortune sincerely hoped the strangers' crime did not consist of eating up all the silver in town.

"After we fed them breakfast," the woman picked up the story, "they just left. We tried to let them know they should stay until Macaw's men came to show them around, but, well, I don't know if they understood anything or not."

"I don't believe the pale one was even trying to understand," said the man.

"The pale one?" Exemplary Fortune asked.

"Didn't anybody tell you?" the man and woman asked simultaneously. They exchanged glances, and the woman continued, "One of them was so pale he didn't even look sick, just very strange—"

"Some people were saying he might be the World Animator come back," the man put in. He shook his head.

"The other," the woman continued, "was a brown so dark as to be almost black. I'd like to try a dye that color sometime."

"They had similar clothes, though," said the man, "so we figure they must belong to the same tribe."

"An albino?" Exemplary Fortune hazarded.

"Not that light," said the woman, "about the color of ground corn, only ruddier." She grinned. "Corn with lots of pepper."

"Lots of pepper," the man cackled.

"So they went out into town," the woman continued, "and wandered around for a bit, looking at things, and then the pale one went up to Guava and tried to say something to her. She just shook her head and then nodded toward Macaw's palace, figuring he wanted to know where it was. He grabbed her and started pulling her in the direction she'd indicated. She hit at him to let him know that wasn't what she'd meant, but he just pulled her toward him. She was too close to kick or anything so she yelled for help."

"And then," said the man, "he put his hand over her mouth."

Had his father heard this? Exemplary Fortune wondered. If these men were the future, then his worries were indeed justified.

"By that time, people were starting to come out of their compounds and houses to see what was happening, but, when they tried to grab him, the pale one just threw them away like they were children's toys. And then he grabbed at Guava again."

"She'd gotten far enough away to kick him," said the man. "She says she got him good, but he just yelled and grabbed her tighter. She's got some nasty bruises."

"By this time, a ten-group from the fortress had heard the commotion. When they came around the corner, and everybody explained what was happening, they ordered the pale one to put her down. He growled at them like a wild animal and held her as a shield. They rushed him anyway, and it took all of them to pin him down."

"Sand-Dune ran for rope," said the man, "and some people wanted to hang him right then, but the Inca captain said they should take him to Macaw, so they tied him up good."

"They dragged him," said the woman, "yelling all the way."

"He wouldn't walk," the man agreed. "Macaw said he'd already sent a message to Young Majesty asking what to do with the two, so we couldn't have a trial until the Unique Inca's answer got back."

The two of them looked at Exemplary Fortune expectantly.

Exemplary Fortune avoided answering their implicit question by asking questions of his own, but he learned little else. The dark stranger had evidently not taken part in the scuffle at all. "Nobody noticed him," said the woman, "so everybody figures he must have been cowering against a wall or something." He had followed the crowd to Macaw's palace on his own; and, after the pale stranger had finished yelling at everyone else, he had yelled at the dark. The couple agreed that the pale must be the dark's superior. "Or else," said the man, "the dark would have got the pale to stop what he was doing." While that made sense, Exemplary Fortune decided to reserve judgment until he saw the two interacting.

He did not tell them he had come to take the two back to the Unique Inca, merely saying that he would talk with both Macaw and the Inca fortress's captain.

His men were excited by the couple's story. Since no one had been seriously hurt, they regarded it as a further scene in the great adventure they were sharing. The women, including Qantu Flower, watched the men's excitement with a rather sardonic acceptance.

In bed that night, Qantu Flower and Exemplary Fortune talked about Young Majesty's worries, and how much of a danger the strangers were likely to be. But they did not know enough to come to any firm conclusions. They decided that Exemplary Fortune would go alone to talk with Macaw and Select Seed. From what the tampu-keepers had said, this mission was far more likely to be military than diplomatic. Qantu Flower would talk with as many locals as possible to gather their impressions of the strangers who had sailed away as well as those who had been left behind. She would stay ready to talk with the strangers if new facts altered the mission yet again.

When they had settled that, Exemplary Fortune sighed a small worried sigh.

Qantu Flower put a questioning hand on his lips.

"My father's worries, the Sun's oracle," he said in answer to her unvoiced question.

"Your father has been worrying for a long time. Perhaps you worry too soon."

"Perhaps."

She shifted on the kumpi quilts, a dissatisfied motion. Clearly she had heard the skepticism in his tone. "If some tribe on the empire's borders had sent these two as envoys, what would you be saying then?"

"Alas," he said, "I would be nearly as worried. But at least it would be possible to spy on them in return."

"Has anyone ever sent such nasty envoys?"

"Not that I know of," he admitted.

"It sounds to me as though these strangers are deficient in strategy."

"Perhaps they are," he said, less skeptically this time. Her reasoning had merit.

She drew him closer. Their lips touched, and for a time all discussion ended. Afterward, as Exemplary Fortune drifted toward sleep, he thought that her strategic skills were impeccable. When he woke on the morrow, he would be rested and ready for whatever the day's revelations brought.

2

ELEVENTH YEAR OF KING CARLOS'S REIGN
DECEMBER 1527

The people who have written actual history do not talk about most of the people in this chapter. Not much is known about their backgrounds or how they lived. We tell the story exactly as it may have happened.

The silver indented cleanly under Hummingbird's chasing tool as he centered a straight line across the groove he had already cut. As he drew the third line, he let up on the pressure at the center so the narrow trough would stay smooth. And then he had formed another perfectly radiating star lined up evenly with the others around the tumbler. He set the tool down and buffed the tumbler with a clean piece of leather so he wouldn't tarnish it against his sweaty skin. He took out the sandbag that had kept the tumbler in shape while he worked, then turned the cup around in his cloth-draped hands looking for imperfections. Finding none, he looked up, looked into his father's eyes.

"It's done," he said.

Fishscale picked the tumbler up and turned it around in his own gnarled, powerful hands.

Outside, beyond the compound walls, Hummingbird could hear no strange noises. Most of that day and the day before, people outside had been talking excitedly, not quite loud enough for him to understand. Many people had marched by while he was absorbed in his work, following his father's advice and example that a piece should be finished while its shape was still clear in one's heart. Then, the sounds had not distracted him. Now, he wanted to go outside to find out what had happened. It was somehow worse that there was no noise anymore, as though he had missed everything. He sighed; he probably had.

Fishscale slowly turned the tumbler Hummingbird had made and its twin he had made, comparing them. Hummingbird found himself fidgeting. It seemed suddenly that he had spent a whole lifetime in this stifling room with its pungent smell of sweat and silver dust. He wanted to go outside, find out what was happening, see Happy Speaker. It had been far too long since he had touched Happy Speaker. If he could, he would not go directly into the Inca fortress; he would stay outside and play a special tune on a flute until Happy Speaker invited him in. But he could not do that. Happy Speaker told him they must keep their affair a secret, that his Inca commander, who led the troops against the Highland Islanders, would punish them for being together. Hummingbird shivered a little with excitement. He must not let anyone at the fortress know he and Happy Speaker were lovers.

Fishscale stopped turning the tumblers and looked up at Hummingbird. "They are not perfect."

He did not say anything more, but he did not have to. Hummingbird knew what he wanted. He sat down again and took the tumblers, one at a time, looking them over carefully, but he could not see anything wrong. He looked back at his father.

Fishscale smiled. "Try again." So he set them down as his father had, turning them together. The first time he did not find anything, and, without really meaning to, he snorted impatiently. He turned them again, forcing himself to compare every tiny detail. And then he saw it, a star arm that looked perfect on each tumbler was noticeably longer on one when they were compared. "Here it is," he said, holding the tumblers flaw up.

"So it is," said Fishscale. He shook his head. "You do fine work, but, when you become an adult, you will need the patience to hold your concentration until you are sure the job is finished."

Hummingbird ducked his head. "I have no excuse."

"Well, my son, we promised the Inca commander his tumblers this afternoon. If I give them to you now, will your fingers know how hard to press, or when to stop the line?"

"I do not think so," Hummingbird admitted.

"Then I will fix them. On our next job, we will allow ourselves extra time. Go now, get ready."

Hummingbird turned and ran from the room, no longer trying to hide his eagerness. He washed quickly, then put on the pale green tunic with the embroidered front and combed his hair down over his shoulders the way Happy Speaker liked it. He carefully tied his blue-and-fawn headband so as not to disturb the smooth flow of his hair. Happy Speaker's hair was short and bristly, and his gold earrings were smooth and cool to touch. Finally, he took the silver tumbler that Happy Speaker had loaned him to study and wrapped it in long folds of cloth.

When he returned to the room, Fishscale had already wrapped the tumblers they had made. He looked at Hummingbird resplendent in his best clothes. "Be discreet, my son."

Hummingbird felt himself blushing. Given the Incas' odd ideas, his father did not really approve of his affair, but he said Hummingbird was old enough to make his own mistakes. He knew, as Hummingbird did, that when the Inca army had finished subduing the Highland Islanders, Happy Speaker would be gone. "I will, father."

He went out into the glare of the midafternoon sun. It was another of the Incas' mad ideas that everyone should worship the hot rays of the sun. Happy Speaker said it was always cool in the uplands, and many Incas could not imagine being too warm. Hummingbird, in his turn, had a hard time imagining cold. Happy Speaker did not make him cool.

Molle Tree, standing in the shade of her family's doorway, called out to him. "Have you heard the news?"

"I have heard nothing. I have spent the last three days laboring for the Incas."

"For your father," she corrected with a smile. "The Incas let people rest occasionally."

He smiled back. The thought of Happy Speaker called to him; but, if the news was about the Incas, he should learn it. Besides, Molle Tree was a good worker and a good friend. When they were older, they would probably marry sometime when the Inca inspector came to match couples up. "My father," he accepted the correction. "Did the Incas win a glorious victory?"

"You and your foreign lover," she said, tossing her head. "My brother thinks you are pretty, I think you are pretty, and you run after him who worships the hot Sun and straight lines. If you keep visiting him, the other Incas will find out, and what will you do then? Stand in the square for punishment while Macaw tells everyone how foolish you've been? I will not marry a man everyone laughs at." She spoke lightly, but Hummingbird knew she meant it. Her opinion was not easily altered.

"He will soon be gone," said Hummingbird, feeling the sadness the words made in his mouth.

"Maybe," said Molle Tree. "It is not an Inca victory."

"A defeat?" he asked, his heart plummeting, though he knew Molle Tree wouldn't tease him first if anything had happened to Happy Speaker.

"Incas," she said scornfully. Then she relented. "A big boat that wasn't a raft came into the harbor the day before yesterday with strange bearded men dressed all in shiny clothes. One of them had a thundering stick that breaks wood. He was a giant, very pale with a thick beard, and he has been going all over the city. Light-on-Water and I watched at the plaza."

Intrigued in spite of himself, Hummingbird asked, "How can a big boat not be a raft?"

"It was shaped like a bowl only narrow and long instead of round."

"But . . ." said Hummingbird, then stopped himself. "I will have to go and see."

She laughed. "I think the boat will leave before you get to the waterfront."

He ducked his head, admitting it was probably true, and ran on toward the Inca fortress, testing Inca words in his heart. He wanted to speak correctly, though Happy Speaker said his accent was pleasantly exotic. He stopped running just before the massive walls of the fortress came into view and walked the last few hundred paces. He did not want to seem too eager. He and Happy Speaker would walk with the tumblers into the back of the storeroom, where it was dark and one could hear only one's partner's quick breath. He could already imagine Happy Speaker's breath on his ear.

One of the guards at the gateway was new. Hummingbird said, "Two tumblers for the commander."

The new one looked at the other and said, "I would like to see."

The other guard grinned at Hummingbird and said, "He's still learning, needs a little practice. Why don't you show him?"

The third tumbler suddenly weighted Hummingbird's bundle so that he could hardly hold it up. He did not know what to say or do. He wanted to sink into Mother Earth where no one could see him. He wanted . . . if Happy Speaker were here, he would know what to say. He should be here, but Hummingbird could not see him in the fortress's courtyard.

The usual guard began to look at Hummingbird suspiciously. "What's the problem?" he asked.

"I was—I was bringing it back," stammered Hummingbird.

"Bringing what back?" demanded the guard.

He did not know what to say to that.

The guard's expression had changed from suspicion to dour unhappiness. "Give me the bag," he said, holding out his hand. Hummingbird handed the package across. The guard carefully unwrapped it just enough to see each tumbler.

"That's not a local design," said the new guard.

"Happy Speaker lent it to me to—to study," said Hummingbird desperately. He didn't want to get Happy Speaker in trouble, but maybe it would be all right. Happy Speaker worked with the accountant in charge of the storehouse. Maybe it was all right if he lent things out.

"Really?" the regular guard grunted, giving him a look that said he didn't believe anything Hummingbird had said, probably wouldn't believe anything he'd ever say again. He looked at the other. "I'll take him to Select Seed. You stay here."

Hummingbird's knees felt like they were going to give way. He did not want to talk with the Inca captain. He walked with the guard across the fortress's courtyard, trying to think of what to say, but his heart was empty of words, a dull pain growing where his thoughts should be. Maybe he would think of something while they waited. But the guard at the doorway to the captain's office nodded them in right away. The office was full of people sitting on brightly colored rugs or standing at ready. Hummingbird stared at the ground, away from their questioning looks.

"Hummingbird was carrying this package," said the guard, "two tumblers that look local and this one." The guard set the package on the ground in front of the captain and opened it to show the third tumbler. "After stammering a bit, he said Happy Speaker had lent it to him 'to study.' If Happy Speaker was involved in some way, I figured you'd want to know."

He shouldn't have mentioned Happy Speaker's name, Hummingbird realized. Tears began leaking out of his eyes, running down his cheeks, and falling to the floor.

"He was carrying the package into the fortress?" asked the captain.

"Yes, sir."

There was a short silence, and then the captain's voice said, "Hummingbird, sit down so we can talk."

Hummingbird's legs gave way, and he sat heavily.

"How did you get the third tumbler?" the captain asked in a voice that sounded calm and patient, like he had all day to get the information out of Hummingbird if he needed to.

Hummingbird began to sob harder. He didn't know what to say. Everything he'd said so far was wrong.

"How did you get the third tumbler?" the captain asked again.

"I don't know," Hummingbird managed between his sobs.

"Did you tell the guard that Happy Speaker had given it to you?"

Hummingbird nodded.

There was silence for a time, and then Happy Speaker's voice said, "Reporting." With just that one word, Hummingbird could feel his heart lift. Happy Speaker sounded as lighthearted as always. He was never at a loss for words or the right action. He would know how to fix everything.

"Do you know who this is?" the Inca captain asked, and this time Hummingbird could hear a bit of annoyance in his voice.

"Why, it's Hummingbird," said Happy Speaker. "What's the matter?"

"I'm not sure," said the captain. "He was carrying an extra tumbler into the fortress."

"How odd," said Happy Speaker with a short pause between the first and second words.

Hummingbird's heart contracted with pain. He felt sick. Happy Speaker was not going to admit he had anything to do with it.

"He has said you loaned the tumbler to him," said the captain.

"But I'm not authorized to do that," Happy Speaker exclaimed in apparent surprise.

"Do you recognize the tumbler?"

Another short pause. Hummingbird could see Happy Speaker's hand moving the package wrappings, but the way his hand moved it could have been anyone's hand. It did not signal to him, not even secretly. "This was part of the last caravan from Navel," said Happy Speaker. "We were saving it as a festival gift for Macaw." His voice was matter-of-fact, with no sign that the tumbler meant anything to him.

His father and Molle Tree had been right. He'd been a fool to get involved with the Incas.

The captain continued to ask Happy Speaker about the tumbler, and Happy Speaker continued to answer in his usual carefree manner. Lying in his usual carefree manner. He said he had not shown it to Hummingbird. He made it sound as though he did not know Hummingbird very well at all.

When the captain finished questioning Happy Speaker, he dismissed him and asked Hummingbird, "Do you have anything you want to say?"

Still looking at the ground, Hummingbird shook his head. He

didn't want to talk to anybody, especially not Incas. He hadn't even stolen it.

The Inca captain said to somebody, "Take him to Macaw, and tell him what has been said here."

The guard helped him up and led him out into the courtyard. Hummingbird rubbed around his eyes and tried to make himself presentable. He didn't want to talk to Macaw either. Another man joined them just before they got to the gate. As they walked through the streets of the city, Hummingbird could imagine everyone's eyes on him. He could almost hear the whispers about him starting to spread. He kept his eyes on the beaten earth of the streets. In his heart he could hear Molle Tree's voice saying, "I will not marry someone everyone laughs at." He looked up along the street. The houses on either side stifled him, and the people who had stopped to watch the three of them made his face burn. Suddenly he was running, he did not know where, just away, away from the Incas, and away from the laughter building around him.

Behind him there was a startled shout, and he ran until he thought his lungs would burst. His feet led him into the older part of the city, where the adobe houses were huddled together in random patterns. The Incas, who liked all lines straight, would get lost in the maze. He was looking up now to see where he was going, and he could see people staring at him as he ran down the twisting streets. Some of them called out after him. He could not get away from them.

He ducked, panting, through a drying shed for fish, and then turned again into an abandoned compound, but he could not make himself go into any of the rooms. He would be trapped inside. He was trapped anyway. There was no place to go. He realized he had not heard any sound of pursuit after that one startled command to stop. Why should the Incas bother? All they had to do was to wait until he showed himself, or someone found him and told them where he was. Or let Macaw catch him and punish him instead. By now he must have convinced the Incas he was guilty of something dreadful. When they captured him, they'd probably ask him if he was planning a revolt or something. Even if Happy Speaker hadn't already suggested it.

And then he was running again, back toward the waterfront this time. Maybe the strange boat would still be there; and, if it wasn't, or, if they would not take him, he could drown himself. There was no other escape except to join the Highland Islanders, and he would not do that.

He could see the masts of the strange boat high above the water almost as soon as he turned toward it, but it was far out in the bay, maybe too far for him to swim, probably far enough for the Incas to catch him on a raft if they wanted to. He kept running. People lined the shore, watching the boat. They might not know yet that the Incas wanted to question him. He could see no Incas, and Macaw's men were all down at the far end. He eeled his way through the crowd, trying to make himself small and unnoticed.

There was a small boat between the shore and the big boat, pulling away toward the mother boat. He ran down the causeway straight into the water, then swam out to the smaller boat. The strange bearded men on the boat saw him coming, and they all sat very still with their hands at their waists as though they had weapons there. Hummingbird grabbed at the side of the boat with his hands. He hung half out of the water, not knowing what to do next.

Suddenly a giant man laughed and grabbed his arms, saying something to the others in the boat as he did so. The giant pulled him into the boat and sat him on a bench. Hummingbird sat trembling, unable to move. He did not look back.

3

THIRTY-FOURTH YEAR OF YOUNG MAJESTY'S REIGN
MAJESTIC FESTIVAL MONTH

Most say that, in actual history, the two Spaniards left behind in the Inca Empire died or were killed soon after they reached Recognition.

In the morning, Exemplary Fortune dressed in a deep rich green tunic with yellow embroidery at the throat. It was the only tunic in the tampu's stores that was appropriate to his day's business. The other ornamented tunics were all scarlet or heavily decorated with scarlet, clearly designed for ceremony, not diplomatic work.

He went first to Macaw's palace. He knew the chief had met the two strangers, and they were his main concern. He would talk with Select Seed when he knew more. Because it appeared likely that the strangers were indeed enemies of the Four Quarters, talking to the fortress's captain would be a delicate proceeding. He wanted to be as prepared as possible before the two of them sat down to discuss what should be done and who, or which one of them, should do it.

The adobe walls surrounding Macaw's palace compound were painted in bright green jungle scenes with monkeys hanging from imaginary branches just above the wall's top. The monkeys suspended in midair gave the mural a rather comical appearance, but Exemplary Fortune did not know if the effect was intentional. He decided not to comment. If Macaw for some reason asked his opinion of the artwork, he would say it was well-done, which was true.

The guard at the gateway did not ask Exemplary Fortune's name but led him directly through the main courtyard to the largest building in the compound. The doorway of that building was guarded by a pair of jaguars, again painted rather than real but with their heads turned out to watch people coming and going nevertheless. The guard at this doorway, when the gateguard bowed Exemplary Fortune over to him, again did not ask for a name. Clearly, the tampu-keepers had been talking to Macaw's courtiers.

The doorguard did, however, ask Exemplary Fortune's opinion of the murals, apparently as polite chitchat, before handing him off to the next official, and Exemplary Fortune said that the jaguars appeared alert and that he liked the style of the artist who had painted them. The doorguard named the clan responsible and told Exemplary Fortune where he could find other murals in Recognition that were painted in the same style. Another of Macaw's courtiers appeared then and led Exemplary Fortune into the large room within just as Macaw finished talking with his latest petitioner.

Macaw wore a blue tunic that matched the blue in his blue-and-fawn headband as well as the blue of the blue-and-scarlet rug he sat on. When his courtier announced Exemplary Fortune, he rose from his rug to give Exemplary Fortune full obeisance. The bow was proper, but the blown kiss was in questionable taste when given to anyone save the Unique Inca. Still, Exemplary Fortune was pleased with the smoothness of Macaw's organization. No one had had to wait, neither the Inca prince nor the local petitioner. "I am delighted to see you," said Macaw. "I have tried to do all as your father would wish."

He nodded Exemplary Fortune to a scarlet-and-green rug at his side, and the green matched the color of the tunic Exemplary Fortune wore. When they were both comfortably seated, Macaw said, "Please forgive me if I overstepped my bounds by giving the two strangers into the army's care, but I have no facilities to hold them."

So the strangers were already in the fortress. The tampu-keepers had not known that. "I have heard enough about these men to be grateful that you were able to keep them alive. The Unique Inca is most anxious to see them."

With that encouragement, the chief related his own version of what had happened. It added little to what Exemplary Fortune had already heard. Macaw did emphasize the pale's ferociousness. "All who brought him here have bruises to prove that they met him. He would not stop fighting. I think maybe he is a madman, and the dark assigned to care for him. But the others should have told me."

"So you met some of the other strangers?" Exemplary Fortune asked.

"I met two more," said the chief, "and both were most courteous. The first one walked up the causeway the afternoon the boat came into the harbor. He looked around the city like someone who wanted to learn what goods we had to trade. He was the one who brought the birds and animals. I sent supplies to the boat at that time, for he indicated that they were low in foodstuffs. I also sent them some metalwork to show the quality of our craftsmanship."

"What did the first man look like?" Exemplary Fortune asked.

"Very pale with an extraordinarily heavy beard, but that describes the other, too. The first one, though, was of average size, while the second was a giant."

"A giant?" This sounded like an expedition the empire might put together with many different kinds of people, except that in the Four Quarters, the people were of similar build and their hairstyles indicated their tribal diversity. The tampu's couple had said that the two strangers who had stayed there wore matching clothes. Maybe Lakefoam, or the World Animator as the coastal peoples would say, had somewhere created an inverse of the Four Quarters, and these were its inhabitants.

"A giant," Macaw repeated. "He came the next day, and he was not only taller than anyone I have ever seen, he was also quite husky. Excuse me, but I shared a drink with him. I know that I do not have the right to conclude treaties with other peoples, but he expressed great interest in all our metalwork. I thought it would be in the Four Quarters' best interest to be as cordial as possible."

From his demeanor, Macaw clearly believed that he had been

friendlier with the strangers than the Unique Inca would approve of. With the subsequent actions of the pale man who had stayed in the city, he was probably wondering if his overtures had been wise. Exemplary Fortune found himself secretly amused. This chief, like his predecessor, clearly believed that Recognition should be a much more important trading center than it was. But the problem would not be solved by treaties with outsiders.

As long as the Highland Islanders made the harbor unsafe, the empire would not even consider increasing Recognition's share of coastal trade. Of course, it was possible Macaw believed the strangers might be better able to subdue the Islanders than the Four Quarters. Exemplary Fortune said neutrally, "I will tell the Unique Inca of your actions."

The chief nodded in resigned acquiescence. He had probably not expected endorsement. "Then let us share beer in recognition and praise of the Four Quarters' most wise sovereign, Young Majesty."

And his actions also explained why Exemplary Fortune had not been offered a hospitable drink immediately. Macaw had wanted to confess how he had overstepped his authority before reaffirming his ties with the Four Quarters and its representative. "For myself," said Exemplary Fortune, "I will be glad to share a drink with you."

A barely perceptible quirk of the chief's mouth admitted himself overmatched as he sent servants to get a jar of beer, matching tumblers, and "the ring."

The tumblers the servants returned with were of wood carved in ceremonial scenes in the style of Navel's crafters, clearly a gift from the Four Quarters, probably from Royal Reckoning Inca's commander at the time the Matrons were incorporated into the empire. Macaw was clearly courting the favor of the Unique Inca's representative with all his wiles. The chief poured them each a tumbler of beer and handed one to Exemplary Fortune with his right hand as was befitting to a superior. "To our friendship," he said.

"May the two of us always be able to talk peaceably," Exemplary Fortune replied.

Macaw smiled and drank.

When they had each drunk a sociable amount, Macaw opened the small wicker box that had arrived with the beer. The circlet inside was much too large for anyone's finger and too small for the wrist of anyone but a baby. It was dull gray and had a line on one side where the two ends had not been properly aligned.

"The first stranger gave this to me. I thought I had indicated I wanted something like the shiny suit he wore, and so I was disappointed; but, since this is what he chose to give me, this is what I took. I had largely forgotten about it when I sent the message to Young Majesty. Afterward, when a courtier reminded me, I had one of the local silversmiths test it. The ring's metal broke two of his tools when he tried to dent it, and only with the greatest difficulty was he able to scratch it at all. Then, with my permission, he tried to melt the ring in his furnace. As the ring grew hotter, it glowed, first a dull red, then brighter and brighter until it was a brilliant orange-yellow, but it would not melt. When the silversmith pulled it out of the fire, it was soft enough that he was able to dent it with a hammer blow; but, as it cooled and darkened, it became as hard as it had been before." Macaw held the ring out for Exemplary Fortune to take.

Exemplary Fortune squeezed it, gingerly at first and then with all his strength, and tried to pull it out of shape between his hands, but he could barely make it give. Now that Macaw had pointed the mark out to him, he could see the flat dent the silversmith had made. He pouched the ring thoughtfully. If the strangers made their clothes from this metal, they would be a formidable foe. "Did the strangers, either of them, seem disappointed that you did not have any of this metal? Did they in any way indicate they would like some?"

Macaw thought for a heartbeat and then shook his head. "They were both delighted with the gold and silver work I showed them, but, when I touched the metal of his clothing with my hand, the first man seemed surprised I would ask about it. He thought for a bit and then pulled a straight knife out of a tight-fitting leather pouch on his belt and cut the ring off a leather thong."

"What was the knife made out of?"

"It wasn't silver, and it was shiny white like his clothes. I would guess that it was the same metal."

Which meant the strangers did know how to make weapons out of their hard metal—which still led nowhere. If they had weapons of the metal, then they could only want the silver and gold for decoration—or as a cover for a scouting expedition that would later lead to a war of conquest. The Four Quarters did that. He needed more information. "Were they interested in bronze or copper?"

Macaw shook his head immediately. "Not at all. I showed the first man some bronze ware, and I had the feeling that, if he weren't being polite, he would have scorned the pieces utterly."

But that made it only slightly less likely that the interest in gold and silver was a cover for something else. Those two metals were the more decorative.

Exemplary Fortune took another swallow of beer to ponder the information he knew, and all that he didn't know. "The quipu said the strangers took three of our people. Who were they?"

"I sent Young Fox, one of my advisors, with them," said Macaw too casually, "to be the Four Quarters' representative. Now, though, given the way their man has been acting, I wonder if I did the right thing." He shook his head dolefully.

So the chief really had been trying to make a separate deal with the strangers. When he talked with Select Seed, Exemplary Fortune would have to find out how competent Macaw's son was.

"The second man we are well rid of," Macaw continued. "He had been married to a fine woman, but she died three years ago, and he has always managed to be sick or otherwise unavailable when the Unique Inca's inspector comes to marry people. He's supposedly a courier, but he's so unreliable most people won't have anything to do with him. I had already had to chastise him publicly for laziness, and he wasn't reforming. He has three children, but his wife's parents took them in when she died. I don't know that anyone is going to miss him." He fidgeted with his tumbler for a few heartbeats. "If you don't mind, I'd rather you asked the Incas about the third."

Now that was interesting. Macaw seemed sincerely upset this time, and, although Exemplary Fortune could push if he wanted, he decided to wait. If he needed to, he could come back to the chief's compound after he visited the fortress.

Taking his silence for acquiescence, Macaw got up from his rug. "Let me show you the menagerie we've acquired."

They strolled out to the compound's ornamental garden. The garden was filled with fragrant yellow oleander, heady purple heliotropes, and other sweet-smelling flowers, but the air was tainted with a strong undertone of rank dung. A gardener was frantically scooping up a reeking pile of apparently fresh dung as they walked into the area. Following Macaw's lead, Exemplary Fortune pretended not to notice as the birds and animals were duly displayed for his edification. The birds were about the size of partridges and came in two varieties, one of which was red-brown all over with a red fleshy line on the top of its head, and a single bird like the others but with long brightly colored tail feathers and a big red lump on its head. That one, said Macaw, had to be the male since all the others had laid at least one egg. They all made soft clucking noises that reminded Exemplary Fortune of a cui's soft murmurs. Except for the lumps on their heads, they were quite ordinary, a game-type bird that could have come from some remote corner of the empire.

The animals, on the other hand, were astonishingly grotesque. Their bodies were as big as a llama's, but they had no neck, and their short stumpy legs ended in hooves like a deer's. Their scanty body covering was in the form of thick stiff hairs, and their muzzles ended in a perfectly round flat circle. They grunted and dug in the ground for roots, which drove their caretakers frantic because they did not care whether the plants they dug up were otherwise useful or not. It soon became clear that they were also the ones that voided the stinking dung.

"The birds," said Macaw, "may turn out to be good eating when we have enough to kill one, but unless the Unique Inca would like them as an exotic animal, we see little use for the grunters." A note in his voice implied the animals were considerably more trouble than he was saying. Having overstepped his bounds on the issues he felt most important, he had evidently decided to stay within self-imposed limits on this.

Exemplary Fortune promised blandly to ask the Unique Inca for his decision on the strange animals as soon as possible. And that was that. Exemplary Fortune left the chief's compound with far more information on the strangers than he had arrived with, but he was not even close to a coherent whole. He could see, though, in his mind's eye, the bewildered face of the speaker. First a dreadful omen, then a good one. If the pattern held, his final understanding of the strangers should be both good and terrifyingly waka at the same time—if they were what the omen had referred to.

He headed for the Inca fortress, but there were rafts starting to unload warriors onto the causeway at the harbor. Locals lined the route to the fortress. They cheered as the first warriors marched down the causeway to dry land, and the warriors grinned back. So Commander Shrewdness had already defeated the Highland Islanders. Excellent.

However, now would not be the time to try to talk with the fortress's captain. Besides, if Exemplary Fortune waited until the warriors were settled into the fortress, he could talk with Shrewdness instead of Select Seed, whom he hardly knew. Shrewdness, as an army commander, was of higher rank than Select Seed and would have more authority and means to carry out any plans they made. Exemplary Fortune watched the unloading for a while, judging the extent of the victory from the warriors' demeanor, genuinely elated, and checking the number of wounded, not very many.

His father would be pleased. The Unique Inca's grudge against the Highland Islanders, who were most to be feared when they smiled and treated you hospitably, was fierce. Once before, the Four Quarters had gone to Highland Island with an army and defeated the Islanders. That time, after the Islanders had feasted the empire's army and sworn eternal friendship, the Incas and their troops had accepted a ride back to the mainland on the Islanders' rafts. None of those warriors had reached shore alive. Young Majesty had sent another expedition to the Island and killed hundreds of the Islanders for their treachery, but the Islanders had still not learned to honor the empire's peace. So the Incas had to do it all again, and the Incas had learned. This time Taciturn rafts were ferrying the warriors back to the mainland.

Not only the rafts came from the coast. By their headbands and hairstyles, about two-thirds of the celebrating warriors were from coastal tribes, a mixture of Matrons from the Recognition area, Chimu from the central coast, and Taciturns and Dolefuls from the area just north of the Fortunate Soul Desert. That was not his father's doing. In a real sense this was not Young Majesty's victory. The Unique Inca had expressed displeasure when he learned that the Highland Islanders were once again raiding the coast, but he had done no more than that. If Whence Grasping and Shrewdness had not developed a campaign strategy without his authorization, there likely would have been no battle and no victory. Exemplary Fortune bit his lip. He did not want to doubt his father, especially not now.

Exemplary Fortune went back to the tampu in a thoughtful mood. He found that Qantu Flower was still out in the city doing reconnaissance. The Glowing men were in the garden behind the tampu, giving each other bad advice on how to stop somebody who was trying to either beat them up or get away. In lieu of the things he could not do, Exemplary Fortune changed tunics and joined them at their practice.

"See," one of the men was saying as he walked back out into the garden, "even if you get the knife away from me, I can jump on you like this." Exemplary Fortune winced as the man crossed his legs when he stepped in to swing his arm around and grab the other man's forearm. It worked on his fellow Glowing, but would not have worked against even a well-trained turn-warrior. Against a skilled enemy such a tactic would have certainly gotten him killed.

Exemplary Fortune walked into the eager gathering. "Let me play enemy for a while," he suggested.

The Glowings all looked at each other, half with an anxious enthusiasm, half with real worry. "Ha," said the tampu-keeper who was watching them, "now you get to find out how your tactics work against a professional."

The Glowings took this as encouragement. Smiling self-consciously, one untied the cords they had bound around the latest "enemy" 's wrists and brought them over to Exemplary Fortune. Exemplary Fortune had to stop himself from throwing the cord-bearer to the ground and tying him up with the rope. The pale stranger would certainly not play by their rules and wait patiently until they had bound his wrists before beginning to fight back. But this was also a kind of diplomatic session, and throwing the man immediately would just convince the Glowings that he did not play by the rules, not that their tactics were unsound. The man bound his wrists and stepped away.

"This is a knife," said one of the other men, showing Exemplary Fortune a short shaped stick.

Exemplary Fortune nodded. The man stepped back a pace, then came at Exemplary Fortune from the front, his face in a silly, half-concealed grin. Exemplary Fortune waited for the right moment, then kicked his right foot into the man's shin, not as hard as he could but hard enough to hurt fiercely. As the man froze in shocked and pained surprise, Exemplary Fortune spun him to the ground. The man nearly impaled himself on the stick as he went down, and Exemplary Fortune had to pull him up at the last instant to keep him from killing himself.

"I believe you're dead," Exemplary Fortune observed mildly.

"You didn't even take the knife," said the man.

"I didn't have to," said Exemplary Fortune. "If I had wanted it, I could have pulled it just as quickly from your dead body."

The man sat up and rubbed absently at his sore shin. He still looked rather stunned.

Exemplary Fortune picked up the stick from the ground where the man had dropped it. "It is not a wise idea to leave weapons around where miscreants can get at them," he said.

The man he had defeated opened his mouth to protest, then shut it again. One of the other Glowings came over to help the man up off the ground.

Exemplary Fortune looked at the rest of the men, and one began circling in from behind him. He was, foolishly, not carrying a knife. Without having to worry about weapons, Exemplary Fortune pivoted around low to the ground, attacking with his shoulder and using the man's momentum to sweep him off his feet. The man flipped completely over and landed on the ground with a solid thunk.

It took the man several heartbeats to get his breath back. "You didn't use the knife," he got out finally.

"So," said Exemplary Fortune, "do you want me to kill you with it now, or have you surrendered?"

"I've surrendered," said the man hastily.

Exemplary Fortune looked at the remaining six men, but it was obvious that they had lost all interest in going after him. That he had not used the knife in either encounter had probably demoralized them as much as anything else. "Is there anything else you want to try?" he asked the group.

"Maybe we could all attack you at once, or something," one man offered without enthusiasm.

"And all get in each other's way," said Exemplary Fortune. He started picking at the knots as he talked, and one of the men came over to untie him. "I have been playing gently, as a real enemy would not. I do not have time to teach you hand-to-hand combat, so I am going to teach you one vital rule instead. Do not let anyone who might be an enemy get close enough to touch you."

"But what happens if he's attacking someone else?"

Good question. "First, leave it to me. If that's impossible, then aim for the legs or the body with your sling, but only as a last resort. We want both of these men alive and as unharmed as possible."

The men looked at each other unhappily, all their fun ruined.

Exemplary Fortune smiled. "Since sling stones are usually slung at the head, I suggest you set up a target and practice aiming for legs."

The men's interest revived.

The watching tampu-keeper said, "We've got a kind of target in the tampu. We could use that."

The kind-of-target was a wooden frame behind bins of supplies in a far corner. Its function was not totally clear to Exemplary Fortune, but it had obviously been battered around. It took a bit of bracing to make the frame stand up securely. The Glowings adapted to this new practice much more easily. They had obviously had a great deal of experience downing the birds who raided the cornfields and were nearly as skilled as Exemplary Fortune. They also adapted to aiming low more quickly than he did. Exemplary Fortune praised their skills lavishly.

After an hour and a half of practice—not enough time to wear him out, but definitely enough to work up a lather of perspiration in the heat—Exemplary Fortune said, "We clearly have divided the defense correctly. Keep practicing as you will. I will be back by nightfall."

The men grinned at him, and Exemplary Fortune decided he would emphasize again, before they started out, that slings were only to be used as an absolute last resort. Still, it was heartwarming to see them so enthusiastic about their duty. He took another bath, put on the formal clothes again, and headed to the fortress.

The guards at the gateway to the fort wore the blue-and-gold headbands of Taciturns, and Exemplary Fortune saw Dolefuls and Chimu as he crossed the courtyard to Commander Shrewdness's office. Since the lowlanders had not yet proven their trustworthiness, the uplanders were all either Incas or Warm Valleys, who were honorary Incas.

Shrewdness had cleared his office of lower officials by the time Exemplary Fortune reached it, but his gold earrings were still the pair that he called "two clubs crossed" and wore only on military expeditions. He smiled warmly as he greeted Exemplary Fortune and kissed him on both cheeks. "It's good to see you, or—" his eyes twinkled "—have you been sent to check up on me? If you'd like, I can provide you with accommodations on Highland Island for however long it takes to be sure the Islanders are behaving properly."

"I am sure they have all been properly chastened and will never misbehave again," Exemplary Fortune replied with mock seriousness.

Shrewdness snorted. "Then you're more optimistic than I. As soon as we killed a few of their so-called leaders, the rest swore undying devotion to the Four Quarters, the Unique Inca, the

Unique Inca's favorite llama, his favorite cui, his favorite piss pot, and my nephew's little left toe. I expect they've already gotten over it. That's why they are currently building a garrison for the troops I left behind."

Exemplary Fortune grinned. "So the coastal troops worked well."

"Mostly. The Chimu kept trying to command, and then I'd have to chide them, and they'd get annoyed. The other coastal tribes would be amused, and the Chimu would get even more annoyed." He shook his head. "I thought they'd gotten over their empire."

Exemplary Fortune raised an eyebrow. "So no more Chimu in the Four Quarters' armies for a while."

Shrewdness nodded glumly. "Which they've already figured out. We'll have to come up with some honor to mollify them."

"Maybe we could send some Chimu to join Bright Rainbow's army against the Colddungs."

Shrewdness contemplated Exemplary Fortune. "Now that is a possibility I hadn't considered."

"And then, to complete their ecstasy, we move the Colddungs to Highland Island and put the Chimu in charge of civilizing the lot."

"You tell your father."

"And you tell Bright Rainbow."

A man came to the doorway with beer as Shrewdness's lip quirked up. The man offered to pour, but Shrewdness nodded for him to leave. "Sorry about the tumbler," he said as he poured. The tumblers were fine silver, but one had the design obliterated along one side. "The silversmith told me it'd be easier to make new ones than repair the old so I just had him take the dent out." He sighed unhappily.

"Local trouble?" Exemplary Fortune asked sympathetically.

"Actually," said Shrewdness, "I'm still not sure what happened. The silversmith's son, who delivered the new ones, was also mysteriously carrying a silver tumbler from Navel into the fortress."

"Into the fortress?" Exemplary Fortune repeated.

"Indeed. When Captain Select Seed asked the youth how he had gotten it, he started crying." Shrewdness paused.

"And so Select Seed sent him to Macaw," Exemplary Fortune prompted.

Shrewdness gave him a wry grin. "And he ran away. Before anyone realized what was happening, he'd swum out to the strangers' boat as it was leaving. Macaw's upset, the silversmith . . . well, actually, I don't know how the silversmith feels, but I know how I'd feel if one of my children went somewhere on a simple errand and inexplicably vanished."

Perhaps, thought Exemplary Fortune, this was Macaw's way of getting another local onto the Beard boat. No, that didn't make sense, especially since he'd been fairly open about sending Young Fox.

"Anyway, the new tumblers are in a storeroom until I talk to Macaw." Shrewdness rubbed absently at the pitcher's handle and then asked, "So what did Young Majesty send you about?"

"He's worried about the strangers."

Shrewdness regarded him with interest. He, unlike most of Young Majesty's courtiers, had been willing to tell Exemplary Fortune how mistrustful he was becoming of the Unique Inca's judgment. He knew Exemplary Fortune would provide information to explain whether or not he believed the Unique Inca's worries to be accurate and why.

"I'm beginning to think he may be right to be anxious," said Exemplary Fortune carefully. He was not sure how much persuasion it would take to convince Shrewdness that his father's worries were reasonable. "The Divine Speaker was given an unfavorable omen at Majestic Festival—he said it meant drought—and the speaker at Throat Town received an omen so strange he didn't know how to interpret it when my father had me ask for an augury at the Sun temple there." Shrewdness still looked skeptical, so Exemplary Fortune continued, "Certainly what I've heard about the strangers so far is not very hopeful."

"That's true enough," Shrewdness said. He filled the tumblers and offered one to Exemplary Fortune with his left hand. Exemplary Fortune grinned and took it. He was the petitioner here, and, be-sides, Shrewdness was still both far wiser and higher-ranking than he. He liked the easy honesty of their relationship, and Shrewdness knew that.

Shrewdness took a swallow of beer and said, "I did see something of the strangers myself. Their boat was impressive, I will admit that, but, frankly, I wouldn't be surprised if they stole it. They were as motley a crew as I've laid eyes on, loud, dirty, and with little apparent discipline. Their clothes, though similar from one man to another, appeared to be randomly decorated, with no sign of rank that I could discern. There was no way to distinguish the captain from the other men; and, although a few may have had order in their hearts, most acted as though they should have been hung long ago."

"How closely did you observe them?"

"I was actually on the boat. They came in as we were rafting off Highland Island, and I took the time to go aboard to see what I could learn. The boat was made of wood cut into even boards joined firmly side to side and end to end. The boards were curved somehow, and two curves joined to make a kind of bowl, a huge bowl. The boat had one floor made of flat boards open to the air, like a raft's floor, only much higher above the water, and under that, it had a big room filled with stores. The floor of that room was again flat boards. Since all the boat that I could see above water was made of curved boards, I thought there might be another layer below that. I bent down to feel around the slabs to see how they were fastened."

"You might have ended up in the water," said Exemplary Fortune.

Shrewdness shrugged. "The boat was wood. Wood floats."

"Generally," said Exemplary Fortune.

"Generally," Shrewdness conceded. "And actually, the man who was showing me around didn't want to go any further down at first, so I was taking a bit of a risk. Still, I was curious. When I started tugging at the edges of various boards, my guide laughed, and lifted one of them up." Shrewdness smiled lazily at Exemplary Fortune. "I really was half-expecting water to come gushing out, but nothing happened. I gathered my courage—it was dark and smelly where we were, and the man's laugh hadn't been that friendly—and looked in. The bottom storey, assuming that's what it was, was even darker than the one we were in and fetid smelling. It was also dank, too low to stand up in, and filled with stones."

"Stones?" Exemplary Fortune asked, startled from his other questions. They seemed an awkward thing to carry by boat.

Shrewdness grinned. "Stones. I've been thinking about it, and I ran a couple experiments while on the island. I think they keep the strangers' boat from tipping over. It has all these big sails and masts up top, and I'm pretty sure that if they didn't put stones in the bottom, the whole thing would turn topsy-turvy."

Exemplary Fortune was intrigued. "Did you talk to the Taciturns about whether they could make a boat like that?"

Shrewdness snorted. "They didn't want to think about it, and I do admit their rafts work disgustingly well." With Exemplary Fortune's questions and comments, Shrewdness went on to talk about the bearded strangers' clothes, their possible tribal diversity, their command structure, the reasons they might have come to Recognition.

As Exemplary Fortune shared his surmise that the bearded strangers might soon be returning to invade in force, Shrewdness's eyes grew thoughtful. "I hadn't considered that," he said when Exemplary Fortune finished, "because they didn't seem to have the discipline necessary to carry out a sustained invasion. It hadn't occurred to me until now, but their seeming disorder might be as much of a ploy as our scouts' gifts. Though what that implies about their homeland . . ." He shook his head.

"Disordered groups would have to be commonplace," said Exemplary Fortune. A heartbeat later, he added, "and accepted."

"A disordered group of clans," said Shrewdness tentatively, "spilling out across the world."

"The Colddungs," said Exemplary Fortune, though, as he thought about the analogy, he was less sure. The Colddungs did have some order, and they were not dirty. But they had once had a bearded stranger with them.

"I did look for weapons," Shrewdness said. "Most of the men wore swords that looked as though they were made of the same material as the shiny clothes some wore. I didn't see any slings, though, or bows or spears. At the time I decided they didn't carry long-distance weapons. Now that I've heard about the thunder-sticks, though . . . I wish I'd seen them demonstrated."

Indeed. Exemplary Fortune pulled the ring Macaw had been given from his pouch and told Shrewdness about the silversmith's tests.

Shrewdness turned the ring over in his hands and rubbed the hammer mark. "This makes them a lot more formidable. I didn't want to start a fight just to see how good their weaponry might be." He rubbed the ring against his tumbler and regarded both.

"They're just too different," he said then. "What I thought I learned on the boat, what we think we know about them now, everything is suspect." He stared pensively at the ring, and Exemplary Fortune, respecting his mood, didn't speak.

After some heartbeats, Shrewdness looked up. "The Taciturns say they've met boats like these twice before. Once, some years ago, a similar boat is said to have sailed up the coast from south to north. Last year, a few miles north of here, another similar boat highjacked a Taciturn raft, stole just about everything except the logs it was made of, and also either stole or killed three of the men aboard." He made a face. "When I asked the Taciturns why the Unique Inca hadn't been informed, they said that, though they were eternally grateful for the Four Quarters' protection of their land, the Incas were not known for their skills on water. They seem to think having everything stolen out from under them is just another hazard of coastal trading."

"We've helped them against the Highland Islanders," Exemplary Fortune said slowly, wondering about the Taciturns' motives.

"True," said Shrewdness, "but only because we know where the Islanders' base is. Admit it, the reason the Highland Islanders were able to destroy our first expedition was because we literally could not make a boat to save our lives."

"We trusted them," Exemplary Fortune retorted.

"We had to," Shrewdness said quietly.

Exemplary Fortune bit back the words he wanted to say and forced himself to think calmly. The water, lakes. All the water in ancestral Inca territory was in swiftly flowing rivers. Within the empire, the largest body of water was Lake Titicaca. All others were but a fraction of one tribe's territory, all except the Great Lake, which so far they had conquered only one shore of, indeed, knew only one shore of. No one had ever come from lands on the Great Lake beyond Inca knowledge. No one until now. The Taciturns should have told them about it. No, they wouldn't have been believed, and, if the Taciturns had been believed, their words would have been dismissed as unimportant. Exemplary Fortune realized he had always imagined the world simply ending somewhere beyond sight of land. There was no reason to believe it did that, and now there was reason to believe it didn't. "Maybe they come from the other side of the Great Lake."

"That's one possibility," Shrewdness said.

"And the others?" Exemplary Fortune asked. His heart was beginning to feel stretched out of shape by a world suddenly much larger than he had ever imagined.

"We don't know how long the coast is on this side of the Lake," said Shrewdness.

Another heart stretch. Lake Titicaca's shores were settled by Eminences, Covereds, and Belows; but the coast of the Great Lake had tens of tribes in the part the Four Quarters controlled. He had assumed, they had all assumed, that the lands they knew, the tribes they knew, were most of the world. Unreasonably. Every time they brought a tribe into the Four Quarters, there was always another tribe beyond the tribe beyond that one. He had not thought how far the process could go. Maybe beyond the reach of even Young Majesty's great-grandson's conquests, there were more tribes, and, somewhere among them, there was a tribe that used a metal harder than anything the Four Quarters mined.

Because Incas did not use boats, that tribe had now come looking for the Four Quarters before the empire even suspected such a people could exist. The idea was hard to keep in his heart because everyone knew there was nothing beyond the Great Lake, that nothing lived out there except fishes. That it was the end of the world. For the Incas it was. For someone else it clearly was not. "We will have to build more fortresses along the coast."

"We have to find out what that metal is," said Shrewdness.

"Maybe they are traders, after all," said Exemplary Fortune smiling thinly. "They appear to have all of it."

"They may well be traders," said Shrewdness, "but, whoever or whatever they are, they've come looking for us rather than us for them. I don't like that."

Exemplary Fortune agreed. "Perhaps you and your troops should stay at Recognition's fortress until I present my father with the information we've gathered about the strangers, and let him decide whether to recall you or keep an army here."

Shrewdness frowned a bit, thinking. "Given his current mood, he will doubtless want to keep an army in the area. And this time I agree that it does sound like a useful precaution. Do remember that Young Majesty's other courtiers will need careful reasoning to be convinced of the threat. He may well not be willing to give the necessary orders himself."

Exemplary Fortune sighed and nodded. "I will be both cautious and firm."

Shrewdness nodded in his turn. "Good. Now let's see the actual evidence we've got." He stood, and Exemplary Fortune stood with him.

As they walked through the fortress's main courtyard, Shrewdness said, "From what I've heard—I haven't visited them yet myself—the pale one isn't very impressive-looking at the moment, but then, we got him somewhat worse for wear, as it were. Since the dark didn't do anything wrong, Captain Select Seed has given him the run of the fortress's compound. Didn't want to let him out, though. Frankly, I'm glad you'll be taking them off our hands. I don't like caging people."

They went into a small room that had evidently once housed pumas, for there were two wooden posts of the kind they were normally tied to. Now there was a man, his arms spread wide, tied between them. He sat on a blanket on the floor, and someone had put a large box at his back for him to rest against. Except for a cape around his shoulders, he was naked, revealing an astonishing variety of scratches and bruises over most of his body and one particularly nasty scrape along the front of his right leg around the knee. His left leg was also missing some skin but was not nearly as damaged.

He had evidently been sleeping, but his eyes popped open as they walked into the room. They had the wary look of a caged wild animal unsure whether to snap or not. They were a lighter brown than Exemplary Fortune had ever seen in a person before. His nose was small and thin, and his face narrow. The promised beard ran from the point of his chin halfway back to his ears. His upper lip was also covered with hair. His head hair was shorter than most tribes' and cut to show his ears like the Incas' hairstyle did, though, since his ears were not adorned with earrings or painted, it was difficult to figure out why they were highlighted.

Shrewdness crouched down next to him, and the man jerked his head back as though he expected to be hit. "Captain Select Seed tells me it took a whole ten-group to subdue him," he said. "Do you know what happened to his leg?"

"I was told they had to drag him to Macaw's because he wouldn't walk."

"And nobody was feeling kindly disposed towards him right then anyway. Makes sense."

A figure suddenly appeared in the doorway, and Shrewdness rose quickly to his feet. It was the dark man, his eyes wide, his glance darting between his companion and the two of them. On impulse, Exemplary Fortune put a hand to his chest. "Exemplary Fortune," he said.

The dark licked his lips. They were full and richly colored by the darkness of his skin. He put his right hand to his own chest. "Ginez," he said.

"Ginez," Exemplary Fortune repeated carefully. Then, touching himself again, he repeated his own name.

Ginez used his hand to point at Exemplary Fortune and repeated that name, mangling it only slightly. Exemplary Fortune smiled approval and then, using his hand to point as Ginez had, indicated Shrewdness and gave him that name, which he duly repeated. Then Ginez hand-pointed at the man on the floor, and the man growled exactly like a wild animal. Ginez pulled his hand back as though he were afraid it would be bitten off. He looked helplessly from Exemplary Fortune to Shrewdness and back.

"I take it you're stuck with him," said Shrewdness sympathetically to Ginez.

Ginez shrugged and looked at the floor.

Shrewdness looked appraisingly at the pale man. "Looks like he's over fourteen to me."

"He does that," said Exemplary Fortune, guessing what Shrewdness intended.

"And he needs a loincloth."

"He certainly does," agreed Exemplary Fortune.

"So it's about time he had an adult name, don't you think?"

"Seems so."

Ginez looked from one to the other of them in bewilderment, probably confused by their jocular tone.

"And we're his closest relatives in Four Quarters," Shrewdness continued.

"Also his furthest," said Exemplary Fortune, giving them both a little time to decide if they wanted to carry through this bit of disorder.

Shrewdness tossed his head, getting rid of that objection. "His closest," he repeated.

"His closest," Exemplary Fortune conceded, hoping none of the trickier wakas were listening.

Shrewdness hand-pointed to the man on the floor. "Your name is Tamed Ocelot." He looked up at Ginez and repeated slowly, "Tamed Ocelot," with his hand still pointing at the pale man.

Ginez backed up an anxious half-step and said nothing.

Exemplary Fortune had only seen one ocelot. It had been a spitting ball of fury, clawing at anything that moved. To tame that ocelot would have been an impressive feat, as impressive perhaps as taming the man on the floor. It was definitely an appropriate name, and as full of good omen as any name this man could have. Exemplary Fortune repeated the name in his turn.

"Now," said Shrewdness, "we have to figure out what kind of name presents he gets."

"A loincloth and a tunic would be a good idea," said Exemplary Fortune.

Shrewdness nodded. He went to the door around the skittish Ginez, who followed his movements with his eyes. Once Shrewdness had cleared the door, Ginez darted to the back of the room and crouched there watching warily. If he were choosing a name for Ginez, Exemplary Fortune decided, he would name him after a small woodland bird. The two of them appraised each other. Ginez's beard was similar to his companion's, as was his hairstyle, though neither was as conspicuous against his dark skin.

Exemplary Fortune also had his first look at the strangers' clothes. They were as Shrewdness had described them, an oddly shaped top with coverings for the arm and closely fitted coverings for the whole leg. Between the top covering and those for the leg was a bulgy something that made it look as though the man had a large symmetrical tumor from his upper thigh to his midriff. The foot coverings were of animal skin and covered the top of the foot as well as the bottom. Ginez, like his companion, wore no headband or other head covering. Still, if a people's degree of civilization were measured by how many clothes they wore, then these people were even more civilized than Incas.

With that thought, Exemplary Fortune found his glance straying almost reassuringly to the figure on the floor, who clearly fit no one's definition of civility. The man was even spotted like an ocelot, he thought with amusement, even if the spots were bruises rather than natural coloring.

Shrewdness returned with a bright yellow tunic and a matching darker loincloth. He crouched down near Ginez. "This is for Tamed Ocelot." He pointed at the man on the floor. "Tamed Ocelot." He hefted the clothes. "Tamed Ocelot's." He held the clothes out to Ginez, who took them and folded them to his chest without otherwise moving. Shrewdness stood up without turning away from Ginez. "I also talked to the healer who's been working on Tamed Ocelot, but she's busy with men who were wounded on the Island." He turned to Exemplary Fortune. "I assume you're not leaving until tomorrow."

"Probably not," Exemplary Fortune admitted. It was already almost too late to make it to the first tampu east before dark.

"Good. I told her you would meet her here a half hour after sunrise." He took another look at Ginez, who hadn't moved since he had taken the clothes. "Something's sure worrying him," he observed.

Exemplary Fortune agreed, but there seemed no way to calm him without another few days of language lessons.

They left the room, and then, after Shrewdness took care of various administrative chores, went together to the Sun temple, where they told a speaker how they had named Tamed Ocelot. The speaker pursed his lips, clearly displeased at the irregularity, but agreed to sacrifice a cui to seal the new name with the gods. Tamed Ocelot's omen was entirely adequate, the organs coming out intact, though the lungs were not still pulsing. Exemplary Fortune found himself annoyed that a nonentity like Tamed Ocelot should get a tolerable omen without any effort when the omens his father got were fraught with foreboding.

He went back to the tampu, where the Glowing men were relaxing and the Glowing women were starting to cook dinner. Qantu Flower was not yet there, but she came in shortly after he did. She reported that she had talked to Macaw's wives, some of the other local women, including Guava, and a few of the Mothers. "Most of the women I talked with said the strangers made them uneasy even before the mad one grabbed Guava. Though they did not say so directly, it was clear that Macaw's wives felt he was much too willing to interpret the strangers' actions in the most positive manner possible. One woman said that she thought the first strangers looked as though they thought everything in town would soon be theirs." As she gave him a more complete report of what various women had said, her words kept resonating with what Exemplary Fortune had learned.

When she finished, Exemplary Fortune told her what he had learned and surmised. She got a rather disgusted look on her face when he repeated Macaw's words about the first two strangers.

Qantu Flower thought for a few heartbeats after he finished speaking, and then said, "We may not have learned everything we need to know, but certainly it is much easier to believe that these strangers are inimical than that they are friendly. What worries me most about the strangers is that they are all men. I keep wondering why the women have all stayed home."

Exemplary Fortune nodded. "It does sound as though the men expected to be waging a war as soon as they got on their boat."

"But they would still need someone to cook for them," Qantu Flower protested.

"Shrewdness says they have an open box on their boat that is filled with a slow-burning fire. He says it appears that one or some of the men cook for the others."

"How absurd," said Qantu Flower. "Men don't know how to cook."

Exemplary Fortune grinned. "Maybe that is the strangers' talent, that the men know how to cook."

"And the women, I suppose, fight all the battles," she replied derisively.

Exemplary Fortune wondered if that really was so impossible. Maybe that was the hidden secret of the strangers, that the men conducted the scouting missions, and then, if the group decided to fight, the women would come to wage war. Given what else they knew about the strangers, it sounded absurd enough to be likely.

4

INTERREGNUM
MAJESTIC FESTIVAL MONTH

In actual history, Exemplary Fortune traveled to Recognition
only after civil war started and so never met the two Spaniards.

The next morning Exemplary Fortune took his men and a
stretcher to the fortress, where the healer showed them how
to care for Tamed Ocelot's leg. Ginez watched anxiously. Anxiety
seemed habitual with him.

Looking at Ginez, Exemplary Fortune realized that he was
wearing the only undamaged strangers' clothes in the Four Quarters. He would have to start wearing local clothing sooner or later.
It might as well be now. But Exemplary Fortune didn't want to
make him more frightened than he already was. He had one of his
men get an outfit to match Tamed Ocelot's and put that outfit
down on the floor next to Ginez, saying clearly, "Ginez's." Then
he picked up the bundle they'd given Ginez yesterday, which had
been put neatly in a corner. "Tamed Ocelot's." He carried the
clothes over to the stretcher and set them down there.

Exemplary Fortune crouched down next to Tamed Ocelot. "We
are going to untie your bonds now. You can fight us or not as you
wish, but since you are in the middle of an Inca fortress, I recommend that you do not try anything."

Tamed Ocelot watched him warily.

Exemplary Fortune signaled two of his men to untie the man. Tamed Ocelot watched the process carefully but made no other move than to bring down each arm as they untied it. When they had both his arms untied, he rubbed his wrists and moved his shoulders as though to loosen them.

Exemplary Fortune hand-pointed at the stretcher. "Now we are going to put you on the stretcher."

Tamed Ocelot allowed two men to help him to his feet and limped heavily to the stretcher. He allowed them to dress him and sat where they wanted him to. Once he was fully clothed, Exemplary Fortune looked back at Ginez. Ginez had backed into a corner and wrapped his arms around himself. So much for that idea. Exemplary Fortune picked up Ginez's new clothes and held them out to him. Ginez shook his head and hugged himself tighter. Exemplary Fortune took the bundle over to the stretcher and showed it to Tamed Ocelot. "Ginez's," he said, using the clothes to point in that direction; and then, when the man said nothing, "Would you kindly tell your friend that the new clothes won't hurt him?"

Tamed Ocelot still said nothing.

Exemplary Fortune had no idea how to get the strange clothes off. They found out. They wrestled Ginez to the floor and worked at the strange fastenings until they figured out how each one worked. Some were rather ingenious. Ginez fought, but he did not fight hard, and, once they found the first silver pin in his clothes, he stopped fighting altogether. He cried, though, as they found a remarkable number of gold and silver objects secreted in various places on his person. He tried to gather them back up whenever they let go of him.

Exemplary Fortune had one of the men pile the trinkets they found in a far corner; and then, since Ginez was apparently no threat, and Tamed Ocelot wasn't moving, he sent another man for an accountant to record the lot. The accountant exclaimed over several pieces he had noticed missing from the storerooms in the past several days and said he should have no trouble returning them all to their proper owners. Once they had Ginez thoroughly undressed and had checked his tightly curled hair for rings and other small objects, and the accountant had taken everything away, Ginez willingly put on the new clothes.

Exemplary Fortune looked at his charges with disgust. This was what he would bring back to his father, a thief and a would-be rapist. They packaged the clothes, Ginez's and the ruined set Tamed Ocelot had been wearing. Then, with some misgivings, because Ginez was so upset already, Exemplary Fortune had a man get rope to tie Ginez's hands together. It was obvious they could not trust him. When they produced the rope, Ginez fell to his knees and started crying again. Two of the men were so distressed that they said they would be happy to watch him. Exemplary Fortune shook his head. "We will see how he behaves today, and then tomorrow, when we're in the countryside, we may let him walk free."

Exemplary Fortune also decided to tie Tamed Ocelot to his stretcher; but, when they approached with rope, Tamed Ocelot was on his feet and half out the door almost before anyone could move. Only Exemplary Fortune's trained reflexes took him over the stretcher to tackle the man in the doorway. Under him, Tamed Ocelot tried to use his legs to lever Exemplary Fortune around, but his bad leg hampered him, and Exemplary Fortune was able to climb up his body and get an arm around his neck. He applied pressure to Tamed Ocelot's windpipe. The man went limp. When he released the pressure, Tamed Ocelot tensed again, positioning himself for a throw. Exemplary Fortune pressed down harder on his windpipe. "No." This time when he let up, Tamed Ocelot stayed still, not unconscious but quiescent.

Exemplary Fortune looked up to face the interested gaze of a number of Incas and Warm Valleys.

"Having trouble?" one asked.

"A little," said Exemplary Fortune, "but I think we can handle it." He'd learned something. Whatever else Tamed Ocelot was, he was a trained warrior. He had thought about that run out the door beforehand, had known how to pull himself up to avoid the men, and exactly the right angle to run for the door. He had also been shamming earlier about how bad his leg was. Though they had not had a serious fight, Exemplary Fortune was beginning to understand how he had been able to stand off a whole crowd of townspeople.

He lifted Tamed Ocelot's head by the hair—fortunately long enough to provide a grip—to show him the interested warriors watching them. Then he pulled him to his feet, marched him back over to the stretcher, and held him down flat on his back until he was tied hand and foot. They recleaned the wound on his leg and slathered it with the salve the healer had given them.

They carried the stretcher and led Ginez to the tampu, where the women were waiting. Qantu Flower's gaze explored Exemplary Fortune's now-wrinkled tunic. "Tamed Ocelot is, alas, not yet tame," he told her.

She surveyed him again with a trace of humorous pride in her eyes, then nodded. The tale of their fight would doubtless grow in the next few days as it was told and retold at the various tampus. Right now, she did not ask further, and the group set out immediately for the mountains and home.

They made reasonably good time the first day, but, on the second day, they had to carry the litter on the narrow and winding road along the cliffs, which slowed them considerably. Tamed Ocelot endured his often-amateurish ride stoically—like a warrior. Ginez, released from his bonds and out of the city, was much happier than he had been, though he hugged the cliff edge in any stretch with a drop-off on one side. From his reaction, it seemed likely that the strangers did not live in an area with high cliffs or mountains.

The third day of their journey they would reach the Majestic Road and begin to make better time. They needed to talk to Young Majesty as quickly as possible. Exemplary Fortune did not believe the bearded strangers' intentions were peaceful, not when they had left Tamed Ocelot behind as a representative. He understood his father's worries better now and could help the Unique Inca's other courtiers understand too.

From what he had observed so far, if they separated Ginez from Tamed Ocelot, Ginez would be willing to help them. They would need his help. If most of the strangers fought like Tamed Ocelot, finding strategies to defeat them would be a test of even Thorniest's skills. They would also have to station a permanent garrison at Recognition against the day when the strangers returned.

The third day, as the group climbed into the uplands, the air became cool and moist. Ginez shivered and wrapped his cloak tightly around himself. They would have to get extra clothes and coverings for both Ginez and Tamed Ocelot in Heads-of-Corn. Lowlanders sometimes died in the cool uplands. Exemplary Fortune did not want that to happen to these two, not with the information they had to be carrying in their minds.

The group reached Heads-of-Corn about midday. Exemplary Fortune had expected the town to be quiet, with most of its people working their fields. Instead, the whole population of the area seemed to have gathered in the plaza in front of the Sun temple. They all looked dazed, and some were crying. Exemplary Fortune could feel his heart plummet. The first person he addressed confirmed his worst fears. "Young Majesty is dead," he sobbed. "Our Unique Inca is gone."

Exemplary Fortune exchanged a stunned look with Qantu Flower. "I need . . . ," Exemplary Fortune started. He was too numb to figure out what his next words would have been.

"I'll take the group," said Qantu Flower, her voice sounding strained.

Exemplary Fortune nodded blindly. He turned and made his way through the crowd in front of the temple. No one stopped him as he walked into the temple or asked him his business. Maybe the speakers recognized him; maybe they no longer cared. He found the room with the gold band around its walls and the statue of the Sun, who ordered the Four Quarters and whom the Unique Inca embodied.

Exemplary Fortune sat down on the floor and stared blankly at the walls for a time. His father was not old enough, he thought. He was not old enough to be dead. Unique Incas did not die young. There had to be a mistake. But another thought whispered that Young Majesty had expected this. He had, in some measure, passed on that premonition. Ever since Exemplary Fortune had left Throat Town, it had been in his heart that he would never again see his father alive. For a long time, these two thoughts held his heart, blocking out all else. He made a picture of his father in his mind. It was his father as he had last seen him, a man grown old too young, worn down by something he could not name.

"I can name it for you now, Father," Exemplary Fortune said. "They travel by boat. They are warriors. They like gold and silver. They have a metal stronger and harder than anything we know. They do not have any honor. They do not cherish their families." He did not know if everything he told his father, told the Sun, in that quiet room was the truth, but most of it was. He had no one left to tell it to. He cried, but he did not lose himself in wailing, for he had information no one else in the Four Quarters could put together as he could. He had received a burden. Until he could pass it on, he had to keep functioning. He could not break down, not scream his loss. He would have to let the rest of the people in the Four Quarters mourn for him.

He had to communicate his knowledge. Not in Kitu Dove. With his father's death, Kitu Dove would no longer be the center of government. He would go south to Navel. In Navel, the learned elders of the empire lived, and soon, in Navel, Bright Rainbow would be installed as Unique Inca. He and Bright Rainbow had gotten along well for brothers, but this would not be information a Unique Inca would want to know so early in his reign, before he had time to consolidate his power. It was bad news, and it was bad news Bright Rainbow might well not be expecting. It was possible Young Majesty had not even sent him word that a strange boat had come to Recognition. Exemplary Fortune would have to be careful to present the information both clearly and believably. He had the ring, he had the clothes, and he had the two men. Especially he had Tamed Ocelot. Tamed Ocelot would make a believer out of almost anyone.

Exemplary Fortune kissed his fingers to the Sun's statue on the west wall. "Guide me in my journeys, o glorious Sun," he prayed. Then he left. Outside, the Sun was hidden by clouds filled with moisture He had drawn from the Earth. But it was not raining. Even the Sun was in mourning.

Exemplary Fortune found his charges at the edge of the crowd in front of the temple. The Glowings were huddled together in a sodden heap. Qantu Flower stood staring blankly at nothing, her hands clenched tightly in front of her. Ginez was off to the side, staring around anxiously at everyone. Tamed Ocelot watched them all with his calm hunter's gaze from his spot on the ground.

Exemplary Fortune went to Qantu Flower and put an arm around her waist. "We have to go to the tampu to talk," he told the group quietly.

None of the other mourners seemed to notice that he had said anything, and the Glowings did not move either. Exemplary Fortune went to them, talking to each man individually as Qantu Flower talked to the women. The men moved stiffly to pick up the stretcher, and the women followed them. Exemplary Fortune and Qantu Flower led them to the tampu. Once there, the women went to the stores to gather knives to chop off their hair and brown dye to smear their faces.

Exemplary Fortune sat down on the floor, and his charges gathered in front of him. Their eyes were downcast, and their movements were both listless and aimless. Only Qantu Flower showed any animation, and her eyes were fixed fiercely on his face. He focused equally on her. His cheeks were tear streaked, but he was no longer crying. "I mourn my father," he said, "as we all mourn our Unique Inca, but he has given me a commission, a task that I must complete beyond even his death." Exemplary Fortune blinked away new tears, waited until he could speak again.

"I was ordered to learn everything I could about the strangers who came to Recognition and to take that information to the Unique Inca so he could act on it. I have gathered the information, but the information is useless until I deliver it. The Unique Inca who gave me the task is no more, but soon, in Navel, a new Unique Inca will be fringed. I must carry this information to the new emperor. When I asked Tobacco for turn-workers, I asked for men who could be gone for a month." His gaze surveyed the Glowings, who were now all watching him. "I know you are unfamiliar with the center of the Four Quarters. I have no right to ask you to stay away from your homes longer than you orginally agreed, or to travel to more territory. All my authority was given me by . . ." He could not say his father's name. He choked and went on. "I have no authority to recruit new workers. If you feel you cannot go with me . . ."

The men and their wives were now looking at each other.

"We will go with you," one of the women said and then another. Soon all the couples had concurred.

Exemplary Fortune looked at each of the men and women in turn, asking them to affirm their decision individually. Llama ducked his head and said nothing. "Llama, what is it?" Exemplary Fortune asked.

Llama looked uncomfortable but still did not speak. Exemplary Fortune looked at Llama's wife. "His youngest brother," she said, "he will soon receive his adult name. Llama is supposed to choose the name for him."

"Then he should be at home with his family."

Llama shrugged uneasily, and his wife looked unsure as to what she should say.

"We need someone to carry a message to our families telling them where we are and why we have not come back, so they will not worry," said Exemplary Fortune to both of them.

"But you will have to help carry the stretcher sometimes," Llama said uneasily.

"I am a warrior," said Exemplary Fortune. "Warriors do much worse things than carry stretchers."

Llama and his wife exchanged another look. "If you think it's proper," she said. She looked both distressed and relieved.

"I think it is important," said Exemplary Fortune.

"Thank you," said Llama. "I—I am in your debt." They said good-by to the others and left. They did not ask for a wand of official business. Exemplary Fortune had none to give them, but they should be all right. The group was still very close to the lands they knew.

Exemplary Fortune looked at Qantu Flower, who nodded slightly. She took up a knife and, grabbing a handful of her hair, chopped it off as close to her scalp as she could. Exemplary Fortune took some brown dye and smeared it on his cheeks and forehead above his headband. The Glowing women took down their hair, and Qantu Flower helped them hack it off. The men and women all smeared their faces. When they were done, the men picked up Tamed Ocelot's litter, and they all went back to the ceremonies, watching the speakers reaffirm the order of the Four Quarters in this time of instability. The speakers prayed to the Sun to preserve the empire and to Lakefoam and to the Unique Inca Majestic Head-band, who came from the Earth with his siblings as the first Incas.

Exemplary Fortune watched speakers and the ceremonies with a heart that was numb with grief. The speakers' words and actions did not penetrate his sorrow. He let the others wail their grief away, but he felt nothing except a hollowness where his heart should be. Nothing here could touch him. He took Qantu Flower's hand, but he was acting by rote. He could not truly feel it or her.

At sunset, Exemplary Fortune led his charges back to the tampu. "We need to eat," he told them, "so we will be able to travel again in the morning."

They accepted his words, and together they ate a dinner, which Exemplary Fortune, at least, could not taste. After dinner, the Glowings and Qantu Flower went back to the mourning ceremo-nies, but Exemplary Fortune did not want to be with other people, especially other people who had never known Young Majesty. The mass of his friends and relatives with whom he could share his sorrow were all beyond his reach. And Young Majesty was dead; nothing anyone could say or do would change that.

After a while, Ginez hesitantly came over to Exemplary For-tune. Exemplary Fortune looked at him. At least Ginez was not mouthing words that meant little to him. If he could not be with his father's court, he would rather be with someone to whom the Unique Inca meant nothing. Besides, getting to know Ginez was part of his duty, part of his pledge to his father. The more infor-mation he had, the more likely it was that Bright Rainbow would listen to him.

Ginez gently touched a tear track on Exemplary Fortune's cheek in obvious question. "My father," said Exemplary Fortune, but that wouldn't help. He found a pick in the stores and, on the smooth-packed earthen floor, drew a picture of a man, naked, since with the strangers' odd clothes, there was no other certain way to distinguish the sexes. As he drew it, he labeled it with his voice, "Man."

"Man," said Ginez obediently, and then he said another word that Exemplary Fortune didn't understand.

Exemplary Fortune looked at him.

Ginez repeated the word.

It was the strangers' language, Exemplary Fortune realized; Ginez was giving him a word. Exemplary Fortune repeated the word as best he was able, and Ginez said it again. Exemplary Fortune corrected his pronunciation. Tamed Ocelot said something that sounded nasty, and Ginez blinked and swallowed. Exemplary Fortune drew a woman, and Ginez and he exchanged that word, with another nasty comment from Tamed Ocelot. Then Exemplary Fortune connected their hands and said, "Couple." This time Tamed Ocelot merely growled at their exchange of words. Exemplary Fortune drew a baby at the couple's feet, and Ginez and he exchanged words for "baby," "father," and "mother." Then Exemplary Fortune pointed at the baby and said his own name. When Ginez understood that, Exemplary Fortune rubbed out the father with his hand, which terrified him as though he were making it real.

Ginez looked at him, looked sad, and then, in wild surmise, looked toward the door, where the laments of the local populace could be heard. But Exemplary Fortune didn't want to talk anymore and held his hand up when Ginez made to ask him. He was crying again. The hollow space inside of him seemed to keep getting bigger as though it would swallow him. He put his head down on his knees and stopped trying to do or think anything until sleep overtook him.

For the next two tendays the turn-workers performed beyond any reasonable asking. They did not complain about bad weather, about missing their families, about traveling ever farther from home into lands where the customs were often strange to them, and the language spoken on the street was not always one they understood. Ginez gradually became part of their group, helping to carry the litter in turn and learning every day a little more of Humanity's

Mouth while teaching them all the strangers' language, which he called Spanish. Their watch on him in the larger tampus, where there would be trinkets he might want, became more and more perfunctory, although they always kept one man with him. The men, including Ginez, kept the worst aspects of caring for Tamed Ocelot from Exemplary Fortune; but, when they turned him every day or two, Exemplary Fortune was the one who stood over him to make sure he didn't hurt anyone. Tamed Ocelot watched them with his waiting gaze and said nothing.

Qantu Flower and Exemplary Fortune talked about Young Majesty, the wives left behind in Kitu Dove, Young Majesty's other courtiers, and Bright Rainbow, whose presence drew them south. But their words to each other provided little comfort. When Qantu Flower cried at night, he held her, and she did the same for him, but it did not seem to help much. He did not know how to comfort her. He wished at least that some of his other wives were with them to help her with her grief.

As they traveled south, they heard news of Young Majesty's funeral procession, which traveled behind them at the slow stately pace of a Unique Inca's court, so that, as they traveled, the group moved ever farther from Exemplary Fortune's father. Something else traveled south, though, that moved faster than either of them: the disease that had killed the Unique Inca. At first they heard of it as the Kitu Dove disease or the Inca's Death, and then it was the epidemic. Soon, in the villages they passed through, there were people mourning family members who had died of the Spotted Death, but it did not touch their small group, as though they were in a separate world unaffected by anything outside.

They also heard news of Bright Rainbow in Navel: how he had been approved by the gods and the council, how he had started his fast, how he had been fringed with due ceremony. Even with the epidemic, chiefs from all parts of the realm traveled to Navel to swear their allegiance to the new Unique Inca.

Slowly, step-by-step, day by day, life, which had only been a duty in the first terrible days after Young Majesty had died, became again something that was good in and of itself. Exemplary Fortune began, haltingly at first, to find the words and gestures that comforted Qantu Flower. He himself still cried at odd moments over something that unexpectedly reminded him of his father, but he also found himself smiling. He had been his father's favorite son and had basked in the warmth of his father's approval all his life, but he was also grown up, married, and able to take care of himself. He would go on.

With the lessening of that terrible pain, other worries began to gnaw at his awareness. Qantu Flower and he began to discuss more fully and intimately their worries about the other wives and children, and slowly their words of worry and sorrow brought a measure of peace into their hearts. Exemplary Fortune would also like to have been able to comfort Owl Pattern, who was probably with his father on the Majestic Road he himself traveled. He wondered if Shrewdness was still at Recognition or if the epidemic had left the coast unwatched. He did not, could not, know so much that he needed to know about his family, friends, and the health of the Four Quarters.

In midafternoon, a few miles south of Lynx Lake, Qantu Flower stumbled; and, when one of the women caught her arm, she said faintly, "My head hurts."

Exemplary Fortune went to her. "Can you walk?" he asked anxiously.

She was leaning lightly on the woman who had grabbed her, and a faint sheen of perspiration covered her forehead. "I'm not quite sure. I was all right . . ."

Exemplary Fortune could feel his heart contract painfully. He moved automatically to do what had to be done, putting the travel wand in his pouch and scooping her up. To the Glowings, who were standing dumbstruck in the road waiting for new instructions, he said, "We will stop at the next tampu." He turned and led the group as quickly as he could up the road to the next place of refuge. Qantu Flower was a heavy burden against his shoulder, and he could not move as fast as he would like. She lay quietly, not burdening him with more movement than she had to, though she swallowed occasionally as though her throat hurt. The road was steep and occasionally stepped. It was a long, long two hours to the tampu. Stunted Sapling, the town it lay in, was a small way-station between two provincial capitals. Exemplary Fortune carried Qantu Flower straight into the tampu without a word and set her down gently on the floor. He turned then to the two older women who had been sitting just outside the door and were now standing in the doorway staring at him with their spindles still in their hands. They wore the red-and-yellow headbands of the local Lynx Lake tribe. He pulled the travel wand from his pouch. "I am Exemplary Fortune," he said, "sent on a mission by Young Majesty. Where can we find a healer?"

The two women shook their heads.

"The healers have all died," said one sadly.

"They could not do much," said the other. "My husband . . ." She bit her lip. "They said it might help if I put cool cloths on his head, but it did not seem to."

Exemplary Fortune nodded stiffly. His heart was in turmoil, and he did not know what to do next. The Glowing women began to pull food and bedding out of the stores, and one of the Lynx Lakes joined them. The other went to where Qantu Flower lay. She put a hand on Qantu Flower's head and then felt her wrists.

"I have it, don't I?" asked Qantu Flower in a thick whisper, then half sat up and vomited clear liquid.

The woman held her and called for the other woman to bring wiping cloths. Exemplary Fortune took the cloths and wiped off Qantu Flower's chin and dress. She looked so very fragile.

The Glowing women brought over quilts striped with brown, green, red, and yellow. Exemplary Fortune picked Qantu Flower up so they could slide the bedding under her. Together they took off her dress. When they had her in bed and wrapped up, everyone else went to the other end of the tampu for a time. Exemplary Fortune sat beside his most beautiful wife, held her hand, and stroked her strange short hair, ragged with mourning. There was too much mourning, and he was helpless to stop it. Qantu Flower's head felt burning hot under his hands, and rivulets of perspiration ran down her face.

"I'm so thirsty," she murmured.

As though that was a signal, one of the older women brought over a tumbler of water. Qantu Flower sat up, and Exemplary Fortune put his arm around her shoulders so that she would not have to support herself. She drank as though the effort hurt her. When she stopped, Exemplary Fortune felt that it was from exhaustion rather than satiation. She lay back quietly for a time then with her eyes closed. The older women who had delivered the water brought a cloth to wipe her face. "She looks like my daughter," the woman said.

Exemplary Fortune knew she was trying to be friendly, but he did not know what to say to her, was afraid if he spoke he would find out that her daughter had already died in the epidemic. He muttered an awkward thanks, and the woman left again.

Qantu Flower opened her eyes, watching him intensely. "You have to go on," she said thickly.

"As soon as the illness has run its course."

She shook her head against the smooth kumpi quilts she lay on. "Now."

"Qantu Flower, my beloved, it is evening. We have never traveled at night, and I am not going to start now."

She managed an almost smile at his words, but what she said was "Tomorrow."

Exemplary Fortune looked around the tampu. The Glowing women were preparing dinner, and the men were caring for Tamed Ocelot. They hardly needed him. He looked back at Qantu Flower. "I cannot hear what tomorrow will bring," he told her.

"Death," she said and closed her eyes.

Exemplary Fortune stroked her hand and then looked up again at the only member of their party who was watching the two of them closely. Ginez's face wore its usual anxious expression, and he was staring at Exemplary Fortune with a strange intensity. At Exemplary Fortune's look, he crept over to the bedside as though expecting at every heartbeat to be ordered away. When he reached the two of them, he looked at Qantu Flower, and then at Exemplary Fortune.

"She is sick," said Exemplary Fortune, maybe as a continuation of language lessons, maybe because he wanted to deny worse fears.

Ginez said, "Maybe cold cloths help her?"

He did not sound at all certain, but it was the same suggestion the tampu-keeper had made. "Where?" asked Exemplary Fortune.

Ginez touched his own forehead and said, "Qantu Flower here."

Exemplary Fortune nodded permission. He did not really believe the proposed remedy would work, but it did not seem probable that it would hurt either. Most likely, Qantu Flower had predicted the outcome of her illness correctly. She did not comment on their exchange.

Ginez went away and came back with a cool damp cloth, which Exemplary Fortune laid across Qantu Flower's forehead. She gave them another almost smile, then took Exemplary Fortune's hand and squeezed it tight. She did not say how frightened she was, but she did not deny fear either. Every now and then, she moved a little on the bed as though something hurt, but she did not ask for anything to ease the pain. Exemplary Fortune wanted to ask if he could help, but the answer was probably no. He was not a healer, and there were no healers anywhere within several hours' walk that he could call upon; and, in any case, from what they had heard, even the healers were helpless against the Spotted Death.

Eventually, the Glowing women brought over soup, which Exemplary Fortune forced himself to eat. One of them fed Qantu Flower as much broth as she would eat—not very much. All that evening, the Lynx Lake who had brought the first tumbler of water kept bringing more liquid to slake Qantu Flower's continuing thirst.

Qantu Flower told the woman that her back hurt, and the woman said that was one of the symptoms of the disease that had caused the epidemic. "When the disease goes away, then the pain will leave too."

Qantu Flower did not ask how long the disease would last, and the woman did not tell her.

Exemplary Fortune forced himself to talk with the woman. If nothing else, their words would give Qantu Flower something to think about besides her pain. She would not have to listen if she did not want to.

The woman's name was Guanaco. "In my youth, I was the

fastest runner among all the Lynx Lakes," she explained proudly. "Some people said I could actually have outrun a guanaco." She laughed. "I was never foolish enough to try." Her daughter was not dead but had lost two of her children, and the daughter's husband had been blinded in one eye by the disease. Guanaco had come to live with her friend in the tampu after all the other tampu-keepers died as the epidemic flew through the town. "But a large number of adults recovered and are fine now except for some scars," she said. "Others are still recovering. We have had to abandon some of the potato fields because so many are too weak to work the fields."

Perhaps the Divine Speaker had been right after all, Exemplary Fortune thought. Evidently there would be a drought this year, but it would be a drought of labor rather than rain.

Qantu Flower listened to everything the two of them said, and Exemplary Fortune had the feeling Guanaco had reported the townspeople's recovery specifically to give her hope. That night they both slept with Qantu Flower, Exemplary Fortune at her side and Guanaco crossways just above her head. They both woke whenever Qantu Flower stirred, and they tended her needs as best they were able.

The next morning Qantu Flower was much the same, both much too hot and thirsty, but not able to keep down solid food. Exemplary Fortune ate breakfast sitting at her side.

While they were all eating, a young woman came running into the tampu. "Bright Rainbow has died," she wailed. "Our young Protector is dead."

Exemplary Fortune stood without moving from his place. "Stop it," he said sharply. "I will not have you spreading these malicious lies."

The woman collapsed in a heap, but she would not stop wailing. Exemplary Fortune looked around at the men and women in his care, who were staring at her wide-eyed, ready to believe any rumor as long as it was bad. "Watch her," he ordered and strode out of the tampu.

As soon as he was outside, the sound of a general wailing struck his ears. All the people on the streets were crying the same news. It was impossible. Bright Rainbow was younger than Exemplary

Fortune and favored by both the gods and Young Majesty. But the town's clan chief showed him the quipu brought by official messenger. It was true.

The whole world was dying, Exemplary Fortune thought. Soon all would dissolve back into the chaos under the earth. All his efforts were useless. He took his heart and squeezed from it everything but the thought that he had to complete his father's last command. Then he turned and walked back into the tampu. He apologized to the young woman.

He sat back down in front of his now-cold bowl of soup, and told the turn-workers that what she had said was true. "We will finish breakfast," he said, "and then you may go to the mourning ceremonies. I will stay here with Qantu Flower." There was no Sun temple in this small town, but there would be mourning ceremonies, and he was sure they would be easy to find. The Glowings all stared at him in shock. They had not eaten anything since he had left. He picked up his own bowl and forced himself to choke down the rest of the soup. Slowly, the others followed his lead, but none of them finished their bowlfuls.

As the Glowing women cleaned up from breakfast, the tampu-keepers got knives from the stores and shaved away the hair that was just beginning to grow out on their heads. Then they gave the Glowing women the knives to cut their hair. Everyone smeared their faces with brown, and one of the Glowing men brought the dye over to Exemplary Fortune. Exemplary Fortune smeared only his own face. Qantu Flower was too sick, and it was not medicine. Exemplary Fortune found himself wishing that, if she were to die, the disease had killed her before she had had to learn about this newest calamity. She was watching him with all her attention.

After the others left for the mourning ceremonies, Qantu Flower said to him in a hoarse whisper, "Now you can be Unique Inca."

He looked at her and did not know what to say. Was she close enough to death that she could already hear the future, or had she always been secretly ambitious? "I doubt Bright Rainbow named me as his heir."

"He died too soon. No one will heed his words." Qantu Flower's voice held scorn, and she looked more animated than she had since she had been struck down.

She was right. A cold knot of fear wrapped itself around Exemplary Fortune's heart. He could almost hear the tens of his brothers in Navel squabbling over the succession. If his brothers started fighting about which one should be emperor, they would likely not pay any attention to reports of hostile strangers unless those enemies were actually marching through the heart of the Four Quarters.

Qantu Flower was watching him closely. She said, "You must leave . . . now."

He shook his head. "Now is the time for mourning. We cannot leave."

She pursed her lips in frustration, looking very ill once again. Exemplary Fortune wondered if he should try to continue the discussion, if it would give her strength to focus on the future. But he did not want to tire her. She closed her eyes and did not speak for a time. Ginez continued in his self-imposed duty of bringing cool cloths for her burning forehead. The tampu-keepers came back from the ceremonies after a time and got clean quilts from the stores. Together they replaced the quilts Qantu Flower was lying on, which were sodden with her sweat. Exemplary Fortune got up from time to time to tend to Tamed Ocelot's needs, though he had to force himself to care enough to do it. What use was there in keeping Tamed Ocelot alive when the whole empire was dissolving?

As the day wore on, Qantu Flower became restless and began to moan with pain. There were few painkillers in the tampu to give her, all of them having been used for the townspeople who had been struck down by the Spotted Death. Guanaco shook out the bags that had held dried coca leaves and made the leaf dust she found into a weak tea. They gave it to Qantu Flower, as much as she would take, every hour or two. Nothing they did seemed to help. She moaned and tossed, quieting only when Exemplary Fortune talked soothingly to her and sometimes not even then.

In late afternoon, when Exemplary Fortune went to help Guanaco get another set of quilts for Qantu Flower's bed, Guanaco said to him, "Usually the disease does not kill people until the spots appear."

He understood that she was saying she did not know if Qantu Flower would live that long, but nevertheless he asked, as though he believed the information mattered, "And how long will that be?"

"About three days from the time the fever started," she replied. Her look was sympathetic and sad. He could tell she held no hope for Qantu Flower at all.

The Glowings came back after sunset, and they all ate a dispirited dinner together. Again that night, Exemplary Fortune and Guanaco cared for Qantu Flower. This night their patient moaned and cried and would not be comforted. She was too weak, Exemplary Fortune thought, to know that her complaints could not help. He could no longer comfort her with either his voice or his touch. In the morning, after breakfast, most of the Glowings again went to the ceremonies to mourn Bright Rainbow, but a number of the women stayed to help care for Qantu Flower. She needed all their attention because she could not help herself anymore.

In midmorning, Qantu Flower suddenly opened her eyes and asked fretfully, "If I am going to die here, who will I become?"

Exemplary Fortune did not know how to answer, and he looked helplessly at Guanaco. That woman said, "The ground here is rocky and steep, and there are few comfortable places to sit, so when we die, we all eventually go to sit in the ground under Lynx Lake, from which we originally come. The lake's water is cold and very dark. The soil underneath is likewise dark and soft and rich. It will seem comfortable to you, I promise."

Qantu Flower was listening intently to this, not moaning or crying for the first time in many hours.

One of the Garlands touched Exemplary Fortune on the arm. "You need to mourn," she said. "The ceremonies are just outside. We will tell you if you should come back."

Exemplary Fortune nodded without saying anything. When he stood up, he was very stiff. He stretched his limbs to be sure he would not fall over, and then went out into the searing brightness of the day. As he left the tampu, Guanaco was saying, "When

Lakefoam ordered all the tribes, she gave the Lynx Lakes . . ."

The day was not really that bright. Thin clouds covered the Sun, though it was not raining. Exemplary Fortune found himself wondering if the Sun were hiding from the sight of the devastation He had allowed to ravage the Four Quarters. It was not a proper thought to have about the Sun, who was the empire's patron, but he barely cared.

The gathered mourners were, as he had been told, standing in a clump near the tampu's entrance. The village elders stood a short way up the Road and were telling tales, not of Bright Rainbow's exploits, but of Young Majesty's. That only made sense. As Unique Inca, Bright Rainbow had not had time to do anything other than die. He had not been able to prove himself or do deeds worth remembering. If there were a future, in that time Bright Rainbow would not even be reckoned among the Unique Incas. He would be forgotten, was already being forgotten, his mourning ceremonies usurped by his father.

Like everyone else, Exemplary Fortune mourned his young brother with only a fraction of his heart, but he did mourn the Four Quarters. Like most here, he had lived all his life within the stability of Young Majesty's reign. His father's death had been a personal sadness, but Young Majesty had ruled the Four Quarters for over thirty years. He had brought peace and stability to the empire and raised up sons to succeed him and to administer the realm. Bright Rainbow had had time to do none of these things. With his death the very fabric of the empire was threatened.

You could be Unique Inca, Qantu Flower had said. But the elders and other Incas and honorary Incas would want to install a full brother of Bright Rainbow, a son of both Young Majesty and Whence Happiness, Young Majesty's sister-queen. Except that choice was not viable either. The queen's only other son was twelve and had not yet even been given his adult name. A long regency would be disastrous for the empire. Newly incorporated tribes, who had joined the Four Quarters only because they knew the empire's might would otherwise destroy them, would regard a regent's control as weak and be eager to test their strength against his. Sons of Young Majesty by his other wives would jostle for position, trying to prove that they were most suited to be Unique Inca before the boy emperor was old enough to show his own mettle.

With the threat of revolt by recalcitrant tribes and fighting among the adult princes, the council would choose someone else, and, for those same reasons, they would choose quickly. They would pick the least controversial candidate who was both over eighteen and had a father and a mother who were both Inca. And he should be in Navel. Given that the need to ensure stability would be paramount in the councilors' hearts, it would be important to them that their choice would be immediately available. As Exemplary Fortune assembled these criteria, Cable's name came instantly into his heart. Cable was nineteen. Chosen Creator, Cable's mother, though not Young Majesty's chief wife, was nevertheless his sister and would therefore give her son's claim validity. Cable had spent his whole life in Navel. But Exemplary Fortune also knew that, if he did not thwart that most likely possibility, his father's last wish was doomed.

He remembered Cable as a thin sullen child. There had been a sling target practice once between the two of them. Exemplary Fortune, older and more experienced, had won easily, but Cable, unwilling to concede defeat, had tried to say that the stones Exemplary Fortune had slung were really his. They had argued, and Cable had attacked Exemplary Fortune with his fists. When Exemplary Fortune had grabbed his hands to stop him, he had screamed that he was being attacked. There had been enough witnesses that his accusation had been laughed at, but some had coddled him afterward. From then on, the two of them had avoided each other. Exemplary Fortune had heard other stories that implied Cable was barely able to control himself, let alone an empire. If Cable had not changed, and he became Unique Inca, he might well destroy the Four Quarters. Some on the council might well feel similarly; but, depending on the situation in Navel, depending on how many had died and were yet to die, they might feel they had little choice. At best, their doubts would likely delay the decision only until some revolt or rumor made them feel they had to act.

Exemplary Fortune could feel the despair he kept from the front of his heart threatening to overwhelm him again, and he fought it like a physical being. If he failed, the empire would be lost, swallowed up by treacherous barbarians. He could not stop.

You could be Unique Inca, Qantu Flower had said. It was unlikely. He had no political base in Navel or with the Incas and honorary Incas in the provinces that surrounded the capital. His mother was not even Inca. Few in Navel had fought with him or knew his abilities.

For the first time, he regretted spending so little time in that city. He did not know how disrupted the government in Navel was or how quickly the council could reconstitute itself to make its decision. Perhaps, if he reached the capital in the next two tendays, he could influence the council's choice. He was one of the oldest princes, and it was well-known that his father had favored him. If he were in Navel, he would give his support to whichever prince had the best chance to stop Cable and become Unique Inca himself. If the new Unique Inca owed his selection in part to Exemplary Fortune, he would surely listen when Exemplary Fortune talked about the strangers who had come to Recognition. It was a frail hope. He could not even name this brother whom he might aid, nor could he be sure that the council, or some tattered shreds of it, had not already made its decision or was going to make its decision today, tomorrow, or the next day. It was the only hope he had, his only reason to keep moving.

You must leave now, Qantu Flower had said. You must leave. Exemplary Fortune took a deep breath past the tears gathering in his throat. He could not abandon her, but he knew as an almost certainty that soon his most pressing services to her would be done. Once she died—today, tomorrow, or maybe, frailer hope even than the other, long years from now—his immediate ministrations would matter less to her. If the world did not end, he could come back later to tend to the rest of her needs.

If he were to obey her last command to the best of his ability, he should find a way to travel faster. The Glowings were sturdy and faithful workers, but they were not trained to carry a stretcher quickly. He could stop in Narrow Valleys, the next provincial capital, and ask for a trained fifty-group to help him. But then I would be alone, his heart told him. I could not go on.

He sat with that despair clogging his heart for a time, staring blankly at dark shapes that would be his fellow mourners could he but see them. The tears that threatened to overwhelm him ran down his cheeks. Slowly, though, another thought came into his heart. If the Glowing turn-workers, who had served him beyond any hope or reasonable expectation, wanted to stay with him, he could not turn them back after they had come with him so far. It would not be his decision. They would decide whether to stay or return. But what if they decided to go home? his heart asked. That was not this day's decision. If that time came, he would find a way to survive it. He sat in silence for a while longer, reconciling himself to the latest decision he had been forced into, half listening to the drone of the elders' words. Finally, when he was sure he could function without collapsing, he went back into the tampu.

Qantu Flower was quieter, her protests against the disease that was killing her muted by weakness. But the disease had not relented. Her forehead was still much too hot, and her breathing both quicker and shallower than it had been when he had left. Her skin felt dry, and Exemplary Fortune knew that the fever was driving all the moisture from her body, readying her to be a mummified corpse. The Glowing women fed him soup and forced a little broth between her dry lips.

Guanaco told him, "She listened to everything. She will be ready."

He nodded. He did not have energy to talk, but he could sit at Qantu Flower's side and listen as her breathing grew shallower and then rougher. He did not talk to her. She could not hear him anymore. He did rub her hands and wipe her face, but he did not believe she could feel that either. She died at sunset without ever waking up again. He let go of her hand. Guanaco and her companion began preparing her body for burial. "We will take care of her," Guanaco promised.

"Thank you," said Exemplary Fortune thickly. He could barely talk around his grief.

"In this time," said her companion, "we all have to look out for each other."

Exemplary Fortune did not even know her name. He nodded

mutely. He went to walk outside the tampu for a time, to walk enough of his grief away that he could think again. They do not even know who she is, he thought. They will not be able to celebrate her life. Maybe someday, in a future he could not hear, he or one of his other wives could come back and tell them her life's stories. She had told him to go on. He could do nothing else. He walked back into the tampu and told the Glowings that the next day they would continue their journey as she had requested.

He slept that night as though hit hard by a blow to the head. He remembered no dreams. Qantu Flower had already given him what omens or advice she could.

In the morning the group got up as it always had, ate breakfast, and set out on the road. There was nothing else to do. All that day Exemplary Fortune had to force himself to slow to the pace of the others. Even when he was helping to carry the stretcher, he walked too fast. Maybe he believed that somehow he could outrun the desolation that was threatening to take over the world.

That night they stopped in Narrow Valleys. It took all Exemplary Fortune's heart-strength to ask after the governor, but the tampu-keepers said that he had died in the epidemic. There would be no way to ask for any turn-workers from this province. Maybe the disorder that threatened the empire would keep him from finding turn-workers all the way to Navel. Nonetheless, the next evening Exemplary Fortune asked the Glowings if they would like him to ask for new turn-workers in Great Granary, the next provincial capital. They all looked at each other with hesitant and furtive glances. He knew their answer before anyone spoke.

One of the women finally said, "We would like to see our families again, to know if they are still alive or not. If you need us, we can go on."

He did need them, but he could not say that. What he did say was "If there is no governor in Great Granary, I will ask again at Stronghold and then at Hawk's Shrine."

The Glowings all looked relieved, and Ginez looked even more distressed than usual. He knew something more was going to change, and to him, it seemed, all change must be disaster. When the Glowings explained to him that they would soon go back to their homes, he cried. The Glowings did their best to comfort him, as Exemplary Fortune could not, but they could promise him nothing, not even that he could visit them later.

Great Granary was at the head of a large terraced valley surrounded by snow-covered mountains. On the steep slopes above the city, row upon row of storehouses for corn, potatoes, cloth, and everything needful embodied the empire's promise that everyone under the Unique Inca's care would have plenty in drought and frost as well as in good weather. Through the city, the Unfolding River wound its way, bound by three bridges that unified the neighborhoods. Exemplary Fortune and his group crossed the main bridge into the giant plaza. The local Field Guardians, the men still wearing the chin-length braids that were fastened with red-and-green ribbons, had their faces smeared brown in mourning. Large numbers of people were going into and out of the Sun temple. Maybe Bright Rainbow had been especially popular in this city.

The traffic in and out of the governor's compound looked normal. At the tampu, Exemplary Fortune asked if the governor was in good health. The tampu-keepers said he was, and Exemplary Fortune kept his face steady only with effort. That meant he had to follow through on his offer. He busied himself with detail to keep his heart from stifling him.

From the stores he selected a deep blue tunic with embroidered brown-and-yellow squares around the bottom, a matching loincloth, and a cream-colored cloak. He bathed and dressed and went across the plaza to the governor's compound.

The guards at the doorway to the compound did not recognize him, but, at his name, they bowed deeply and welcomed him in. While one man went to inform the governor's advisors that Exemplary Fortune had come to visit, others spread a kumpi rug in an inner courtyard for him to sit on. Exemplary Fortune turned his heart to reviewing what he knew about the governor. He was Magnanimous Strength of the Loom lineage, descended from the Unique Inca Left-Handed Reckoner. Exemplary Fortune had talked with him several times and knew that his father considered him a competent administrator, but he had not formed any ties with the man. He could not remember any experiences they shared that would make the governor more inclined to listen to him. Still, he would only be doing what he had planned to do with Bright Rainbow—less, since Magnanimous Strength would not have to decide on the merits of his case, only to help him on the mission ordained by Young Majesty. One of Magnanimous Strength's assistants came back in about half an hour to escort him to the governor.

Magnanimous Strength greeted him cordially. "It is good to see you."

"It is good to see you," Exemplary Fortune replied almost automatically. "I wish that we could meet in happier times."

"Indeed," said Magnanimous Strength. "It is Bright Rainbow's death everyone mourns now, but it is your father's untimely death that struck the hardest. He was a great leader. I could not but think of you with compassion when I heard the sad news."

"It has been difficult," said Exemplary Fortune and could hear his voice crack just a little. He could not even try to tell the governor just how difficult. "One of the hardest parts for me was that I was not able to be with him."

Magnanimous Strength cocked his head. "I did not know about this."

Exemplary Fortune took a deep breath. He had to say this without faltering. He had shaped the words he wanted to say, but he was not sure he could mold his voice to sound convincing. "Shortly before he became ill, my father sent me on an errand to learn everything I could about strangers who had come to Recognition in an oddly shaped boat carrying unknown animals. The boat had left, but two men stayed behind, and my father wanted to talk to them. When I arrived in Recognition, I found that one of the men was a malefactor who had tried to rape a woman. This in itself told me something about the strangers, and, talking to the people of Recognition, I found much a Unique Inca should know. The men are both unusual, and a prolonged study of them would clearly reveal more. Since he had been wounded in the fight he had caused, I had to strap the malefactor to a stretcher, and then, with turn-workers from Throat Town, I set out for Kitu Dove."

Exemplary Fortune paused both to give Magnanimous Strength a chance to comment if the governor wished and because the next part of Exemplary Fortune's speech was going to be harder for him to say. It was also a plea, and that was not something Exemplary Fortune was used to doing. Perhaps, if he faltered here, the governor would think that was the reason. "Then I found out that my father had just died. I still had the information and the turn-workers, but there was no longer a Unique Inca in Kitu Dove. I wanted to go to Kitu Dove to mourn my father, but the new Unique Inca would be in Navel, and it was to him that the information must go. I turned away from my longing and have ever since been following duty toward Navel. The turn-workers who originally agreed to travel with me only a month have helped me all this way. They are worried about their families, and so I would ask you to lend me others to help me get the two strangers to Navel."

Magnanimous Strength did not say anything for a number of heartbeats, digesting the news. "I had not heard anything about this before," he said finally, "but your request does not sound unreasonable. I would like to see these two strangers."

"They are at the tampu," said Exemplary Fortune, feeling his heart a little comforted. The governor at least was trying to be helpful. Probably his turn-workers would be experienced and maybe even kind to an Inca prince who had no strength left to reciprocate. "I can have them here whenever you wish."

"Bring them here with your men," said Magnanimous Strength, "and I will give the turn-workers a travel wand back to Throat Town. By the time you return, I should be free to attend to you. You, of course, will stay in the governor's compound for the night."

Exemplary Fortune bowed and left.

The Glowings were delighted with the news in a quiet way. They clearly knew this was difficult for him and did not do much more than smile at him. Some of them hugged him good-bye.

Ginez kept asking, "Will they treat me well?"

"I will stay with you," said Exemplary Fortune. He found Ginez's useless worrying annoying, but to snap at him would only make the situation worse. Exemplary Fortune could not imagine Ginez volunteering to get off a boat in strange territory. Maybe he had been forced off, or maybe his time in Recognition with only

Tamed Ocelot as a companion had turned him into a chronic worrier.

The Glowings and Ginez washed and put on clean clothes. Together Exemplary Fortune and the men washed and dressed Tamed Ocelot. Then they went across the plaza to the palace.

Magnanimous Strength received them all in a room away from the main audience chamber. He looked Tamed Ocelot over carefully. "It looks as though his wounds have almost healed."

"They have," said Exemplary Fortune. "We did not have enough men to risk letting him walk around with only bonds on his arms."

"Then you regard him as a continual danger?" Magnanimous Strength asked.

"I do," said Exemplary Fortune firmly. He did not want Magnanimous Strength to underestimate Tamed Ocelot. There was no reason to believe Tamed Ocelot would scruple at attacking and killing anyone. There had already been too much death.

Magnanimous Strength nodded and turned toward Exemplary Fortune's faithful turn-workers. "You have served the Four Quarters well. Go back to your families firm in the satisfaction of a task well-done." He held out an official wand to them, and one of the men stepped forward to accept it. The Glowings bowed to them both as they turned to go out the door. And then they were gone. Exemplary Fortune bit his lip to keep himself from calling them back or otherwise breaking down.

Turning to Exemplary Fortune, Magnanimous Strength said, "Those kind of people are the foundation of the empire."

"They are indeed," Exemplary Fortune forced out from between stiff lips.

"Now," said Magnanimous Strength, "we have to decide what to do about you."

That was an odd way to say it. "I require very little special care," said Exemplary Fortune.

"That's not what I mean," said Magnanimous Strength. This time there was definitely a sharp note in his voice. "You admit that you have been traveling around the countryside with a dangerous criminal and an inadequate force for containing him. You also admit that you intended to take this criminal into the Unique Inca's presence, where he could do whatever damage he wished."

The room was filled with men who were loyal to Magnanimous Strength. There were hundreds more outside willing to do his bidding. He had walked into a trap. Go now, Qantu Flower had said. He had not listened, had not understood. But a part of him still struggled automatically against the trap's noose. He heard his voice say, "That's a rather strained interpretation of the facts."

"Perhaps," said Magnanimous Strength, his voice giving Exemplary Fortune less than his words, "but, since you are an Inca prince, I am not qualified to judge your case. It will have to be judged by the Unique Inca himself." He inclined his head slightly. "Since there is no Unique Inca at the moment, I shall put you up until there is. I shall endeavor to be a good host."

Exemplary Fortune felt numb. Magnanimous Strength had obviously done the same calculations as Exemplary Fortune and had come up with the same answer. But he had decided his best interest lay in helping the probable next Unique Inca. He undoubtedly knew Cable far better than Exemplary Fortune, knew just how much the removal of one of his rivals would please him. With his ears open and of his own free will, Exemplary Fortune had delivered himself into the hands of his enemies. He tried once more. "If I am to be tried in Navel, the law of the Four Quarters says that I should be taken there immediately."

Magnanimous Strength smiled. "The roads are too dangerous at present for me to risk any of my men in such a journey."

"I have traveled them with no trouble," said Exemplary Fortune.

"Then you have indeed been fortunate." Magnanimous Strength sounded as though he were enjoying this. Perhaps he was.

There was nothing more to say. He was going to die. Alive, with a justified grudge against Cable, he would be dangerous, too much of an attraction for those who would be dissatisfied with Cable's reign. He could not even hope that some other brother would be chosen and save him. Magnanimous Strength had gone too far. If Cable were not selected, Exemplary Fortune would have to disappear; while, if, as they both expected, Cable were chosen, then, to win the new Unique Inca's favor, Magnanimous Strength would reveal his helpful capture of one of Cable's rivals, along with an almost reasonable-sounding excuse for Cable to execute him. When the strangers returned, there would be no one left to stop them.

Magnanimous Strength had his men untie Tamed Ocelot and then left. As he walked out the door, there was the rustle of men positioning themselves on the other side of the doorway, and then the thwack of spear butts being set firmly on the hard floor.

5

From the conquistadors' point of view, this is the story of how the youth we follow got his name. No one in actual history bothered to record the name his family gave him. Probably they never learned it.

In the small boat the giant sitting next to Hummingbird slapped him on the back. The man seemed friendly, but Hummingbird was not ready for the blow, and it nearly knocked him off the bench he was somehow sitting on. All the men in the boat had pale skins with a reddish tint and thick face hair on their upper lips and their chins. Their chin hair came to a point.

The men rowed to the big boat; and, as they rowed, the big boat kept looming higher and higher over them. When they reached the big boat's side, the men clambered up ropes hanging down. The giant waved with his hand for Hummingbird to climb up ahead of him. Hummingbird grabbed the rope with his hands, and that was easy. But when he tried to climb, it swung away from his feet. He had to reach up as high as he could with his hands and then jump up with both feet at once. He was moving a lot more awkwardly than the others had. He had never even seen a boat one had to climb into before. In fact, the only boat he had ever been on before had sunk to just under the water when six children all tried to climb on at once. He had thought he was going to drown. He couldn't think about that. He concentrated on the rough rope between his hands and feet. Slowly, he worked his way upward. He reached the top and put a foot over the edge of the boat, but the floor was so much lower than its edge that he almost fell. The giant, climbing up the rope just behind him, steadied him.

Once they were on the big boat, the giant went up to a tall thin man who was already there and started talking very fast, waving his arms back at the city. Hummingbird did not move from his place by the edge of the boat. No one seemed to notice he was there. The boat was made entirely of wood—the side, the floor, the towering masts and yardarms. It was more wood than Hummingbird had seen in his whole life. The men all talked very loudly. They worked hard to pull the little boat up, and Hummingbird helped with that. Then they fastened the small boat upside down on the floor of the big boat.

The men moved quickly all over the big boat, even climbing to the top of the highest mast, pulling on ropes and yelling at each other. The sails on the boat moved, unfolding and turning and puffing out with the wind. Such big sails, like clouds against the bright blue sky.

The giant was yelling at him, waving for him to come over. Hummingbird ran over, and the giant turned to his companion as though introducing them. Maybe this thin stranger was their leader. He looked older than the others, with deep lines on his face, sunken cheeks, and hair that looked as though it were starting to turn gray. He also had less facial hair than most of the other men.

Hummingbird did full obeisance to him, bowing low with his hands above his head and then bringing his right hand back to kiss his fingers and send the kiss palm forward to the man. When he stood up again, the man's eyes were approving, but he was not grinning like the giant was. The giant slapped the man on the back—so he couldn't be the leader then—and the man said something while looking at Hummingbird.

The giant waved at two other men. They were men Hummingbird recognized: Young Fox, one of Macaw's advisors, and another man Hummingbird had seen sometimes around the waterfront. Maybe he had not escaped. Maybe they would take him back. Hummingbird took a step back and turned toward the city. It had moved away since he had last seen it, had gotten smaller until it looked like a toy one could hold in both hands. Hummingbird found that his eyes were full of tears again as though he really did not want to leave, as though he would rather be laughed at than live among strangers. He watched the city go still further away, watched the water spread out between the boat and the land.

Then a man touched him on the shoulder. Hummingbird jumped and turned, very frightened. The man laughed and gestured that Hummingbird should come with him. The giant and the tall thin man were gone. Hummingbird followed the man down a ladder. Inside, the boat was very dim and smelled of decay and damp. The room they climbed into was almost as big as the whole boat. The ceiling was low enough that the giant would have to duck his head to walk around. The man led him along the room to the end and then moved a piece of wall away so that a small room was in front of them. He had Hummingbird go into the room and then put the wall back in place so it was between them.

Hummingbird looked around the new room. The floor was wood, the ceiling was wood, and the walls were wood. So much wood. There was a platform against the wall of the room. It was covered with a big cloth like a rug or a blanket. Above the platform was a cross with a statue of a tortured man on it. He was hanging from the cross as though he were dying. It was a terrible thing, but Hummingbird could not take his eyes from it. The sculpture was well-done. You could tell the man had been starved first because you could see his ribs. Maybe they were going to torture him like that, and this was his warning.

He should not have left Recognition, except he still did not know what to say. He did not want everyone to laugh at him. He did not want Molle Tree to turn away with scorn whenever she saw him. He kept thinking, though, that, if he died here, no one would know. Not even Happy Speaker, he told himself, but the thought did not make him feel any better.

He did not know what to do. He looked at the piece of wall that had moved; but, even if he could figure out how it worked, he could not swim all the way back to Recognition. His parents would worry about him, and maybe even Molle Tree. They would never know. He wanted to pray to Mother Earth, but he knew how far from Her they were. He did not know how to pray to the water like the fishermen and the sailors. And the World Animator was so far away even the speakers could not always hear him. He turned away from the image finally, sat down on the floor, wrapped his arms around himself, and waited for whatever they would do to him. He tried not to think about his family and friends.

After a long time the wall opened again, and the man who had been with the giant came in with another man. Hummingbird stood up, waiting for them to hurt him. The man who'd been with the giant gestured him to the other man, and so he followed that man back through the big room and up the ladder to the top, where men were cooking in a kind of box. There were no women. The man he'd been following gave Hummingbird a tray and put food-filled plates on it and a pitcher. Then he led Hummingbird back to the room where the man he knew was. It was hard carrying the tray down the ladder, but the man showed him how.

In the small room, the man he knew was sitting on a high seat at an even-higher wooden platform that had not been there before. The man he knew gestured for him to put the plates and the other things on the higher platform. The other man had gone, and the wall was closed again. The man on the seat even had a tumbler of wood. The Incas made wooden tumblers too sometimes, he could not help thinking, but this was not an Inca tumbler. It had no designs and was rather crudely made.

The man ate and drank without offering Hummingbird any-thing. He had Hummingbird take the things off the tray and set them on the higher platform and pour his drink from the pitcher. He used a pointed knife and a spoon to carry the food to his mouth. When he was done, he gestured Hummingbird to put the things on the tray again and then go through the wall, but Hummingbird did not know how to do that. He stood there with the tray in his hands and did not move. The man frowned at him angrily, and Hummingbird bowed his head, ready to cry. Then the man laughed. He pulled up the flat wooden platform he had set his food on so he had space to get up from his seat. He showed Humming-bird how to make the wall open.

Hummingbird swallowed his tears and went back to the top floor of the boat. The men there gave him food and something to drink. The food was tasteless, and the drink was sour and thin, but he was both hungry and thirsty and ate and drank it all. Then, when they indicated he should leave, he went back to the room where the man had been. He did not know if he should, but the man had showed him how to move the wall so he could get in again, and he did not know where else to go.

The room was empty. Hummingbird sat back down on the floor. He was not so frightened now. The tall thin man wanted him for something, and so he would not kill him. He kept his face turned away from the waka statue and surveyed the rest of the room. On the wall directly across from the waka statue, there was a thing that looked like a sword, long and thin with a handle. There was the high seat in a corner with the piece of wood that had been a food platform standing up behind it and a big box in front of it between it and the door. Hummingbird unfolded himself and lifted the lid of the box. The top layer of things was mostly clothes. Hummingbird didn't touch anything. He did not know what the man would do if he found him looking at his things. He closed the lid gently so it didn't make any noise and sat back down where he had been.

After a while, the wall opened again, and the man who'd been with the giant came back in. He smiled thinly when he saw Hum-mingbird, and Hummingbird smiled back. The man sat down on the platform with the cloth on top of it and patted the spot next to him as though he wanted Hummingbird to sit there. Watching the man carefully to make sure he was doing what he wanted, Hummingbird got up from his spot on the floor and sat down where the man indicated.

The man smiled his approval, and then, putting his hand on his chest, said, "Francisco Pizarro."

Hummingbird tried to repeat the name, but it was long and did not mean anything to him so he mangled it badly.

The man repeated his name, and Hummingbird tried again.

The man laughed and patted him on the back. Then he held up a foot and said something. Hummingbird repeated it. At first Hummingbird thought the new word meant foot; but then, when he indicated his own foot, Francisco Pizarro shook his head and tugged at his foot covering, repeating the word. "Boot," Hummingbird repeated, touching the soft hide of the boot gently with his hand. Francisco Pizarro put his hand over Hummingbird's and showed him how to take the boot off, and then turned onto the platform so Hummingbird had the other foot in his lap. Hummingbird took that boot off. Then Francisco Pizarro took Hummingbird's hand and showed him how to undo the fastenings that connected the arm pieces to the tunic. And then the fastenings down the front of his tunic, which were entirely different. Under the first tunic was another. Maybe Francisco Pizarro just wanted Hummingbird to help him undress, but he was touching him when he didn't have to. Before Hummingbird started undoing the undertunic, he let his hand slide down Francisco Pizarro's hairy arm, and the man drew him closer.

The strangers had so many clothes.

In the next few days, Hummingbird learned the simple things Francisco Pizarro wanted him to do: to dress and undress him, to get his clothes out of the box, to get his food for him, to fetch things, to have sex with him when he wanted it. That seemed to be what pleased him most, and Hummingbird was careful to learn how he liked it done.

When Francisco Pizarro did not want him for any of those things, Hummingbird would wander the boat, trying to figure out what each of the men was doing and looking at all the many things on the boat. The giant was in charge of a number of complex pieces of metal that were kept in specific places. Though the giant tried to explain it to him, Hummingbird did not understand what the things were supposed to do. They were called *artillería,* and the giant spent a lot of time cleaning and fussing over them. In that way, the giant reminded Hummingbird of his father. He wanted to make sure his things were perfect.

When he wasn't helping the giant clean his *artillería,* Hummingbird would help the other men with the ropes that were connected to the sails. Though he had worked with metal all his life, he understood the cloth and ropes of the sails far better than the metal of the giant's *artillería.*

He also spent time at the side of the boat, looking down at the water but seeing only the people he would never see again. His family, Molle Tree, Macaw and his court, even the Incas with their customs that did not seem quite so odd now. Once, when a fish jumped, the silvery flash of its scales against the sun brought the dear memory of his father too close, and he sobbed helplessly until he had no more tears left. But Francisco Pizarro had been looking for him and was angry, yelling at him with words he did not know. After that, Hummingbird tried not to cry anymore because, once he started, he could not stop.

Hummingbird had thought that when the boat left Recognition, it would sail away from the Four Quarters back to wherever it had come from, but it didn't do that. Instead, it sailed farther south along the coast, deeper into the Incas' territory. Sometimes Hummingbird wondered if he should jump off the boat and try to swim to shore, but they did not sail very close to land, and, besides, he still did not know what he would say to the Incas, to his father and mother, to Macaw. It was better that he didn't try to go back. He told himself that, but his eyes still stung whenever the desert landscape gave way to irrigated fields as they sailed past a river valley. A few times, when they came to a green valley with its towns and fields, Francisco Pizarro asked him with a gesture what the place was, but Hummingbird had never been outside of Recognition before. He knew only that the valleys south of Recognition were all Chimu territory. The third time he said Chimu, Francisco Pizarro stopped asking him.

For the first few days, Hummingbird avoided Young Fox, unsure what to say to him, wondering if Macaw might have sent him to bring Hummingbird back to face justice. But the only other person he could talk with was the other man from Recognition.

His name was Adobe, and he spent all his time complaining about how everyone in Recognition had mistreated him. The men on the ship would ask Adobe to help sometimes the way they did with Hummingbird, by taking him and showing him how to do what needed to be done, but Adobe would just wander away and not do it. Finally, one day, when Adobe stared to leave, the man who had asked him grabbed Adobe and started hitting him. Adobe yelled, and the men around the two of them laughed. The man who had started hitting Adobe kept beating him, even when Adobe fell to the floor. Only when he started kicking at Adobe did Francisco Pizarro come over and get him to stop. They made Adobe do the job anyway even though he had blood all over his face and could hardly use his right arm. They laughed when he cried out in pain because they made him do something that hurt his arm.

Hummingbird looked away and found Young Fox soberly watching the scene. Later, when he was free, Hummingbird went to look for him and found Young Fox in the big common room where the men slept in hammocks over the stores. He was sitting on a hammock holding a small version of the awful waka statues that were all over the boat. He was not moving, and Hummingbird wondered if the statue had done something to him, but then Young Fox looked up and saw him.

"Ho, my little bird," said Young Fox.

"Hello," said Hummingbird, unwilling to move closer to the statue.

Young Fox held it up. "What do you think of these?"

"I think they are terrible," said Hummingbird with feeling.

"They are well made."

"Everything on this boat is well made," said Hummingbird. It came out as an angry complaint, and it wasn't even true.

"What does it mean, I wonder, when a people worship someone who is being tortured?" This was asked quietly, almost reflectively, and it terrified Hummingbird. He did not want to know that Young Fox did not understand this place either. Hummingbird didn't say anything, and Young Fox put the statue down. "I thought you were avoiding me."

"I was," Hummingbird admitted. "I thought maybe you had come after me."

"Oh?" said Young Fox.

Hummingbird shrugged. "I was having an affair with an Inca, and then they thought I stole a tumbler, and I ran away," he confessed.

"Ah," said Young Fox, "and now you are having sex with the ship's leader."

Hummingbird shifted uncomfortably, waiting for Young Fox to scold him about it.

Instead, he said, "Be very careful. I do not think we know yet what our hosts are capable of doing."

Hummingbird bit his lip. He wanted reassurance, not vague warnings that echoed what he already felt. He said, "They are very sure of themselves."

"Yes," said Young Fox, "they are." And he asked Hummingbird to tell him about what he had learned. They talked about sails and oddly shaped boats and *artillería*. Young Fox did not have answers, but Hummingbird found he felt better having somebody else to talk with who felt the same way he did.

The giant, after some time, told Hummingbird his name was Greek, which meant someone of a different tribe than the others. After Hummingbird asked Greek what his name meant, Greek started calling Hummingbird Felipe. He laughed when he said it. The other men changed the name to Little Felipe, and they did not laugh. Greek would not tell him what the name meant, and nobody else seemed to know, although they all seemed to think it was a fine name. Soon everyone was calling him Little Felipe.

Even though Adobe was now doing what they told him to, the men still kept hitting him. They gave him all the hardest, dirtiest jobs, the tasks no one else wanted to do. Sometimes even when he was working, they would hit him anyway. They had decided he was a person of no worth, and maybe he was, but they did not have to treat him like that. He cried and grew thin and did not talk much at all.

As the ship sailed down the coast, the men would exclaim at the cities they saw, and, after a while, Hummingbird realized that, at each new valley, they would talk among themselves about whether they should go ashore. They would show Young Fox the tumblers and bracelets they had gotten in Recognition to ask if he thought those things would be in the cities they passed, but Young Fox always just shrugged his shoulders and shook his head. Francisco Pizarro would frown at Young Fox when he did that. He believed Hummingbird when he said he didn't know anything, but he did not believe Young Fox.

Hummingbird asked Young Fox why he did not tell the men where the craftspeople lived, and Young Fox said, "I don't know these valleys, either." And then he said, "Macaw thought, like you did, that they would sail back to their own land after leaving Recognition. I am supposed to make sure that Recognition gets the trade with them." He did not say anything more, but he looked worried. Hummingbird felt there was something he wasn't saying, some private reason for not telling Francisco Pizarro and the other men what they wanted to know.

After some months, they finally decided to stop at another valley. This valley did not have a lot of green fields along the shore, but there were a great many rafts in the water and several well-traveled roads leading from the city they could see. The men thought there might be other cities in the area. They thought maybe this city was the chief city for a whole province or kingdom.

Hummingbird helped haul on the ropes to bring the sails in and get the boat into the harbor. When they were close enough, Francisco Pizarro had him ask the men on the nearest raft what valley it was. It was Taciturn, but, of course, that did not mean anything to Francisco Pizarro, so Hummingbird tried to explain that they were people who traded things up and down the coast. Francisco Pizarro nodded and looked pleased.

Taciturn's chief sailed out on a raft bringing gifts of food and silver and gold ware, and the strangers in return gave him beads and chickens. The chief came aboard, and Francisco Pizarro escorted him with great ceremony onto the ship. He took him to his room, where he had Hummingbird get out from the box two tumblers of a strange material, neither stone, metal, nor wood. They were smooth like obsidian, but they did not look as though they had been shaped by chipping. The light came through them as though they were made of water. Hummingbird poured Francisco Pizarro and the chief each a tumbler of the Spaniards' sour drink. They drank friendship together.

Francisco Pizarro asked Hummingbird to say to the chief that they needed more young men to learn their language to help them translate. Hummingbird found he did not really want to do this, but he asked anyway, adding he did not know how long it would be before the young men could return home. He hoped that would discourage the chief so he would not send anyone, but the chief promised he would.

Almost as soon as he got off the ship, he sent them two young men named Seaweed and Muyushell. Francisco Pizarro welcomed them aboard enthusiastically. Hummingbird had to turn his head away to keep from showing how much he hated that. There was no reason for him to be jealous of them, and he was ashamed of himself, but deep in his heart the strangers frightened him. He liked Greek, though he was loud, but he needed to know that one of the strangers needed something from him alone.

Maybe that was what really troubled him, that the young men did not know how really strange, how frightening, how waka the men on the boat were. If Young Fox had been there, he would have been able to explain to the chief why the young men should not have come aboard without being impolite. And then Humming-bird realized he had not seen Young Fox since Francisco Pizarro had given the order to sail into the harbor. If he could have, Young Fox would come to talk to the chief about the strangers.

One of the men called, "Little Felipe," and Hummingbird went to help them with the sails. As he hauled on the ropes with the others, he realized they were turning the boat, heading back north. The men laughed as they worked; they were going home now, going to some place called Panama.

Even as he worked, Hummingbird was afraid; and, though he smiled when it was appropriate and did not show his fear, his heart trembled.

Greek slapped him on the back, grinning and saying something about Panama and making Little Felipe into something. Hummingbird signaled his confusion, and Greek just laughed.

As soon as he could, as soon as the sails had been set the way they were supposed to be and no one was looking at him, Hummingbird slipped away to look for Young Fox. Maybe, Hummingbird thought, Francisco Pizarro had had Young Fox tied to his hammock so he could not talk to the chief, but Young Fox was not in the common room, not even tied up and hidden among the stores. He was not down below in the dank space where the stones were. Hummingbird even went back into Francisco Pizarro's room in case Young Fox had been moved there while Hummingbird was working up top to help turn the sails.

Young Fox was no longer on the boat. Hummingbird wanted to believe that was impossible, but he didn't know that. He did not know what the strangers would do. He could ask Francisco Pizarro, except he couldn't. He would not dare to ask even Greek, who liked him. But there was one more thing he could do. It frightened him because he knew Francisco Pizarro would be mad if he found out and because it would tell him something he didn't want to know, but knowing was important. If he was wrong, maybe he could say something to somebody.

In Francisco Pizarro's room, he went into the big box, where down at the bottom, in a small box with many other things, was a key like the key that Francisco Pizarro always carried around his neck. Then he pulled out the boxes hidden under Francisco Pizarro's bed and quickly, before he could become too frightened, started opening the lids. Young Fox's clothes were in the second box right on top, along with the silver bracelet he had worn on his arm.

Hummingbird shut the lids quickly and locked them, then went back to the box that was not hidden. With a wildly beating heart, he reopened the small box and put the key back. His hands were starting to shake, but he made sure that everything in the big box was the way it had been before he closed it again. Francisco Pizarro did not go into the boxes very much now that Hummingbird took care of his clothes, but he wanted to be sure.

After he had closed the box again, Hummingbird sat on the floor, where he generally sat with his back against the bed and his face away from the statue. He put his head down in his hands and cried, and then, because he did not want Francisco Pizarro to know what he had done, he wiped his face on his tunic, smoothed the tunic out, and rubbed under his eyes with his hands until they stopped tearing. After that, he just sat staring blankly at the wall. He should go out to be with the men, but he was afraid he would start crying again. He did not know what he should do next. He kept thinking if only he could talk with Young Fox, together they could figure something out, but that was utterly stupid.

He heard footsteps outside finally and stood up, making his face pleasant. The door opened framing Francisco Pizarro. Hummingbird went over to him. There was nothing else to do.

6

FIRST YEAR OF EXEMPLARY ROYAL HAPPINESS'S REIGN
LITTLE RIPENING TO FLOWER GARMENT MONTH

In actual history, Exemplary Fortune was in Kitu Dove with
Thorniest and other commanders of the northern army while the
Incas in Navel quickly decided who should assume the emper-
orship.

For the first few days, Exemplary Fortune did not even see the
cage he was in. He saw only Qantu Flower. She was talking
to him, but he could no longer understand what she said. Her hair
was long again, and it was very dark where she was. He wanted to
go to Lynx Lake to join her. He did not want to die all alone.

Gradually, the pictures changed. He began to see the court at
Navel, people plotting amid the brocade tapestries and along the
smooth-paved streets. He saw Young Majesty's sister-wives,
Whence Happiness, Bright Rainbow's mother, and Chosen Creator,
Cable's mother, along with Mother Egg, Young Majesty's wife and
niece. He saw Young Majesty's older sons, Beautiful Plowridge,
Reckoning Sadness, Bright Reckoning, Beseeching Cotton,
Whence Reckoning, Exemplary Hawk, Warmth, Hawk Magna-
nimity, and, of course, Cable. He saw members of the highest coun-
cils among the Incas and honorary Incas: Excellent Royalty, Inca
Fox, Shrewd Reckoner, Whence Grasping, Majestic Salviaflower,
Center Hawk, Majestic Quinoa, Royal Reckoner, Royal Greatness,

Royal Anaconda, and other, more shadowy figures, talking and gesticulating with each other, but he could not hear what they said. It was the past he sensed. The future was hidden, as he would soon be hidden in the ground. Mostly he just watched the shadowy figures blankly, but sometimes, as the days went by, he wanted to scream at them. It would do no good. They would not hear him. They would not listen.

The pictures went away only at night, and he welcomed the darkness that was his release from despair. One night, though, men's voices raised in anger woke him. Tamed Ocelot stood in the doorway, facing outward. The two doorguards had their spears inches from his chest. 'Just stay there," said one guard. He sounded a little frightened. So Tamed Ocelot tried to escape, thought Exemplary Fortune calmly. He was not particularly upset. If anything, he wondered that Magnanimous Strength's guards had been able to stop him.

Nevertheless, the next night, Exemplary Fortune found himself moving to sleep across the doorway of their cage. Part of his heart said it would be perfectly fitting if Tamed Ocelot got out and killed some of Magnanimous Strength's people, but the people who died would most likely not be the guilty. Besides, he foolishly felt that protecting people was still somehow his duty. He knew it did not matter anymore, but he could not stop himself.

Over the next few days, he became aware of Ginez huddled next to him, quiet and drawn looking, all his pessimism proven out. Ginez got them both food when it was delivered, and Exemplary Fortune realized that the man had been feeding him when he was too despondent to feed himself.

As Exemplary Fortune sat on the floor with his back against the cold stone wall of their cage, he also began to see Tamed Ocelot instead of the people who moved far beyond his reach. Tamed Ocelot moved cautiously around their shared room, walking, bending, stretching out, and strengthening his bad leg.

He began to notice that the food he ate actually befitted a prince. It included such delicacies as slices of pineapple and avocado, and was rich with both llama and duck meat. It was made with corn rather than the lowly potato. Magnanimous Strength must be worried that someone might ask how he had treated the captive prince before he led him to his death—foolishly. Nobody knew where Exemplary Fortune was, and those who might care would soon be out of power.

As soon as Exemplary Fortune started to reply when Ginez talked to him, Ginez began to ask him about words in Humanity's Mouth; and, for Ginez's sake, Exemplary Fortune answered. As the days went by, the question-and-answer sessions turned into structured language lessons. Ginez had done better than he had, Exemplary Fortune thought. He had not stopped functioning even when there was no hope. And then he thought, Ginez was his responsibility, his only remaining responsibility. He had failed his father's last order in every other way, but he did not have to fail Ginez. Even if Cable had to kill his princely brother, he might yet preserve Ginez for his novelty; but Ginez did not know the rules of the Unique Inca's court. Ordinarily that would not matter, as chief's sons from newly conquered tribes were constantly trickling into Navel to learn civilized ways, but, because Ginez had been with Exemplary Fortune, Cable would be suspicious of him. Exemplary Fortune did not want Ginez to make any mistakes that could be misconstrued.

Exemplary Fortune began teaching Ginez the basic etiquette that everyone should know, along with the customs and lore of the Four Quarters, Navel, and the court. Ginez was an apt pupil, and his questions about this or that custom were often interesting. Exemplary Fortune began to see that all the varied tribes of the empire shared common assumptions. There was this *dinero* that Ginez seemed to think necessary, but which made no sense to Exemplary Fortune at all. Sometimes it seemed to be a record-keeping device like quipus, sometimes a useful item in itself like dried corn. Ginez finally accepted that it didn't exist in the Four Quarters and gave up trying to explain it.

As Exemplary Fortune gave Ginez lessons, Ginez gave him hope, for Ginez knew the bearded strangers' customs intimately. If he could learn enough about the ways of the Unique Inca's court, perhaps he could finish the task Exemplary Fortune had been given. But sometimes Exemplary Fortune's heart would fail again because he did not at all trust the heart of his young brother who was almost certainly receiving the scarlet fringe in Navel. Exemplary Fortune could imagine Cable killing Ginez simply because he had associated with a brother he had executed. Cable could say Ginez was part of a conspiracy against him, and Ginez would not know how to explain his actions in a way to make them sound innocent.

When Exemplary Fortune could not continue, he would stare at the gray stone of the far wall, and always his heart would eventually start uselessly going over his actions to find a mistake. He could never find any. Even the Divine Speaker had misunderstood Majestic Festival's omen, and he did not think he could have saved Qantu Flower no matter what he had done. Perhaps, if she had stayed in the north, she would still be alive, but it seemed equally likely she might have died sooner. His only misjudgment was here in Great Granary. He had not realized he was going into battle with the governor and so had not taken precautions to avoid an ambush.

Sometimes Ginez would rouse him from his despair, and sometimes it would be Tamed Ocelot, moving across his line of sight and rousing his battle-trained heart to awareness. As the days passed, Tamed Ocelot began moving more and more quickly, running and jabbing at imaginary enemies. He ignored Exemplary Fortune and Ginez completely, as though their cage was his alone, given him perhaps as a training ground for a race or a battle.

Exemplary Fortune and Ginez both watched Tamed Ocelot as his exercises more and more came to resemble fighting practice. They stayed as far away from him as possible, but he recognized none of their boundaries; and, since Exemplary Fortune was determined not to let him near the door, they were constantly interacting. Sometimes, it was as simple as Exemplary Fortune putting up a hand, and Tamed Ocelot, without acknowledging that it was there, moving just enough to avoid him. Sometimes, Tamed Ocelot would deliberately brush up against one of them or grab at them and only back off when Exemplary Fortune made to fight. He was testing them, checking their reaction time and methods. Starting a fight would only give him more of what he wanted.

As the days went by, Tamed Ocelot's beard grew longer and

thicker. It also spread back toward his ears to join the hair growing down in front of them. It was a wild black tangle that made his face look both fierce and unhuman. The first part of his name was obviously totally inappropriate, but Exemplary Fortune did find himself wondering occasionally if he would turn into a jungle beast and run off on all fours. He had seen carvings on old stones that seemed to show such transformations and had heard tales of speakers in the eastern jungles who could turn into jaguars. Perhaps only a thin thread held Tamed Ocelot's heart to humanity. Perhaps it would not be his brother who would kill him, but rather Tamed Ocelot who would claw him to death.

Exemplary Fortune and Ginez did not talk much about their roommate, but Ginez flinched whenever Tamed Ocelot started toward him—an activity that seemed to give Tamed Ocelot pleasure. Exemplary Fortune stepped between them as often as he could, but Tamed Ocelot knew that Exemplary Fortune guarded the door, and his eyes lit whenever he maneuvered them so that Exemplary Fortune had to choose between protecting the door or Ginez. Ginez simply cringed in any encounter, and Exemplary Fortune had no idea whether he would act if Exemplary Fortune's life were threatened. He did not ask. Probably such a question would only make Ginez cower and turn away.

Exemplary Fortune's biggest worry was that Tamed Ocelot would attack while they slept. If Cable had astute advisors, such a death might make Exemplary Fortune a hero rather than a traitor; but, even if that happened, Exemplary Fortune doubted that Cable or any other possible Unique Inca would keep Tamed Ocelot alive after he had killed a prince. Likely Ginez would either be killed, too, or, worse, forced to aid Tamed Ocelot in his escape. Exemplary Fortune could easily imagine Ginez stealing food for a fugitive Tamed Ocelot, hiding perhaps in a house emptied by the epidemic or a herder's hut hidden among a mountain's rocks and cliffs. In that case, anyone who did not know the two well would probably fail to understand that Ginez may not have had any choice. Ginez would then most likely be executed for Tamed Ocelot's crimes as well as his own.

Exemplary Fortune's last hope of getting a new Unique Inca

to listen to Ginez could fail in so many ways. That was perhaps what he had not understood when he promised to bring the two men back to his father. He had understood the path that led to success, but he had had no knowledge of the many ways that his mission could fail. He taught Ginez, he watched Tamed Ocelot, he listened for the movements of the guards at the door, and he held no hope for himself. He slept lightly, waking every time Tamed Ocelot moved.

Tamed Ocelot attacked while Exemplary Fortune was showing Ginez the drum dance, charging from just outside Exemplary Fortune's alert radius. Off balance, Exemplary Fortune twisted away, but Tamed Ocelot's right hand gave him a glancing blow, and he moved in before Exemplary Fortune could recover. Exemplary Fortune grabbed Tamed Ocelot's right arm, seeking to lever him around, but Tamed Ocelot was ready for the maneuver, and soon, in spite of everything Exemplary Fortune tried, Tamed Ocelot's hands were around his throat, and his own arms were pinned so he could not fight back. He bucked, his vision blurring. Then suddenly the pressure on his throat was gone. He inhaled and choked on acrid fumes. The pressure of Tamed Ocelot's body on his went away, and Ginez's face appeared above his.

Ginez asked anxiously, "Are you all right?"

Exemplary Fortune took another breath, more cautiously. His windpipe seemed undamaged. "I'm okay," he croaked, rubbing his throat and looking for the source of the awful stench.

The unbroken top rim of the piss pot was on the floor next to him, and shards of its bottom littered the floor around him. Now that Ginez had rolled Tamed Ocelot away from him, the stench had lessened. Tamed Ocelot's hair was matted and filthy. Unfortunately, he had not gotten all the mess. Well, that was one way to win a fight. Thorniest particularly approved of innovation. "Thank you," Exemplary Fortune said to Ginez.

Ginez looked unhappily at Tamed Ocelot's inert body. "He be very mad when he wakes up," he said unhappily.

"He will," said Exemplary Fortune, "but now that he knows we guard each other, he will be less likely to attack." Exemplary Fortune's throat hurt, but his heart felt better than it had since

Young Majesty had died. This battle had been won, and it had been won by Ginez, who did not appear to be any kind of a fighter. It was a very small battle, and, furthermore, Ginez was right. Tamed Ocelot would no doubt be very annoyed. Exemplary Fortune had no idea how the desire for revenge would weigh against prudence in Tamed Ocelot's heart. Ginez and he might be dead as soon as they both went to sleep. That would be later.

Exemplary Fortune checked Tamed Ocelot's breathing, which was deep and regular, then let Ginez help him to his feet. He went to the door to ask the guards for a new piss pot and a bath. They got the piss pot almost immediately, but they had to wait six days for the bath, six days of having Tamed Ocelot trying to wipe himself off on every available surface, especially Ginez's clothes. But he did not attack again, not even while they were sleeping. Maybe he was clever enough to realize that, smelling as he did, he had no hope of hiding anywhere, except maybe in a llamas' communal voiding heap.

On the seventh day, ten guards came to take them to bathe. Ginez explained to Tamed Ocelot what the guards wanted, and Tamed Ocelot, without acknowledging the explanation, went with them, not meekly, but as though he had organized the expedition. They had to cross a large part of the governor's compound to reach the bath. Magnanimous Strength obviously no longer felt any need to hide Exemplary Fortune. The bath was a sensuous pleasure, but it set up a new tension in Exemplary Fortune. That night he woke not only to Tamed Ocelot's stirrings, but also to movements of the guards outside. He started when breakfast was delivered.

It was an actual relief when, shortly after breakfast, an Inca captain came to the door and ordered them out into the compound's courtyard. Exemplary Fortune went first, bringing the apprehensive Ginez with him. There were fifty-one men outside, all save the captain belonging to the Tampu honorary Inca tribe with black-and-red headbands and silver earrings. All of them looked extremely dedicated, as though they had been made fully aware that their task was both important and likely to be fraught with danger. Not surprisingly, Exemplary Fortune recognized none of the men.

Exemplary Fortune turned away from the warriors and watched

the doorway of their room. Tamed Ocelot came out into the open with his eyes darting everywhere, orienting himself, making sure that nothing had changed since the last time he had been outside. When the captain's men produced ropes to tie their hands, Exemplary Fortune said to the guard in front of him, "I assume this means that you agree to accept full responsibility for Tamed Ocelot and his actions."

The man turned uncertainly to the fifty-captain. When the guard repeated Exemplary Fortune's words, the captain asked, "Which one is he?"

"The pale one."

It should have been obvious. Tamed Ocelot had his knees flexed and his hands loose at his sides ready to move in any direction. The guard with the rope for him had already started to turn to the captain.

"Tell him to let us tie his hands," the captain ordered.

"He does not listen to me," said Exemplary Fortune.

The captain had the man with the rope move closer to Tamed Ocelot while a small circle of men surrounded Tamed Ocelot close enough to back him up. Tamed Ocelot went for the side, almost the back, of the circle. It was the spot Exemplary Fortune himself would have chosen. The man there moved hesitantly as though unsure of how he should defend himself. He did, however, hold Tamed Ocelot long enough for the others to come up and eventually wrestle Tamed Ocelot to the ground and tie his hands, but the man had gotten a knee to the gut and had trouble catching his breath. The Inca captain called for a healer and accepted his recommendation that the man be left behind. His wife was summoned and went with the wounded man and the healer.

The captain came over to Exemplary Fortune. "So, he does not listen to you?" His voice had a dangerous edge.

"My bruises have faded," said Exemplary Fortune. "Also, as I am sure you have heard, Ginez used a weapon on him."

The captain nodded shortly and signaled the men to tie Exemplary Fortune. He held out his hands readily.

Once he had them all secured, the captain surveyed his now-disheveled troops with an unhappy eye. Exemplary Fortune could almost hear his thoughts. A troop starting out was supposed to embody the precision and order of the empire, not the disorder of untamed lands. The captain pursed his lips with frustration and then, watching Tamed Ocelot closely, signaled them to start. Tamed Ocelot responded readily to the tug on his rope. He did not, however, have the carriage of someone who had been defeated. He managed to hold himself as though he were doing everyone a royal favor just by being there; he looked, in fact, very much like an Inca. The similarity was disquieting.

The fifty women joined them at the gateway of the compound. Exemplary Fortune expected Magnanimous Strength to join the group as well, but he was nowhere to be seen. The governor would not send Exemplary Fortune to Navel unless he would be in that city to state the case against him. Since he was not traveling with their group, he must already be in the capital. Exemplary Fortune nearly ground his teeth. Magnanimous Strength must have left as soon as he had Exemplary Fortune safely caged. He could have gone to Cable with the good news and worked unhampered and unworried for his accession. All of which he, Exemplary Fortune, had helped make possible. He could not have done more for Cable if he had tried.

The 105 of them made excellent time, and, saying good-bye to the heart of the Four Quarters, Exemplary Fortune found in it a beauty that he had not noticed before. Its precipitous drops from chill wind-lashed highlands to hot stifling river valleys seemed an ironic comment on his own life, but the stone-paved road was lined with molle trees, willows, and the beautiful red-flowered qantu trees, which tore at his heart, in all the valleys. The grassy hilltops were green with the driving rains of the season. In the upper valleys, potato, quinoa, oca, nasturtium, and bean sprouts flecked the fields. In the lower valleys people weeded well-grown corn plants.

Though weeding was not as colorful as the plowing celebrations, the sight of people working the fields filled Exemplary Fortune with an almost enjoyable melancholy. He would never again work the earth, but life would go on. The corn would grow, and people go out into their fields without him. He would get that far in his thoughts, and he would think of Magnanimous Strength, and all his equanimity would vanish. He did not want Magnanimous Strength to go on, especially without him.

He could do nothing about it, and the rage he sometimes felt was useless, but he did think occasionally of whom he would contact if he could somehow get away. In his careful isolation, it was hard to know who was supporting whom and why, but he finally decided that he would try to find Beautiful Plowridge. He was well liked enough that, if it became known that he had talked with Exemplary Fortune, it would not cause him major harm. Also, his main interest was plant-breeding rather than politics; he was not likely to have passionately supported any candidate for Unique Inca. But Exemplary Fortune did not know where Beautiful Plowridge was. Besides, Beautiful Plowridge was a brother, and brothers, though one's closest kin, were too much like one, competing for the same honors, attention, and land. Contacting Beautiful Plowridge might be no safer than talking with Cable.

They reached the gorge of the Commanding Speaker on the morning of the fifth day. Her roar, swollen by rains, had been with them from the evening before. Ginez, who had been walking rain-slicked roads along sheer cliff faces with equanimity, balked at the edge of the chasm until Exemplary Fortune stepped onto the Waka Bridge himself and yelled reassurances that although it swayed, the bridge would not throw them, that the fiber cables were strong enough to support them all. Tamed Ocelot stepped out onto the bridge as though he didn't even notice it. Once on the bridge, though, he did assume a gait that was noticeably straddle legged. The Commanding Speaker roared at them all, but Exemplary Fortune could not decipher what she said, and, in any case, it did not seem likely to help him.

It was still raining, a light cool drizzle as they crossed into Navel's valley two days later. Exemplary Fortune found no joy in the sight of the orderly green terraces of corn and the majestic golden-roofed city on the hillsides to their left. Instead, he found his heart tending toward an anger he could not afford. He had used up all his patience and much of his sorrow while caged in Magnanimous Strength's trap. His heart beat fast, readying him for battle, and his hands clenched. He forced himself to breathe slowly, convincing himself that he needed to at least appear calm. His fists unclenched, and he looked around the city with all the interest he could summon, trying to glean any information that might help him or Ginez.

Now that they were in the city, everyone's mouth was filled with the name of the new Unique Inca, Exemplary Royal Happiness. The reign name meant nothing to Exemplary Fortune, and certainly did not tell him which brother had been fringed. However, since Cable was neither happy nor an exemplar of much of anything, it sounded like a reign name he would choose. Their father, who had taken the fringe when he was twenty, had chosen to acknowledge his youth, to make it an asset. If Exemplary Royal Happiness was indeed Cable's choice of a reign name, that was not the path he was taking. It was depressing to have his worries about Cable confirmed, even in such a minor way.

One man went ahead to contact Magnanimous Strength and came back with fifty-one new guards. Fifty of these men, though, were Field Guardians from Granary with chin-length braids fastened with red-and-green ribbons, clearly Governor Magnanimous Strength's men. Their captain was again Inca, and he carried a wand from the Unique Inca rather than the governor. The Field Guardians and he were to take the three of them to the Unique Inca Exemplary Royal Happiness.

Exemplary Fortune felt a grim satisfaction with the substitution. Maybe the new Unique Inca did not trust Incas or honorary Incas to carry out their orders to kill his brother. Maybe he believed Exemplary Fortune would have convinced his escort of his innocence as they walked toward Navel. In either case, the Unique Inca believed in Exemplary Fortune's power far more than Exemplary Fortune did. Perhaps Exemplary Fortune could find a way to use that belief. The squad took them to Young Majesty's original palace compound and then through the main courtyard into a room Young Majesty had used as an audience chamber before he moved to Kitu Dove.

It was indeed Cable on the Unique Inca's stool. His clothes

were of richly patterned kumpi cloth in gold, silver, and dark orange. The scarlet fringe hung down to the bridge of his nose, and his headband was adorned with flowers. He held the feathered scepter in his right hand. But none of this succeeded in making him look regal. He looked very young and unsure of himself, determined perhaps, but determined with the slightly desperate manner of someone who expects to fail. He was not an auspicious ideal for the empire's future.

A herald announced them. Exemplary Fortune, who had had time to think about the problem of giving obeisance with one's hands tied, gave Cable the full bow and long-distance kiss, bringing both hands to his lips. Ginez went down on his knees and then bowed. Tamed Ocelot, as was to be expected, ignored everyone.

The Unique Inca did not respond to their presence, but the man standing on his right said in a neutral tone, "Exemplary Fortune, a charge of treason has been brought against you. Your accuser, Magnanimous Strength, will speak first." The speaker was Royal Reckoner. He had been with Young Majesty when Exemplary Fortune had left Throat Town and had undoubtedly stayed with him until he died. He would know Young Majesty's last words to his people, who else had died, and how the survivors were faring. As Magnanimous Strength began speaking, Exemplary Fortune shook off the longing Royal Reckoner's presence aroused in him. He could not afford it.

Magnanimous Strength started with a paean to his own love of the empire and his great wisdom in seeing and dealing with the threat that Exemplary Fortune posed. No one stopped him or suggested that he speak only of what had actually happened. When he did finally reach the facts of the case, he gave the same mix of almost correct facts and completely wrong interpretation that he had accused Exemplary Fortune with originally. Exemplary Royal Happiness and his advisors listened attentively and did not ask questions. When Magnanimous Strength finished, Royal Reckoner said, "Exemplary Fortune, you may now speak."

Exemplary Fortune inclined his head. "I have acted with love toward and on orders of our father, Young Majesty." He tried to speak as he would to Bright Rainbow, beginning with his father's worries and not downplaying the very real danger Tamed Ocelot posed. He did understate the camaraderie between himself and Shrewdness and with his faithful turn-workers. Though he wanted the Unique Inca to talk with Shrewdness, he did not wish Shrewdness to be destroyed because of their friendship. Since Cable—Exemplary Fortune could not think of him as anything Happiness—had assumed an air of uninterested boredom, Exemplary Fortune concentrated his attention on Royal Reckoner and the Inca's other advisors.

When Exemplary Fortune finished, Cable said, "So you admit that Tamed Ocelot is a danger?"

"I insist on it."

Exemplary Royal Happiness's lips formed a pout. "Can you talk with this barbarian?"

"I can try."

"Tell him I want him to wrestle one of my warriors."

Exemplary Fortune hesitated. "I fear for your safety."

The Unique Inca's eyes turned dangerous. "Do it," he hissed.

Exemplary Fortune turned to Tamed Ocelot and gathered his Spanish. "The king wants you fight one man with your hands."

Tamed Ocelot surveyed him. "Tell him, if he will give me a weapon, I will kill everyone here."

"He will not give you a weapon."

"I will fight," said Tamed Ocelot.

Exemplary Fortune turned back to Cable. "He will fight."

"You had two exchanges," said Cable petulantly.

Exemplary Fortune shrugged off irritation. The Unique Inca had a right to be suspicious, but he didn't have to act like a spoiled child. "He said if you gave him a weapon, he would kill everyone here. I told him that wasn't what was offered."

Suppressed snickers came from the Unique Inca's bodyguard. Clearly, some of the men would welcome the diversion of a lone barbarian trying to fight them all. Exemplary Fortune would not. He was the only one who thought Tamed Ocelot might be telling the truth.

The Unique Inca picked his champion, a big well-muscled man but lithe rather than burly. Exemplary Fortune found himself curious about the outcome of the fight. If he were betting, he would bet on Tamed Ocelot, but he had not fought Tamed Ocelot in a situation where one or the other of them did not have an advantage. As for hope, he had no idea if anything Tamed Ocelot would do could help him or not. He dared not hope.

The whole of the Inca's entourage—courtiers, guards, and the three prisoners—went out into the main courtyard in solemn procession, and Tamed Ocelot's bonds were removed. Exemplary Fortune held his breath, but, for once, Tamed Ocelot was doing what he was supposed to. He stretched and then took off his tunic, exposing his pallid hairy skin to all. With the dark furlike band around his throat and lower face, he looked even more like an exotic wild animal than usual. He stared at the Unique Inca's champion appraisingly, not, in spite of his boastful words, taking the contest for granted.

Exemplary Fortune's eyes strayed to Cable's bodyguard. The only thing worse than Cable as Unique Inca might well be Cable murdered almost as soon as he assumed the fringe. The Four Quarters did not need another dreadful shock on top of the two it had just suffered. Some of the Unique Inca's bodyguards were watching the two contestants with an intensity that boded ill for their concentration on their task, but most seemed to be keeping at least half their attention on the job they were supposed to be doing. The Unique Inca himself looked impatient. Interestingly enough, Royal Reckoner was watching him. They traded an appraising gaze, and then Royal Reckoner's eyes flicked away at an unhappy cry from the gathering. Exemplary Fortune checked the bodyguard again before he looked at the two fighters.

They had broken away from each other, but the Unique Inca's champion was favoring his right leg and had a slightly panicked air. Tamed Ocelot, on the other hand, seemed almost relaxed. He advanced on the Inca fighter in a leisurely fashion. The Unique Inca's champion backed cautiously, trying to regain his confidence with a slow retreat. When Tamed Ocelot went for him again, he held his ground, trying quick punches to confuse Tamed Ocelot, but they never got to see what his followthrough would be. Tamed Ocelot ignored his punches, knocked him over, and got his hands around his throat almost as though the man weren't even resisting him. Exemplary Fortune looked away as Tamed Ocelot's arms bunched with the effort of throttling the man.

He turned his attention to the Unique Inca, who was staring at the scene with shocked dismay. He had clearly believed his champion would win easily. Think, Exemplary Fortune willed silently. Even if you won't listen to me, think about what Tamed Ocelot is showing you.

Cable's eyes tore away from the fight and came up to meet Exemplary Fortune's. Their eyes locked, and then the Inca blinked and looked away. He did not move for a few breaths, staring blankly at the courtyard's surface. His jaw tightened. Looking around, he said, "This is a difficult case. I would talk with my advisors." With no more ceremony than that, he got up and walked back into the audience room, followed by his advisors and half of his much-subdued bodyguard.

In the courtyard, Tamed Ocelot watched him go with an expression that was almost a sneer. Beside him on the ground was the unmoving form of the Inca's champion.

The captain of the remaining guards came over to Exemplary Fortune. "Tell Tamed Ocelot to let us tie his hands again."

"I can tell him," said Exemplary Fortune, "but I cannot promise he will do it."

"He understood you well enough when you asked him to fight," the captain said.

The captain made it sound as though it were Exemplary Fortune's fault that the man was dead. "When I relayed the Unique Inca Exemplary Royal Happiness's words," said Exemplary Fortune carefully, "I was asking him to fight. He likes to fight. Never before has he done anything I asked him to."

The captain's expression tightened. "Just tell him."

Exemplary Fortune took four steps closer to Tamed Ocelot without anyone stopping him. He said, gesturing with his tied hands, "The captain here wants to tie your hands again."

Tamed Ocelot gave him an imperious gaze. The Unique Inca's men approached him warily. When the man with the rope was a pace away, Tamed Ocelot thrust his hands forward so quickly that the man took a half-step back. Tamed Ocelot gave him a predator's grin and let them tie him. A somber party carried away the body of the Unique Inca's champion.

The courtyard of the Unique Inca's palace compound was quiet. No one there had anything to do except wait for whatever the new Unique Inca and his councilors decided. Exemplary Fortune found an unreasonable sprout of hope inside himself. He had not expected to live even this long after meeting the new Unique Inca. Cable had not listened to his words, but he had been unable to ignore Tamed Ocelot. He was thinking now, reevaluating what he had been told. Maybe he would even live up to the position he had assumed, though that did not necessarily mean he would let Exemplary Fortune live. Prudence might well hold that Exemplary Fortune alive, with a grievance against the Unique Inca, would be too dangerous to the realm's stability. Wryly, Exemplary Fortune had to admit that he did not know how he would advise Cable if he were in a position to do so. He no longer knew what he would do if he were free to act as he wished.

Across the courtyard, the retinue around Magnanimous Strength shifted, giving Exemplary Fortune a clear view of the man. He looked annoyed rather than worried, as though some subordinate had misunderstood orders rather than that the supreme archetype of the land was making an independent decision. Under Young Majesty, Magnanimous Strength had evidently kept himself in line, but now his ambition fairly screamed at Exemplary Fortune. Be very wary of this one, he thought at Cable, with no hope that the Unique Inca would hear him, but the Unique Inca's advisors, if Cable would listen to them, might well say the same thing. Royal Reckoner, for one, had served their father well.

It was a long wait in the courtyard. While the guards and Tamed Ocelot assumed an impassive demeanor, Magnanimous Strength became visibly impatient. Ginez stayed still, keeping his head down and his thoughts to himself. Exemplary Fortune did not know how much of the proceedings he had understood, but he did not ask for clarification. For himself, as the time stretched on, Exemplary Fortune began to be frightened, which meant hope was growing in his heart. There did not seem to be anything he could do about it except to keep his face impassive as the others did.

Finally, a courtier appeared in the doorway to the audience chamber and bid them all enter. Exemplary Fortune found that he was stiff. He had evidently been holding himself very still. Inside the room, all was as they had first seen it, the Unique Inca on his stool with his advisors and guards around him. This time Exemplary Royal Happiness had schooled his features to calm. When the prisoners had gathered in front of him, he said, "After considering all the facts of this case, while I find that Exemplary Fortune has exercised poor judgment—"

Exemplary Fortune bowed his head to keep the sudden, premature joy from showing on his face. His heart turned over, making it hard to breathe.

"—in traveling the Four Quarters with a dangerous individual and no trained guards, I do not find evidence that he intended treason." The Unique Inca paused briefly. "He says that our father believed the stranger he calls Tamed Ocelot might someday be important to the well-being of the Four Quarters. I therefore decree that Tamed Ocelot, an individual with a defective heart, be assigned to Exemplary Fortune to maintain and to keep in conformity with the rules of the Four Quarters." Cable stared at Exemplary Fortune with more impassivity than Exemplary Fortune would have believed him capable of.

Even over the ragged pounding of his heart, Exemplary Fortune heard the trap. While, if he refused the assignment, he would be guilty of disobeying the Unique Inca's orders, if he accepted with no more instruction than Cable had just given him, he could become the danger Magnanimous Strength professed to believe he was. He bowed in acknowledgement. "As always, I am the Unique Inca's faithful servant. Who will be his guards?"

A hint of annoyance crossed Exemplary Royal Happiness's face—did he really think Exemplary Fortune would fall for such a simple trap?—as he continued, "The position of governor in Completion Province is currently vacant. I believe you will find sufficient men there. A regiment of troops leaves for Sundried the day after tomorrow. I will instruct Commander Whence Reckoning to

assign sufficient troops to escort you and your charge past Endward."

Exile. That was what they had decreed for him. Exemplary
Fortune's heart began to sing in unreasonable ecstasy. He could
accept exile. He could, for the moment at least, positively revel in
exile. Exemplary Fortune bowed again. "I hear and obey." His heart
beat as though after a victorious battle. He did not know what to
do with himself. The captain of the guards came over to untie his
hands, and Exemplary Fortune had difficulty realizing that the
hands he held out belonged to him.

"Ginez," said Royal Reckoner, and Ginez looked up, his face
full of bewilderment and fear.

Exemplary Fortune bit his lip, his heart calming a little. He
had worked to provide Ginez with the skills to succeed here, but
Ginez had shown mixed reactions under pressure. And he dare not
try to help.

"I hear," said Ginez. Not the response Exemplary Fortune had
taught him, but not unreasonable, either.

"You came into this land with a dangerous criminal and warned
no one about his problems."

Yes, no one here knew that Ginez had pilfered from Recognition's fortress. He was not a danger. Exemplary Fortune would
not tell them.

"Please," said Ginez. "He does not tell me he is—" he searched
for a word "—rotten. When I find out, so does everyone."

Reasonable.

"Whom do you give your allegiance to?" asked Royal Reckoner.

"I am in the Inca's land," said Ginez. "I worship the High Inca."

"Will you fight for him in his wars?"

"Yes," said Ginez.

"And accept the wife and position he gives you, working always
to promote order and the prosperity of the Four Quarters?"

"This is what I wish for," said Ginez. "I want to stay here
always."

In spite of having spent most of his time here caged like an animal with someone who would just as soon kill him as not. But the Unique Inca and his staff did not appear to be listening to those nuances. Perhaps, though, someone would remember and ask Ginez later. Right now, they all appeared bent only on settling the disposition of Exemplary Fortune and his two charges. That they also needed to settle the disposition of the strangers who had visited Recognition did not yet seem to have penetrated their hearts. In that much Exemplary Fortune had failed, but the Unique Inca had left both him and Ginez alive to make the case another day.

As one of the younger courtiers led Ginez away to continue his education in the ways of the Four Quarters, Exemplary Fortune began to move, rubbing his wrists and looking around the room. On the far side, Magnanimous Strength appeared somewhat stunned. Exemplary Fortune had to fight down a sudden laugh. Magnanimous Strength would not be so ready to assume Exemplary Royal Happiness would be his tool in the future.

The Unique Inca's decree was a good decision, a very good decision. Magnanimous Strength had been given a small but public setback. One of the Unique Inca's rivals for the fringe had been sent into exile at the opposite end of the empire from his sources of political power with enough of a problem to keep him occupied even without the duties of running a recently conquered province. Ginez had his chance to prove himself in the empire.

As for Tamed Ocelot, Tamed Ocelot had obviously come out of this with far more than he deserved. He even had a kind of insurance on his life, for if he died at Exemplary Fortune's hands, Exemplary Fortune would have disobeyed the Unique Inca's express orders and could again find himself on trial for his life. If Exemplary Fortune ever saw Shrewdness again, he would have to warn him about the dangers of idly naming strangers. He would have to remember that Tamed Ocelot always went for the throat.

7

FIRST YEAR OF EXEMPLARY ROYAL HAPPINESS'S REIGN
FLOWER GARMENT AND YOUNG CORN DANCE MONTHS

In actual history, some say the epidemic killed as many as two-thirds of the people in the Four Quarters, some say only one in twenty. No one mentions any of those who died except Young Majesty, his heir, and a few commanders.

As courtiers began urging him out of the Unique Inca's audience chamber, Exemplary Fortune went over to the guard holding Tamed Ocelot's tether and took it from him. Tamed Ocelot gave him a rather wild-eyed look. It was obvious he had no idea of what had just happened.

Exemplary Hawk, who had been another of Exemplary Fortune's brothers in Navel with Bright Rainbow, came over with ten newly vigilant guards. The guards eyed Tamed Ocelot warily, and Exemplary Hawk surveyed Exemplary Fortune with about the same expression. He did not say anything to Exemplary Fortune directly, merely nodding him toward the door. Exemplary Fortune, watching Tamed Ocelot with as much of his attention as he did his brother, followed the prince through the city streets and then on up past the stepped fields of Granary Terrace just above the city to the jagged walls leading into the grounds of Royal Eagle.

Royal Eagle was Navel's storehouse and hilltop fortress as well as a second temple to the glory of the Sun. It was also high enough to be above the tolerance of most crops, and its grounds were therefore the best place in Navel Valley to assemble troops.

Tamed Ocelot surveyed Exemplary Fortune and the rest of his guards with renewed interest as the group turned through the first narrow gateway in the stairway that led up to Royal Eagle's grounds. They traveled single file through the narrow opening. If Tamed Ocelot thought he could propel himself quickly up one of the giant stones that formed the gate's sides, this might be the best place to try to escape. When Tamed Ocelot saw that Exemplary Fortune was watching him, he turned his head away so that Exemplary Fortune could not see his face. Exemplary Fortune kept a wary watch on him as they turned through the second and third gates, but the man did not try anything. As they turned through the highest gateway, though, Tamed Ocelot stumbled. Exemplary Fortune did not try to catch him, and the man recovered his balance and walked on steadily along the dusty road. Exemplary Fortune was not sure if the stumble had been a ploy or if Tamed Ocelot had been stunned by the sight of the veritable tent city spread out before them.

Thousands of tents formed a meadow of bright colors, and the people moving among them were crowded more thickly than in any permanent town. At the edge of the road a group of Black Loincloths were setting up a cluster of tents. A group of women wearing the silver earrings and black-and-red headbands of the Tampu tribe of honorary Incas had just come out of Royal Eagle's massive compound carrying food and water jars on their backs. An Inca captain was instructing an Ichu-Grass ten-group on how to swing a sword in an area barely big enough to avoid disaster should someone stumble. Everywhere people were running errands and talking with each other. Exemplary Fortune found himself feeling as though he had just come home and, without willing it, found himself surveying the encampment to check how it was functioning and the morale of the people within it. But, when he did not see any of his old comrades, the illusion of familiarity faded away.

Exemplary Hawk led his charges to a large scarlet tent in the tent city's center that faced the roadway to the huge compound. At the back of the tent Whence Reckoning sat surrounded by captains and advisors. He evinced both astonishment and suspicion at finding Exemplary Fortune literally at the door of his command tent; and, were it not for Exemplary Hawk and the rest of Exemplary Fortune's rather ample escort, would doubtless have bound him again. Whence Reckoning was even less pleased when Exemplary Hawk explained that the pale bearded stranger, killer of Inca guards and an ever-present danger to all, was now, thanks to Exemplary Fortune's presence, part of the encampment.

When the situation had been made clear, complete with the implication that Exemplary Fortune, though cleared of any serious wrongdoing, was still out of favor, Whence Reckoning said to Exemplary Fortune, "Your devotion to our father is most praiseworthy. I am delighted you are so diligent." He paused, a dour look on his face. "Your companion, however, can hardly be cared for by ordinary turn-workers."

"Of course not," said Exemplary Fortune affably. "And, in any case, the Unique Inca Exemplary Royal Happiness has given him specifically into my care."

That statement was evidently not what Whence Reckoning expected. He shifted uneasily on his rug and tried another approach. "You are not an officer in this army."

"Of course not," said Exemplary Fortune again. He was too relieved at his unexpected release from death to care what Whence Reckoning, Exemplary Hawk, or any of his brothers thought of him. "If you are worried that my presence in an officer's tent would be disruptive, put the two of us in a tent of strong turn-warriors." He could hardly keep from laughing. Whence Reckoning literally did not know what to do with the two of them. As for Exemplary Fortune, he would just as soon be away from his brothers and other Incas who would either sympathize and thereby, if he understood Exemplary Royal Happiness's heart, put themselves in danger, or, more likely, make every effort to properly snub him. In either case, the humblest of turn-workers would make better companions.

"Well," said Whence Reckoning, "if you do not mind, a tent of warriors . . . is Tamed Ocelot's heart strong enough that he will not harm others if there is no possible purpose in it?"

"So far he has seemed to act with purpose," said Exemplary

Fortune. "He will, however, have to be kept away from all weapons."

Whence Reckoning nodded and, without saying anything more to Exemplary Fortune, sent for Splinter. Exemplary Fortune knew the name, though he had not met the man. It was said the Colddungs had given Splinter his name because, in an earlier campaign, he had been a constant irritant to them. That he had chosen to keep the name implied he intended to make the military his career. If circumstances had been different, Exemplary Fortune would have been eager to talk with him, to find out how his heart worked. Now he merely wondered what the man had done to merit Whence Reckoning's disapproval. Or maybe he was becoming too suspicious. Splinter turned out to be the Inca captain of the Flamingo Lake turn-warriors. While Whence Reckoning explained the problem Tamed Ocelot posed without once addressing Exemplary Fortune, Exemplary Fortune practiced a calm gaze at nothing and tried to convince himself that Splinter had been chosen because Exemplary Fortune had never stopped in Flamingo Lake territory and, for that matter, had never known a Flamingo Lake tribesperson.

At least part of the explanation was even simpler than that. Splinter led Exemplary Fortune to a group of twenty people with bright pink headbands. The men wore their hair chin length. The women's hair was still short with mourning for the newly dead. Both the women and the men were unusually burly, and most of the men were also tall. Whether the men were skilled fighters or not, they were certainly intimidating, and their weight alone would crush anyone who tried to resist them bare-handed. Exemplary Fortune felt somewhat ashamed of himself when Splinter fairly explained Tamed Ocelot and the problem he posed. The Flamingo Lake ten-group was delighted to be considered a company of great warriors, capable of controlling this fierce madman, but the men worried about their wives. "How crazy is he?" they asked Exemplary Fortune, and he had to admit that, yes, he would attack even women.

"But," said Molle, their ten-captain, "if we refuse to take you two in, you will have to stay with warriors who are not as strong as we are, and you will be in more danger."

Everyone agreed that they were the best possible group to control Tamed Ocelot. It took them a while, though, to agree on how to take him in without undue danger. Finally, one of the women suggested they adjust their sleeping arrangements so a different two men would sleep between Tamed Ocelot and the rest of group every night. Exemplary Fortune, they decided, would always sleep between Tamed Ocelot and the tent wall.

"Don't hesitate to call on us if he attacks you," said Molle.

Exemplary Fortune assured them he wouldn't.

That settled, the women asked Exemplary Fortune where his wives were. Though from a small village, they were sophisticated enough to know that an Inca prince old enough to be on his own would have more than one wife.

The question tore at a scab that was still fresh. Exemplary Fortune did not want to talk about Qantu Flower's death with strangers no matter how friendly. He said simply, "As far as I know, they are in Kitu Dove. If they are not . . ." He shrugged the rest of the answer away. The Flamingo Lakes looked sympathetic and did not ask further about that topic.

"You should ask the Unique Inca for another wife until they can join you," the youngest woman said instead. "One of our men could sleep against the tent wall one night in ten."

The other women agreed that their men would not miss sleeping with them occasionally, and the men replied that was all very well, but the women would likely be unwilling to forego sex that often. It took a while for them to get back to the main topic, but, in the end, all agreed that Exemplary Fortune needed a wife for the trip. It was true. No one should be single, but Exemplary Fortune was not unpaired. His unwilling partner was Tamed Ocelot; and, however fragmentary and unhappy their relationship, Tamed Ocelot's presence made him refuse to think about taking a wife. Until he knew how quickly the men could move, Exemplary Fortune did not want anyone else to take the more dangerous job of guarding the tent wall.

The women said that cooking another two portions would be no problem, and there was little else to settle. When they retired for the night, the group's yellow tent was totally filled with the twenty-two of them. Just before they unrolled the quilts, one woman produced a tinkling anklet to put around Tamed Ocelot's ankle for the night. They all watched as Exemplary Fortune fastened it. Tamed Ocelot did not resist. It might be that he regarded it as more of a nuisance for the rest of them than an inconvenience for him. Its string was thin and would be easy to part.

The next day the Flamingo Lakes asked Exemplary Fortune if he had been in Kitu Dove when the epidemic started. The epidemic was what they most wanted to know about, not Young Majesty or even Tamed Ocelot, who sat at the edge of the group watching them all warily. When Exemplary Fortune said that he knew nothing about how the epidemic began, the Flamingo Lakes told him their own experiences instead. Fourteen people in their village of three hundred had died, including their chief healer. "It was so sad," said a man. "Fuchsia had only two children in ten years and both of them died." In surrounding villages an even-larger portion of people had died. After they talked about family and friends, they turned to the more general effects of the epidemic. "I heard," said Molle, "of a village that had to be abandoned because there weren't enough people to work the fields anymore."

"There is a village of Copper colonists west of ours," said a woman, "and they have so few people now, they are worried whether they can perform the ceremonies properly for their wakas."

"For a while," said a man, "they even thought about asking the Inca if they could move back to their old province, but no one else knows how to tend the suspension bridge across the Earthbridge River, and besides, the young people didn't want to move."

"It is better in Flamingo Lake," the woman affirmed. They all agreed, and the conversation moved to other topics.

Exemplary Fortune, though, began to feel through his dimming pain an urge to talk to an accountant. Traveling south, he had been so focused on reaching the Unique Inca that he had not seriously thought about the extent of the disaster. Three of the Flamingo Lakes were pocked with massive new scars from the disease. Without the unheard accountant's report, Exemplary Fortune could only guess, but it sounded as though as many as a sixth of the Four Quarters' people might have died, many of them babies and older people, future workers and the communities' repositories of knowledge. If a warrior tribe with no thought for its future members wanted to sabotage a people before trying to conquer them, those were two of the groups it would most want to destroy. It fit somehow with the strange hard metal and the round boats, things the Incas had not thought of, could hardly even imagine existing. The timing was so close. And the disease had spread, the Flamingo Lakes said, person to person.

He had a sudden clear picture of Young Majesty's audience chamber with just the two of them and the messenger with the quipu from Recognition. It was nonsense. The quipu had been handled by many runners in succession, and Recognition did not suffer from the disease first. Still, he could not shake the feeling that, however the bearded strangers had or had not brought the Spotted Death to the empire, that was the moment that sealed his father's doom.

Exemplary Fortune slept even more lightly than usual that night, waking at every change in Tamed Ocelot's breathing, wondering why the man had been left in the Four Quarters, if he held some dreadful surprise Exemplary Fortune could not forehear; wondering if keeping him alive was, after all, a betrayal of the empire. There was no way to know. It could even be his death that would bring the cataclysm.

The next morning, Splinter invited all the Flamingo Lake ten-captains to a meeting, talking mostly, said Molle, about taking down and setting up the tents in the shortest possible period of time. The tents would be the only large supplies the army would carry with them, and, if they were not expeditiously dealt with, they could significantly delay the army. Splinter appeared to have a clear grasp of how to motivate his turn-warriors. That afternoon, all the Flamingo Lake ten-groups held a competition to see who could take down and set up their tents most quickly. Molle's ten-group came in third. "Don't worry," Molle told his people, "we will have months to practice. By the time we reach Sundried, we will be the fastest, not only of the Flamingo Lakes, but of all the ten-groups in the army." They did not let Exemplary Fortune help. "You are our guest," they said, and besides, "The other Flamingo Lakes would not think it was fair."

The next morning, the tents were folded swiftly, and the army set out immediately after making the offerings to the Sun at His rising. The army marched through Navel in approved tribal order, except for Exemplary Fortune and Tamed Ocelot, who were not captaining the Flamingo Lakes and therefore should not, by strict reckoning, have marched with them. There was no other place for their odd coupling, though, and Splinter simply told them to stay in the middle of their row. To Exemplary Fortune, the cheers of the Incas and honorary Incas, who lined the streets to watch them go, seemed subdued.

From Navel, the army followed the southern section of the Majestic Road. In three days they were beyond the lands Exemplary Fortune knew and headed directly toward Lake Titicaca—Rock of the Cat in Aymara, the language of the Eminences and Covereds—but they would not stop there. The army would travel past the southern edge of Lake Titicaca through Sundried to the empire's troubled eastern border with the Colddungs.

When the army turned east where the road split in Sundried, Exemplary Fortune and Tamed Ocelot would continue south. The two of them would travel into Endward and through that province all the way to the end of the empire. They would not stop even there but continue west back over the mountains toward the Great Lake. His journey would end three thousand miles from Throat Town, where the trek had started.

Exemplary Fortune wondered why Cable and his advisors had decided to carry out this campaign against the Colddungs so soon after the epidemic. Were the Colddungs wreaking that much havoc along the border, or did Cable worry about the ambitions of Whence Reckoning or other princes in the army? If Cable sought to lessen the chance that another prince would try to usurp his position, the strategy seemed risky. If the campaign against the Colddungs succeeded, those who led it would come back heroes, with perhaps more power and therefore more ambition. If, on the other hand, the campaign failed, Cable's policy would have been shown to be ill conceived and thus increase the chances someone would try to oust him. Of course, if Cable ordered a campaign to push the Colddungs back into their own lands without totally defeating them, and Whence Reckoning conquered them anyway, Cable would have learned about his ambitions at no cost to himself. He would then have both a valid reason to execute him and have added a new province to the Four Quarters.

Sometimes as they walked, Exemplary Fortune tried to talk to Tamed Ocelot about the landscape they passed through or whether he was warm enough or if he liked the food, but Tamed Ocelot, though he sometimes deigned to look at him, never replied. He ate the food and sometimes wrapped himself in a second cloak. He did occasionally look at the ranks of the troops around them and then at Exemplary Fortune, but he would not ask his questions out loud. Exemplary Fortune wondered what he thought of the army, if he saw it as larger or smaller, more or less disciplined than the ones he was used to, but asking him would be worse than a waste of breath; it would give him information, and that Exemplary Fortune was not willing to do.

Sometimes Exemplary Fortune thought about the wives he had not seen since he had left the north: Skein Reckoner, Gold Share, Esteemed Egg, Sandpiper, Pure Joy, Grasshopper, Coca Neighbor, Happy Balance, Hillstar, Agave Needle, Puku Dove, Elegant Reckoner, White Cereus, and Half Moon. Some of them had died. He did not know which ones, but after talking with the Flamingo Lakes he could not doubt it. His children, too. He had dreams sometimes of the children crying for him or one of his wives trying to tell him what had happened, but none of those dreams were numinous with truth. He saw Qantu Flower, too, but she did not talk to him. He thought sometimes that she appeared in his dreams to tell him that she was satisfied where she was. It comforted him to think so, but he was never completely sure.

He worried too about his mother, though oddly, he did not believe Owl Pattern had died in the epidemic. Instead, he wondered if she would try to come to his defense, but she was a canny politician, and would be unlikely to risk her younger children for her oldest son, who was, after all, out of her control and, if she but knew it, in no serious danger. There was nothing Exemplary Fortune could do for her, nothing he could do for any of them. He tried not to worry about them, tried to focus only on the present and what little he could do about the world around him: care for Tamed Ocelot and occasionally advise the Flamingo Lakes about their fighting techniques.

As the army marched south, time and space were one. Flower Garment was the land to the southern edge of Lake Titicaca, a flat space of cold winds, llamas, raised potato fields, and the metallic glitter of the lake on their right. In Navel, said the messengers, the Unique Inca planned a Carrying Ceremony to make sure the epidemic would not return. The Covereds whose cities they marched through had their confessors searching for the crime the Four Quarters' people had committed to cause such a calamity.

Though Exemplary Fortune did not really accept the beliefs of the Covered confessors, he began having nightmares of a people who could pass to others the punishment for crimes they had committed. His dream figures were dripping corpses on a shadowy raft who stopped secretly to throw glistening gobbets of flesh onto the shore, where they would grow into a disease that destroyed everyone who lived there and so bring the dead sailors back to life. The dreams were not sent by the Sun, but he did not know if Lakefoam, Earth, Lightning, or one of the lesser gods or wakas had sent him the visions. He could not act on those dreams either but held them in his mind until they would be useful.

Young Corn Dance was the province of Sundried. As its name implied, it was drier than the lands around Lake Titicaca. It was equally cold, though, and its terrain more rugged. Here, three days into the first tenday, they reached Sparrow, the capital of Sundried, where the troops' road branched east. The Flamingo Lakes Exemplary Fortune had been staying with said they would be willing to travel all the way south with him and Tamed Ocelot, but Whence Reckoning gave him an Inca ten-captain instead. Exemplary Fortune said good-bye to his newfound turn-worker friends and went on.

From here on, the journey was not as easy as it had been, even though their meals were cooked by the women of the tampus rather than the wives who had stayed with the main body of the army. The group no longer had to set up tents either, even at the smallest tampus. But the Inca captain clearly resented his escort duty. He was middle-aged, old enough that this campaign might be his last chance to prove himself in battle, and, in spite of being an Inca, he was still a ten-captain. Probably he suspected, as Exemplary Fortune did, that he was being deliberately kept away from the battlefield. He talked to Exemplary Fortune more than Tamed Ocelot did, but not much more, and that only by necessity. His men were likewise taciturn.

They traveled into Endward, the province farthest to the south on the eastern side of the mountains. Though the eastern slopes farther north were humid and fell off into jungle, Endward was even drier than Sundried. In the lower river valleys, the corn stood almost ready for harvest, while higher up there were only occasional fields of potatoes or other crops surrounded by vast grasslands as cold as Eminence. The land was filled with long-legged rheas and vicunas and small birds that flew up at their approach. This far from the center of the empire, the towns and tampus were both small, sometimes barely big enough to hold the twelve of them. Sometimes, when the captain passed a tampu early in the afternoon, they would travel far into the night before reaching another. The captain was clearly anxious to be rid of his charges and rejoin the army. He pushed them hard enough that sometimes they stumbled with weariness at the end of the day. If they had been headed for battle, they would not have been ready for it. Day by day, the air grew colder.

The road turned west finally along the north bank of the river the locals called Deceitful. Great ranks of snow-clad mountains commanded the western sky ahead of them. As they climbed toward the river's source, cold air flecked with snow poured down over them. Lowering clouds hid the mountains' midflanks.

They stopped at the town of Spotted Deer for a midday meal. In that at least, the ten-captain was fair to his men. Since he made them travel farther each day than all but dire emergency would warrant, he also fed them more than ordinary travelers. But he would not allow them more than a perfunctory stop at the local temple to celebrate the start of Harvest Song.

The tampu-keepers were horrified when they heard that the party planned to push on to Completion. "The pass is not safe this time of year," they said. "The last supply caravan went over more than a tenday ago."

"How far is the next tampu?" the captain asked.

"Firewood is fifteen miles," the man said, "but it's not staffed, and neither is Icelake, the tampu just beyond the pass."

The names were certainly not propitious, but the tampu-keepers' efforts at dissuasion were in vain. As soon as they finished their midday meal, the captain had them out the door facing the icy wind coming down the pass. They wrapped their cloaks tightly around themselves, bowed their heads against the blast, and walked uphill.

For about three miles. Then the captain stopped. Facing Exemplary Fortune, he said, "I was told to take you and your charge far enough toward Completion that you would not be a danger to the surrounding countryside. I have done that. I will watch you over the next rise. Then I and my men will go back to Spotted Deer, where we will celebrate Harvest Song with due ceremony."

Exemplary Fortune inclined his head slightly. "May I return your sentiments fourfold. I shall be delighted to see my new province." He continued up the slope with his charge in tow. He was furious but not totally surprised. Whence Reckoning had not been friendly and likely knew that Exemplary Royal Happiness would not be upset to have Exemplary Fortune disappear permanently. For that matter, if Whence Reckoning had misjudged Cable, he would probably consider it a blessing to have an excuse to get rid of the ten-captain.

The wind was bitterly cold, and the snow fell ever more thickly. Tamed Ocelot dropped behind him, at his back and out of the wind. Exemplary Fortune went over the first rise, and then turned around. "Now you can make me dead," he said in Spanish. "I cannot stop you."

It was clear he had totally shocked Tamed Ocelot. The man

stood absolutely still for a few breaths, and then said, "It is cold out here."

"Yes."

Tamed Ocelot blinked at having the conversation thrown so abruptly back to him. "If we do not get inside, we will both die."

"That is true."

"I will not kill you until after we find shelter."

Exemplary Fortune grinned predator fashion. Everyone was so generous this day. But all he said was "Do you want me to untie your hands?"

"Can you?"

Exemplary Fortune flexed his fingers. They were already stiff with cold. "Maybe not," he admitted. "You walk in front sometimes."

And Tamed Ocelot promptly walked around him into the fury of the mountain wind. It was warmer in the lee of the man's body. But the road led always up. The Sun was hidden by clouds, and the snow grew ever thicker, confusing the shapes of the cliffs and rocks around them. The day grew gradually darker until all the world was nothing but dim shapes looming up only a few steps before one would run into them. The precipices they could avoid only by keeping one shoulder always at the cliff face and hoping they did not miss a turn in the road. But, even if they did not fall off the edge of the world, they could easily miss the tampu in the darkness, and, however far the next one was, Exemplary Fortune did not think they would survive to reach it.

They found the building only because Tamed Ocelot, in the lead, stumbled over a log and went sprawling. As Exemplary Fortune helped him to his feet, he realized the dim shape to their right was probably a building. "Come," he said, and they ran into its shelter. Great heaps of firewood around the entrance blocked the wind, but the building was cold and very dark.

"Get firewood," Exemplary Fortune said over his shoulder to Tamed Ocelot and began sliding his feet across the floor, searching for the hearth found in most Endward tampus. His feet found a block where his outstretched arms felt nothing. He bent down and found the raised stone shape. He sat on its cold edge.

"Where are you?" Tamed Ocelot called from near the doorway.

"To your right."

As Exemplary Fortune patted the area around the hearth for the firesticks and straw kindling ball, he could hear Tamed Ocelot's feet shuffling toward him. "You are almost here," he said.

"What are you sitting on?" asked Tamed Ocelot from above him in the darkness.

He undoubtedly had firewood in his arms, and Exemplary Fortune's voice would give him the information he would need to crush his skull if he wanted. "The hearth."

"Cold as a" and some Spanish Exemplary Fortune didn't know came from the darkness.

"Yes, it is." The firesticks were in the cloth container, where they were supposed to be. He could not feel its texture, but the bag deformed like cloth under his fingers.

Tamed Ocelot stood close enough to him that he could feel the warmth of his body.

"Do you have a dry wood piece?" Exemplary Fortune asked in the direction of the warmth. He opened the firesticks' container carefully. His fingers were numb, and, if he dropped the sticks, he doubted he would find them again.

"In this *nieve*? Take one from the bottom."

"Can you set one on the hearth?" Exemplary Fortune asked, unwilling to release his hold on the firesticks.

Tamed Ocelot dropped a number of pieces of wood outside the hearth with a clatter, and then one landed on the hearth with a sharp thwack that told Exemplary Fortune exactly where it was. Exemplary Fortune pulled the wood toward him, set the kindling ball on it, and used the wood as a base for his firesticks. He willed himself to calm. If he did not get the fire lit, they would both die, but this was not a task that would be helped by a warrior's excitement. It demanded absolute calm and concentration. The first spark visible in the darkness was gone before he could fan it higher. Next to him, he could hear, almost feel Tamed Ocelot shift in the darkness. Tamed Ocelot had not asked what he was doing, Exemplary Fortune realized. He twirled the sticks again, and this time the tiny spark grew into a real flame fed by the kindling ball.

As it grew, Exemplary Fortune fed it twigs, then sticks. By then, he could feel it warming his hands as he fed it. Neither of them said anything until the fire started to feed on the larger pieces of wood.

Then Tamed Ocelot held out his hands. "Will you get this unholy rope off me?"

"Yes. Will you kill me?"

"Not until we get off this unholy mountain."

Exemplary Fortune stopped what he was doing. He looked up at Tamed Ocelot. "Do not say bad things about the mountain. We are in its care."

Tamed Ocelot growled. Exemplary Fortune sighed and said a prayer to Eagle View Mountain, asking the mountain to forgive Tamed Ocelot's disrespect.

Tamed Ocelot growled again, then stamped his feet and muttered until Exemplary Fortune set to his task once more. Under the cover of his bent head, Exemplary Fortune grinned. Tamed Ocelot might be talking to him now, but he did not seem to have changed much. The rope was tight from being wetted and then frozen, and his fingers were stiff and still a little numb. In the end, he had to cut the knot on Tamed Ocelot's left wrist. Tamed Ocelot did not say anything to that, but he did watch closely.

Afterward, Exemplary Fortune pulled powdered freeze-dried potatoes and dried llama meat from the stores. He gathered pots of snow, melted one over the fire, then brought it to boiling and added two handfuls of potato powder and several sticks of llama meat. When he took the pot off the fire, he found that the powder had clumped into nearly unchewable pieces, some of which were still powdery in the middle, and the llama meat was still hard. The broth was tasteless. It was, said Tamed Ocelot, the worst thing he had ever eaten.

"I am not a woman," said Exemplary Fortune. "I do not know cooking."

"Cooking is not just for women," protested Tamed Ocelot. "I could do better than this."

"Good, then you cook breakfast."

After that they went directly to bed, wrapping themselves in several blankets each. Exemplary Fortune's main worry as he lay down was that he would not wake when the fire died. And it was, indeed, Tamed Ocelot's movements that woke him, not the chill in the tampu. Tamed Ocelot went to the hearth, did things with wood, and then after a time went back to bed. The tampu began to warm. Exemplary Fortune smiled to himself as he drifted off again.

In the morning, snow still swirled around the tampu. Tamed Ocelot cooked breakfast from the stores Exemplary Fortune brought out and some dried leaves he found himself. It was, as promised, a good deal better than Exemplary Fortune's attempt from the night before. When Exemplary Fortune said as much, Tamed Ocelot said, "You do not watch when the cooking is done."

"That is true," said Exemplary Fortune.

After their meal, Exemplary Fortune went out to see if the clouds were thinning at all, but he could see only snow. Even the high profile of Eagle View, whose presence he could almost feel, was hidden. He said another prayer to the mountain and for their safety, then gathered a large armload of wood before going back inside.

When he went back in, Tamed Ocelot was examining a five-foot-long sword from the stores. He looked up as Exemplary Fortune walked in the door and appraised him in silence a short time. Then he threw the sword onto the floor. "It is a bad weapon," he said.

"Oh?" Given Tamed Ocelot's attitude toward Ginez whenever he had given out information, Exemplary Fortune did not want to ask his question directly. He should have time to get the information he wanted from Tamed Ocelot without asking direct questions.

"It has no edge. It is not sharp."

"Oh." He did not appear to think that it was bigger than expected, just too dull. So probably the Spanish did make long weapons from their metal. Exemplary Fortune set the armload of wood he had gathered by the hearth. "I do not think it will clear today.

We will travel again tomorrow." He sat on the hearth, warming his hands above the fire.

Tamed Ocelot was behind him. Exemplary Fortune could almost feel the tension in the man, but he did not turn. Finally, Tamed Ocelot said, "You should not make it so easy for me to attack you."

"We know you are the better warrior, and, besides, it is much easier to kill me when I sleep." Exemplary Fortune still did not turn.

"That is true." Tamed Ocelot sat down next to him, staring at the fire. "The chief of that city lied to me."

Which city? "How so?"

"The first day, he showed me gold and silver. The next day he sent me to stay with this old couple. I thought it was their house."

Ah. "He did not know you were same person."

"The woman lied, too. First she said she would go with me, then she would not."

"She pointed to the chief's house."

Tamed Ocelot looked at him finally. "How do you know this?"

"When I came to city, I asked everyone what happened. My father was curious about you."

Tamed Ocelot did not ask anything more for a time. They took turns tending the fire. Tamed Ocelot rummaged through the tampu's stores, testing all the weapons he found for heft and sharpness. He found fault with each of them, breaking a sword over his knee and feeding it to the fire to make a point about its untrustworthiness. He finally pronounced the lot of them "women's weapons."

Though Tamed Ocelot's assessments of the weapons were revealing, to keep him from destroying everything in the tampu, Exemplary Fortune finally got out the board and some beans to play and-ten. That kept Tamed Ocelot busy until he had the rules mastered. Then he lost interest. "We have no *dinero*," he said, as though that explained why the game was no fun, leaving Exemplary Fortune even more confused as to what *dinero* was.

Toward sundown the snow stopped, and the clouds began to tatter and blow away.

When Tamed Ocelot came back inside with a load of wood just after sunset, he said, "The road goes uphill from here."

"Yes, it does," said Exemplary Fortune from his position on the hearth.

Tamed Ocelot dropped his load of wood by the fire. "We should go back to the last village."

Exemplary Fortune shook his head. "We must go to Completion."

"Why?"

"Many reasons. I will be chief in Completion. I said I will take you with me—"

"Why?" This question was nearly a growl.

"No one trusts you to act civilized alone."

Tamed Ocelot did snarl at that. "You talked to your king."

"Yes, I did. He told me to take you with me."

"Why?"

"I do not know everything in his heart. He does not like me. Maybe he wants you to kill me."

"That is stupid."

"Our father, who was king before, wanted me to find you and bring you to see him. Because he is dead, I cannot do that. But I still have you."

"That does not make sense."

Exemplary Fortune smiled. "I sometimes agree, but it is true."

Tamed Ocelot walked to stand over him. "Tell me what you will do with me in Completion."

"In Completion, I hope you will do for yourself. Completion is new place. It needs good workers."

"I am not a prisoner."

"No, you are free. If you follow rules, you will stay free."

"I do not know the rules."

"I can teach you."

Tamed Ocelot crouched down next to him. "If you will get me women, I will not kill you until the other Christians come back."

"You are not a person who did great things for our kingdom. I will get you one wife to cook and sew and help you in fields."

"I do not want a wife. I will not become a _____ " (some Spanish word Exemplary Fortune did not know).

"What is a payon?" He mangled the word, but Tamed Ocelot knew it anyway.

"Someone who works in the fields."

"Everyone here works in the fields. I work in the fields, the king works in the fields. Children work in the fields. If you have another skill we can use, then most of the time you will do that, but, at plowing time and at harvesttime, you will work in the fields. Or maybe you want me to cut your hand off. People with only one hand do not work in the fields."

"You are a stupid *indio*." Tamed Ocelot stood back up and kicked at the various things he had strewn about the floor of the tampu. Exemplary Fortune gritted his teeth and said nothing. He did not actually want the man to kill him.

After a time, Tamed Ocelot came back. "You will work in the fields with me."

"I will work in the fields with you," Exemplary Fortune agreed.

"I do not want a wife," Tamed Ocelot repeated then. "I want a woman who will let me do what I want and then go away."

"This is not our custom," said Exemplary Fortune, unsure of the exact implications of Tamed Ocelot's words.

"In Castile," said Tamed Ocelot, "if we see a woman on the street, we say to her, we will give you *dinero,* we will give you a piece of cloth, and she takes us to where she stays, and we have our way with her, and then we go away and do not see her again."

Exemplary Fortune found the idea revolting. "Here we only have sex with people we know. Everyone is married. If you are not married, you have no one to make your clothes. You have no children."

"I do not want *indios* children."

Did that mean he was ready to kill everyone here to introduce women who would birth the kind of children he wanted? Maybe the strangers really had caused the epidemic. "Very well. I will find you an older wife, a woman who can no longer have children."

"I do not want an old woman."

"Well then, I will try to find young woman who will birth no children." Actually, it shouldn't be that hard. Everyone except Tamed Ocelot wanted children. A man was allowed to leave a woman who was sterile. What would be harder was to find someone willing to live with Tamed Ocelot and his peculiar and dangerous notions.

Tamed Ocelot did not say anything for a time, staring into the fire and thinking thoughts that were undoubtedly utterly strange. After a time, he said, "When my people come back, I will kill everybody."

And, by implication, he would not kill anyone until then. So he accepted Exemplary Fortune's proposal. Which meant, the Moon forgive him, he had just agreed to find a wife for the man. He hoped there was a large group of strong imperturbable women in Completion. "In morning, we will go to Completion."

"In the morning," agreed Tamed Ocelot.

TWELFTH YEAR OF KING CARLOS'S REIGN
MARCH THROUGH JUNE 1528

From actual history, we do not even know where the man known to the Spanish as Felipe or Little Felipe came from. Some say he was a Taciturn. Some say he was a Wind-Star. Some imply he came from Recognition. Most do not say.

Wrapped in a quilt at the foot of Francisco Pizarro's bed, Hummingbird had nightmares about Young Fox almost every night. Sometimes Hummingbird watched as the other men on the boat carried the bundled shape of Young Fox's body to the rail of the boat and dumped it into the water while he did nothing. Sometimes he stood by and did nothing while they killed Young Fox. The worst, though, was when Young Fox's ghost called out to him, and he turned away, saying, "I am not Hummingbird; I am Little Felipe." Sometimes even when he was awake, he was not sure who he was. He worked on a Spanish ship and spoke mostly Spanish words, though he did not speak well.

Every day, Hummingbird would stand by the edge of the boat to watch the desert coast slip away. They sailed far enough from the coast that he could not see much; all he saw were the gray-brown desert, the green valleys, the dark mountain peaks against the blue sky, and occasionally the black shape of a condor as it soared over the coast looking for dead fish to eat.

As they sailed north along the coast, at each river valley Francisco Pizarro would talk about stopping to pick up more gold and young men to train to Spanish service. But the men wanted to go home. Always, after listening to them, Francisco Pizarro would agree to continue on. Every time, though, when Francisco Pizarro said maybe they should stop, Hummingbird's heart would beat faster, and his palms would start to sweat. He did not know what he would say to a chief; but, if no young men came aboard like Francisco Pizarro wanted, he was sure Francisco Pizarro would kill him.

Francisco Pizarro ignored Seaweed and Muyushell once they were on the ship, and Hummingbird was ashamed of himself for being glad of that. He did not avoid the two of them the way he had avoided Young Fox, but he did not know what to say to them either. When the two of them asked him about Spanish words, he could help a little; but, when they asked him about what the Spanish traded in or what proper etiquette among them was, he did not know what to say. As far as he knew, having Francisco Pizarro want to have sex with you was the only reason the Spanish would treat someone well. They did not like Greek because he was loud, and so they would not talk with him.

The two of them slept in the same hammock together, and the men laughed at them and called them names that were supposed to be insulting and meant they had sex together. But it was not even true. They slept together because they were all alone in a strange place. Hummingbird envied them their companionship.

Eventually, the coast grew familiar, and Hummingbird's heart beat faster as they again sailed past Recognition. The sight of the city he knew made a lump in his throat he could do nothing about. He went below and talked to Adobe about unfastening and stealing the small boat and escaping back to their city. Adobe agreed eagerly, but, when Hummingbird suggested specific times they could get together, he kept asking, "What if we get caught?"

"If we are careful and quick," said Hummingbird, trying not to sound impatient, "we will not be caught."

"I don't think Macaw likes me," Adobe said fretfully.

"The Spaniards hit you," said Hummingbird.

"Yes," said Adobe, "we should leave." But, again, when Hummingbird tried to talk about a time they could meet, Adobe began making excuses and worrying.

Hummingbird went up to the top floor alone and looked at the small boat. There was no way he could unfasten it and get it into the water without help. He thought about asking Muyushell and Seaweed if they wanted to leave, but this was not their land. He had not told them the Spaniards had killed anyone, and they would probably not believe him now when he wanted something from them. They might even try to ask the Spanish if what he said was true.

Finally, Hummingbird reminded himself he had decided it was better if he didn't go home. He still watched Adobe to see if he would head for the small boat or even jump overboard and try to swim for shore. They were too far away to swim, but if Adobe tried, Hummingbird would try to help him.

But Adobe did nothing. They were still both on the boat when the coast was all jungle green and hidden by mangrove trees growing out into the water. It was best this way, Hummingbird told himself. If they had left the ship, Francisco Pizarro would probably have gone ashore to try to take them back. Macaw or the Incas might have gotten upset with the Spanish, and people could have gotten killed. But Hummingbird's heart still hurt. He told himself that, if he just knew his friends and family were safe, it would be all right, but that wasn't true. He wanted to go home even if everyone laughed at him or worse.

As soon as they began to sail past jungle, Francisco Pizarro had Hummingbird arrange all the things in the boxes under the bed. He did not even take Young Fox's clothes or silver armband out of the boxes before he gave Hummingbird the key. It was as though he did not care what Hummingbird thought, as though he knew Hummingbird could do nothing.

Hummingbird was polishing Francisco Pizarro's armor when the men outside started yelling, "Panama." His heart beat faster. He finished putting Francisco Pizarro's armor back in its box and then went up to the deck.

"Is it not beautiful?" Greek asked Hummingbird.

But Hummingbird could not see it. The town was a gash in the greenery, red like a raw sore on Mother Earth. The wound had no shape, no sign that the Spanish had made order out of the wilderness. The men all began bringing the sails in, and, as he worked, Hummingbird kept taking looks at the town, waiting for it to appear more regular; but, as they sailed closer, it just looked worse, straggling and disordered. There was a center at least, a big building with a tall tower on each front corner, but there did not seem to be any flowers or other greenery around the houses. At its edge, the clearing around the town was rimmed with dead trees as though the wound were still growing.

The ship pulled up alongside a wooden causeway that ran right out over the water. Lots of men came out of the town onto the shore. The men on the ship and the men on the shore yelled back and forth at each other. Hummingbird could not understand everything they said, but the men on the ship threw down ropes, and those ashore tied them onto posts alongside the causeway.

Hummingbird allowed himself to be jostled toward the edge of the ship, and then stood there while the men did the things they thought necessary. He did not know what was supposed to happen, but it all seemed to take a very long time. Mostly, it was just people talking back and forth like they did not know what was supposed to happen either. Then a man with a beard and dressed like a Spaniard came leading other people who looked like ordinary people, like they could be anybody. They had coppery skin and no beards, but they were dressed in rags. The bearded man had something like a stick in his hand that every now and then he would flick at the people he led, and they would flinch.

Francisco Pizarro looked around and called for Hummingbird to get the two boys. He went below and found Muyushell and Seaweed sitting on their hammock. They looked up as he came down the ladder and asked him what was happening.

"We are at Panama," he said. "We must go ashore now."

"Will we get a bath?" Muyushell asked.

"I do not know," Hummingbird admitted. It was one of the many questions he had not asked Greek. When he was not with Greek, the questions seemed obvious; but, when he was with him, somehow a lot of the questions he wanted to ask never came up. He did not tell them about the people in rags.

They started together toward the ladder, but Francisco Pizarro and the man with the ragged people came down just then. Together they made the ragged people carry out Francisco Pizarro's boxes with all the things from Recognition and Taciturn inside. The boxes were heavy with gold and silver, and the people looked thin and weak. When the people were slower than the man thought they should be, the man would flick the stick so a string at the end of it would spring out and hit the slow one.

The second time that happened, Hummingbird looked away and found Seaweed watching him. He looked at the floor. He had nothing he could tell Seaweed. He did not know why they hit the people. It was possible that the people had done something wrong and were being punished, but he did not think that was necessarily true. The Spaniards had killed Young Fox because they thought he might say something they did not want him to say, and they hit Adobe because they thought he was insignificant. They had wanted both Young Fox and Adobe to come aboard their ship. People they did not care about, they might very well hit for no reason at all.

When Hummingbird, Seaweed, and Muyushell followed Francisco Pizarro and the others off the boat, Adobe, who was standing on the ship's deck, came along, too. The ragged people carrying Francisco Pizarro's things were in front now, and Francisco Pizarro and the other man talked together without paying any attention to them. Francisco Pizarro did look at Hummingbird and nod, which meant he was doing what Francisco Pizarro wanted him to. No one else paid him any attention at all.

Seaweed, Muyushell, and Adobe were looking around at the town, but there was very little to see. The buildings were shoddily put together and painted mostly a solid white with no decoration like they were still empty and waiting for some tribe to come along and mark them as their own. The buildings had doors like those on the ship. The roofs were odd, red like the earth and shaped in small curved pieces.

What was overwhelming was the smell. The town smelled as if everyone used the streets to defecate in. The stench was overpowering. And nobody seemed to notice.

There were Spaniards in the town with their beards and many clothes. And then there were the other people who could be anybody. Their skin was red-brown, and their hair was black and straight. Most of them did not have very many clothes on, and the clothes they did have were usually dirtier than the Spaniards' and full of holes. Most of them did not wear shoes. Some of them even sat on the ground, filthy as it was, as though they did not care.

Many of the people who were not Spanish looked as though they expected to be hit. They looked away from the Spaniards and down at the ground except when the Spaniards talked to them directly. Some of them had lines of scabs on their backs. As their group walked, they twice saw Spaniards hit ragged people with cords that made red weals across their backs. One of the people fell down when the Spaniard hit him, but the Spaniard did not stop.

There was a ragged man who stood almost in the middle of the street. He had one eye and one arm, and flies crawled around the socket of his empty eye. He held his one hand out whenever a Spaniard came near. Sometimes they would throw him a little piece of something. Most of the time, he would not catch it. Then he would bend down into the muck of the street and grope around for whatever it was. Except for the people who threw him things, no one paid any attention to him either.

The Incas would have him to a healer. They would have the town cleaned up. They would stop the Spanish from hitting people and making them so afraid.

The other three crowded close to Hummingbird, but they did not say anything. Adobe was breathing in short little bursts as though he wanted to cry.

An animal that was bigger even than a llama stood at the edge of the road, and Hummingbird eyed it warily. He did not know what Spanish beasts would do. As he watched, the beast defecated right into the road. Maybe it somehow knew he would be upset by the filth. He turned his head away.

The man with Francisco Pizarro barked, "Here," to the ragged people ahead of them, and they turned into a big white-painted building. It was wood like the other buildings, but that, at least, made sense. It obviously rained a lot here, and so adobe would not last.

The whole group walked into the building, and Hummingbird had to stop himself from cringing as they went through the door. He did not know why he wanted to cringe. The ragged people set the boxes down on the floor in a big room, and then the Spaniard with the stick led them out of the house again. Francisco Pizarro looked at Hummingbird. Hummingbird helped him take off the cloak he was wearing. Francisco Pizarro looked at the four of them, and said, "You'll need rooms."

He walked toward the back of the house, and Hummingbird nodded for the others to follow. A woman, who moved like she was young even though she was so old she had gray hair, came up to them as they walked through the house. She had dark brown skin like the cook on the ship and wore many clothes like a Spaniard. Francisco Pizarro said to her, "They need beds made up." No more than that.

She nodded to him and then looked the four of them over. "Will they need clothes?" she asked.

Francisco Pizarro looked at them and nodded. "Little Felipe."

"What do you wish?" he asked. He wanted to be back on the ship. He did not know what the rules were here, but everything was somehow different.

Francisco Pizarro looked back at the woman. "He can advise you on what they need. He's pretty good with clothes."

The woman nodded and went away somewhere while Francisco Pizarro led them to a room. "The boys and he," nodding at Adobe, "can sleep here." Another room. This one already had a bed in it and a chair. "You'll stay here. Help them get settled." Francisco Pizarro walked away, and Hummingbird did not follow.

Instead, he turned to the others and led them back to the first room. As he repeated what Francisco Pizarro had said, the older woman came back with a young woman with copper skin and fewer clothes as though she were not a Spaniard. Together they made beds, the older woman telling the younger what to do in a manner that said she was the superior, very much like Francisco Pizarro sometimes. Hummingbird wondered if she was somehow related to Francisco Pizarro, but he did not dare ask. She was the first Spanish woman he had seen, and he did not know how to talk with her. He did discuss with her, as best as he could, the clothes the four of them would need. In spite of what Francisco Pizarro had said, she knew much more about Spanish men's clothes than Hummingbird did.

When she left, none of them knew what to do. Hummingbird thought that they should not wander around the building until Francisco Pizarro said it was all right. There was nothing much else to do, though, and even the boys did not seem to want to talk about what they had seen on the street.

A long time later Francisco Pizarro came back and said, "Come on."

He led them back to the front of the house, where several Spaniards were. Or at least the men were all dressed like Spaniards. As they came in, a young man said something to Seaweed and Muyushell in a language Hummingbird did not know. They smiled eagerly at him and said something back. The young man turned to one of the strange Spaniards and said in good Spanish, "These two are from my town. I can help them learn proper behavior."

The man he addressed had a patch over one eye. The man nodded and said, "That is good, eh, Francisco?"

Francisco Pizarro's face had clouded over when the young man started speaking in the unknown language. Nevertheless, he nodded and said, "It is good." The one-eyed man introduced the young man who spoke Spanish so well as Martin, and Francisco Pizarro introduced Hummingbird as Felipe. For the whole rest of the evening, Francisco Pizarro would every now and then look at Martin speculatively, and Hummingbird's heart would contract with fear. He did not know what Francisco Pizarro wanted with the young man, but he wanted something.

The one-eyed man said, "So now, let us see these treasures you have brought us."

Francisco Pizarro smiled. Together they opened the boxes, and the men all exclaimed at what was in them. But they did not talk about how beautiful the plates and tumblers, the statues and jewelry were or how fine the craft that had gone into them was. Instead, they would lift a piece and talk about how much it weighed and how pure the gold or silver that made it was. The other men kept asking Francisco Pizarro, "And they just gave it to you?"

Francisco Pizarro would smile and say, "They have so much gold and silver, they do not even think about it. Everyone eats on gold and silver plates. They have gardens with plants that are all made out of gold and silver. The important buildings are covered with gold and silver."

That was all they talked about all afternoon and evening, gold and silver—not how pretty it was, not how smooth it felt, not what a person could make with it, just the mere fact of its existence. If the gray-haired woman had not come in and started setting out food, it seemed as though they might not even have eaten, so excited were they about gold and silver. They did not ever ask any of those who came from the Four Quarters about how much gold and silver they had or how they used it. They did not talk to them at all, as if they were statues to set off the shiny metal, nothing more. Martin did go over to Muyushell and Seaweed and talk with them quietly, but he did not talk to Hummingbird, and Muyushell and Seaweed did not invite him into the conversation.

Only when the men had all left, and Hummingbird was helping Francisco Pizarro get ready for bed, did Francisco Pizarro say anything to him. He said, "Tomorrow we'll have to see that you all get properly baptized. I'll take you to the church. You'll be able to find your way home, won't you?"

Hummingbird licked his lips. He did not like it that Francisco Pizarro would leave him so easily as soon as they were in the strange town. "The city is not very big," he said.

"Not yet," said Francisco Pizarro, and Hummingbird fumbled the next fastening on his clothes.

•   •   •

The next morning, before they set out for the church, Martin showed up at Francisco Pizarro's house and asked if he could help with anything. Francisco Pizarro smiled at him and said, "They need to be baptized."

Martin nodded easily. "I will be glad to stand as their godfather."

"Good," said Francisco Pizarro. "I have business with Diego." Who was Diego?

Martin led the four of them out of the house and along the filthy mud street toward the towered building. As they walked, he said in Humanity's Mouth, "Felipe, you have a Christian name already. Have the rest of you been given Christian names?"

None of them had, and so Martin decided that Muyushell would be Francisco and Seaweed would be Diego. Adobe, he said, would become Juan.

The church was dark inside and cooler than it was outside. The building was big and dark and empty; but, as Hummingbird's eyes adjusted to the dimness, he could see that above the high platform on the far end was one of the horrible waka statues, huge, the dying man hanging over them like a mountain ready to avalanche down on them.

"What is that?" he asked Martin, his voice much shriller than he wanted it to be.

Martin looked at him and then at the statue, without any expression. "That is a crucifix," he said. "It is a reminder of how the Lord Jesus Christ gave his life for us."

It was an ancestor, a true waka who had somehow sacrificed Himself for the tribe of the Spaniards. But it was still wrong to have that horrible thing everywhere. It should be brought out for festivals when He was celebrated and then put away again.

A man in a long black robe came down to them and talked to Martin. Martin explained that the four of them were from a *pagano* land and needed to be baptized into the true faith. The man, whom Martin called father, seemed happy at this, and took them over to a stand with a basin on top. Hummingbird tried to hang back. He

did not want to become Felipe. He did not want to become a
Spaniard and not care about anything anymore. But, if he did not,
he would have to go outside and become one of the ragged people
whom the Spanish hit whenever they wanted to.

Martin's new father put water on Muyushell's head. He said
words that Hummingbird could not understand and gave him the
name of Francisco. The new Francisco did not say anything, but he
was shaking a little and looked as though he might faint. Martin's
father did the same thing to Seaweed-Diego, and he looked equally
frightened. Only Adobe-Juan did not change when they put the
water on him.

Both the priest and Martin looked at Hummingbird when they
had finished with Juan. He went forward to where Martin's father
was and let him say the words over him. When he saw the father's
hand coming at him with the water, he flinched, though he knew
he wasn't supposed to. The water hit his head and then ran down
his hair, covering him. Father said his name, "Felipe." He cried
because he was now a Spaniard. Martin looked annoyed, and the
speaker said words that did not make any sense. Martin said polite
words to his father, took Felipe by the arm, and pulled him out of
the building.

When they were outside, he said, "You must not do that. They
will think an evil waka infests you and kill us all."

"I'm sorry," said Felipe. He blinked his eyes to stop the tears.

Martin kept his hand around Felipe's arm all the way to Francisco Pizarro's house, and then, inside the house, he pushed him in
the direction he wanted him to go. The older woman said that
Francisco Pizarro was not at home, and Martin asked if there was
a crucifix Felipe could wear until Señor Pizarro returned to his
house.

The woman looked Felipe over. "I think maybe there is one he
could borrow," she said.

She came back with an awful waka statue on a chain of beads.
Martin took it and put it around Felipe's neck. Felipe bit his lip
so that he would not start crying again, but tears still ran down
his cheeks. When Martin walked away from him, he slid down to
sitting on the floor because it was too much work to stand up. The

others went with Martin when he walked out of the room, but the woman stayed, looking at him. "You can't sit there," she said. "You go to your bed. I'll bring you something."

She left the room then, too. Felipe pulled himself to standing and, leaning against the walls for support, walked back to the room he and Francisco Pizarro shared. He felt like the beads with the statue were digging into him, eating him up. The bedroll he had slept on had been folded onto Francisco Pizarro's bed, and so there was no place for him.

The woman came in with a tray full of things. She put the tray down and came over to him. She picked up the crucifix from where it hung down on his chest and asked, "Were you a religious?"

"No."

"It is making blisters on your neck. You must not tell anyone. I will do a ceremony and make a salve that will help." She had him take his shirts off.

"Aren't you a Spaniard?" he asked, confused.

"I am Massi," she said, looking very proud. "They stole my mother from her home, but they could not steal her memories. I am the great-granddaughter of a famous king, and I remember." Her eyes blazed, and Felipe saw she was right, that somehow in spite of her Spanish clothes, in spite of the fact that she could handle the waka statues without flinching, she had kept her inner self, her heart intact.

She lit candles around the room and started incense smoking in a small bronze container. She chanted low and fierce in a language Felipe could not understand, but it was not the language of the Spaniards, not even the strange language Martin's father had used. She lifted the incense container and swung it around the room. Then she set the incense down and picked up a small squat jar. "This is medicine," she said. "It will help." She rubbed it on his back, chest, and neck where the crucifix rubbed him. "Now," she said, handing him another small jar, "rub this on the crucifix as you wish, and then go to sleep with the crucifix in your hand. Maybe you will see what you need." Before she left, she opened all the windows of the room. "He must not know," she said.

Felipe nodded, and, after she left, since she had said it was all right, he took his blankets off the bed, wrapped himself up, and went to sleep. But the dreams did not help. They were full of bright terrible things he could not quite make out waiting for him in a fog where even sounds and smells blurred.

Francisco Pizarro came back late and did not seem to notice anything wrong. For many days after that, Francisco Pizarro spent most of his time away, talking with the one-eyed man, who was Diego Almagro. While Francisco Pizarro was gone, Felipe spent most of his time in the room, sitting on the floor and not thinking about anything. The woman's salve had helped him, so he could do the things he had to do, but it was not enough. A few times he tried to talk to her, but she was always busy or with someone else. Maybe she could not help him anymore. Maybe she was afraid if she talked with him, somebody would think something was wrong. He did not know, but she would not help.

He did not see the others from the Four Quarters. They seemed almost to have vanished. He had nightmares about that too, but, when he sat in the hall, sometimes he would see them. They would walk by him without saying anything, as though they could not see him.

Finally one day, sitting in Francisco Pizarro's room, he had a dream about the salve the gray-haired woman had left separating itself into various leaves and roots, which ran back into the jungle and attached themselves to the plants where they belonged. "Come find us," they called. "Come see where we live."

He got up and walked out the door, down the filthy street, and out through the fields. The fields outside of the town were filled with people in ragged clothes hoeing corn and manioc. They looked as unhappy as they did when he saw them inside Panama. In some ways that was the worst of all. He did not understand how the Spanish could make people unhappy about working in their fields. He kept walking, but he half-expected some Spaniard with a whip to tell him he had to stop, and then make him start doing whatever the Spaniard wanted. He forced himself not to run, to walk like a Spaniard would, as though every step he took was more important than anything else.

He was very frightened. The town was where Francisco Pizarro was, and Francisco Pizarro was the only one who was keeping him alive. If he somehow could not get back to Francisco Pizarro, or, if he changed so Francisco Pizarro did not want him anymore, he would become one of the ragged people; and, because he did not know how to survive when everyone beat him all the time, he would die.

Outside of Panama, the road did not smell so bad, but it still made an ugly gash in the earth. He walked past all the fields and into the jungle, where even the road began to smell only of earth and the green growing things that surrounded it. He turned into the dark woods at a rich flowery scent that might have been in the gray-haired woman's salve. He stepped carefully through the underbrush and into the warm dark, where trees roofed the world. He found a place to sit on a tree root that jutted a little above the surface of the earth. It was damp, but he did not care. The jungle was very quiet except for bird cries, and those did not hurt his heart. He put his right hand on the earth and said, "Mother, I do not know what to do. I cannot go home. The Spanish are so awful that it hurts to be with them, and I am afraid that I will become like they are."

He started crying, and Mother Earth comforted him. *Endure,* She said, *you have a place.* She assured him that She would always be there, that no matter what the Spanish did with their knives and defecations, they could not destroy Her. *I will be here when you need me,* She said.

A bird in various shades of gray with a small head and neck and almost no tail walked past Felipe with firm steps. It did not seem afraid of him or what he would do. It pecked at the ground and then continued on until it disappeared from sight behind a hanging vine. He watched the place it had disappeared for a long time. Then he looked around at the quiet green and said quietly, "Thank you."

He got up and walked back to the road and down to where he could see the town of Panama. It was very small, like a rotting ugly flower in a jungle clearing. It was only the Spanish with their self-importance that made it seem so big. He walked back into the city. There were still the ragged people, the Spanish animals, and the smell, but under everything was the Earth. He could feel Her now, bigger than all of them, quiet and enduring.

The house was worse. It was a brooding malevolent presence. He could feel tentacles of corruption spreading out from it into the city. From the quiet rooms of Francisco Pizarro's house, terror and filth spread everywhere. He had been hiding, trying to get well in a place that was the very center of infection. He walked into the house, murmuring, "Mother Earth protect me." The miasma of the house pushed at him, but it no longer penetrated him. He went to Francisco Pizarro's room and put in order all the things that he had been neglecting in the weeks he had been sick. Francisco Pizarro might not care if his things were chaotic, but it was still not right.

The next day he returned the jar with the salve to the woman. "Thank you," he said.

She smiled at him. "Sometimes it helps."

After that, he started going around town with Martin like the others did, but Martin thought only that they should become good Spaniards. He had useful information on how to survive, but he did not know how to keep his heart intact. He did not care if he kept his heart intact. Francisco and Diego hung on his every word.

Francisco Pizarro was gone every day, talking to people. Sometimes he and Diego Almagro would come to the house late and complain about how this or that person did not understand what they were trying to do. They would drink and talk. Felipe was not sure what they wanted to do or what they thought people should understand. But he was still glad when they complained, because, whatever they wanted to do, he was sure they would hurt his people.

Then one day, Francisco Pizarro said, "Pack my things. We are leaving."

In Spanish one could never tell if "we" included "you" or not. Felipe said, "Where are you going?" He would walk back to Recognition if Francisco Pizarro was leaving him here. He would die in the water, but he would start back first.

Francisco Pizarro looked at him. "You are coming with me. The other boys are coming, too. You will need to pack clothes for them."

"I will do that."

Martin already knew they were leaving. "We are going to Spain," he said, "to Castile." That was all, and Felipe suspected that he did not know any more, but Francisco and Diego were, as always, impressed.

It wasn't until they were all ready to go, with a line of the Spanish animals called mules instead of ragged people to carry the luggage and the gold and silver, that he found Greek was coming too. He had not even known Greek was in town. For the trip, Greek was dressed in fancy frilled clothes and wore a hat with feathers in it.

Francisco Pizarro looked at him sourly. "Your fine clothes will get all muddy."

"Ah, well," said Greek, "at least I will start out in style." Greek spoke with an accent. Felipe had not noticed that before.

"I did not know you were coming," said Felipe. "I did not know you were still in Panama."

Greek laughed. It was a pleasant sound, and Felipe did not mind that Martin gave him a foul look. "I would not miss this trip for anything," he said. "I have always wanted to see the king."

They started out, and Martin soon made himself useful with the mules. Felipe decided he did not mind. He hated the Spanish animals that shit all over everything. Francisco Pizarro still needed him, and he could not do all the things that needed to be done. During the day he would rather talk with Greek, who described the wonders of Spain. "Seville is the richest city in the world," he said. "Every year hundreds of ships travel into its harbor, bringing gold, silver, esclavos, and jewels. There are buildings in Seville so big all of Panama could fit into them."

Of course, he had also said Panama was a wonderful city. "How far is it?" asked Felipe. "How long do we have to walk?"

"Oho," said Greek, "does that worry you? Well, Little Felipe, do not fret yourself. One does not walk to Spain. We merely walk a short way up these hills and then down the other side. Then we board a ship, and the ship carries us to Spain. If we had to walk, on the water, hey? I think it would take years."

Felipe's heart beat faster at these words, but he did not let his distress show. This was another thing to make him terrified. He had to have contact with Mother Earth to keep his heart from breaking. He tried to pretend to himself that he didn't believe Greek; that, if he just waited, that would be enough. But Greek was right. When they got to the top of the hills, at a break in the trees by a river he could see an expanse of water in the distance. He could almost see boats in the harbor. He could not see the road down, but he knew Greek was right. His breathing got faster. He had to find a way to keep in touch with Mother Earth.

At first he was so frightened he could not think of anything. When he lay down at night, he could not sleep and got up and walked into the jungle farther than the men walked when they went to defecate. He had to be alone with Mother Earth again. This time She told him how to make a small hole in the statue he wore. Into the hole he stuffed a bit of rotted wood the Earth had made almost one with Herself. He rubbed the statue until the hole was smooth, and then Mother Earth led him back to the campsite. The waka did not do anything to him because of the damage he gave it.

9

FIRST YEAR OF EXEMPLARY ROYAL HAPPINESS'S REIGN
HARVEST SONG MONTH

In actual history, too, Cable was chosen as Unique Inca. It is unclear, though, whether the choice was made by the council who would ordinarily select the emperor or simply by those with power who happened to be in Navel. We do not know how much the epidemic disrupted the process.

Morning dawned clear and cold. Exemplary Fortune cleaned up the mess Tamed Ocelot had made and recorded the damage, as well as the food they had eaten, on a quipu blank, while Tamed Ocelot made breakfast.

"You act like a servant," said Tamed Ocelot. From his tone, this was a bad thing to be.

"One part of my job is to keep everything orderly," said Exemplary Fortune.

"Maybe you will carry my things for me when we get to your kingdom."

"Not kingdom. What things will you have?"

Tamed Ocelot pursed his lips and said nothing, which was too bad. Exemplary Fortune would have liked to know what things Tamed Ocelot expected a person to have.

The weather stayed sunny, if cold, and they reached Ice Lake by early afternoon. There was again a line of logs across the road, which Tamed Ocelot pronounced stupid even when Exemplary Fortune reminded him that such a row had saved their lives two nights earlier. They were almost comfortable at this tampu, though Tamed Ocelot complained that they should have some light-making devices of fat-soaked cord. The way Tamed Ocelot described them, they sounded quite ingenious and quite unlike anything the artisans of the Four Quarters made. Exemplary Fortune said merely that they couldn't waste fuel.

Tamed Ocelot got a knife and a bronze mirror from the stores and carefully cut away at his bushy beard until his chin hair came to a neat point in the middle and was trimmed to invisibility halfway to his neck. He also cut back the hair on his upper lip. This, thankfully, took much of the evening so that Exemplary Fortune did not have to figure out ways to keep him entertained. He did leave the cut ends scattered all over the floor. As Exemplary Fortune swept them out, he wondered if the strangers had to leave home because they filled up their houses with debris until they could not get in.

As the Sun brightened the tops of the commanding Eagle View Mountain behind them, they started out again and walked the steep road downhill. The road was clear and well marked. The air warmed as they walked and a small stream that grew rapidly into a river paralleled their path. Soon only the deepest rock shadows held snowdrifts.

It was about noon when they reached a small village surrounded by highland grasses and llama herds. As they walked into the village, small children stared at them and then ran for their parents. Soon they were surrounded by people with copper earrings and dark-green-and-yellow headbands. They were Pollens, honorary Incas sent to settle the new province and bring with them the customs of the Four Quarters. The villagers exclaimed with wonder at Exemplary Fortune's report of their trek over the mountain pass and looked only slightly nonplused when he said he was the new governor, sent out too hastily to bring assistants. But they did ask where their wives were.

Exemplary Fortune said, "Tamed Ocelot has not yet found a wife in the Four Quarters, and I had to leave mine in the north."

Then he added, because this land was now his home and these people had a right to know, "The one wife who did come with me on the journey was killed by the Spotted Death." Exemplary Fortune could feel his voice grow gruff as spoke. Qantu Flower may have accepted her death, but he had not entirely done so. When he could, he would have one of the speakers perform a mourning ceremony.

"Ah, yes," said the villagers, murmuring sympathetically. Exemplary Fortune could see the grief of recent losses in their eyes.

An elder said, "The world has been very unsettled lately. We have all seen too much death. The whole world has been disordered by it. We welcome you and wish you a long quiet service."

They asked the two of them to stay the night at the tampu, but Exemplary Fortune found himself strangely ill-at-ease in their company. The village was too homey, too much like a glimpse back into another world, the world before his father had sent him away. As he talked with the villagers, he had a sudden clear vision of himself lying in a delirium in Young Majesty's Kitu Dove palace, the healers rubbing his body with herbs and his father anxiously saying his name. He shook off the vision and asked about the next tampu. The fort of Eagle View was, they said, eighteen miles downriver. It was also served by Pollens.

Eighteen miles should be reachable before sunset. Exemplary Fortune thanked them for their offer of hospitality and pleaded the press of his waiting duties. The villagers let him go reluctantly, warning, "Sunset comes early in the river's gorge." He acknowledged the warning, and the two of them went on.

As they walked, Exemplary Fortune mulled the vision he had received. That it was a true vision he did not doubt, but visions were often tricky with hidden meanings. He had barely thought about his new assignment since Cable had given it to him. Even now, he could feel the tug of the vision on him. If he could make the events of the last few months go away, he would gladly die of fever. But that was not what his father wished of him. His father had sent him off into the future while he had, in some measure, chosen otherwise. His father had sent him to find Tamed Ocelot, who strode in unhappy step beside him. Whatever else existed in his present or future, whether his family was still alive, whether Completion Province needed him, he had sworn to protect Tamed Ocelot and any secrets he might hold that the future would need. The Sun, his past in Young Majesty's court, went before them; behind were shadows of the future lengthening invisibly as they walked downstream away from the river's source and, as the villagers had promised, into shadow, dark like death, like the future, in a canyon of Earth where the dead dwelt, where the future dwelt. They avoided the river's noisy maw and hugged the valley wall.

Concentrating on staying on the road in the darkness, they did not see any sign of the fort until a man in the shadows called, "Who is it?"

Beside him, Tamed Ocelot tensed, and his breathing became faster, but he did not jump.

"Exemplary Fortune on assignment from the Unique Inca Exemplary Royal Happiness with one companion."

"By the Sun," said the other of the two guards. "You're not from Riverhead."

"Three thousand miles further," said Exemplary Fortune.

The men laughed and took them up the hill to their captain, a Pollen named Anaconda. Exemplary Fortune had fought in one short campaign with him when the man was a one hundred–captain but did not know him well. He greeted Exemplary Fortune with cordial enthusiasm and ordered beer for them all and a meal for the two of them. "Though," he warned, "we're not set up for unexpected after-dinner visitors, especially now with the pass closed. The food may not be what you expect."

Exemplary Fortune laughed. "I have been eating tampu-prepared food from Lynx Lake south through Endward. I no longer have any expectations, and, as Tamed Ocelot would tell you if he knew Humanity's Mouth, whatever you serve will be far better than anything I could prepare myself." He introduced Tamed Ocelot as a scout from a far land, and Anaconda's eyes narrowed, but he did not ask any questions. Exemplary Fortune found himself relieved at his restraint because any explanation would surely lead to a description of his own disfavor, which he did not want to reveal immediately.

When the welcoming beer came, Anaconda offered Exemplary Fortune beer with his right hand while Tamed Ocelot was served by a subordinate. Tamed Ocelot was, of course, oblivious to the implications. If he had known of his implied lower status, he might have been annoyed, but probably he would at least claim he did not care. In any case, he drank the beer.

Anaconda reported that the fort held five hundred men who served as guards and turn-warriors as necessary. The fort currently acted as a checkpoint and last resupply depot for the gold caravans traveling over the pass. The river valley was too narrow to grow much food and the lands above too cold for all but llamas and potatoes, so the people living in the fortress brought in corn and most of their other supplies from the fields of Completion's lowland towns as well as other provinces, Commanding Blue to the north and Endward "when the pass is open."

Anaconda asked about news from the capital and was disappointed at how little Exemplary Fortune knew. "I was in the north," Exemplary Fortune said, "until just before my father died. Since then I've been almost constantly on the Road. I spent only two days in Navel."

Anaconda didn't ask any more about that either, but Exemplary Fortune had the strong feeling that the first spring caravan from over the mountains would be squeezed for all its news and gossip. That was all right. Exemplary Fortune was not trying to hide his status at court, just not broadcast it either. By spring, he would have had six months to prove himself as governor. The news should matter a lot less then.

Exemplary Fortune and Tamed Ocelot's late dinner came then, and was, as Anaconda's narrative would imply, filled with potatoes. It was also considerably better than Anaconda had led him to expect. When he said as much, Anaconda replied, "We've had people complain about the preponderance of potatoes."

Exemplary Fortune did not reply to that, but he did wonder if the statement was literally true or if Anaconda had been worried that an Inca prince would expect more-elaborate fare. He would have to be careful with his personal requests until he had become familiar to the people of the province and knew they would not put too much into them.

After dinner, Anaconda and he continued to drink beer and talk. With Anaconda's third tumbler of beer, he became expansive. "You know," he said, "I'm glad to see Exemplary Royal Happiness put a warrior in as governor. Ever since I got here four years ago, I've thought that the Four Quarters should take the border to the Little Fruit."

Exemplary Fortune had thought the border did go to the Little Fruit River. All the epics certainly said so.

"Acting Governor Black Hawk thinks so, too, but Highest Strength thought we should wait until we'd got things more built up around here. It's not going to be easy, I will give you that. Those Pormocos know how to fight, and they know the terrain. That's how we got beaten the first time. Too cocky." He stared at his beer for a time, then looked up at Exemplary Fortune. "What exactly are your plans for winning the Pormoco over?"

Exemplary Fortune shook his head. "Sorry to disappoint you, but my current plans are to go slow and learn as much as I can about the situation before I decide anything." Yes, there had been talk at school that the Inca forces had been repulsed by the Pormocos, but that class had been over ten years ago. Though no one at the Unique Inca's court had ever talked about waging a new compaign in the area, he had somehow assumed the Poromocos' resistance had been dealt with.

"Well," said Anaconda, "conquest will need more than the two of you, that's for sure." He chuckled, but his eyes were watchful, almost wary.

"I will need to know much more about the local people as well as the terrain," said Exemplary Fortune, wondering what other important facts he didn't know about his new assignment. He had been thinking too much about Tamed Ocelot and not enough about the governorship, but his new job had not seemed as pressing. It had not yet tried to kill him.

"Well," said Anaconda reflectively, "as you know, the locals call themselves Pichunche, but I'd call them Governmentless. They have clans, but no ordering among the clans, and even the individual clans often lack a recognized leader. It takes a lot of patience to talk to them. You have to make sure every single person agrees with what you're saying. Once they agree, they'll stay with their word, but no one of them will ever agree just because everyone else does. Highest Strength was good at waiting until they were all ready to act together."

So Highest Strength had been the last governor. He thought of asking more about him, but Anaconda seemed ready to keep talking, and Exemplary Fortune was curious about what he thought about the situation the new governor had walked into.

"Black Hawk's not nearly as good. He talks to two or three people, and then he starts to get impatient. He wants a nice neat hierarchy so he can say something to just one person and then have everyone agree."

Well, yes, that was the way government was supposed to work. How, for instance, could one collect tribute if everyone could argue with the assessment? Exemplary Fortune kept his face composed, but inwardly he wondered. It was beginning to sound as though Anaconda condoned this chaos.

"Maybe in a generation or two." Anaconda said blithely. He stared at his tumbler. "Black Hawk's a disgustingly good warrior, though. Complains, in fact, that he doesn't have enough to do. Maybe we should have put somebody else in as acting governor." He looked up at Exemplary Fortune. "He's a Ten. That tribe's not known for its diplomatic ability."

So what had he done? And, if Anaconda felt order was not important, what could he have done that Anaconda would condemn?

"Beautiful Orchid might have done better. But, since the Sun didn't favor him . . . actually, I don't think we even considered him. You should, though. He's a good accountant, knows where everything is; everybody, too. Better yet, he knows why." Anaconda poured them each another tumbler of beer and took a long draught.

Exemplary Fortune tried to decipher what the name Beautiful Orchid was supposed to mean. Since the only thing he knew about orchids was that they were prized for their beauty, it sounded redundant. Maybe the man had planned to become an ornamental plant breeder. Or maybe the new governor was missing something. That fit with his general feeling of being lost in this informal not-quite-briefing.

"So," Anaconda continued, "we've got the Pichunche. We've got Ten colonists; voluntary that was. Black Hawk said he asked the Unique Inca to be the military trainer of a province, and Young Majesty told him this was the only place open. So, even though it's mostly lowlands, he accepted the position and brought his whole village with him, along with about two thousand other Tens. So we've got a little under three thousand Tens and then the Wild-Sands from north of here, another thousand of those, and about two thousand of us Pollens in the highlands, the capital, and further south by the gold mines—the Pichunche aren't much good with stone or metal. About a hundred Incas, working at the temple mainly. The Tens are split between the Narrows and the capital.

"Let's see, did I give you the number of Pichunche? About eighteen thousand. Not a small number of people for an out-of-the-way province, but we haven't done much with it yet. It's not what you're used to. We rough it out here. The gods and the wakas get their share, but the highest sacrifices are generally of cui, and the libations are from wooden bowls. For people, it's about the same. We get by, but it's not the navel of the world; more like the fingernails." He chuckled at his own witticism, and then said, "Well, I'm keeping you up. You had a long day today, and you'll want to start out early tomorrow." He stood up, leaving Exemplary Fortune no polite way to prolong the conversation.

Exemplary Fortune had the strong feeling that Anaconda didn't want to say more. He had laid out his hints about the situation the new governor found himself in and wanted Exemplary Fortune to take it from there. Exemplary Fortune could push for more information but only at the risk of alienating the man. There were other ways to get information.

As Exemplary Fortune got ready for bed, he wondered if the Unique Inca Exemplary Royal Happiness were even less merciful than he had believed. If Completion was as chaotic as Anaconda implied, the Unique Inca could send an inspector at any time to prove the province's anarchy and then take the governor back to Navel on charges of blatant malfeasance to finish what Magnanimous Strength had started. As for Exemplary Fortune charging anyone in the province with misgovernment, he had the strong feeling that Cable and his administrators would believe almost anyone's word against his. He had not thought about the bind he could be in, caught between incompetent officials in the province and administrators in Navel who would not listen to him. Although, so far, he had only Anaconda's word for how the government here functioned. He would find out tomorrow. Until then, there was no use worrying.

It wasn't until he was settled down on a bed that did not have to be assembled from scratch, on quilts that were above freezing when one climbed into them, that Black Hawk's name finally registered. It had been early in the Caller campaign. The Inca forces had surrounded one of the Callers' unyielding fortresses, and, secure in the knowledge that the defenders were not moving from behind their walls, a sentry had gotten careless. The first warning they had had that other Callers were coming to rescue their kin were the yells of the onrushing attackers.

The army had not been ready. The Unique Inca and his bodyguard had immediately grabbed weapons and started rallying the men, but caught between the attackers in front and the defenders behind throwing missiles down onto their heads, a number of the turn-warriors had started to panic, ready to run if they could find an opening.

Exemplary Fortune had been fifteen, just months past having his ears pierced. The din of the unexpected attack had confused him. Though he had, almost by instinct, grabbed weapons, in the press of bodies and with the cries of frightened men running in all directions, he had not been able to act with direction, choosing instead each movement, each target, moment by moment. Backing, he had tripped over a dead man's outflung arm and nearly fallen, saving himself by that much from the blow of an onrushing warrior's club. He had killed that attacker and avoided the blows of two others, but he was fully aware that they were being pushed into range of the defenders behind them when yet another group coming from the side had fallen on the Caller attackers. Like the Callers before them, the new attackers' yells and unexpectedness had more of a demoralizing effect than their actual numbers, and the Caller attackers had soon been routed. The saving group had, in fact, been a small supply train, a group of men and llamas coming with food and other supplies for the besiegers.

Black Hawk had not even been the leader of the caravan's guards, but he had been the one who had refused to retreat from battle, saying simply, "The Unique Inca needs me." Willing to attack alone if necessary, he had shamed the fifty-captain into rescuing the empire's troops. After that, Black Hawk had had his own fifty-captaincy, and, when the Callers had finally been conquered, Young Majesty had taken the unusual step of asking him to choose his reward. Exemplary Fortune had not been at that audience, but thinking about it now, he would guess that Young Majesty had expected Black Hawk to ask for another wife or a promotion or to be stationed in the capital. What kind of man would pass on conventional honors for a command at the end of nowhere? Not the kind Young Majesty would want in his court. Probably the Unique Inca had been quite glad to send him to the far end of the empire. Thinking of his father, Exemplary Fortune smiled ruefully to himself. He seemed to be inheriting all his father's misfits. With that thought, he fell asleep.

The next day, a ten-group under Captain Cornstalk was detached to take him and Tamed Ocelot to Great Completion, the provincial capital. They spent the first part of the day walking down the Eagle View River's valley to join the main road south. The Pollen warrior-colonists told him about the problems of keeping llamas in the tree-covered lowlands, about the deer that lived in forests, about the strawberries that grew in profusion in some parts of the wood, about the hot springs to the east of the road between Redbridge and Warbler.

"The governor used to visit the hot springs a lot," said one of the warriors.

"Then I'll have to try them myself," said Exemplary Fortune. "What happened to him anyway?"

There was a flat unhappy silence. All the other Pollens gave sidelong glances to the indiscreet one.

"Well," he said, "I'm not sure really."

If the Unique Inca had been looking for a replacement for Highest Strength two months ago in Navel, the governor had to have died at least two days before that, definitely enough time for Black Hawk to have carried out an investigation. If the Pollen colonist did not want to answer, though, a complete investigation must not have been done, so there was no official, and therefore easy, explanation. Now, whatever the local rumors, they would have become accepted as fact and be almost impossible to remove from people's minds. "What do people say happened?"

"Well," the unfortunate Pollen said again, "some people say the locals killed him."

Exemplary Fortune took a deep breath to calm himself. Out of the corner of his eye, he could see Tamed Ocelot look at him oddly. "I see." So that was one problem Anaconda had been hinting at. Black Hawk had definitely mismanaged this. Talking to Black Hawk, which had always been his first order of business, suddenly became much more urgent. Maybe Anaconda had assumed he already knew this. It was not at all unlikely that a preliminary report had been sent to Navel. Maybe Cable had a sense of humor after all—nasty, of course, but even that was better than nothing.

Their march south was very quiet after that, and rather than embarrassing the colonists further or fuming silently at Black Hawk, Exemplary Fortune forced himself to look at the scenery. It was mostly wilderness, one giant forest of unfamiliar trees interspersed with grassy plains. He could hear birds in the trees, and occasionally one would run or fly across the road. Sometimes, the road was completely overhung with trees, the branches of the trees on one side meeting and mingling with those on the other side over their heads. Exemplary Fortune had the feeling that they were talking with one another, murmuring tree thoughts just below his level of perception. Sometimes the murmur intensified so that he could catch a glimmer of meaning. *Come play with me,* a grove of trees would call, or again, others would demand, *What are you doing here?* with the strong implication that he and his companions should go away and leave them alone. The trees were much easier to hear than the waka stones of the highlands. All together, they made a drowsy contemplative music that was far different than the muted but busy essence of the rocks. It was as though the stones, communing with the future hidden in the earth, existed to be shaken by earthquake or worn by water, while the trees lived only in the present, which had everything they wanted and needed—sun, water, and other things Exemplary Fortune could only guess at. He would have to talk with the local speakers about the trees—if Black Hawk hadn't already destroyed that option.

They reached the fields around Redbridge in early afternoon. The corn was almost ready for harvest, though shorter and less healthy-looking than most fields Exemplary Fortune had seen. Men and women with a single thick braid down their backs bound in scarlet-and-brown yarn stood at the edge of the fields. They gestured vigorously as they talked with one another in a language Exemplary Fortune didn't know.

"The next town's Warbler," said Cornstalk. "It's twelve miles south, with quite a range of hills between here and there. I recommend we stop now."

That was logical, and, if Exemplary Fortune did not already know of one crisis way overdue for resolution, he would have welcomed the suggestion. It would be pleasant to talk with the villagers. "How well do you know the terrain?"

"We walk it all the time, sir," said the captain uncertainly.

"Can it be traversed in the dark?"

"If a person is careful." Cornstalk's voice was full of unspoken objections.

"Is walking along the road at night dangerous?" Exemplary Fortune asked.

"Not usually, but, well, we have had one governor die."

That was true, and it was also true the problem he had to face had already waited over two months. But he did not want to begin his administration as the interim administration had been run. "Walking on the road?"

"No, sir." The ten-captain was obviously unhappy.

"Any other objections?"

"No, sir."

"Then we go on."

They crossed the narrow wooden bridge over Redbridge's stream, and walked up gradual slopes into late afternoon, when the path began climbing abruptly over the Warbler Hills. The hills were rocky, and their covering of trees made the road hard to see. The warriors from the fort divided themselves, half in front and half in back of the two of them. For much of the way over the hills, the road was little more than a footpath, a narrow line worn down to earth through leaf mulch and wildflowers. The group reached the summit at sunset and made an offering to both the heightshrine and the Sun.

"The road goes consistently down from here," said Cornstalk, "and there are a couple stretches where it jogs a little. The slope is just too steep."

It *was* steep, considerably steeper than the other side. About halfway down, Tamed Ocelot asked, "Did the captain tell you to do this?"

"No," said Exemplary Fortune, feeling for the next step with his foot, "he told me not to."

"Crazy *indio,*" muttered Tamed Ocelot.

The stars were considerably dimmer than in the uplands, and, under the trees, the ground was totally dark. Not knowing the terrain, he and Tamed Ocelot could not tell if the next step was safe with flat ground all around or if a small drop-off to one side or the other meant they had to place their feet exactly. It made for slow going.

By the time they reached the bottom of the hills, all the people in Warbler had gone to bed, and Exemplary Fortune cravenly let Cornstalk wake the couple who ran the tiny tampu. He was simply too tired to be political. Cornstalk and his men had to set up a tent outside because the tampu would only hold five. Exemplary Fortune and Tamed Ocelot ate a quick meal and went straight to sleep.

In the morning the people of Warbler were likewise out in their fields, discussing the corn and how soon it would be ready to harvest. Tamed Ocelot looked at him.

"Not these fields," said Exemplary Fortune.

Tamed Ocelot said nothing.

Cornstalk said that Great Completion was another fifteen miles, but they had only gone about five miles through the forest when a group of twenty men came up the road to meet them. They all wore the long braids with twined yarn in red, orange, blue, scarlet, green, and yellow that designated Tens; and, though Exemplary Fortune would not have recognized Black Hawk, their leader's scarlet tunic was elaborately embroidered.

"Black Hawk," Cornstalk confirmed his guess.

Black Hawk gave Exemplary Fortune a deep bow. "I am Black Hawk, military trainer and interim governor of Completion. I am delighted to meet you." He sounded sincere.

"I have been most anxious to see you," returned Exemplary Fortune.

"I am at your service," said Black Hawk. "If you would like us to escort you to Great Completion . . ."

"I will be glad to travel with you," said Exemplary Fortune. He thanked Cornstalk and the rest of the ten-group for their services and promised to stop by the Eagle View Fort for a longer visit as soon as his duties permitted.

Exemplary Fortune had Black Hawk send his escort several paces ahead so they could talk more privately. After exchanging the minimum of pleasantries, Exemplary Fortune said, "Tell me about the death of the last governor."

"Well," said Black Hawk, "actually, a tree fell on him."

Not the usual way to die. Maybe trees were more dangerous than he had thought. "Tell me the full story."

Black Hawk sighed and nodded. "I take it people have already been talking to you."

"They have."

"The governor, Highest Strength, was rather close to the, ah, most influential individual in one of the local villages. They don't seem to have any permanent leaders." Frustration leaked around the edges of Black Hawk's report voice. "Anyway, this individual— her name is Chalomongo—invited the governor to watch them cut down a tree. It's quite important to them. They reverence the waka of the trees the way we do stones, and so they had quite a ceremony beforehand to ensure, so they said, that the tree they had chosen was ready to serve them. They specifically said that they knew which way the tree would fall. It fell on Highest Strength."

"Then what happened?"

"They acted quite upset. Chalomongo gathered everybody to lift the tree off him, but he was already dead."

"When did this happen?"

"The middle third of Corpse Procession."

Five full months ago. "What type of investigation have you done?"

Black Hawk swallowed. "I haven't done any investigation." He said this in a frozen tone that indicated he knew he was in the wrong.

"None at all?"

"None at all."

"Why not?"

Black Hawk licked his lips. "Well, at first I wasn't really sure I had the authority and then, when that had been clarified—"

It sounded as though Highest Strength had been a better diplomat than an administrator.

"—I kept thinking Navel would send someone." Black Hawk stopped, took a deep breath, and admitted, "I've been using the various mourning ceremonies as an excuse. I did not—do not have the faintest idea where to start."

"Why not?"

"Too many witnesses. Everybody saw what happened. I saw what happened, and I still don't know if the Pichunche really intended to kill him or not."

"Have there been any other incidents with the locals?"

"Not at that time. Lately, some of the young men of the villages around here have been, oh, I guess you'd say harassing people—suddenly jumping out in front of loaded llamas and yelling at them, coming into colonist villages as though scouting them out, not saying anything to anyone but looking over the houses and the crops."

"How long has this been going on?"

"Less than a month," said Black Hawk. "It's not easy to pinpoint an exact day. There has always been travel between the villages for one reason and another, but about two tendays ago people started complaining that the young men were making them apprehensive. I've been thinking I should go to Chalomongo's village to talk about the problem with her, but I don't feel I should go without a decision on Highest Strength's death. . . ."

No wonder he was glad to see the new governor. "Sounds as though you've backed yourself to a cliff's edge," said Exemplary Fortune.

"Yes sir, I'm afraid I have."

An honest man. "What do you think the end result of your actions is likely to be?"

Black Hawk swallowed. "I think if events continue the way they've been going, eventually somebody will have to reconquer the whole province."

And a brave one to admit that to the incoming governor. "Would you find that easier than ruling it?"

Black Hawk took the question as the rebuke it was. "Perhaps I would, but it's definitely not better."

So much for recriminations. Now to figure out a way out of the mess. "How much time do you think we have?"

"I honestly . . . Beautiful Orchid would have a better idea than I."

The same individual Anaconda thought should have been named acting governor. Interesting. And yet Anaconda had said the Sun didn't favor him. A curious juxtaposition. "What do the Pichunche value?"

"Courage," said Black Hawk without hesitation, "honesty, generosity." He thought a little. "They don't value going along with everybody else, and sometimes they positively like show-offs."

"As in the current rash of incidents?"

"I've been thinking in that direction. Beautiful Orchid definitely thinks so."

He had to meet this person. "Any other comments you can think of that might be helpful?"

"Sir," said Black Hawk fervently, "I have been unable to think of anything useful in this connection whatsoever."

So much for that line of questioning. They spent the rest of the way to the capital talking about lesser problems. Given Anaconda's hint, Exemplary Fortune did not bring up the chaos of the Pichunche's command structure. There seemed quite enough immediate problems for him to deal with in any case. As they talked, Black Hawk gave Exemplary Fortune the additional information he needed to understand why Black Hawk, with his obvious deficiencies, was governor. A group of Inca governmental advisors had left Completion a month before Highest Strength had been killed, leaving little resilience in the provincial governmment. It made sense then that Black Hawk, the highest-ranking official, should have become acting governor. Two months later, about the time it would have taken for his weaknesses to become obvious, the epidemic had struck, killing three more officials. If the Four Quarters' own hierarchy had not been so badly battered at the same time, the deaths might not have caused as much of a problem; but with so many gaps throughout the empire, this one, at least, had been allowed go untended far too long.

Undoubtedly, there were other rips throughout the fabric of the Four Quarters . . . the clan leader and other wise elders of a lineage all killed in the epidemic, the chief and his most promising heir dead. The epidemic was like a giant landslide that destroyed villages, tore off topsoil, destroyed terraces, and left the land next to it destabilized and ready to come crashing down. All one could do, even as one mourned lost friends and kin, was to begin rebuilding and hope that one's efforts to restabilize the ground succeeded before the loosened soil killed more people.

Another unfortunate side effect of this province's troubles was that the Pollens, who had originally expected one of their own would be governor when the Inca governor retired, would have reason to resent Exemplary Fortune before they even met him. He would have to be very careful indeed not to precipitate any new slippages.

About noon he and Black Hawk reached a sturdy log bridge over the Completion River. There was a moderate-sized town on the other side.

"Great Completion," said Black Hawk with a nod at the town.

The village had a long way to go to live up to its name. Most of its buildings were little more than tents, domes of cloth or skin with wood supports. Only two buildings facing the mud plaza were made entirely, even, of wood. The one on the west side was clearly a Sun temple of sorts, and the other, since Black Hawk led him straight to it, was the governor's compound. There was another wood framework with logs around it nearby, but it looked abandoned, as though it had not been worked on since the last governor had died.

That made an ugly kind of sense. A tree had killed the governor, and, if the Pichunche had not set out to make it fall on him, then the trees themselves must be upset with the Incas; but, since no one had determined the Pichunche's innocence, they could not be consulted about how to appease the forest. Therefore, no more trees could be cut down, and no more work could be done on any buildings in the provincial capital. And whenever people looked at the unfinished building, they would think of the Pichunche. Just what the province needed to guarantee its instability. Black Hawk had a lot to answer for.

The room in the governor's compound that Black Hawk led him to was floored with wood and had bright tapestries on three walls. The fourth wall had been worked and polished to bring out the grain of the wood.

On a rug three men sat adding figures from quipus. The one in the middle, a Pollen, had a withered leg and arm. He looked up as they came in. "Black Hawk," he said.

Black Hawk nodded acknowledgement. "This is Exemplary Fortune, the new governor, and this is his companion, Tamed Ocelot."

The middle man did not try to get up. It was a breach of etiquette, though understandable. "Exemplary Fortune. I am delighted to meet you," said the man. "As you may have heard, I am Beautiful Orchid."

"An excellent name," said Exemplary Fortune, accepting the situation and sitting down on the floor facing the man. It was indeed. Orchids derived a great deal of their beauty from their controlled asymmetry. Beautiful Orchid's uncle or whoever had given him his adult name had shrewdly made his weakness meritorious. "I have heard good reports about you."

Tamed Ocelot did not sit down, looking around the room with his usual suspicion and disdain.

"My companion," said Exemplary Fortune to Black Hawk, "should be shown the tampu. He likes fighting and will appreciate being shown fighting practice. He does not understand Humanity's Mouth." Exemplary Fortune translated for Tamed Ocelot and sent them off without any warnings, trusting his perception that Tamed Ocelot would not try anything without provocation at least until the pass reopened. However, he himself was obviously not going to be able to study Tamed Ocelot and his reactions nearly as much as he needed to.

Exemplary Fortune spent the next two days under Beautiful Orchid's tutelage, trying to understand the dimensions and problems of the province he'd been entrusted with, trying especially to find the information that would allow him to deal with the one major crisis he had been handed all unready. Beautiful Orchid, as everyone said, had a clear insightful knowledge of where and who everyone was and how they all interacted, though, like Anaconda, he was astonishingly indifferent to the Pichunches' lack of regularity.

Even a small province like Completion was a complex entity, and Exemplary Fortune found himself constantly oversimplifying everything: geography; climate; the Pichunche's social structure; the Wild-Sands' social structure; the architectural problems of a land where all the quarries were tens of miles away, and it rained too much to rely on adobe. By midmorning of the third day his heart felt full to bursting with facts.

"I will need a break soon," he told Beautiful Orchid. "I don't think I can hold much more new information right now."

Beautiful Orchid nodded. "I will give you just one more fact, and then we can discuss action."

There was a note in Beautiful Orchid's voice that implied this might be the information Exemplary Fortune needed. "And what is that fact?"

"We have not yet gotten the monthly census figures from any of the Pichunche villages between the Completion and Eagle View Rivers."

"Ah," said Exemplary Fortune. It had been six days since the festival that began Harvest Song. Though one would not expect everyone in the province to attend the festival in the capital, at least one person from every village would deliver the month's quipus to the Inca governor or his accountant. Not to do so was a clear act of defiance. "So, what do you think this means?"

"I think it means several things," said Beautiful Orchid. "The young men who are dissatisfied with the stability of the Four Quarters' rule have obviously gained some power. But also—" he hesitated "—this means that someone will have to go to the villages or at least one of the villages to talk to the Pichunche. Chalomongo has her greatest influence in this area. She has always welcomed the empire's overlordship. I think this is an invitation or a plea for someone to come and talk."

"Yes," said Exemplary Fortune, "and I have been looking for a reason to do just that. I think you knew that."

"I did," said Beautiful Orchid, and then he said, "I want to go with you."

"No, and it is not that you would slow me down. I need you here. You will be my acting governor while I am gone."

The ready-made protest that had started forming in Beautiful Orchid's expression was replaced by utter blankness for a moment, and then he managed in a rather strangled voice, "The Sun."

"The Sun," said Exemplary Fortune, "likes order and beauty. Black Hawk may be a perfectly formed figure, but he has been making chaos out of this province. You have a heart of great orderliness."

"If you're sure it's all right," said Beautiful Orchid, still looking rather stunned.

"I'm sure," said Exemplary Fortune firmly. He turned to Cui, a young man with an Inca father and a Pichunche mother whom Beautiful Orchid had recommended as an assistant, and said, "Please have Black Hawk come talk with us."

The rather plump young Inca got up from his place on the floor and went out the door. Watching him go, Beautiful Orchid said, "Black Hawk will want to come with you."

"Will he behave?"

Beautiful Orchid considered. "He is not really a very good subordinate, but, if you can get him to endorse what you are trying to do, he will do almost anything to achieve it."

Exemplary Fortune smiled. "I do not think that you are a good subordinate yourself. You did not tell him about this."

"He would have started a war," said Beautiful Orchid.

Exemplary Fortune nodded. "He does not seem to see the other options."

Beautiful Orchid sighed. "He certainly doesn't." And Exemplary Fortune had an insight into how trying it must have been for Beautiful Orchid to work for Black Hawk in the months since Highest Strength had died.

"I would put an extra task to you while I am gone," said Exemplary Fortune. "I have promised Tamed Ocelot a wife. He wants a woman who is not too old and who will not bear him children."

Beautiful Orchid blinked. "Not bear children?"

Exemplary Fortune nodded.

"Well," said Beautiful Orchid, "that does make it easier. What are his virtues?"

"He's a good fighter," said Exemplary Fortune and stopped. There was really nothing else to say in the man's favor. He grinned wryly. "Other than that, he has promised me he will not kill anyone without my permission until his friends show up."

Beautiful Orchid was silent for a bit, then gave a wry grin in his turn. "I was going to ask about his defects next, but . . ."

"He knows nothing about our customs or language, hates farming, and thinks we are all worth considerably less than he is. I am not leaving you the easiest task."

"Ah, no. How urgent is this?"

"Fairly. His promise of conditional nonviolence was based on my finding him a wife, and I would really rather not kill him."

"I will work on it," said Beautiful Orchid. "Will he accept a trial marriage?"

"I believe so," said Exemplary Fortune as Cui came back in with Black Hawk.

Black Hawk's tunic was dirt stained and somewhat disheveled. "I didn't know if I should stop to change," he said.

"That's all right," said Exemplary Fortune. "This shouldn't take too long. I just wanted to tell you that I am going to Chalomongo's village, and that Beautiful Orchid is in charge until I get back."

Black Hawk opened his mouth and then shut it again. He looked at Beautiful Orchid and away. "Do you think this is wise?" he asked finally.

"Obviously I do."

Another pause. "How did you decide that the Pichunche were innocent?"

"I didn't. I have tentatively decided that, since there were more-secretive ways to get rid of Highest Strength, they are probably innocent—" Beautiful Orchid said that Black Hawk had already rejected that argument "—but absolutely establishing guilt or innocence is no longer the main issue. After five months, what matters is rebuilding Completion province. Though each tribe remains distinct, a province must be a unity of peoples to function. Completion is disintegrating." He watched Black Hawk carefully as he spoke and did not see any signs of understanding or a change of heart.

"But you can't . . . I want to go with you."

"Why?"

Black Hawk struggled with his reasons. "You will need someone with you in case the Pichunches are not as friendly as you hope."

"This is a diplomatic mission. I will not need someone with me who is searching for ways the mission can fail. If I am killed, Beautiful Orchid will decide what to do next." He paused just long enough for Black Hawk to absorb that, but not long enough for him to think of a suitable reply. "More importantly, there is something you need to do here. I believe Tamed Ocelot has been watching your fighting practices."

"Sneering at them," corrected Black Hawk almost absentmindedly.

"Exactly. I want you to invite him to join the practices, and then to watch him, to study his moves and tactics. I believe that his people plan to invade the Four Quarters. We need to understand their fighting style. And you personally must make sure that he doesn't kill anyone."

It was Black Hawk's turn to blink. Exemplary Fortune had clearly distracted him from his worries about the latest governor's safety. What he said, though, was "I hardly think that's likely."

"I hope not," said Exemplary Fortune, "but the last person who underestimated his fighting prowess did die. I urge you not to be careless."

New concerns surfaced in Black Hawk's eyes. "I will watch him carefully."

"Good. It may be of utmost importance."

Black Hawk bowed and left.

Now that, thought Exemplary Fortune, was a use he had not imagined for Tamed Ocelot, as a distraction, and yet, everything he had said to Black Hawk was true. The rather sardonic look in Beautiful Orchid's eyes indicated that he knew exactly what Exemplary Fortune had done.

Exemplary Fortune sent messengers to the Eagle View and Narrows fortresses saying that he had chosen Beautiful Orchid to act in his stead when he was not available. Then he went to the practice field, where the men were standing around gesturing at Tamed Ocelot and told Tamed Ocelot that he would be gone for a while.

Tamed Ocelot nodded and said, waving a hand at the group, "They think they want me to fight them, but I do not think they will like it."

"How is practice for fighting done among your people?"

"Better than this."

"I meant, what are the rules of when to stop the fight?"

Black Hawk and his turn-warriors were watching their discussion with great interest.

"When the other steps away from you or puts his weapon down or stops trying to move or is injured."

"Those are like our rules. These men will respect you if you follow them."

Tamed Ocelot nodded with a sudden predatory look in his eyes that made Exemplary Fortune wonder if he was doing the right thing. Well, the problems Tamed Ocelot caused should at least be those Black Hawk was good at. And it would keep him occupied. He told the others Tamed Ocelot's rules and left.

Then he put on a clean orange tunic with butterflies of purple, yellow, and red embroidered in even squares around the hem and over the shoulders and went to join Cui, who was waiting for him in the plaza. As they walked through the forest to Twotree, the village of Cui's mother's people, Exemplary Fortune asked, "Is there some phrase of respectful greeting that I could say when we come into the village?"

Cui gave him a phrase, but, after Exemplary Fortune had repeated it several times, Cui said, "I think you will need longer practice to make those words more pleasing than grating to the ear."

"I will rely on your translations, then."

Cui nodded. He seemed remarkably phlegmatic about the whole adventure.

They had gone about three miles when Exemplary Fortune became aware that there were at least one or two moving bodies in the trees off to the right of the road. They were being very quiet, quieter than Exemplary Fortune himself could have been on leafy ground, but the movement paralleled their path, and it seemed unlikely animals would do that. He was not at all surprised when a young man with a spear in his right hand stepped directly into their path. Exemplary Fortune stopped and said, "Greetings," which Cui duly translated.

"Why do you not know our language?" the young man demanded through Cui's translation.

"Because no one has taught it to me," Exemplary Fortune replied.

There was still a person in the woods off to the left and another on their right.

The young man took another step forward, uncomfortably close, but Exemplary Fortune did not back up. "I can teach you something," said the young man.

"I expect you can teach me more than one thing," said Exemplary Fortune. "I have much to learn."

The young man's eyes narrowed as Cui translated this. He stepped back and said, "I will show you later." He turned and was gone or rather out of sight. There were still rustlings in the forest around them.

As Exemplary Fortune started walking again, he said to Cui, "We did not introduce ourselves. Who is that young man?"

"That is Michalongo, Chalomongo's grandson."

Which meant he almost certainly understood Humanity's Mouth.

After another three miles, the forest opened into cornfields surrounding a village of perhaps two hundred people. Coming in from the south as they were, a high hill to the north crowned with several large trees framed the village. Children on the edge of the cornfields ran back into the village at their approach, yelling phrases Cui did not translate. In the village itself, everyone seemed to be standing along the path to watch them walk in. A number of people were sitting on woven mats in the small plaza at the village center, and two mats on the far side were empty. They had clearly been announced.

Exemplary Fortune walked to the right-hand vacant mat and sat down. The gathering watched him with seeming interest, but no one said anything, so Exemplary Fortune started speaking, pausing to give Cui time to translate between each of his clauses. "I am Exemplary Fortune, the new Inca governor. I am most delighted to be here. . . ." A somewhat longer pause to give anyone who wished to speak the opportunity to do so. Apparently no one did. "But I find that in the months before I came here, this province has been most poorly governed. Buildings that were started a long time ago have not been built. Festivals have not been performed properly, and so on. I am here to ask your help."

This time when he paused, a woman said, "It's not our fault if everything is messed up."

"Forgive me if I implied it was," said Exemplary Fortune. "I did not mean to do that."

"When the Incas made peace with us," said an older man, "they said that they would make sure that we would always have enough food to eat, that they would show us better ways to grow our crops, and that, even if the crops failed, we would be fed. They said they would build bridges that would not fail. They said they would defend us from the Pormoco. They said they would treat us always as one of their own kin. In the last few months, the people of the empire have refused to talk to us and treated us as though we were a spot of dirt that they wanted to be rid of. If they do not keep their promise in this, how can we believe they will keep their promises in other areas?"

From the murmurs around the circle and the approving cries of those outside it, the man had echoed the sentiments of a large portion of the populace.

Exemplary Fortune allowed himself a few heartbeats to put his planned speech in order. "We Incas," he said, "have built a structure. We have rules for how someone should be chosen as governor. We have guidelines on who should be his substitute if he dies in office. We like to believe that with these rules, we can ensure the succession will always go smoothly. But sometimes, in spite of our rules, things go wrong, the wrong person gets chosen, there is a misunderstanding about what has happened. We would like to believe that, with the Sun as our guide, and, with our knowledge and rules, we can guarantee that the proper actions will always occur, but this is not so. Most of the time, we succeed at making people better-off than before they met us.

"Everyone in all the empire is well fed; that we have accomplished. All the suspension bridges and all the stone bridges in the empire have successfully supported everyone and everything that have traveled across them. I know of one basket bridge that failed. Occasionally on the eastern edge of the empire, along the jungle's fringes, a wild tribe will briefly overrun a town or a fort. We have not yet found ways to stop this entirely. We do not always know what people will do. Sometimes, in spite of our best efforts, disasters happen that we cannot forehear." He paused. He had more words, but this was one of the places an alert ally could come in.

"Sometimes, in spite of our best efforts, disasters happen that we cannot forehear," the gray-haired woman sitting on a mat across the circle echoed.

Even through Cui's interpretation Exemplary Fortune could feel how, with the emphasis the woman gave them, the words changed meaning, referring now to the death of the former governor. Exemplary Fortune felt a bit of the tension that had seized his heart untwist. He inclined his head to her, and her eyes, deep with knowledge, caught him in their depths. She nodded just a fraction to him, and then looked around at the other villagers, allowing him to think again. Around them others affirmed the truth of her statement in a sustained murmur of approval, but at first no one said anything that asked for comment.

Finally a skinny old man said, "Well, I have lived a long time and met a lot of Incas, but this is the first time I've ever heard one admit they could be wrong."

There was background chuckling at this, and Exemplary Fortune allowed himself a smile. "It is not something we like to admit, but it is true. I have made at least three mistakes in my life."

"Oho," said the man, "then you are wiser than Highest Strength, who never made any."

Interesting. "Forgive me, but I had heard that people liked Highest Strength."

"Oh, he was pleasant enough," said the man, "but I could never quite trust him. He always knew all the answers. Even the wakas are occasionally stumped, but not Highest Strength."

"This is all very pleasant," said a younger man. In Cui's translation the emphasized "pleasant" held scorn. "But what are you going to say to people back in Great Completion? What will happen to us when you are among the Incas and Pollens again?"

"That is a good question," said Exemplary Fortune. "In the five months since Highest Strength died, much ill will has built up among the people of this province. I do not believe I can cure that overnight. But I have started. I have told the various captains and the people in the capital that, if anything happens to me, Beautiful

Orchid will be the acting governor." There was a great sigh at this, like the wind in the trees. "As soon as possible, I would like to have a ceremony, in Great Completion if possible, to appease the trees and to understand their feelings toward us. I would like to go back to Great Completion with several people who can help us work on the buildings that have been abandoned half-built in that city. I would like to reinstate the joint fighting practices with all the peoples in the province. When the harvest is complete, I want to have a great harvest festival with much dancing and feasting in Great Completion." As he talked, people nodded, and the atmosphere relaxed another few degrees. He had the approval of at least most of the people here. "These are the actions I know of that will start to heal our province. Please tell me if you know others."

A middle-aged woman said, "We have been told about the school in Navel that teaches boys Inca ways, but Highest Strength said that we could not send our sons there. He did not say why."

This was an opening for a complaint about the Pichunche's lack of structure, but Exemplary Fortune did not yet have the credibility or the power to make that complaint. He hid his feelings about the Pichunche's anarchy from his demeanor and carried the calmness he had been building into his reply. "It is not that you cannot send your sons there; it is rather that your structure—" Exemplary Fortune gave her the most positive phrasing he could imagine "—confuses us. Usually, a son of the local chief, the tribe's main elder, is sent to the school in Navel. But, as I understand it, you do not have a single chief."

"That should not stop us from learning your rules."

"That is true, and so I say this: if all the Pichunche can agree on a boy candidate approximately twelve years old, then, no more than once every five years, such a student may be sent to the school." And I will break this to Exemplary Royal Happiness very carefully, Exemplary Fortune added to himself.

"A lot of our children won't be able to go."

"That is true in every province. There are not enough places in the school to take more than a few children."

The woman nodded, satisfied.

Another person spoke up with a problem he wanted addressed.

The mood of the gathering had shifted. They were no longer a crowd of angry rebellious people; they were individuals bringing up grievances to their overlord. Exemplary Fortune answered their complaints and concerns as best he was able, occasionally asking for information or even advice. Some problems he could not solve without more study, and he told them so. People drifted away from the gathering and came back again.

As the westering Sun sent long shadows across the group, the gray-haired woman said, "There is so much to discuss, and there are so many plans to make for the tree ceremony, that I wonder if you would be willing to stay for the night?"

"I would be glad to," said Exemplary Fortune, "but I must send a quipu with my intentions to prevent further misunderstandings."

The youth who had accosted Exemplary Fortune in the forest said through Cui, "I will take the quipu to Great Completion."

Exemplary Fortune queried the woman with his eyes, and she gave him a barely perceptible nod. He had Cui give him a quipu blank, and, as he assembled his message, he said to Michalongo, "Whenever anyone asks you what you are doing, tell them that you have a message from the governor to Beautiful Orchid. Do not give this quipu to anyone except Beautiful Orchid."

"I will do that," said Michalongo in Humanity's Mouth.

Exemplary Fortune smiled at him, and the young man smiled back, clearly pleased with his cleverness at having fooled the Inca governor, who had not known until that moment that Michalongo knew his language. Exemplary Fortune finished the message and handed it to Michalongo, who, without another word, turned and ran back along the path Exemplary Fortune had walked in on.

When he had disappeared between the trees, the woman said, also in Humanity's Mouth, "Now that we have invited you to stay in our village, we should introduce ourselves. I am Chalomongo."

"Chalomongo, I am pleased to meet you," said Exemplary Fortune. He did not add, as he usually would, that he had already heard of her. The situation was still delicate enough that he did not know if that would please her or not.

Others introduced themselves, mostly in Humanity's Mouth. It was amazing how many people had suddenly found knowledge of that language. Food was brought out and cooked on great wood fires in the plaza. The large open fires seemed wasteful, but there was so much wood here that the forest would probably not be diminished by them. After dinner, people danced, and at their urging, Exemplary Fortune demonstrated an Inca dance and one of the Kitu Doves'. They asked him to play a song on the flute, but he laughed and said, "I have spent too much time on the battle-fields. I have not had time to learn to play properly."

So they had him tell them a story about battle instead. In the flickering light of the fires, people's faces were hard to see clearly, but they seemed pleased with his story. When he asked, they told him local tales in return. It was very late when they all went to bed, but Exemplary Fortune was well pleased with the day's work. Only in the very depths of his heart did a niggling voice remind him that he should be remaking the Pichunche's structure, not reinforcing the current unworkable system.

Now was not the time for that. First, he had to prevent a revolt, and then slowly reaffirm the empire's authority. Only when that was done would he be able to develop a more regular arrangement. But he did not expect Cable to understand if he found out. It did not matter. He could only do his best for the province day by day. If the new Unique Inca killed him, well, that had always been one of the more likely outcomes.

In the morning he woke when the Sun cleared the trees. The skin-roofed hut filtered the light coming to his blinking eyes and made his situation unreal. In that half-dreaming confusion, he knew what his father would say to him. Young Majesty would command him to rise up and bring order to the world. With hundreds of thousands of troops and officials, he should reform those who were disorderly, killing any who stood in his way. His father could have done this, but he himself must now work on a much smaller scale, eschewing help from Navel and relying instead on those who were themselves ill regulated. He silently promised his father he would talk to him later, and then, to recover a sense of reality from the confusion he felt, quickly got up and went outside.

The village's population seemed to have at least doubled during the night. Spilling out of the plaza, an assemblage of men and women animatedly discussed the details of the tree ceremony they planned. Cui translated pieces of the debate for Exemplary Fortune as they ate breakfast and afterward. For quite a while it seemed to Exemplary Fortune as though it was impossible that everyone would agree on what exactly was needed for the ceremony and how it was to be done. As Anaconda had said, everyone participated, even young children. There seemed to be no point at which a wise elder could interject their authority with more power than anyone else. Exemplary Fortune stayed impassive, listening quietly to the bits that Cui gave him, trying to find a pattern or logic to the course of the discussion. There were hints, but either Cui was not translating the relevant parts, or much of the logic was incomprehensible to an outsider. Villagers who became bored by the debates wandered off to do chores.

Exemplary Fortune found himself envying them, but he did not wish to make demands or, worse yet, break whatever continuity the discussion did have and so prolong it. Finally, shortly before noon, this person agreed to that adjustment, and that person decided they could incorporate two variants into that part of the ceremony, and suddenly everyone was ready to go.

A man took Exemplary Fortune's arm and said in Humanity's Mouth, "I am Tolacache. Come. You must go with us."

Seven of them went into the woods. The villagers told Cui to stay behind in the village. "Exemplary Fortune has reason to participate in the ceremony, but we should not have more than one person who does not know the ritual," they explained. It was a perfect setup to kill the new governor, and Black Hawk would have been horrified. Exemplary Fortune merely nodded to Cui to accept their directive.

While they were still in the village, Tolacache demonstrated how to walk "so as not to disturb the trees." As they moved into the woods, everyone except Exemplary Fortune began chanting to let the trees know that they were looking for a sapling who wanted to come live with the Incas.

The chant seemed somehow to amplify the silence of the woods, to manifest the listening quiet. The trees pressed in on them, surrounding them with alien leafy thoughts of Sun and Dark, Earth and Water, of slow patient unfoldings.

"Can you hear?" Tolacache asked Exemplary Fortune in perfect rhythm with the chant.

Exemplary Fortune nodded, unwilling to risk breaking the rhythm.

"Is there a direction?"

Trying to focus destroyed his sense of the trees altogether. Exemplary Fortune shook his head.

The group walked from sapling to sapling, asking each if it wished to go to Great Completion to learn about the empire and to teach the Four Quarters about the forest. Exemplary Fortune finally stopped in front of a waist-high tree, for no clear reason except that he'd noticed it. The others all crowded around, chanting their questions, and this time, though Exemplary Fortune could not hear any specific response, they agreed that this was the right sapling. Carefully, with their hands, they dug the tree with some of the dirt it embraced out of the ground and set it on a piece of deer hide they had brought. Singing a new song, they wrapped the roots in the hide and bound the skin gently with thongs. Then they set the tree on a stretcher and had Exemplary Fortune and a woman pick it up and carry it back to the village. It was surprising how heavy such a little tree was.

At the village they poured liquid on the tree, and then had Exemplary Fortune and Cui pick it up to carry it back down the path to Great Completion. As the two of them walked, people dancing in front of them strewed the ground with herbs and river water. The whole village followed along behind, singing and, as much as the narrow path would admit, dancing. The procession stopped for a time at the bridge over the Completion River while the speakers introduced the tree to the idea of traveling over water. It was not a long-enough stop, however, to justify setting the tree down, which Exemplary Fortune regretted. His arms and shoulders were getting very tired.

On the other side of the river, half the city had come out to see what was happening. Black Hawk was there with several turn-warriors, but so were Beautiful Orchid and the chief speaker from the Sun temple. It was the speaker who came forward to embrace one of the leaders. "Iwagante, how I have missed you," he said.

"Potato Flower, I have longed to talk with you again." Iwagante embraced the Inca speaker in turn, and then, while everyone waited, explained the ceremony they were performing. Cui's arms were starting to visibly tremble, and Exemplary Fortune was relieved by that much when the Inca speaker came to take the other end of the litter. He did not want to have to do this twice. Besides, he rather liked this tree. It was compact, interestingly leaved, and seemed friendly. He and the speaker carried the tree into the Sun's compound and around to the various spots where a tree might grow in the temple. But none of the places seemed right.

"Come," said Exemplary Fortune finally. It might not be part of the ceremony, but his arms hurt. "It has known me longest. Maybe it wants to live where I work."

So they carried the sapling into the governor's compound and found a spot near some salvia flowers where the tree seemed content. The spot was visible from outside the compound and would get morning sun. When the tree grew to full size, its trunk might make getting into the main office difficult, but quite likely the buildings would have been rebuilt before then anyway. At that moment, Exemplary Fortune would have agreed with almost any place the tree was willing to stay as long as he could set it down. He did not know if this was part of what ordinarily made the ceremony work or not, but he suspected it was at least possible.

Potato Flower and he set the tree down next to the designated spot. While other Incas dug the hole for the tree, Exemplary Fortune, as the Pichunche requested, explained to the sapling what life would be like for it in the governor's compound and promised to faithfully water it in droughts. When the hole was big enough, Exemplary Fortune and the speaker again picked up the tree, by the root ball this time, and the Pichunche made several slashes in the hide covering. Then the tree was carefully set in the hole, and the dirt that had been removed from the hole was piled up around its base. To chants and dancing, river water was poured on the piled-up dirt, and all those who worked or otherwise might have reason to visit the governor's compound were encouraged to spit on the dirt and say their name. Black Hawk, looking offended, did so, but Tamed Ocelot would not. The little children were delighted, and several of them spit on the dirt more than once.

When Exemplary Fortune asked Tolacache if that was proper, he said, "This sapling is learning about the Four Quarters and about children. In the future, those children will come back to talk to the tree and cherish it. It is a good thing."

Exemplary Fortune imagined his home and office invaded by children who wanted to talk to the tree. The thought was pleasant with the promise of life and continuity.

The actual ceremony over, the speakers of the Sun and the Mothers brought out enough beer to share with the multitude. Beautiful Orchid had planned hopefully. The speakers, the Mothers, and Beautiful Orchid and his staff circulated freely, and the gathering stayed congenial. Black Hawk disappeared early, and so Exemplary Fortune drank only the absolute minimum for sociability. Tamed Ocelot was encouraged to drink by various of Black Hawk's turn-warriors, and then began looking calculatingly at the women in the group, but the warriors, thankfully, stayed with him, and there seemed to be enough to stop him if he tried anything. Various people, mostly Pichunche, volunteered to massage Exemplary Fortune's arms, shoulders, and even his legs, which did not really need it. When he asked if other people got tired carrying their village's trees, the Pichunche said, "Oh, everybody," and laughed. Exemplary Fortune joined in the laughter.

A Pichunche said to Exemplary Fortune and Potato Flower, "We think we have finally figured out what happened to Highest Strength. We had the ceremony to keep the tree from falling on people, but we had not introduced the trees to the Incas, and so the tree did not know he was there."

It seemed as likely an explanation of what had happened as they would find.

In late afternoon, the Pichunche began to leave in order to reach their homes by sundown, and everyone else began to drift off to the fields. Exemplary Fortune went in search of Black Hawk.

Black Hawk was cleaning weapons in the room where they were

stored. He looked up as Exemplary Fortune came in, but he did not say anything or stop what he was doing.

"So," said Exemplary Fortune, "you are not happy with peace."

As Black Hawk turned to him, his eyes blazed with anger. "You did not go to the village to find out what happened," he accused Exemplary Fortune. "You went to make an agreement with the Pichunche. Never mind that they may have killed the last governor, or what they may be plotting now."

Exemplary Fortune seated himself comfortably on the floor. "About a hundred years ago, a federation of people who called themselves Tens attacked Navel—"

"We were not part of the empire then," Black Hawk shot back.

Without acknowledging that Black Hawk had said anything, Exemplary Fortune went on. "After the Unique Inca World Reverser had defeated the Tens and put Navel in order, he decided that he needed an experienced commander to train his troops and help him with his conquest of the surrounding territory. As there were none in his command who had experience conquering other tribes, he invited Ear-Chopper Eagle, the chief surviving commander of the Tens, to come to Navel with all his relatives. Together he and Ear-Chopper Eagle conquered many of the surrounding tribes until the day the Ten commander broke the agreement and fled away to the jungle."

Black Hawk glared at him.

"Say it," commanded Exemplary Fortune.

Angrily Black Hawk said, "It was the Incas who broke faith first. Commander Majestic Reckoner planned to kill Ear-Chopper Eagle by treachery."

Exemplary Fortune nodded. "The Tens have forgiven the Incas all the men killed in battle, all the prisoners killed after the battle, even the prisoners whose bodies were made into drums still played on the appropriate feast days. But all of them are upset that, after the war was over, one of their people had to flee the Four Quarters.

"It does not really matter who is right about what happened, that resentment weakens the empire, and the Inca commander who caused that weakening committed a great crime that even his execution could not expiate. To be an Inca is always to think how to strengthen the empire. In a very real sense, it does not matter if the Pichunche killed Highest Strength. The important question is, will punishing them strengthen the Four Quarters?

"When Ear-Chopper Eagle fled away into the jungle, World Reverser could very easily have decided that those who had helped organize his escape should be tracked down and punished. Since it is clear that Ear-Chopper Eagle had help, and without question those who helped him betrayed the empire; from an Inca point of view, did World Reverser do wrong in not finding and punishing the people who had helped Ear-Chopper Eagle?"

Black Hawk threw down the rag he had been using to clean the weapons. He stared at Exemplary Fortune, the ready answer in his eyes giving way to doubt as he struggled to formulate an answer. He looked down at his hands, stained with grime from the weapons, and said finally, "The Tens would have revolted."

"What would happen if I punish the Pichunche?"

"They'd revolt I'd guess, but we—"

"And after you'd defeated them, what would the other people of the province do?"

"What?" Black Hawk looked nearly stunned. He had not expected that question, but he did not, as he would have earlier, disgorge an automatic answer.

"Suppose I kill the three people who could most likely have plotted to kill the governor," Exemplary Fortune said. "The Pichunche revolt, and your forces put them down. What will the Tens do?"

"Well, they wouldn't trust the Pichunche anymore," Black Hawk said.

"Will that help the empire?" Exemplary Fortune pressed.

"It would hurt it," admitted Black Hawk grudgingly.

"And how will the Pichunche feel? Remember, whatever happened, most of the Pichunche did not even know where the governor was when he died."

"They'd feel betrayed," said Black Hawk slowly. He sat down facing Exemplary Fortune. He scratched at the dirt with a fingernail. "They might even make up a story about how it was all the Incas' fault."

"They might," agreed Exemplary Fortune.

Black Hawk gave him a rueful grin. "You are a terrible person. Beautiful Orchid has lectured me for months about how it would be wrong to punish the Pichunche. I never believed him. You . . ." He shook his head.

"I saved a couple tumblers of beer," said Exemplary Fortune. "Do you want some?"

"I'm not really in a festive mood. You've made me doubt the tribal history I learned as a child." He paused again. "I suppose I've missed the festivities."

"You have." Exemplary Fortune stood up. "If it helps at all, I do know how you must feel. I've had my view of the world stretched a couple times. Since it's been a while, I've decided it was useful."

"Ha," said Black Hawk as he followed Exemplary Fortune to where the beer was hidden. They drank the beer in silence, each with their own thoughts.

"Do you want me to resign as military trainer?" Black Hawk asked finally.

The true answer was that Exemplary Fortune did not want anyone to resign or to do anything that required confirmation by the current Unique Inca. He did not want to do anything that would unnecessarily remind Cable of his existence, but that was not the right answer. He said, "Who would be a good replacement?"

"Captain Anaconda up at Eagle View Fort," said Black Hawk promptly.

"And how would the Tens feel about having a Pollen trainer?"

Black Hawk shook his head ruefully. "I thought I was done with your questions." He considered. "They came with me. Most of them came because they knew I'd be military trainer for the province. They wouldn't like it. They'd blame the Pichunche."

"Good, you're thinking," said Exemplary Fortune. "From what I've heard and seen, you are a good trainer. I do not want your resignation. If the Pichunche ask me to find another military trainer, I may have to think again, but I don't believe they will. Already, some of them have asked to join fighting practice."

"And you said yes."

"And I said yes."

Black Hawk nodded. "That does make sense, I guess. Besides—" his lips quirked into an almost smile "—you've already given us Tamed Ocelot."

"Ah, dare I ask?"

"Have you ever fought him?"

"Twice."

Black Hawk raised his eyebrows. "I would like to see you fight."

"I am good," said Exemplary Fortune, "but I am not that good. The first time, I caught him at a disadvantage, and the second, someone else saved me. I take it he's been behaving?"

"Well, he hasn't seriously hurt anyone. Having him in the practice sessions does give them a certain realism. No one is ever sure if he will stop or not." Black Hawk appraised Exemplary Fortune. "Come to think of it, he resembles you in that regard, although at first sight, you do not appear as deadly as he does. You're much sneakier."

Exemplary Fortune grinned. "That is one of my strengths."

That night, as Exemplary Fortune dreamt, Young Majesty came to him. When his father appeared, Exemplary Fortune said, "I am sorry, father, that I cannot reorder Completion's government—"

"My son," said Young Majesty, "you must . . ." He dissolved into a red haze redolent with the smell of blood. Exemplary Fortune woke with his heart brimming with the scent and sound of Blood Lake filled with the dead who had surrendered, and then, at Young Majesty's orders, been slain and thrown into its waters. It was shortly after that that Young Majesty had set the bounds of the Four Quarters and retired to Kitu Dove to administer the empire, shortly after that that he had become afraid of the future. Exemplary Fortune had never before tied those deaths to his father's fear of the future. He still did not know if he should. His father's warning-plea was not clear to him.

After he ate breakfast in the tampu and before he went to the governor's compound to work, Exemplary Fortune went to the Sun temple and prayed to the Sun and to Lightning for his father. Potato

Flower greeted him as he came out of the Sun's room. "That was very well-done yesterday. I have been heartsore with the disorder that has been threatening our province."

Exemplary Fortune thanked him, but he knew he was more subdued than Potato Flower likely expected. The images of his father were still too vivid. "I have a request of you," he said. "I would like you to do a sacrifice for my father. I was on the Road when he died, and, though I know there have been many state ceremonies and sacrifices for him, I have not been able to pay my proper respects as his son."

As he spoke of sacrifices, his heart chilled within him. His father had asked in Throat Town for an omen to cover a decade. So far only one-twentieth of that dire prediction had been made manifest. Perhaps his father's warning was not about the past at all. Maybe he should discuss this apprehension directly with Potato Flower. But his father had chosen to talk with him rather than with someone else. He wanted to try to decipher the dream's meaning himself before he talked with anyone else about it.

Beautiful Orchid and his assistants were surrounded by piles of quipus. "Don't touch anything," Beautiful Orchid said as Exemplary Fortune came to the door, and then, "Excuse me, but for some reason everyone who comes by today wants to sift through the piles and find out what's here." He grinned. "They've been coming in all morning."

"Good," said Exemplary Fortune, "I was hoping we wouldn't have to go back and say, 'Ah, by the way . . .' Have we got them all?"

"I'm not sure," said Beautiful Orchid, looking around at the colorful piles. "No, as a matter of fact, I know we're missing a few from villages in the north along the coast. They'll probably take a while. No roads down there."

10

FIRST YEAR OF EXEMPLARY ROYAL HAPPINESS'S REIGN
HARVEST SONG THROUGH EARTHLY PURIFICATION MONTH

Some chroniclers of actual history say that, before he died, Young Majesty ordered the empire split between the northern half, which Exemplary Fortune should rule, and the southern half, which Cable would rule. Given the disorder that would inevitably follow such a division, this seems unlikely.

It was another tenday before the corn was ready to harvest, and, in that time, Exemplary Fortune's father came to him in dreams not once, but twice more. Whatever he wanted had to be urgent to him, but his warning-pleas fragmented into incongruous and clashing images. Sometimes Young Majesty seemed to command Exemplary Fortune to take some specific action for the empire, and sometimes he seemed in pain that must be stopped. He did not respond coherently to Exemplary Fortune's queries. With each vision, Exemplary Fortune woke filled with memories of Blood Lake, as though the ghosts of those he had killed, not in battle but in cold blood, haunted Young Majesty; as though those ghosts, vowing vengeance, had somehow brought his death, had maybe even brought the Spanish here. As though Young Majesty had decided that with that action he had weakened the empire rather than strengthening it. After the third dream visitation, Exemplary Fortune told Potato Flower about his father's visits. Potato Flower tried to contact Young Majesty to find out more about his worries and what he wanted, but Young Majesty would give him no clear omens either.

The province itself was far calmer than Exemplary Fortune would have believed possible when he first talked with Black Hawk. There was still tension under the surface, but it was not nearly as bad as it could have been. If no one did anything stupid, they might actually wash away the bad feeling Black Hawk had let fester without further incident.

Tamed Ocelot had started to pester Exemplary Fortune about his promise of a wife, but, when Exemplary Fortune said it was extremely difficult to find a marriage partner for someone who refused to learn the local language and hated farming, he growled wordlessly and dropped the subject for a time.

He growled similarly when Exemplary Fortune said the corn was ready to harvest, but he got up early on the appointed day and went with everyone to the fields. Exemplary Fortune, as governor, cut the first bundle, and then, as Tamed Ocelot's mentor, showed him how to tie the bundle. Some of those who practiced under Black Hawk showed Tamed Ocelot where to carry the corn. Though a governor usually rested after cutting only a few sheaves, Exemplary Fortune worked the whole day. The physical exercise was heart numbing, and he knew if he quit, Tamed Ocelot would do likewise. As it was, Tamed Ocelot grumbled, dropped cornstalks, and nearly ran into other harvesters many times as he worked. But he kept at it. By the end of the day, he was nearly proficient. He refused to join in any of the harvest chants, though, and, whenever anyone smiled at him, he growled. By the end of the first day, he had earned the nickname "Growler."

"What is it they are calling me?" he asked Exemplary Fortune as they drank tumblers of beer that those unable to do the heavy work brought out to the fields. When Exemplary Fortune told him, he growled again, and then his face froze, and he looked away. He did not say anything for quite a while after that. It was, thought Exemplary Fortune, only just that he should take away whatever pleasure Tamed Ocelot had gotten out of his day since the man had done much the same for him.

He watched Tamed Ocelot in the festival that followed partly to learn his reactions, to figure out what he thought anomalous or expected, and partly to make sure he didn't cause trouble. Tamed Ocelot was also watched by Black Hawk's turn-warriors, who had, in a fashion, adopted him. Even so, with all the surrounding villages crowding into the plaza, there were simply too many people for anyone to keep a close watch on him. But Tamed Ocelot did not cause problems.

The trouble came instead from the tribal divisions Exemplary Fortune worried about. Three Tens began pushing people, not actually hitting or kicking but shoving people, particularly Pichunche, with enough force to knock them over. Before they were stopped, they had nearly started a full-scale riot.

Black Hawk's warriors wedged themselves between the angry groups and hustled the offenders off to the side. The three young men went willingly, almost cockily. Clearly, they had not been taught they were doing anything wrong. And it did not seem likely Exemplary Fortune would convince them quickly. The plaza was once again quiet, too quiet; with people waiting to see how the Inca governor would handle this situation that the Incas themselves had in some measure caused.

Exemplary Fortune said to Beautiful Orchid, "Make an inventory of all the damage. Black Hawk, bring those three into the compound with the witnesses." He turned and walked into the governor's compound, leaving the governor's place at the festival vacant. That normally happened intermittently with the press of administrative duties, but trials of misdemeanors were held over until after the festival. It was his first statement that he considered the Tens' actions serious.

That the three did not believe him became clear as the trial progressed. "Okay," said one of them, "we had a little too much beer. We were clumsy. It happens."

There was no sign of remorse or understanding of why their actions were serious.

Everyone agreed as to what had happened. The only question was that of motive. The case was in that respect an echo of Highest Strength's death. When everyone who felt they had an interest had spoken, Exemplary Fortune said to the three, "Before I pass sentence, now that you have heard the witnesses, I would remind you for the last time that it is your right, if you wish, to ask for a factfinder to research the case. Do you so wish?"

The young man who had been the spokesman of the three looked at the older man who'd been advising them, his uncle, and then shook his head. "Everybody knows what happened."

Exemplary Fortune turned to his Ten military trainer. "Black Hawk, you have had experience as governor. How would you evaluate this case?"

There was a sudden frozen silence in the court. This was not standard procedure. Black Hawk turned to look at the new governor in a heartbeat of surprise and then, before Exemplary Fortune could make any sign to him, said, "This is not a case of drunken clumsiness. This is a case of treason. These three deliberately attempted and indeed succeeded in disrupting a festival ordered by the Unique Inca's governor. They acted to foment ill will and mistrust between the groups making up this province and thereby to weaken the Four Quarters." Black Hawk's voice shook with emotion. "For such actions, the prescribed penalty is death."

The three Tens had gone wide-eyed and pale. Their uncle had his mouth literally hanging open. The rest of the people in the court, Tens who were mainly family and friends of the defendants, the Pichunche, the Wild Sands, and a few Incas who were all hostile witnesses, looked nearly as stunned. The one thing that had to be clear to them all was that the Inca governor had in no way signaled his Ten military aide what to say.

Exemplary Fortune let the silence lengthen just enough to be sure everyone had gotten the message and then said, "Black Hawk has indeed named the crime correctly. These three have deliberately worked to destabilize this province and therefore the empire. Normally, I would also agree with his sentencing. It appears, however, that these three have been woefully misinformed about the duties of the people of the Four Quarters. We are not here today to punish the instruction that the various people of the province have received. I cannot judge, with the information at my disposal, how wide this misinformation has spread or who is responsible for it. I can only say that these young people are not wholly responsible for their misdeeds, as their elders have failed them in this area." Exemplary Fortune's eyes swept the courtroom. Everyone, including the Pichunche, had become wary, waiting almost without expectation for what he would say next. "Therefore, I hereby order that these three be publicly whipped and that, for the next year, all that is produced by the works of their hands be given over, not to their families, but to the government's stores to reimburse it for the damages it will have to cover. I have spoken."

Next month at the great Sun Festival and the month after at Earthly Purification, there were no incidents at all.

11

TWELFTH TO FOURTEENTH YEAR OF KING CARLOS'S REIGN

JUNE 1528 THROUGH JANUARY 1530

Before the Spanish swept across the sea, they had conquered the Iberian peninsula. Then they banished everyone whom they felt was not truly Spanish and perfected the Inquisition to keep themselves true to their beliefs.

J uan was somehow not on the ship when it sailed. He had been with them all the way down to the town by the ocean, and he was with them for the first night or two while they negotiated for space on a ship, but somehow in the confusion of boarding he was left behind. Or more likely, there was no confusion at all. Felipe did not know if Francisco Pizarro had had Juan killed or if he had merely left him behind to become one of the ragged people, but Francisco Pizarro did not mention Juan or look for him, though after the first few hours he must have known he was not on board. Felipe did not even like Juan much, but Juan was of the Matron tribe like he was and, therefore, partly his responsibility. Besides, the Spanish kept making people disappear, and he was afraid he would be next.

As they sailed out onto the vast water, Felipe would feel his heart beat faster with fear whenever they came near an island. It was stupid. The Spaniards had killed Young Fox on the water, but

Felipe knew the Spanish ships and their routine. He still did not know what they might do on land.

Diego and Francisco followed Martin around the ship, drinking in his every word and not talking to Felipe at all. Whenever Felipe came near, Martin would turn away, not hiding his face with respect but refusing to acknowledge Felipe's presence. Francisco Pizarro spent much of his time arranging and rearranging small pieces of variously decorated stiff paper with other men. It was a game, he said, and something about *dinero*.

Eventually, the islands disappeared. They were on open water with no land anywhere around. That was frightening too, but this fear made Felipe stronger instead of weaker. He would clutch the crucifix with Earth in it and stare out over the water for hours. Whether the waves were high and fierce, or the air was so calm the ship barely moved, the water was always itself. The ocean did not even seem to know the Spaniards traversed it. Even the Spanish admitted the ocean could destroy them whenever it wanted to.

The other passengers all thought he was very fond of their ancestor, which made them pleased with him, but they did not talk to him. The sailors did not talk to him because he was a passenger, and the other passengers thought he was not worth talking to because he was an *indio*. Some of them looked at him as though they thought he should not be wearing clothes without holes.

Only Greek treated him like a real person, talking with him and trying to explain about *dinero,* which, even when he finally understood how it was used, did not make much sense. When Greek talked about machinery, that eventually did make sense. Wheels, once Felipe understood how axles worked, seemed especially ingenious. Greek also spent a great deal of time talking about Greece, the Turks, Italy, and Castile, which was both a country and a province of Spain. Mostly, when he talked about those countries, he talked about war: the wars they had fought, the wars they were fighting, and the wars they would probably fight in the future. As he talked, Felipe realized the people he talked about had no stabilizing force like the Four Quarters. Everyone—pope, kings, the emperor, other nobility, even the common soldiers—were in constantly shifting alliances. Greek did not even know if Castile was currently fighting with or against Greece. It did not bother him. "Everyone needs a good artilleryman," he said, "and I am very good. So I go where the pay is good, where the excitement is. In Peru I think we will all get rich."

Felipe did not say anything to that. By Peru, Greek meant the Four Quarters, and Felipe did not think he meant to trade for what he wanted. He and Francisco Pizarro meant to steal or fight for it. Young Majesty would stop them, Felipe thought, but they were so confident, and somehow they had destroyed the hearts of the people in Panama so they did not even try to fight anymore.

He held the Earth and stared out over the great water that made even the Spanish seem small.

Felipe was not pleased when they sighted land again. They saw islands first; the last stop, said Greek, before Spain. Everyone else on the ship seemed excited by how close Spain was, even Martin and the boys, but Felipe wished he could think of some way to stop the ship from ever reaching Seville. Maybe if he knew more about ships he could figure out a way to make them get permanently lost, or, if he were a speaker with Water, maybe he could convince the water to take them far, far away.

Nothing like that happened, and, sooner than he hoped, they reached the foot of the Guadalquivir River. Seville was sixty miles upriver, and the men who had sailed the ship across the ocean did not know how to guide the ship on such a small body of water. A riverman came on board and took over. The river was not very deep, and all the men worried that the ship would scrape bottom, but again the water was good to them. Maybe the terrible ancestor was a water waka. That would explain why the Spanish poured water on people to make them one of His followers.

It took several days for the ship to maneuver up the Guadalquivir River to Seville. Felipe did not understand why the Spanish couldn't have built a harbor on the coast, but he did not ask. It seemed sometimes that the Spanish actually liked doing things in the most difficult possible way. If they had not thought of putting their harbor city on the coast, he did not want to suggest it to them.

Felipe spent most of the time as they maneuvered upriver looking around at the country of the Spanish. The area they were traveling through seemed to be all marshland. At first Felipe thought it must be salt marshes like the coastal area north of Recognition, where nothing would grow, but the farther inland they traveled, the more he wondered if the swamp couldn't be drained or built up and made fruitful. He tried to talk to Greek about the earth, but Greek just snorted and said, "I am not a farmer."

The first view they had of Seville was a tall tower that Greek said had been built by *paganos*. Soon they could see sturdy-looking walls that seemed to curve all the way around the city. Felipe wondered whom the city-dwellers were afraid of. Were the Spanish fighting each other? Did they have enemies in the countryside? From the stories Greek had been telling him, both of those seemed likely. There were no enemy troops in the fields outside the city, though; just the usual Spanish confusion of people jostling each other as they came and went.

As the ship followed the river in its curve around the outside of the walls, Felipe could see ships and boats of all sizes tied up alongside its banks. Some of them were only half-finished, and men moved around on them, obviously putting them together. There were also piles of boxes and other things out in the open on the bare ground. If the boxes were full of things the Spanish valued, it could not rain very much here.

The man who was now in charge of steering the ship maneuvered it in close to the riverbank. By then Francisco Pizarro and some of the other men were yelling back and forth to men on shore. As usual, it took the Spanish a long time to decide what to do and how to do it.

Seville was, as Greek had promised, a big city, but most of the people on the streets were furtive ragged-looking people. They wore Spanish clothes, though, and most of them were pale, though a number were dark brown like the woman in Francisco Pizarro's house and some of the other people he had seen in Panama. The men generally had short black beards like Francisco Pizarro and the other Spaniards. Many of the people who were not ragged wore sharp swords on their hips. These were all men. The people dressed in fine rich clothing hid from everyone else, moving about in closed boxes on wheels. The city stank at least as badly as Panama. In the first hour they got off the boat, Felipe saw a dead dog lying in the middle of the road. No one seemed to notice. People pissed against the walls of the finest buildings in broad daylight. At night the innkeepers threw the slop from the piss pots out the windows into those same streets.

Francisco Pizarro stayed in Seville only a few days, long enough to buy pack animals to carry the boxes full of the Four Quarters' gold and silver. He was going to take the metalwork to Toledo, the capital of Spain, where King Carlos was staying.

On the road to Toledo, Martin got sick. He threw up and had diarrhea. He complained about cramps in his belly and his legs, and Felipe could tell that he did not complain willingly. He was almost doubled over with pain. His heart beat weakly, and his skin was cool. Francisco Pizarro recognized the illness and said it was a summer disease. That Martin would get sick in Spain somehow surprised Felipe. Maybe he had thought Martin was so Spanish he would be protected from Spanish diseases. It was also frightening that Martin, who acted so thoroughly Spanish, was the one who got sick. It was like the Spanish ancestor did not really care if anyone reverenced Him or not.

All the rest of them, Diego and Francisco and he, tended Martin, and in a few days he was well again. By then Diego was sick, and he did not get better even though Francisco Pizarro let them ride in the wheeled boxes, the coaches, instead of walking. He got steadily sicker, until, three days later, he died. By then, Felipe himself was sick, and Francisco Pizarro was irritated with all of them. "I didn't bring you here just so you could die," he complained.

Felipe was so sick he barely even noticed when they crossed into Toledo. All he noticed was that Francisco Pizarro let him lie in bed and did not make him move again for quite a while. It took nearly a week before he could start to take care of Francisco Pizarro again. By then, they had found a place in Toledo where they could stay without using too much *dinero,* and Francisco Pizarro was visiting the king's officials to explain why the king should see them.

Martin had taken care of Francisco Pizarro's clothes while Felipe was sick, but, as soon as Felipe was well enough, Francisco Pizarro insisted he do it again. "Martin likes too many frills," he said. But there were some things he trusted Martin with. He took Martin with him to talk to the king's officials and not Felipe.

Felipe tended Little Francisco, who was still sick. He was sometimes delirious, and then he spoke in a language Felipe did not understand. It would be better if Martin, who knew his language, took care of him, but Martin said he had to go with Francisco Pizarro. For a time Felipe was afraid that Little Francisco would die like Diego had, but eventually he began to get better. By then Francisco Pizarro had an interview with King Carlos, and, although Little Francisco was still pale, he was able to go with them.

Francisco Pizarro said that Felipe, Francisco, and Martin had to wear the clothes of their homeland for their audience with King Carlos. Martin's eyes flashed anger, but he bowed and smiled and said he would be happy to. When Felipe opened the chest with the clothes from Recognition, he found that it was hard to even touch them. He could not bring himself to put on the tunic and loincloth he had been wearing when he ran away, and he did not want to wear Juan's clothes either, so instead he put on the clothes that had belonged to Young Fox. It felt almost right somehow. Young Fox should be the one who was here. When Francisco Pizarro saw him in those clothes, he did not comment.

As they walked down the street toward the palace, Francisco Pizarro reminded them that everyone who was announced into the presence of the king must go down on their knees and then bow. It seemed odd to Felipe that the Spanish, who violated the earth so casually, should respect Earth by touching Her more fully when they wanted to honor their king, but he did not complain.

King Carlos's palace was a large compound, with the usual Spanish high walls all the way around it. The compound was bigger than Macaw's headquarters, maybe even as big as Young Majesty's palace in Kitu Dove. The floors were all smoothly polished and the ceilings very high. Near the ceilings were large open furnishings with many candles that looked as though they would fall down and set the whole building on fire in even a small earthquake.

All the people in the palace wore black with frilly white and metallic cuffs and trim and jewels like Francisco Pizarro wore. Greek, who was this day Pedro of Crete, wore black tights but had insisted on a bright blue-and-yellow doublet. "Something festive," he had said, "to show the king we think this is a momentous occasion." Francisco Pizarro had frowned and said nothing, but there was a look in his eyes that said he was not totally displeased. Maybe he thought Greek's outfit would help King Carlos realize who among them should be taken seriously.

Felipe's first sight of the man on the ornate raised seat was a shock. He had seen others among the Spanish who had colorless hair and had assumed they were recovering from some serious illness. But Francisco Pizarro had not said the king had been ill, so his thin hair the color of dead bleached plant stalks must be usual with him. But that was not the worst. His lower jaw was huge and deformed, so his voice sounded strange and some of his words were hard to understand. Felipe bowed his head to hide his face so he would not show his shock. Maybe he should not have been surprised. People who would worship torturedness would do anything, even take a deformed person as their model.

Francisco Pizarro brought out the chests of gold and silver they had gotten in the Four Quarters while Greek told about how he had gone ashore at a place that had to be Recognition. "First," he said, "the chief's men sent out a lion and a tiger to scare me, but I shot in the air with my arquebus, and they both ran away."

That did not sound quite right. It was true Macaw had pumas and a jaguar, but there was no reason to set them on a guest who had come into the city.

"After that, I went up into the city, and the chief took me into his palace. All the walls of the palace are covered with gold, and there is a beautiful garden with plants made of solid gold. The plates the chief eats off of are gold, and his clothes are of the finest silk. Next door to the chief's palace is a palace filled with all the most beautiful women in the land. This building is also covered with gold. . . ."

Greek was obviously taking what he had seen and making it more like what he thought the king wanted. None of the buildings in Recognition were covered with gold, and, though most of the women in the Mothers' House were good-looking, they were not all beautiful. That was not how they were chosen.

As Greek talked and gestured expansively, Francisco Pizarro began to get a closed look. As the king asked questions in his deformed voice, Greek's descriptions began to get more and more elaborate, and Felipe began to hope that the king would not believe anything he or anyone with him said. Francisco Pizarro finally interrupted, saying, "Pedro of Crete was in Peru only a few short hours. Martin was born and raised there, the son of a local king. Let him tell you about the riches of Peru."

Greek looked indignant but did not say anything more.

Instead Martin talked, speaking plainly and clearly about the gold of "Peru." When King Carlos asked him, he said many of the local rulers did not like the Incas and that, with the proper inducements, they would be glad to support the Spanish.

It was possible Martin was trying to make the Spanish overconfident so they would be defeated when they came to conquer the Four Quarters, but his explanation did not sound like that. It sounded as though Martin meant what he said, and Martin knew far more about how the local chiefs felt than Felipe did. Felipe looked over at Little Francisco to see how he was reacting. He had his eyes on the floor, and his face was blank. The king sounded pleased as he talked with Martin, and soon he told his officials to make an agreement with Francisco Pizarro to authorize an expedition to Peru. They were given an appointment to talk with the king's officials and ushered out.

"See," said Greek, "the king liked us."

Francisco Pizarro smiled thinly and said nothing.

Felipe and Little Francisco did not go back to talk with the king's officials. Sometimes Martin went and sometimes Greek, but mostly Francisco Pizarro went alone. He did not talk about what he and the king's high officials said to each other. Greek said that the officials had promised they would all have much land and many servants to take care of them so they could sit at ease and drink wine on their estates.

A person could not trust what Greek said, but Martin talked

with Little Francisco, and Little Francisco talked with Felipe about what he said. Little Francisco also said the king's officials planned to give the Four Quarters to Francisco Pizarro. "Martin does not care," Little Francisco said. "He can see how badly people live here, how badly they treat the land, but all he thinks about is how well he will do if the Spanish win. Seaweed and I used to think Martin would help us, but Martin does not care about anything except himself. I think he would betray his parents to help the Spanish." His voice was bitter, but he was polite and diffident around Martin like he always had been, like Felipe was around Francisco Pizarro.

Little Francisco did not go out much, staying mostly in their room at the inn and eating only what Felipe brought into that building. When he did go out, he would tire quickly and have to sit down to rest before he could walk back to the inn. Felipe worried about him, but, with no healers available, he did not know what to do. He listened to what people said at the inn, and, from their words, he decided he did not trust the Spanish doctors. Greek too said Francisco was better off on his own. Besides, Felipe did not think Francisco Pizarro would want to give *dinero* to a healer for Little Francisco.

Unlike Little Francisco, Felipe could not bear to sit all day at the inn. When Francisco Pizarro was out, Felipe would walk around Toledo just looking at things. Sometimes ragged people, men, women, and children alike, would beg him for *dinero*. At first he would try to talk with them, but, usually when he did that, they would scream at him when they found out he didn't have what they wanted. Eventually he learned to shake his head and keep walking, the way the Spanish did. Sometimes he didn't even do that. Sometimes he would walk by as though he didn't see them, and, after a while, sometimes he didn't.

When the group had come to Toledo, Felipe had not noticed any walls around the city. Maybe, he thought, Seville had a wall around it only because of all the ships from faraway places that visited it. Maybe Greek was wrong about that too, and the Spanish weren't really fighting all the time. Felipe walked south from the inn, looking for the main road into town. He soon found himself standing at the top of a steep-sided gorge with a river far below.

To Felipe the valley's walls looked unclimbable. He walked west around the edge of the town, getting lost in alleys and streets that ended in courtyards, but staying always as close to the ravine's edge as he could. At last, he found the bridge he vaguely remembered. It was made of stone and had towered gates on each side where guards could watch everyone and everything that came and went across it. Felipe continued walking around the edge of the city and soon came to a wall that was even thicker and taller than the wall around Seville. He followed the wall north and east. The wall ended in another bridge across the deep running river. Clearly Greek was right about this. Every city in Spain was a walled fortress. It did not matter whether it was on the coast or far inland. He did not know what battles had been fought here, but he was sure the Spanish had been fighting each other. The Spanish did not know how to do anything else, he thought. If they invaded the Four Quarters, they would bring their fighting ways with them.

When he told Little Francisco what he had seen, he cried and would not eat for a day. Little Francisco's heart was obviously very weak, and Felipe resolved not to share any more bad news than he had to until Little Francisco recovered his heart strength.

Felipe spent many days walking around inside the city and looking at all the buildings, which were sometimes very well designed and made. The ancestor's cathedral was the biggest compound in town, more than twice as large as the palace of King Carlos. He wondered if it could be bigger even than Young Majesty's palace in Navel, but Little Francisco said even Martin had never seen that palace, and so he had no way of knowing. The great high walls that made the outside were of carefully fitted stone. When Felipe peered into the main door, the inside was so beautiful that he had to walk in farther. The whole compound of buildings was elaborately decorated, all in vertical lines that led the viewer's eyes up to look at the ancestors' pictures high on the walls. The decorative work was of wood, many different kinds of stone, including precious stones, and various metals. The windows were made of brightly colored glass that tinted the light inside as though it shone through flowers.

It all made Felipe very sad. If the Spanish could build something like this, then they should be able to keep their streets clean and take care of themselves. If they did that, they would not have to steal land from other people. But, even in the cathedral, not all the carvings and other pictures were of the Spanish wakas. Some were of people fighting and killing one another.

When he could not stand to look at the cathedral anymore, Felipe wandered the markets. Here people stood or sat in rows with the things in front of them that they wanted to trade for *dinero*. There were many strange fruits: grapes, oranges, melons, figs, lemons, and pomegranates. There were much garlic and onion and many different kinds of olives. Felipe ate olives, but they did not taste like very much to him beyond the salt and vinegar they were prepared with. In small buildings along the streets, people displayed different kinds of cloth woven in many styles, though none of it was as fine or as bright as the best of the Four Quarters' cotton and alpaca wool. The metalwork displayed in other shops ranged from outstanding to mediocre. Many of the cups and plates would have been rejected by his father. When Felipe thought about his father, though, or how Molle Tree would like the glassware at another shop, he would move on.

There was a blacksmith's forge not far from their inn. The smith would let him watch for hours as the man worked the strange hard metal of the Spanish. The bellows were most ingenious, and after some weeks the smith let him work them. But even with all that wind to make the furnace very hot, the metal would not melt, and the smith had to hammer and anneal it over and over again to shape and texture it properly.

Sometimes, when Greek was not with Francisco Pizarro, he would take Felipe outside the city walls. Most of the time he would show Felipe artillery, explaining how he decided what he wanted to buy when the king's officials finally authorized their expedition.

As the two of them were walking outside Toledo one day, Felipe exclaimed happily at a field of bright white flowers with violet centers. Greek smiled at him and said, "Those are poppy flowers. They grow where I come from, too. Their seeds make a fine oil, and the pods have a juice that stops pain and brings sleep." Felipe was happy to know the Spanish cared enough for each other that they would grow medicinal plants, but he was still disappointed. He had hoped they grew the flowers simply because they were beautiful.

Much of the rolling land seemed barren and empty. In some places there were prickly bushes and in some places nearly empty ground. In other places, there were well-tended fields and gardens, many of them around farmers' homes. The farmers he saw all looked worn-out, most of them were dirty, and some of them even looked hungry. Only the Spanish, he thought, could so order their world that the people who provided the food went hungry. Herds of sheep roamed the land with herders and dogs guarding them. They had sharp hooves that cut into the ground, and, when the wind blew, dust from the ground blew all over everything.

Soon after they had their audience with King Carlos, the air began to get colder and darker each day. Sometimes Felipe would find himself shaking he was so cold. Probably, he thought, Happy Speaker would be delighted if he died of the cold. But he found he could not even be mad at Happy Speaker anymore. All thoughts of home just made him sad. Greek told Felipe where he could buy warm cloaks and said that eventually the air would get warm again. And, after several months, it did.

Once Greek took him to a house where there were women who would have sex with them for *dinero,* but, when they got there, Felipe panicked. The women were all Spanish. They acted friendly with him, but none of them were saying what they really meant. They scared him, and, when one started to undo his clothes, he ran outside. Greek was annoyed, but he still told Francisco Pizarro what had happened as a funny story. Francisco Pizarro smiled with his lips, which meant little, but he also smiled with his eyes, which meant he was pleased. He liked Felipe only having sex with him. In Spain, though, he often went to find women who were willing to have sex with him. Francisco Pizarro had one set of rules for himself and one set for everyone else. Sometimes Felipe thought Greek did not understand that, but he did not talk to Greek about it, about many things. Greek, too, was one of the people who wanted to destroy the Four Quarters.

As the time wore on, Francisco Pizarro went to the town of

Trujillo in the province where his family came from and where his brothers still lived. He took Martin with him, but left Felipe behind with Francisco and Greek. When he came back, he had his brothers with him: Gonzalo, who was Felipe's age; Juan, who was actually pleasant; and Hernando, who was terrifying. Like Francisco Pizarro, he did not seem to care about other people, but unlike Francisco Pizarro, who was willing to be pleasant to get his way, Hernando was always overbearing and haughty. If King Carlos ever met Hernando, he would probably kill them all for his insolence. Gonzalo taught Martin to ride the Spanish horses, and, though Martin was clearly pleased, he was always reserved and watchful around him. When Felipe could not stay away from them, he was very quiet and polite.

King Carlos stayed away in other lands, and Mad Queen Juana—Felipe could not imagine anyone but a Spaniard calling their ruler that—signed the papers Francisco Pizarro needed at the end of July. Still they did not leave. Instead, Francisco Pizarro went back to Trujillo with his brothers and Martin to find more people to help them conquer the Four Quarters.

Greek went to buy artillery. Felipe had figured out that artillery was supposed to kill people, and, for the first time, he got to see how it actually worked.

Greek let him fire an arquebus. The arquebus was almost too heavy for him to hold by himself. When Greek propped the muzzle up with a forked stick, it took Felipe a long time to figure out how to light the cord, and then to find the touchhole, where the cord would light the powder. Then, when he finally got everything right, the arquebus knocked him over, and the loud sound right next to his face made his ears hurt. Greek laughed when he said he did not want to try any of the other weapons. "A little noise is not any problem," he said, "and, here, I can show you how to stand so the arquebus will not knock you down."

Felipe just shook his head. Maybe the arquebus had scared him too much. Maybe he could all too easily imagine his friends or relatives in place of the target. When Greek had said everything he could imagine to make Felipe change his mind, he threw up his hands and shook his head. "You should not ask so many questions if you do not want to know the answers."

Felipe apologized, and Greek took him to look at the hole his shot had made. It was a nice round hole that went all the way through the board holding up the target. Greek said, "Well, it is not too bad for a first shot. Remember, if there is a whole army coming at you, you can always hit somebody."

Felipe bit his lip and tried not to cry. He was sure his shot would have killed anybody it hit.

Greek did not stay upset very long. He was always happy around his beloved artillery. He did not buy an arquebus, though. He bought a cannon. "An arquebus," he said, "makes a hole in one man. A cannon makes a hole in the army." He hit Felipe on the shoulder. "You will see."

After he bought his cannon, he took Felipe to see a tower with sails atop. The sails turned in the wind, and there were many wheels inside that all fit cunningly together so the wind could grind grain. "You can even saw logs with the right mechanism," said Greek, "or whatever else you want to do."

Greek laughed at how excited Felipe got about the windmill, but he also shook his head. "It will not do you any good to know about these windmills unless you also know about fighting."

Felipe did not contradict him, but he did not agree either.

The air began to get cold again, and Felipe realized that, in Spain, this happened every single year. It also rained more in the cold season so that the cold soaked into one's clothes, and, even inside, the air was chill and uncomfortable. It was enough to make anyone mad. Perhaps Mad Queen Juana was the most sensible person in Spain after all.

When Francisco Pizarro came back to Toledo, he had about a hundred men with him. They were not all soldiers. Some of them were shoemakers or clothes makers or those who took care of horses or who took what one person made and passed it on to someone else. Seeing them, so few and so often unsoldierly, Felipe began to be less frightened for the Four Quarters. The king also sent men: men to handle the *dinero,* fathers and brothers of the waka who would make sure they all worshiped the ancestor properly, and more soldiers. Soon they had enough to fill a large ship, and Francisco Pizarro looked no more.

Felipe packed their possessions and began to talk to Little Francisco about leaving the inn and going back to Seville and then home, but Francisco just shook his head and said, "Francisco Pizarro will not take me with him. I am too weak."

"We will be taking carts for everyone's belongings to Seville," said Hummingbird.

Tears filled Little Francisco's eyes. "That is all I am, cart baggage. If I do not die in the cart or on the water, Francisco Pizarro will have to carry me through the jungle. He will not do that."

"You can become strong again," said Felipe, but he was not sure he could. Something was clearly broken in Little Francisco's heart, and Felipe did not think he could be cured as long as he stayed among the Spanish. "I will walk with you on the deck of the ship. We will have months on the water for you to recover."

"I will not be on the ship," said Francisco. "I do not know how . . ."

When Felipe brought him food that evening, Francisco did not eat it.

The next morning, the day before they were to leave, Francisco's forehead was very hot, and he turned his head away when Felipe tried to give him food. When Felipe, having done everything he could think of to get him to eat, turned to go, Francisco grabbed his arm. Felipe turned back, and Francisco whispered fiercely, "You have to get home. You have to warn everybody. Promise me you'll tell them."

Felipe wanted to ask what to tell them, but that was stupid. He already knew. He didn't want to know. "I will tell them," he said, and, saying that, he realized he had admitted Little Francisco was going to die. He had not even thought of saying, "You tell them." All that day, whenever he had time, he went to Little Francisco, and once he got him to drink a little water. In the morning, Francisco Pizarro kept Felipe doing things until they had to leave. Felipe was out on the cart with all their things, and they were starting to move, and he had not yet even been to see Francisco, did not even know if he were alive or dead. He put his head down and did not say anything.

He did not feel like saying much of anything all the way down to the ship and out onto the Atlantic Ocean. Sometimes he thought it would be better if he died like everyone else, but, if he died, there would be only Martin, and Martin would say whatever the Spanish wanted him to. When he thought of Martin, Felipe wondered how many *indios* Francisco Pizarro thought he needed. If he only needed one, would he chose to keep Martin or Felipe? When Felipe thought like that, he resolved not to be the one who died.

But what Little Francisco had wanted was not enough. By the time Felipe reached the empire, the Incas would already know the Spanish army was coming. Most likely, he would be with it. If he were to have a reason for living, somehow he would have to stop the Spanish before they reached the Four Quarters.

12

FIRST AND SECOND YEARS OF
EXEMPLARY ROYAL HAPPINESS'S REIGN
MAJESTIC PURIFICATION THROUGH HARVEST SONG MONTH

In actual history, some chroniclers say that, when Young Majesty's body reached Navel, Cable was furious because Exemplary Fortune himself had not come south. They say he killed all those in Young Majesty's escort who might be sympathetic to his half brother.

Young Majesty was not quieted by any ceremony Potato Flower tried. When Exemplary Fortune was overbusy, his father, perhaps respecting the press of his duties, did not visit him more than once every few days. When he had time to do more than move from crisis to crisis, as work settled into routine—settling disputes, administering rules, and consulting with architects and tribal and village leaders such as those were—his father began to visit him nearly every night with oracles of disaster. Exemplary Fortune's dreams were full of blood and words of ruin that he could not quite make sense of. Potato Flower's auguries told of a prosperous future for the province and an ambiguous future for both the empire and Exemplary Fortune, but they did not provide any clue as to how Exemplary Fortune could appease his waka father.

"Since his body and brother-figure are both in Navel, he should be there," said Potato Flower. "I do not know why he is here with you, and he will not talk to me. If you are to mollify Young Majesty, you must go to Navel, where his body is, and have the speakers there talk with him on your behalf."

Which did not help at all.

That was a major worry, but there were petty irritations as well. Sleeping and eating in Great Completion's tampu rather than a home filled with kin was beginning to wear on him. The tampu-keepers, though kindly, were not and never would be part of his lineage nor he of theirs. As the province's emergencies and tensions resolved themselves, Exemplary Fortune realized he was lonely. His brothers and others of the Incas might want to kill him, but at least they shared a common background that made communication easier and more satisfying. He understood their motives without any briefings or explanations.

Sharing his living quarters with Tamed Ocelot also grated, especially since Tamed Ocelot seemed to be thriving, glowing with his superiority in arms to Black Hawk and his men and their ac-knowledgement of it. "Today," he would say, "I beat four of them, and they all asked me for lessons." Or he would say, "The three women who watched fighting practice yesterday watched again to-day, and one of them smiled at me with her eyes." Even if Tamed Ocelot were intransigent, it would not have helped to snap at him. Moreover, since, as Tamed Ocelot talked, he gave Exemplary Fortune insights into the way the Spanish thought and functioned, Exemplary Fortune had to encourage his boastful monologues. He should go to fighting practice to learn still more, but he could not force himself to spend more time with Tamed Ocelot than neces-sary. If his father was the center of his nighttime misery, Tamed Ocelot was the focus of the unhappiness of his days.

Chalomongo hinted that she would be happy to have Exem-plary Fortune marry Ganichalo, a granddaughter of hers who had been married less than a year when she was widowed in the epi-demic, but, with Tamed Ocelot as his charge, he could not marry. He did not know what he would do when the pass reopened and his family, if any of his family had survived, rejoined him. He had bad dreams about the wives and children he had left behind in Kitu Dove, but he did not feel them reaching for him. Those dreams were merely his worries become manifest. And he did worry. He worried, and he played with Beautiful Orchid's twin five-year-old daughters and the other children of Great Completion when he could. He also found himself sometimes staring at women, any woman, with unseemly intensity.

His situation was not that much different from many people in the province, in the Four Quarters, cut off by unexpected death from their family and friends, haunted by a loved one who was restless with untimely death. But their common position did not seem to make him more sympathetic toward others. Instead, he grew increasingly irritable, unable to stop himself from spreading his pain to others.

After the second time he had to apologize in one day for angry words, Beautiful Orchid said sympathetically, "It is a long wait until spring, and you can travel to Navel to appease your father."

"I cannot go to Navel," said Exemplary Fortune shortly.

Beautiful Orchid did not say anything further. The next day, though, when Black Hawk walked into the office during a midday break in fighting practice, Beautiful Orchid asked when Exemplary Fortune planned to take his first tour of the province.

"I can't leave Tamed Ocelot," he said, and he could hear the irritation in his voice. Beautiful Orchid already knew that.

Beautiful Orchid and Black Hawk exchanged a look, and Black Hawk said, "We can handle him."

Exemplary Fortune opened his mouth for a nasty reply, and then, without saying anything, shut it again. He trusted his subordinates with the welfare of the people of Completion. Why couldn't he trust them in this? He was becoming accustomed to misery, even starting to expect it, which was stupid. He asked, "Do you have enough men to watch him at night?"

"We'll take care of it," said Black Hawk in a voice that was almost too cheerful. Exemplary Fortune was nearly certain he had not thought about that part of the problem until that moment.

"Very well. Beautiful Orchid, if I am going to efficiently govern this province while traveling, I will need you with me, so we'll need an extra litter." As he talked, Exemplary Fortune could feel his mood begin to lighten. "How long will it take to get ready?"

"I can have everything ready for a tour of the northwest sector of the province by morning," replied Beautiful Orchid. His tone had none of Black Hawk's false bravado. He had thought everything out ahead of time, and, if his voice contained barely suppressed glee that the governor was taking him along, that was only just.

"Don't forget arrangements for one of your wives; I cannot provide someone for women to talk with about their concerns." Exemplary Fortune regarded Beautiful Orchid and found himself smiling. "If you can, bring the twins. Children provide a point of mutual interest, and I have none with me at the moment."

Beautiful Orchid's face lit with the grin he'd been trying to suppress. "They'll love it."

Exemplary Fortune looked back at Black Hawk, who was beginning to look a bit pensive, and said, "I believe you and I should go to the practice field."

Tamed Ocelot did not seem at all dismayed by Exemplary Fortune's imminent departure. On the contrary, he nodded and said, "You have been surly lately."

Exemplary Fortune swallowed his irritation. Probably he should be delighted that Tamed Ocelot even noticed. Expecting him to sympathize was beyond reason. "Yes, I have."

Exemplary Fortune stayed most of the afternoon to watch the practice. It was fiercer and more determined than any turn-worker practices he remembered, and a number of the moves were strange. Instead of studying the best way to strike their opponent's head, the fighters often tried for body blows. That might work on a practice field but did not seem likely to disable an enemy in battle. Still, when Exemplary Fortune went out onto the field and then convinced his opponents to fight him as aggressively as anyone else, he was constantly defeated, more because of the new moves than because he was out of practice, though the latter was true, too.

Because the new moves had to be those of Tamed Ocelot, who was the only one who could teach Spanish tactics, and because Black Hawk had accepted them, Exemplary Fortune did not express his misgivings. Instead, he praised the men's skills and suggested a match against the men at either Narrows or Eagle View fort. When he translated the suggestion for Tamed Ocelot's benefit, Tamed Ocelot said, "In another six months, I will teach them to defeat both armies at once."

Black Hawk said, "We will, too. Whatever his other skills, Tamed Ocelot is an excellent fighter. When he first suggested these moves, I did not believe they would work. We are all learning Spanish to communicate with him. If the other warriors where he comes from are anywhere near as good as he is, any army of theirs could easily defeat any Inca army of twice its size."

Exemplary Fortune carried those words away with him to ponder on the tour, but there was not much time to think quietly. The governor's entourage included architects, agronomists, road designers, bearers, messengers, and various courtiers. Since the tampus were rudimentary, the group also had to carry most of their supplies. With that crowd, the minimal footpaths made even the stately village-to-village daily advance a trek. Sometimes Exemplary Fortune got down from his litter to walk, but, while an hour walk in the morning helped focus his heart, it was nearly impossible to concentrate on the duties of government while walking for extended periods.

The core of the tour was a visit to each village to talk with the people about their problems and hopes. Because each village and clan were bound to a tree, Exemplary Fortune had assumed that the villages had fixed locations, but it was not so. Instead, people would farm a clearing for a few years, and then, as yields fell, move on to a new clearing, sometimes in a circle around their chosen tree, sometimes to another tree they had chosen previously, sometimes choosing a new tree at each site while releasing the previous tree from its duties to them.

To make the villages permanent, the Four Quarters would have to find an easily accessible source of fertilizer. Since llamas did not thrive in the woods, they would have to find new guano islands or sources of seaweed or fish heads. The expedition spent several days camped in the hills along the shores of the Great Lake while the architects discussed the possibilities of settlement, but in many places, the land fell from high cliffs straight into the water, an excellent defense, perhaps, against the Spanish, but hardly suitable for a waterside village. The architects made their recommendations, which involved moving masses of earth and stone that would require thousands of men and decades of labor. Exemplary Fortune would send their recommendations to Navel, but he did not hope Cable would seriously listen to them.

Personally and politically, the tour was a success. Exemplary Fortune thoroughly enjoyed talking to the villagers, eating local foods, learning local dances and stories, gradually developing the shape of the province's life in his heart. And the people seemed pleased with him, even if quietly amused by his Inca mannerisms.

He found himself dreading his return to the capital for the ritual plowing ceremony of Queen's Festival, dealing with Tamed Ocelot, becoming the somewhat dour individual he had been before starting the tour. But, when he returned to Great Completion, Tamed Ocelot met him at the tampu to say he was not living there anymore.

"I'm staying with a woman named Oca at her parents' place. It's better than living at this inn," he explained. "Black Hawk set it up. She belongs to his tribe. She had two other men who died, and all the other men were afraid to marry her. Black Hawk made pictures to explain that, if I work for her family until next harvest, I can leave if I want to."

"Service for a year," said Exemplary Fortune, amused that Tamed Ocelot should be justifying himself. His explanation of why Oca was single sounded a little odd, though. Probably he had misunderstood Black Hawk's words. Still, if the explanation made him happy with his new home, Exemplary Fortune would ask no questions.

Tamed Ocelot frowned. "You didn't tell me about this service-thing."

"No, I didn't. I apologize, but day-to-day living includes so many actions, it is hard to know which might be strange to you and which automatically understood."

"She is strange," Tamed Ocelot muttered thoughtfully.

"How so?" asked Exemplary Fortune, hoping Tamed Ocelot would deign to answer the question since he had brought the matter up.

Tamed Ocelot regarded Exemplary Fortune. "Perhaps such things do not matter here."

Exemplary Fortune shrugged. "It is hard to know."

But that was all Tamed Ocelot would say.

Exemplary Fortune walked back to the governor's compound in a thoughtful mood, wondering if he should go directly to Two-tree or if he should find out first whether Chalomongo was still interested in him as a relative by marriage. His question was more than adequately answered when he was met inside the entrance to the governor's compound by Ganichalo herself. She smiled at him and said, "Beautiful Orchid and my grandmother think you'll want to marry me now."

He smiled back and said, "I was just going to talk to Chalomongo about that very thing. I wanted to be sure you were still interested."

"I am," she said simply.

At their words, waiting staff, led by Black Hawk, headed for the tampu. Ganichalo led Exemplary Fortune to the long-empty governor's quarters inside the compound. As they walked inside, Black Hawk and his fellows returned, carrying Exemplary Fortune's clothes and other accumulated possessions. Ganichalo's belongings were already in a neat pile near the doorway, but she had diffidently not yet put them in niches. He smiled at this hesitation. She and her grandmother had already involved enough of the people of Completion in the proposed union that it was a foregone conclusion. The others left, and together the two of them arranged their belongings in the wall niches. It gave each of them a chance to watch how the other moved. He was well pleased, and she seemed to be also. She made them dinner, a tasty collection of local dishes. "I asked the chief Mother if she could teach me how to make any Inca dishes, but she said it would take practice."

Exemplary Fortune grinned. "And, in any case, I have likely forgotten how Inca food tastes. Pichunche food tastes homelike to me now."

She smiled back and did not contradict him.

The night was pleasant with sex and talk, mainly of families, her sisters and grandmother and dead husband, his wives and children and dead father.

"Everybody thinks it strange that the Incas have more than one wife," she said, "but, since I have five sisters, I'm used to living with other women, and I don't think I'll have any problems." Her name, she told him, translated as Red Deer.

Morning came much too early, which was an excellent sign.

Together, they took a tour of the southeast part of the province. She constantly gave him new understanding into the way the Pichunche thought, so the villagers he stayed with this time had to make fewer allowances for Inca ignorance of their ways. And yet, Red Deer did not, as he had worried she might, interrupt when he asked villagers for information she certainly already knew. They visited the Pollen-worked gold mines, and she was genuinely delighted to become acquainted with another people's culture. Chalomongo had chosen well.

Water Festival came and corn-planting season; and, as the first sprouts dotted the fields with green, the pass reopened. The first person to bring the news to Great Completion was a messenger bearing word from Anaconda that an inspector from the Unique Inca was on his way to the capital along with at least some of Exemplary Fortune's family. Anaconda had sent the message without a quipu to indicate numbers. Most likely a runner from Riverhead had arrived at the fort with only that basic information.

For Anaconda, it would be the Unique Inca's inspector who would be the main news and Exemplary Fortune's family an adjunct. Perhaps the same should be true for Exemplary Fortune. The inspection could be a normal check to see how the new governor was doing, or it could be that Exemplary Royal Happiness had decided he had been overhasty in letting Exemplary Fortune go and was looking for some malfeasance to justify bringing his brother back to Navel for execution. In any case, there was nothing he could do about Cable's actions. Instead, he found himself worrying anew about his family. In his reawakened apprehension for his family, he had little anxiety to spare for what the current Unique Inca might be plotting; not a healthy attitude for talking with an inspector.

But the Inca's inspector did not seem anxious to visit him. Three days after the message came from Anaconda, nine of the fifteen wives he had left in Kitu Dove and seven children came over the wooden bridge into the city. Exemplary Fortune hugged them all and then carried Chatterer, the only child who seemed to remember him well, to the governor's compound. "I was sick too," Chatterer informed him gravely, "but I got better. Leafy and baby died instead. Baby never got a name. Grandmother's taking care of them because we had to leave."

Exemplary Fortune hugged him tighter and didn't say anything. Red Deer met them all at the doorway of the governor's quarters and welcomed them in. She and Skein Reckoner exchanged hugs, and soon seven of his wives were talking eagerly with her, asking questions about the province, its living conditions and people. Grasshopper gathered the children around her, giving them the time and security they needed to adjust to yet another strange place. That left Esteemed Egg and Exemplary Fortune to talk about their eleven months apart. They sat down together on a rug, but for a time they didn't say anything, looking at each other and touching each other's hands and hair gently.

Esteemed Egg said, "It seemed as though as soon as you left, everybody started dying. Coca Neighbor got sick first, but the baby was the first one in our family to die, and then Leafy got sick and Chatterer and Young Majesty and some of our neighbors. Sometimes it seemed as though everyone was dying, almost as though it was wrong not to."

She was crying, and Exemplary Fortune pulled her close and wiped a tear from her cheek with his hand. "Qantu Flower died in the tampu just south of Lynx Lake. The women there said they would care for her. I have seen her in dream, and I think she's satisfied with where she is now. I was on the Majestic Road the whole time. When we stopped in villages, we would hear of the sickness, but until she died it never became real to me. I missed you; I missed you all."

"We missed you. We worried about you, and then when Bright Rainbow died too . . ."

So long ago. "It's been a long road, but this province makes a pleasant home. We can be happy here."

She nodded, still crying, and he hugged her to him. He held her for a long time, listening to his other wives talking, getting to know each other, watching the younger children solemnly watching him, trying to decide if he really was one of them or not. Remembering his wives and children who had died so long ago.

Two days later, Anaconda, somewhat out of breath, appeared in person at the governor's compound. When they had exchanged greetings and drunk a ritual swallow of beer, Anaconda said, "I've been talking to the inspector for three days. He is Majestic Quinoa of the Loom lineage." He stopped, waiting to see if the name meant anything to Exemplary Fortune.

The name was indeed familiar. When Exemplary Fortune had been in school, Majestic Quinoa had come in to discuss government, but he had talked mainly about communication by messenger and by fire, which hardly applied in the current situation. He had been involved in government so long that Young Majesty had deferred to him as an elder. However, he also belonged to the same lineage as Magnanimous Strength, and that, for Cable, had probably been the determining factor in his selection. "I have met a relative," said Exemplary Fortune blandly.

"I answered all his questions as I normally would," said Anaconda, "but, when I praised you, he was impatient; and, if there was any implied criticism of you in my words, he sought it out and asked for more."

"I am not totally surprised," said Exemplary Fortune. "My younger brother in Navel and I have never gotten along well, and I would expect him to be severe."

"But fair?" asked Anaconda.

Exemplary Fortune shrugged, smiling a little.

"Indeed," said Anaconda in enlightenment. "When you first arrived, I thought that, for your lineage, you were a long way from Navel."

"I was glad to come here," said Exemplary Fortune.

"Good," said Anaconda; then, "Is there anything we can do to help your case?"

A supportive and reasonable question, but one Exemplary Fortune had no answer for. "I must talk with the inspector myself. Until then, I have no idea what will or will not help." All very true, but Exemplary Fortune could feel himself tense as he spoke. Since his wives had reached him, he had stopped thinking about Majestic Quinoa or his plans. Anaconda had stirred up suppressed feelings from the bottom of his heart. Useless ambition, useless bitterness, useless anger. He had done well by Completion. He could do no more.

Anaconda eyed him a few heartbeats, then took another swallow of beer and said in a lighter tone, "I have also been hearing rumors of interesting plans afoot here in Great Completion."

"Plans?" asked Exemplary Fortune.

"I have heard that Black Hawk intends to test his turn-warriors against those at both Narrows and Eagle View forts."

Ah. "True enough. I have approved the contest, but it will not happen until after harvest."

"But, if Black Hawk has time to get ready, then so should those of us who are forts' captains. Shrine Tree and I have little way to coordinate our efforts."

"All very true."

"So I would like permission to send messages back and forth between the forts without any possibility of Black Hawk intercepting them."

Exemplary Fortune raised an eyebrow. Competition was not necessarily a bad thing, but this sounded as though it might be too serious. On the other hand, he had not heard of any conflict between Black Hawk and the others. He turned to Beautiful Orchid. "Will you sanction this, ah, intraprovince privacy?"

"I certainly will," said Beautiful Orchid looking amused.

"So then, I will count on you to see that no messages leak." Exemplary Fortune turned back to Anaconda. "You may reckon it accomplished."

Anaconda stayed the night and returned home the next day.

Majestic Quinoa, the Inca inspector, was much more languid. He spent much of Corpse Procession thoroughly inspecting the northern half of the province. Then, instead of coming to pay a call on the governor as a minimal politeness, he took the mountainous back trails through the mining areas along the eastern border. Using those trails, he could both inspect the mines and avoid visiting the governor before he traveled south to investigate the rest of the province.

Exemplary Fortune began to wonder bitterly if the inspector would bother to visit Great Completion at all before going back to Navel to give his report. Perhaps the governor would have to camp out in the middle of the pass to learn what the inspector was thinking—not that he had much doubt. Word about the inspector's progress trickled into the capital along with complaints that he tried to twist people's words to make Exemplary Fortune sound either stupid or corrupt. The complaints diminished as the inspector's travels continued, but Exemplary Fortune did not know if that meant Majestic Quinoa was starting to disparage him less, or if he were less popular in the south.

Exemplary Fortune's family, wives and children together, kept him almost calm, but they were, in their diminished numbers, a reminder that he was not immune from disaster. He introduced them to the Inca families and to Black Hawk and his family, who would acquaint them with the Tens. Red Deer introduced them to the Pichunches who lived in the capital. Skein Reckoner and Red Deer together became almost immediately a focus for the community life of the village, while Grasshopper quietly made a safe place for the children, for the whole family. It was good to see them settling in so well.

He hoped they would not be uprooted again to go to Navel to watch him die. He served Completion to the best of his ability; but, if Majestic Quinoa were determined to find fault, that would not matter. The chaos of the Pichunche social structure was still in place. He had not even started to try to rectify it, and, for someone who wanted to find him guilty of a capital crime, that would be enough.

He took out his tensions in fighting practice and earned a grudging respect from Tamed Ocelot, who said, "You learn faster than most of the stupid *indios*."

Majestic Quinoa finally came to Great Completion on the first day of Majestic Festival. Though it was annoying he had chosen such a momentous day to arrive, Exemplary Fortune decided that, all in all, he was relieved his ceremonial duties kept him busy enough that he did not have much time to worry about the Unique Inca's inspector. During the four days of the ceremony, Majestic Quinoa did not in any way try to push himself to the forefront. He looked as wiry and vigorous as he had when he had visited the school, though his hair had turned gray. He must be at least seventy-five, if not considerably older.

The day after the ceremonies ended, Majestic Quinoa lined up the unmarried men and women of Great Completion to make official the marriages that had been arranged since the last time an inspector had been through. With the epidemic, there were many more widowers and widows than usual, so the line was long. Majestic Quinoa very properly asked Exemplary Fortune about those who did not line up with a chosen partner, and Exemplary Fortune made the recommendations Beautiful Orchid and he had discussed. No one complained, not even the two leftover women.

After finalizing the marriages, Majestic Quinoa accepted Exemplary Fortune's invitation into the governor's compound. He stopped briefly at the small tree beside the doorway to the main audience room. Touching a leaf gently with one finger, he asked, "What is this?"

"A local custom," said Exemplary Fortune. "Every community has a tree as a kind of local waka." He was glad Majestic Quinoa had started his questions with this subject and in this place. It was a calming nonconfrontational situation that allowed Exemplary Fortune to subdue his anxieties and answer forthrightly.

"How long has this tree been here?" Majestic Quinoa asked. From his tone, it was impossible to tell if he were truly seeking information or not.

"Nine months," said Exemplary Fortune. "I helped plant it myself just after I arrived."

When they had settled themselves inside, Majestic Quinoa asked, "How would you describe the situation in Completion when you arrived?"

"It was a disorderly mess," said Exemplary Fortune frankly and told the exact circumstances.

"And yet you kept Black Hawk on," Majestic Quinoa said when Exemplary Fortune finished. It was a teacher's comment, which made Exemplary Fortune's response easy. Majestic Quinoa asked a few more questions, and again Exemplary Fortune had easy answers. "How would you judge the situation now?" Majestic Quinoa asked then.

"Better. There is still a fair amount of tension but much less than there was. The Pichunche's social structure still needs to be regularized, but I have deferred working on that until the tension is gone."

"How would you rate the province as a power base?"

This was not a teacherly question, and Exemplary Fortune gave it a nonstudently answer. "As a power base, it's utterly stinking. Its virtues lie in other directions."

"Such as?"

"People, gold, trees."

"Trees?" asked Majestic Quinoa. He sounded honestly interested.

"I'm not sure yet how. I keep seeing the trees as a timber crop, but I'm not sure that's where their true virtue lies. There is a honey palm that produces, from each tree, as much honey as tens of thousands of bees. Many of the trees have medicinal properties. The leaves of the boldo tree are used to make a refreshing hot drink. The Pichunche treat trees as people or earth or stone. I am treating the whole subject as a research project."

"And the problems?"

By now Exemplary Fortune was calm enough that he answered this one honestly, too, though the answer was not one Cable would want to hear. "Mainly I worry that we may fail them. Aside from minimal tampus, there are no storage facilities anywhere this side

of the mountains and south of the Fortunate Soul Desert. The province could probably deal with a slowly developing disaster; but, if,
say, a hailstorm hit the crops just before harvest in a year with early
mountain snow like last year, then, if we allow eight days to get
the message to Navel across the Fortunate Soul Desert, how long
will it take to get relief? A month and a half, two months, three?
We might, just might, have enough food to last that long if we
ration it carefully, but at the very least the delay would arouse
uncertainties as to whether we Incas can keep our promises. In a
province where those doubts have already been raised, I can very
easily forehear panic, riots, hording, and starvation."

He had surprised Majestic Quinoa; Exemplary Fortune could
see that in his eyes, but all the inspector said was, "So do you think
we should build storehouses here?"

Exemplary Fortune shook his head. "Here, perhaps Commanding Blue, I don't know. That is a policy decision I don't have
enough information to make. Anywhere within a tenday of resupply." This was the right answer, and it came glibly into his mouth,
but a part of his heart protested that this was the area most at risk
and therefore the proper location. But he could not allow himself
any answers that sounded at all assertive.

Majestic Quinoa nodded. "I expected you to be clever, but
denying that your province is automatically the right place to put
official storage facilities is not the statement of an ambitious man."

Exemplary Fortune shrugged, keeping his manner light with
little effort. His chosen role in this interview, in his life here, had
become natural. "There are at least a few people in Navel who do
not like me very much. My recommendation might well mean the
death of an otherwise good idea."

"Then do you want me to say the storage facilities were my
idea?" There was a note of maybe banter, maybe testing, in Majestic
Quinoa's voice.

"Yes, that should help," said Exemplary Fortune. He could feel
the anguished wail of some ambition deep in his heart, but he
ignored it. Those ambitions were no longer relevant to his life.

"I will do that then." Majestic Quinoa took his first swallow
of beer. "The people here like you, and I have come to believe that

you care about them. I will give you a favorable recommendation in Navel. There shouldn't be another inspector through for several years. As long as you stay on this side of the mountains and the desert, I think you will be secure."

Which meant that, though Majestic Quinoa had been sent to make a case against him, the Unique Inca had sent an honest man. For the rest of the time Majestic Quinoa stayed in Great Completion, to check Beautiful Orchid's records and talk with Black Hawk, they discussed many topics. Majestic Quinoa said Highest Strength had recommended a harbor town along the coast, a project that had been indefinitely postponed.

Exemplary Fortune took Majestic Quinoa to a fighting practice, which left the inspector uneasy with Tamed Ocelot's skill and predatory mannerisms, most definitely the proper attitude. The bearded strangers, though, had not been heard of since their visit to Recognition. Majestic Quinoa said that the Unique Inca and his court no longer believed the strangers were seriously interested in the Four Quarters. "I will tell them about Tamed Ocelot's skill in group fighting," said Majestic Quinoa, "but I do not believe they will care."

Exemplary Fortune frowned at that. It was no more than he had expected, but he had to try again. "It is not just his fighting skill," he said. "He is also doggedly determined and generally pugnacious. I cannot believe his people would abandon a project even if they met massive resistance, and we were friendly. We do not know how far away they are, or how long it will take them to assemble the men, boats, and supplies they would need for a full-scale invasion. In fact, the longer before they come back, the more likely it seems that they will return with an invasion force."

"Your arguments have merit," said Majestic Quinoa neutrally.

One last try. "My father has been trying to contact me in dream about something that troubles him deeply having to do with blood and destruction. I know everyone in Navel must be consulting him, and I believe you would have told me if he were spreading oracles of disaster. I do not know why he would talk to me rather than someone closer to his body or trained in interpreting the words of the dead. I would like one of the speakers in Navel to ask him directly about his worries for the future, maybe even to use my name if that is the only way he will respond. He is troubled about something, and it worries me."

"You do not believe this could be your own worries made manifest?"

"I have had other bad dreams," said Exemplary Fortune wryly. "This is not the same."

"I will do what I can," said Majestic Quinoa. "You are aware, however, that any request I make in your name will lessen my credibility in other areas."

"I am aware of that," said Exemplary Fortune. "He is my father."

"I will relay the message. The Divine Speaker will listen to me."

"Thank you," said Exemplary Fortune. He was not certain his father's messages concerned the Spanish, but there was nothing else he could do to warn the empire.

They talked about other things: a new variety of oxalis flower the plant breeders had developed; Exemplary Fortune's half brothers, the princes of the realm, Reckoning Sadness, Whence Reckoning, Beseeching Cotton, Beautiful Plowridge, and all the rest; Owl Pattern and Exemplary Fortune's youngest full siblings, who were living in Tampu on the Spiderplain River, all but Riverfork, who had died in the epidemic. Too many dead, too many pieces of his life, of the Four Quarters, gone.

When Exemplary Fortune asked what Shrewdness was doing, Majestic Quinoa smiled diplomatically and said, "I have not heard anything about him for a long time."

Which meant that, however friendly Majestic Quinoa was willing to be, there were still some things he would not talk about. By implication, Commander Thorniest and Exemplary Fortune's other northern friends were among them. Asking about Flowerbud would doubtless be just as fruitless. With an inward sigh, Exemplary Fortune asked about Ginez instead.

"Partridge," Majestic Quinoa corrected with another smile. "He is doing well. He lives in Clayhearth in Copper and is a member of the full-time army, a ten-captain, I believe. He stands out when you first see him, but after that he is very good at fading into the background."

That sounded like Ginez. He would not enjoy being the center of attention. Exemplary Fortune wondered briefly what woman had been chosen for him. He would need someone gentle and quiet.

For Exemplary Fortune the strangest part of their discussions was his own attitude toward Majestic Quinoa's acceptance of him. It was a bittersweet melancholy. He had thought he was reconciled to being the governor of an out-of-the-way province for the rest of his life, but evidently some part of his heart still held greater ambitions. Majestic Quinoa's confirmation that he really was unwelcome in the capital hurt.

And then Majestic Quinoa was gone, leaving Exemplary Fortune only with an awareness of his own restlessness, an ambiguous gift at best. He focused that restlessness into fighting practice, which left him always tired and bruised. Sometimes, when he fought Tamed Ocelot, the Spaniard's eyes held a look that said he was fully aware he could kill Exemplary Fortune anytime he wanted, and that it would not take very much for him to decide to deliver the fatal blow. With that constant threat, Exemplary Fortune decided it was not at all surprising that Great Completion's turn-workers were becoming excellent warriors.

Tamed Ocelot had his own reason for restlessness. Every day he tried to teach the men to fight in formation like a dance, but, with the crops constantly needing care, only about a quarter of his pupils would show up for any given practice, ruining whatever pattern building he had established the previous day. Also, no one understood the reason for the dance fighting, which made them slow learners. Finally one day, when Tamed Ocelot had been yelling at them in a Spanish so furious even Exemplary Fortune couldn't understand it, Exemplary Fortune asked him what the smallest group his formation would work with was.

"If I had ten unholy real warriors, I could conquer your whole shitty empire," Tamed Ocelot snarled back.

"Very well," said Exemplary Fortune, "I will find ten men who can come to practice two hours every day. We will learn your fighting method."

"You are too stupid," said Tamed Ocelot, but he wasn't yelling anymore, which meant he accepted the plan.

The ten included Black Hawk and Exemplary Fortune himself, which meant he could not go out on any provincial progresses until after harvest, but the farming season was not the proper time to travel anyway. It took not quite a month for the ten of them to get a feel for how two men next to each other could protect each other in battle and to understand how their weapons could work together. It took longer than that to actually make the line work, particularly since the weapons they used were not those Tamed Ocelot was used to; but, long before harvest, the ten of them could take on thirty or forty turn-warriors and consistently beat them. By harvest, they were much less successful because the others were starting to use the same tactics.

Exemplary Fortune was beginning to get a real feel for how the new fighting method worked. Like Black Hawk, he was also beginning to be fundamentally frightened. They were the only two serious fighters in the whole of the Four Quarters who even knew these tactics existed, and Exemplary Fortune could not think of any way he could convince those in power about the kind of threat that might be facing them. He feared that to tell Navel he had better fighters than theirs, no matter how he phrased it, would invite only his death and a large army coming into the province to destroy it. And yet he was doing what both his father and Cable had told him to do, learning about the Spanish and their capabilities.

The harvest was good, for which Exemplary Fortune received more credit than he had earned. Potato Flower was the speaker who convinced the gods to bless them with good weather, but Potato Flower did not meet as many people as closely as the governor did. Exemplary Fortune was basking in people's approval on the last day of Harvest Song's festival when Tamed Ocelot came storming up toward him so vehemently that the governor's guards pounced on him. With some difficulty six of them wrestled him facedown onto the ground. Exemplary Fortune relinquished his seat of honor to Beautiful Orchid. He knelt down next to Tamed Ocelot, who was still trying to throw off the guards, and asked him sympa-thetically, "What is the problem?"

"That cursed . . ." Tamed Ocelot stopped struggling to get his breath back. With two guards' full weight on him, it took a while. "She says everything is hers."

The guards had not relaxed their holds, and Tamed Ocelot's muscles had not relaxed either, as though he were waiting his next opportunity to throw them off.

"Every what thing?" Exemplary Fortune asked.

"I should have hit her," said Tamed Ocelot. "Black Hawk said she would not agree to be my wife if I hit her."

She would if she were Spanish? Exemplary Fortune wondered. However, that did not seem to be the current issue. "The things that she brings into the marriage are hers. The things she makes and that are not for the empire or the Sun are hers."

"That's what she said." Tamed Ocelot sagged onto the ground, and Exemplary Fortune signaled the guards to release him. Cau-tiously, they did so. Tamed Ocelot rolled onto his back. "She said she was going to take them to her sisters."

"That is normal," said Exemplary Fortune agreeably, though, if, as Tamed Ocelot implied, she was taking all her possessions, it was not. "Relatives share."

"It is not right," said Tamed Ocelot, sitting up with enough vehemence that one of the guards made a grab for him.

Black Hawk grabbed the guard from behind and pulled him over before he could touch Tamed Ocelot's arm. The other guards cushioned his fall so it made no noise that Tamed Ocelot would hear. The guard looked up at Black Hawk in total bewilderment, and Black Hawk put a finger to his lips.

Exemplary Fortune gathered what he knew about Oca's sisters and made a pattern with it. "Babies are often weaned after the harvest festival," he said, seating himself comfortably on the ground. "At that time, a baby's relatives come to give the baby gifts of clothes and other things to welcome the child into the community. Each person cuts a lock of the child's hair. The child is given their first name by an uncle or aunt."

Tamed Ocelot stared at him. "Who chooses?" he demanded.

Exemplary Fortune was out of guesses as to what Tamed Ocelot's problem was. "Who chooses what?"

"Who comes?"

"All the relatives come. The whole clan. It is a party with feasting and singing and dancing—"

"It is not right," yelled Tamed Ocelot. His breathing was fast, and his pupils were dilated, eyes staring at nothing. His hands clenched and unclenched. He was clearly on the very edge.

But of what? "Does this have anything to do with strangeness?" Exemplary Fortune asked, tensing himself in case that were the wrong question. Black Hawk, too, was poised to grab Tamed Ocelot again.

Tamed Ocelot's eyes slowly focused in on Exemplary Fortune again. Then his gaze went up, looking over Exemplary Fortune's head and around at the gawking crowd. "There are too many people."

"Then come, let us go to my office." Exemplary Fortune held out a hand, and then stood, drawing Tamed Ocelot up with him. He made eye contact with Black Hawk, signaling the trainer to come with them. Black Hawk passed a signal to his men to stay and to keep the crowd outside before falling in behind them.

Exemplary Fortune led Tamed Ocelot to an empty room, but when he tried to get the man to sitting again, Tamed Ocelot started to breathe faster, so they remained standing. "Tell me about strangeness," said Exemplary Fortune.

Tamed Ocelot looked from him to Black Hawk standing in the doorway. "I could kill both of you."

"We know that."

"Oca is supposed to be my wife."

He paused as though waiting for an answer, and Exemplary Fortune said, "That is true."

"But she does not act like a wife," Tamed Ocelot cried out, and then went on, working himself into a rage. "She acts like a woman of the streets."

"A woman of the streets?"

Tamed Ocelot's eyes bored into his. "The women who sell themselves to every man who comes along. She does not wait for me. Sometimes when I have not shown that I am interested, she will start to act as though she is ready for sex. She knows things, does things. She is not supposed to know things like that." He was back to the fist-clenching stage.

"She likes you. A woman shows she likes her husband by showing him the various ways she knows how to have sex, to find out together the ways that they fit together most joyously."

"It is not right," said Tamed Ocelot again. It was like a litany. "What should she do?"

"She is my wife. She should do what I want, when I want and no other time. She should not . . . do things. She should let me do to her."

This was difficult. They were very close to the center of his madness, Spanish madness here. "If she does this, what is the joy—?"

"She should not enjoy it," Tamed Ocelot roared. He swung not exactly at Exemplary Fortune, but close enough that he had to lean back to avoid it.

Exemplary Fortune was very glad he did not fall.

Tamed Ocelot continued, no longer talking to Exemplary Fortune. "How can I trust her when I know she enjoys it, how can I know she is not seeking other men? How can I know?" This last was an anguished shout.

"All the women here enjoy sex," said Exemplary Fortune into his momentary silence, "especially the wives. It is fun getting to know what someone else enjoys, sharing ever-developing knowledge about each other. This having sex with strangers in the street sounds like no fun at all. I cannot imagine how anyone who'd been married would be interested in anything like that."

"All the women," Tamed Ocelot repeated sounding dazed. He turned to Black Hawk. "All the women?"

"All the women," Black Hawk repeated in Humanity's Mouth.

Tamed Ocelot seemed to understand it. He folded onto the rug like a half-empty sack. Exemplary Fortune sat down facing him. "I have been mad at her for a long time," said Tamed Ocelot. "I thought she was just making believe that she wanted to be my wife. I thought that when the year was over she would go to . . ."

He shook his head, staring at the rug. "And then tonight when she said that everything was hers, and she would take it . . ." He looked back up at Exemplary Fortune. "All the women do this?"

"All the women," Exemplary Fortune agreed.

"I have to talk to her," said Tamed Ocelot. He got up and headed rather unsteadily for the door.

Exemplary Fortune nodded at Black Hawk, who went ahead to clear the way for Tamed Ocelot. Exemplary Fortune followed more slowly, feeling drained. He wished there were some way they could get to Oca before Tamed Ocelot, to explain a little, but there was no way to do that without Tamed Ocelot finding out. And that, Exemplary Fortune judged, was about the worst thing that could happen right now. He would send Skein Reckoner over later to talk to her, much later. He walked to the entrance of the governor's compound and, with his eyes, followed Tamed Ocelot and Black Hawk's progress across the plaza. Others, too, watched with curious eyes. Exemplary Fortune could almost hear the gossip spreading behind them.

Potato Flower and Beautiful Orchid had kept the closing ceremony going, but tomorrow Exemplary Fortune would apologize to the gods. Now he walked over to the guards and said, "That was very good work, fast reflexes. I appreciate that."

"He wasn't actually going to attack you, was he?" Siskin asked tentatively.

"We will never know now," said Exemplary Fortune. "I'd just as soon keep it that way."

"But . . ." said Siskin, looking in the direction Tamed Ocelot and Black Hawk had gone. He looked back at Exemplary Fortune. "Ah, yes sir," he said.

Exemplary Fortune smiled. "It's a long story." He went back into the compound and sat down next to the tree. It didn't seem to say anything, but that was perfectly all right.

A few minutes later, Black Hawk came in and sat down next to him. "They're talking."

"Good."

"Ah, what do all women do?"

"Like sex."

"That's it?"

Exemplary Fortune nodded. "If you ever get a chance to go to Spanish land, don't take it. They all have foul hearts there."

After Skein Reckoner visited Oca a day later, she reported, "Oca is a truly stubborn woman. I think they'll be all right. Tamed Ocelot is starting to talk with her. It sounds as though he knows far more Humanity's Mouth than he admits."

13

The Spanish first reached the Isthmus of Panama in 1502. The people there had no way to resist the conquistadors, and the whole region became part of the Spanish Empire nearly as fast as the invaders could hack their way through the jungle.

On the way back to Panama, Felipe sometimes helped to sail the ship, and he enjoyed it, though he didn't really want to. He kept thinking there should be some way to foul the ropes that moved the sails so no one could control the direction they would go or how fast, but it took many men to pull the sails into place, and the ropes were so thick it would take a long time to cut through them. He did start to cut one rope, but he could only crouch down to saw at it for short periods of time. The cut was discovered before he got even a quarter of the way through. The men were upset, and the ship's captain and Francisco Pizarro asked everyone if they'd seen anybody looking suspicious by the rope. Everybody said no, but they all looked at each other warily for a time. Felipe kept his head down and did not talk much. After a while the men stopped talking about it like they had forgotten. Felipe did not try that again.

Many of the men from Trujillo became sick from the rocking of the ship on the water, and, for a while, Felipe thought maybe he could poison them; but he did not know very much about poison, and he certainly did not know enough about Spanish poisons to use any of them. Besides, he kept wanting to take care of the men who were sick rather than hurting them more. He kept volunteering to bring them food and wine and even empty the piss pots when they were too weak to get out of their hammocks.

Some of the men had brought horses aboard, and the horses were even more distressed by the way the ship moved than the Trujillans. Martin and Gonzalo and some of the other men spent all their time keeping the animals calm and making sure that their cradling slings were not hurting them. If there were not so many people around the horses all the time, it might have been possible to let one loose or kill it, but that seemed impossible too.

Since Felipe was with Francisco Pizarro so much, there should be some way he could kill the man, but Francisco Pizarro was a trained fighter, and, even if Felipe had a knife and Francisco Pizarro did not, even if Francisco Pizarro was asleep at the start, he thought it would be Felipe who died and not Francisco Pizarro. Besides, he did not want to kill him. He did not particularly like him, but that was no reason to murder him.

On the ship with only the men and the vast water all around, it was too easy to forget why all these men were traveling. When they talked about getting gold and silver and land, it sounded almost like a children's game or playacting. With the ship rolling in the waves, the men could not practice with their weapons, and many of the men were even too sick to quarrel with each other the way the Spanish usually did. All some of the men talked about was going home again. Maybe, when they reached land, when the men were actually getting their weapons together, maybe then it would be easier to know how to fight them.

This time, traveling through the islands on the way to Terra Firma did not scare him, and, when they reached the port, the stink of the town and the sight of all the cringing ragged people did not bother him. He did not turn away when the pack animals shat right in front of him. He was becoming too Spanish, too used to the horrible things they did. It was too easy each day to go along with what everyone around him expected, to get out Francisco

Pizarro's clothes and dress him, to serve him his meals, to do the other things he wanted. It had become routine now, something he knew how to do wherever they were. Home was a fading image during the day and bittersweet dreams at night. Fighting the Spanish was less than that, a void he knew nothing about.

The men were all happy to be on dry land again. It was several hours before some of them started complaining about how hot it was and how the sweat stuck to their bodies. They complained about the food and the insects and the lack of gold. Greek did not complain because he was too busy fussing with his cannon and the rest of the artillery. Francisco Pizarro did not complain because he was talking to other men in the town, trying to convince them to travel with him to Peru to scoop up the gold there. Hernando Pizarro did not complain because he was too busy swaggering around among the men, making sure he was the one who got credit for settling any disputes and lending them *dinero* for food and the other things they needed. Most of the men from Trujillo, though, looked a little lost. They all seemed surprised that none of the buildings or the plants looked like those in Spain, and, though some of them talked about leaving right away, none of them really had enough *dinero* to travel back to Spain.

It only took five days to organize everyone to start up the trail to Panama. The straggling group climbed into the jungle with fearful looks all around. Even the carpenters looked at the giant trees with suspicion. When rain started to fall, they all complained as giant drops fell off the trees and landed on them.

Felipe's heart beat faster when he thought about how much closer his home was. Sometimes he was terrified that this army was coming to ravage his homeland, but sometimes, in spite of everything, he felt glad because he was going home or even just to someplace familiar that was not Spain. At night, Felipe prayed for a jaguar or a poisonous snake to come out of the trees and kill the men while they were sleeping, but nothing happened, and soon the group reached Panama. Francisco Pizarro found places for everyone to stay, though they all had to promise to give him *dinero* for their lodging when they got their shares of Peru's gold and silver. Francisco Pizarro's brothers each took a room in his house along with men from the ship who acted as their servants.

The Massi woman watched them all and said nothing. Felipe smiled at her, but she was wary with him. Maybe she could see how living in Spain had changed him.

Francisco Pizarro sent a servant to fetch Diego Almagro to tell him about his success with King Carlos and his officials. He had the Massi woman put a cloth on the table in the dining room and set out three bottles of wine. Diego Almagro came into the house with smiling eyes. He had with him two other men who had often visited before.

"We have full authorization," said Francisco Pizarro.

Diego Almagro grinned. "Tell me about it," he said.

But as Francisco Pizarro talked, telling how the king had named him governor and captain-commander of all Peru, Diego Almagro's face darkened, and, when Francisco Pizarro said that Diego Almagro would be commander of the fort at Recognition, Diego Almagro's fist crashed down on the table between them. "You miserable cheat. Ruis and I have been working here in this goddamn miserable jungle getting money and men while you loll around the king's palace, and what do we get for our efforts? Nothing, a stupid goddamn border town. Or maybe I'm wrong. Maybe it's just me you gypped. What did you get for Ruis? cogovernorship of Peru? or maybe just the right to steer a ship?" He stormed out.

Francisco Pizarro had not said anything. He did not look angry, just thoughtful.

One of the other men quietly asked to see the piece of paper that Mad Queen Juana's men had given them. Francisco Pizarro's eyes grew wary. With a look at Hernando, he handed it over. The other man took the paper and slowly moved his eyes across and down the sheets, following his eyes' progress with his finger. After a time, he rolled the paper up, but he did not give it back to Francisco Pizarro right away. Instead, he said, "You will have to give him more than this."

"It is what the king gave me," said Francisco Pizarro.

"It is what you asked for," the man replied.

Francisco Pizarro leaned back in his chair and regarded the man evenly. "What are you suggesting?"

For more than a month Diego Almagro stayed away from Francisco Pizarro's house. Sometimes he even refused to talk with the messengers that went back and forth between Francisco Pizarro and him. Felipe began to hope that they would never talk again and that the whole idea of invading the Four Quarters would be dropped. But, even when Diego Almagro did not talk to Francisco Pizarro, other men came to his house, and many of those men also wanted to go to Peru to steal its gold, silver, and land. Felipe's hope was fruitless anyway, because, in the end, Diego Almagro agreed to continue working with Francisco Pizarro.

When Felipe was not helping Francisco Pizarro, he talked to the Massi woman, and eventually she began to accept him again. He helped her keep the house in order, making up beds and setting up and cleaning off the tables. One day when he was setting out shallow bowls for dinner, he suddenly realized that the bowls had not been made by Spaniards. The Spanish knew how to make pottery, and he had always assumed somehow that the pottery cups and bowls used in Francisco Pizarro's house were Spanish ware. These bowls, though, were covered in animal and bird designs completely different from any he had seen in Spain. They were painted in a bright rainbow of red, purple, brown, and deep blue quite unlike the somber colors the Spanish preferred.

His hands shook, and he had to set the bowls down. He should have known better. The Spanish had stolen everything they owned. He wanted to go and smash everything in Francisco Pizarro's house. Instead, he put out one gentle finger and traced a design on a bowl. It was a stylized bird, maybe even the bird Mother Earth had shown him. He looked up, and the Massi woman was watching him. He set out the bowls and went to get more. Neither of them said anything.

Felipe sometimes watched the Massi woman tend the garden at the back of Francisco Pizarro's house. She grew the Spanish garlic and hot peppers like the ones that grew in the Four Quarters, and a lot of other plants that Felipe knew nothing about. When he asked her, she said many of the plants were from the area around Panama. After a while, Felipe found time to talk privately with her. He found it hard to even talk about what he wanted to do, but at last he blurted out, "Do you know of any plants that kill people?"

She looked at him for a short time with no expression on her face, and then turned back to the plant she had been trimming. Without looking at him, she said, "There are people here who say I am an evil wizard. Sometimes I use herbs in ways the Spanish do not think is right, but I am always careful. If someone should die of a strange disease in this household, particularly someone who is important to the Spanish, they would first come to me, to find out how I had done this. I think you mean well, so I tell you this, but you must not ask again."

And he didn't. He became, in fact, ashamed of himself for asking the first time. He had not thought about what would happen to her if Francisco Pizarro died, where she would go, how she would live if she helped him. He could not offer her safety or anything else she might need.

He went up into the jungle again and sat on the ground to ask Mother Earth for advice. Again She spoke to him of endurance. She accepted him and gave him strength, but She did not tell him any way to save the Four Quarters from the Spanish. When he thought about Her role, that made sense. She went everywhere and supported everyone, even the Spanish. She did not care about governments or boundaries. She would have no interest in the dispute of one group against another. She gave the Spanish mostly bad harvests, but, since they simply stole from everyone they met, that would not help him. Maybe eventually the Spanish would have destroyed everyone who knew how to farm and so would die of hunger, but, long before that happened, they would have destroyed his city and his people along with the empire that protected them.

Maybe there was no way he could stop the Spanish, or maybe he would have to get to the Four Quarters before he could do anything. He tended Francisco Pizarro and listened to him talking to his brothers, Diego Almagro, and the other men from Panama.

He was very quiet. They were going to take him home. Once he was there, he would somehow find something to do.

The Spanish took so long to do everything. He was months listening to negotiations about ships and supplies and men and *dinero*.

One day, as he watched Francisco Pizarro working with one of those who made and understood marks on paper, like quipus but strange in form and pattern, he caught Francisco Pizarro's sidelong glance. Suddenly, all the little mistrustful glances Francisco Pizarro had given his scribes made a pattern in Felipe's heart. Francisco Pizarro could not interpret the marks on paper, he suddenly knew, and so he mistrusted anyone who made the marks that controlled his life. This too made sense. If Francisco Pizarro made the marks, he would undoubtedly make every attempt to cheat anyone who could not interpret them.

At first Felipe did not know how to use this knowledge, but Hernando Pizarro was the one person who could understand the marks whom Francisco Pizarro did trust. And nobody else liked Hernando. Hernando would cheat even Francisco Pizarro if he could; Felipe was sure of it. So Hernando would be the worst scribe the expedition could have. If Felipe could find a way to discredit another scribe, he should do it.

He began diligently keeping an inventory of all Francisco Pizarro's belongings, especially those things that would someday go south with the expedition. He soon realized counting the things in Francisco Pizarro's house was not helpful. Even if he found something he could use, revealing a mistake there would only get the Massi woman in trouble, and he did not want to do that.

But, eventually, Francisco Pizarro and Diego Almagro and the rest of the expedition's organizers had built and bought the ships they needed, and Felipe could count the things going onto the ships. There came a day when a scribe listing inventory on Francisco Pizarro's ships reported how many bottles of wine were aboard. It was the right number, but Francisco Pizarro was interested in this, so Felipe said apologetically, "Excuse me, but I made a mistake. I had counted two more."

Francisco Pizarro looked at Felipe, and then looked very stonily

at the scribe. "Continue your list," he told the scribe, without showing that he was upset.

That scribe did not sail with the three ships when they set out
from Panama. It was not much, not nearly enough, but it gave
Felipe a little hope as they sailed south.

Sailing south with all these men intent on destroying his homeland was terrifying. They did not seem to think of him as one of
the people who lived there, for they talked about how they would
take the women away from their families, how they would torture
the *indios* to make them tell about their gold, right in front of him.
There were women on the ships, too, *indios* from Panama, some
with young children. They, like Felipe, did what the men wanted
and did not say much. Felipe spent as much time as he could with
Greek and his cannon and the other artillery.

He half hoped that the Spanish would meet a Taciturn trade
raft that could tell Young Majesty or the Incas in the fortress at
Recognition that they were about to be invaded, but he knew that
hope was stupid. Even if a Taciturn raft did meet them, there would
be no reason for the traders to worry. Spanish ships had come to
the Four Quarters before, and nothing had happened.

When he thought about the ships that had come to the empire
before, though, Felipe wondered if Young Majesty had figured out
that the Spanish were not to be trusted, if maybe the empire was
ready for them. Maybe, since Felipe had left, Young Majesty had
had more fortresses built along the coast. Maybe the whole empire
was anxiously waiting for the Spanish to come back. Maybe they
would be met by a ready army.

But, when the 180 Spanish men with their thirty-six horses
landed in the jungle far north of Recognition, no one was there to
meet them or give the alarm. The small army slogged south. Usually they stayed within sight of the coast, but sometimes they would
detour far inland to avoid wide rivers. They marched through
swamps and over tree limbs. The ground was always soggy, and
strange insects buzzed around them. The cannon kept getting
stuck, and everyone would have to push and pull and sometimes
dig or chop at branches to get it out. The jungle was dark, and the
flying insects got into everything. It rained constantly, making fires

almost impossible to light and hard to keep going. Any pack left unopened for more than a day or two was likely to be full of mold or rust when someone looked into it again. The men snapped at each other and got into fights.

But when they came to small villages, the men stopped arguing with each other and instead bullied the villagers, demanding gold and food. The villagers in the jungle did not have much gold, a few trinkets sometimes. They willingly gave food and shelter as common courtesy. The Spanish did not understand that. Since the people were nice to them, the Spanish assumed they were submitting to their overlordship. They did not understand being nice for no reason at all. Some of the men wanted to rape or steal the women, but Francisco Pizarro said that they could not afford to get the villagers mad at them, that first they had to conquer the Inca empire with all its gold and silver. Then they could have all the women they wanted. Sometimes Felipe wished Francisco Pizarro would not say that. If the Spanish got the villagers mad at them, if they had to fight their way through every foot of jungle, then, by the time they reached the Four Quarters, there would be so few soldiers left that the people in the empire could defeat them easily.

The men began to get sick with the nodule disease. They asked Martin about it, but he said that the disease did not infect people where he had lived. Then they asked Felipe if the disease was serious. He did not know what was best to say. He stammered, trying not to say anything, until the men became very frightened, convinced it was such a dreadful disease he did not want to tell them about it.

Some of the more seriously ill asked to be bled. Since so much of their blood was already in the nodules, this made them ever more sick, so they died. But the Spanish did not decide from this that they should stop bleeding the men who were sick. Instead, they decided it was such a dreadful disease even bleeding could not cure it. Many of them looked themselves over fearfully every night for signs of the disease; and, as soon as they found any, they asked to be bled right away. Though he did not know if the World Animator was the proper god, Felipe prayed to Him every evening that more Spanish would get sick. The men cursed Francisco Pizarro for bringing them to such an awful place, but they had no choice except to keep going, carrying the sickest men on stretchers.

They finally came to a small city with straight streets and a plaza with an Inca Sun temple on the west side. As they marched into town, a small group of warriors with an Inca captain at their head came to meet them. Francisco Pizarro told the horsemen, with his brother Hernando as captain, to go talk to them. Martin, also on horseback, went with them. Felipe bit his lip. He could not try to warn the Inca captain. He could not even hear what they said. For a few minutes, Hernando and the Inca captain talked peaceably together. Then the captain nodded and returned to his men.

One of the Spaniards rode back to where Francisco Pizarro waited. "They say we can stay the night," the man reported. There was a half smirk on his face as though they had done something clever.

The Spaniards walked proudly to the tampu on the plaza, the men commenting loudly on the richness of the town. Felipe thought they were loud because they were scared, but he knew the Incas would think they were being impolite. Still, the Incas usually made allowances for others' strange customs. Martin did not tell them to be quiet, and neither did Francisco Pizarro. When they got to the tampu, its keepers were already laying out food for them and pulling bedding out of storage.

They stayed in the Inca city, the city of Incense, for over a month arguing over whether they should stay or continue on.

"This is only the furthest outskirts of Peru," Francisco Pizarro would say. "It is the smallest of the emperor's possessions. It is no place to either stage a conquest from or to defend."

And Captain Cristobal de Mena or one of the other men who were not from Trujillo would say, "There is much gold here. We can't just leave it."

"That is right," Francisco Pizarro would say. "We should take the gold and then leave."

"We cannot travel fast laden down with gold," one of the others would say.

Finally, after weeks of debate, they decided simply to watch the coast. They would wait until a Spanish ship landed with reinforcements, then kill the local soldiers, take the town's gold, and load it onto the ship. Felipe began to look for a way to warn the Inca captain, but Martin was always watching him as though he knew Felipe was not really loyal to the Spanish.

Incense's tampu was a giant hall, big enough for all of them to live in. During the day, most of the Spanish would go outside to take care of the horses or look at the gold in the Sun temple. Taking care of Francisco Pizarro's gear and helping to care for the sick kept Felipe inside or at least under the watchful eye of the Spaniards loitering around the plaza. There were always Spaniards guarding the plaza and the doors to the tampu. Felipe thought he could convince most of them that he had legitimate business in the town, but, whenever he made to go, either Martin would be there or Hernando de Aldana, whom Martin was teaching Humanity's Mouth. Hernando de Aldana did not seem to be suspicious of Felipe, but he always asked enthusiastic questions, and he was impossible to get rid of.

Once, when Felipe thought he had gotten away unobserved, Greek was suddenly beside him. "This is a good town," Greek said amiably, "well built, clean, full of gold," he laughed, "maybe too much gold for the people who live here. Well, we can take care of that, eh?" Together they wandered around the town, and Greek had Felipe ask people about how they built the houses and if they ate the plants growing beside them.

Sometimes the Inca captain would mingle with the Spanish, to study the men and horses and look at the weapons, but that was even more hopeless because the Spanish always watched him so closely. Once Felipe tried to sneak out at night, but a sentry stopped him, and he had to pretend he was dreaming. After that, some of the Spanish watched him suspiciously, making it even harder for him to talk with the Inca captain.

It was months before a Spanish sail appeared on the horizon, time enough for the men to have divided the gold many times in their hearts, time enough for them to start grumbling about not being able to take the gold right now, but not time enough for Felipe to talk alone with the Inca captain. Still, the Inca captain was obviously suspicious of the Spanish and their motives. What could Felipe say to him that the captain did not already suspect? Felipe prayed to the World Animator and Lightning and hoped the Inca captain had a plan to stop the Spanish if they tried anything.

The Spanish ship anchored offshore, and all the Spanish and the curious townsfolk went down to shore to watch the ship's boat pull in. The Spanish who came off the boat looked at the locals suspiciously, and, at the sight of them, the Inca captain's face hardened. He called an accountant over to compose a message. Most of the Spanish were watching the new men wade to shore, but Captain Mena was watching the Inca captain. He did not say anything to anyone, though, and turned back to the disembarking Spanish when the messenger ran up the road toward the uplands.

Thirty-six men and twelve horses got off the ship. Francisco Pizarro smiled at their leader and said it was good to see him, which meant he had been worried about how few men they had. Their leader was Sebastian de Benalcazar, and with him was the scribe who had not gone on one of the first boats. The scribe and Francisco Pizarro looked at each other, but they did not say anything. It did not make sense, but Felipe was suddenly very frightened for the Inca captain and his men.

All that day, there was much going back and forth between the ship and town. Then, just before sunset, Francisco Pizarro had Felipe tell the Inca captain they were going to give an exhibition of their skill with the horses. Felipe said to the captain, "The Spanish are going to show you how good they are with their war beasts. They call this an exhibition of skill."

The Inca captain said, "I have been wondering what they are skilled in," which Felipe translated as, "He would like to see this."

Francisco Pizarro smiled thinly. "Tell him we will be ready in about half an hour."

Felipe said, "They will be ready for you in a half hour," emphasizing carefully the "for you."

The Inca captain seemed to understand. There was a sardonic look in his eye as he turned away. While the Spanish mounted up, the Incas and the other men of the town vanished into their various compounds and houses. About the time the Spanish finished their preparations, they reappeared with their slings wound about their waists like an extra sash and their sashes weighted down with bags full of stones. Some of them carried spears in their hands as though they were walking staffs. The Inca captain set bundles of something at the doorway to the government compound. The men all stood about three-fourths of the way down the plaza in a group that was arranged like men ready to march out either in a parade or to battle. Some of the women came to watch the Spanish, but they stayed behind the men or at the far side of the plaza from the tampu.

Hernando Pizarro told the men to mount up. As usual, Diego of Trujillo had to help him onto his horse. It looked silly, and Felipe began to hope that his fears were unfounded. Captain Mena pranced on his horse to the front of the line. Greek called Felipe away from the doorway to help him move the cannon into place facing the plaza. Felipe's heart was pounding furiously, and he did not have to pretend to keep fumbling things. He could hear the pounding of the horses on the hard-packed earth and the cries of people outside, and he could not concentrate. Greek finally told him to go back to the door.

Captain Mena had led the best Spanish riders in a charge down the plaza that stopped just in front of the Inca warriors. Some of the warriors had evidently turned to flee because the Inca captain was berating them furiously. Captain Mena was grinning. After they had ridden back to the other end of the plaza, he sent Martin forward on his horse.

"The Spanish captain would like to know if our entertainment is too much for you," Martin said. "If it is, we can present the show we usually put on for small children."

In his heart, Felipe begged the Inca captain to accept the children's show, but the Inca captain was too angry at his men to be thinking clearly. "Your show is most educational," said the captain. "I would like to see more of it."

He reassembled his men, and the best of the Spanish horsemen again charged down the plaza. This time the Inca captain's men stood firm as the horses bore down on them. At the last instant, the Spanish turned their horses and rode back down the side of the plaza. The Inca captain nodded at his men as though to say, "Well-done."

At the other end of the plaza, the Spanish horsemen reformed, but this time all the horsemen formed up, even Hernando Pizarro and the others who were not that skilled. Felipe bit his lip. There was no way Hernando Pizarro could turn like Captain Mena and the others had been doing. Felipe looked back at the Inca captain, but the captain was not watching him. He was watching the Spanish instead. Felipe did not even know if the Inca captain would listen if he yelled at him, or if the noise would just distract him so he could not concentrate properly on what he had to do.

And then there was no time. The Spanish started down the field at a medium pace, and then kept urging their horses faster. At the last instant, the captain realized they were not going to stop or turn this time. As the captain started to yell something, Captain Mena's horse reared and came down on the man's shoulders, bringing him hard to the ground. He did not move again, though Felipe watched until another horse stepped on him. Captain Mena drew his sword, yelling in Spanish, as he sliced downward and in an arc. Wherever he cut, men fell over. When the city's warriors tried to flee, the horses ran them down. Whomever the horses didn't kill, the swords did. When some of the men ran back across the plaza, Francisco Pizarro and his foot soldiers poured out from the tampu. Some men tried to surrender, but the Spanish cut them down anyway. The horsemen chased the men and women who fled along the side streets, cutting them down as they ran. By the time they returned, no one was moving anywhere out-of-doors in the town who was not with the Spanish.

Bodies were piled in bloody heaps at the end of the plaza. Some of the Spanish went from body to body making sure everyone was dead and stealing any gold or silver from the bodies. They stole the earrings from the captain's ears and ripped the necklace from around his neck.

Francisco Pizarro organized the looting of the Sun temple. When the speakers and the Mothers tried to fight them, they cut them down too. Sometimes they killed people because they ran away, sometimes they killed them because they did not run. It did not seem to matter. Felipe stayed where he was in the shadow of the tampu's doorway. The Spanish carried the gold and silver from the temple down to the boat, which took it out to the ship.

After the Spanish had looted the temple and the government compound, they began stealing from the houses of the people in the town. And always they killed people. They killed people if they did not find enough gold and so thought the people were hiding gold from them, and they killed people if they found large amounts of gold and so thought the householders were important people who would have even more gold. When they finished killing people, they told the tampu-keepers to make dinner and complained because they were slow.

In the morning, the Spanish made one last sweep through the city to see if they had missed any gold. Then, stepping over the bodies still lying in the plaza, in the streets, and in the fields, they headed south again, back into the jungle.

Felipe had not eaten anything since the attack. He had not slept either. He was afraid to. No one seemed to notice, though, if he was quieter than usual. He did not know what to say. Anything he would have told the Inca captain would have been wrong. What he had said had not helped. Even the scribe he had gotten Francisco Pizarro mad at was with them again. Maybe Little Francisco had taken the right path. There were many dangers in the jungle. It would not be hard to die.

In the jungle, the men started getting sick again. The cannon still was hard to pull over the rough roadless ground. A man died when he bled to death after he cut himself in the leg while chopping underbrush. None of it made Felipe feel anything. He did not believe anymore that any of it would help the Incas. He did not feel bad because people were dying.

One night he woke late and went out into the brush to piss. The sentry saw him but did not say anything. Felipe thought that maybe he would not come back. He did not know how to survive in the jungle or how to get anywhere he wanted to go, but it did not really seem to matter. The jungle was friendly in its dark quietness. He took another step away from camp, and a lighted figure suddenly shone ahead of him. He choked down his startled excla-mation. He was still close enough to camp for the Spanish to hear him.

"I am sorry if you are not strong enough for the path you have chosen," said the figure quietly, "we have need of you."

"Who . . . ?" said Felipe, but the figure was gone again as though he had never been. "The path you have chosen," the waka had said, and that was true. He had joined the Spanish of his own free will and without expectation. He went back to camp.

"Who is it?" the sentry challenged as he came near.

"Felipe," he replied.

As the sentry waved him in, Felipe had the strong feeling the sentry had not expected him to return, had maybe wanted him to desert. So maybe some of the Spanish thought he could do some-thing to harm them. But what?

It kept raining, and the leather on the horses' harnesses began to rot, the Spanish clothes to dissolve, and the food they had stolen from Incense to mold. Felipe, when he was able, loosened the covers on the food or made tiny holes in them.

One day at breakfast, one of the men said to him, "Last night I thought I saw something flying in the dark. I couldn't see very well, but it was bigger than any insect I've ever seen. It looked like it was swooping down on me."

"So he yelled," said his partner, "and woke up half the camp."

"It flew away," said the man defensively. "Have you heard of anything like that?" He stared earnestly at Felipe.

"It sounds like . . ." but he did not know a Spanish word for vampire bat. "They are dark flyers who drink blood," he said.

"Some kind of insect?" one of the other men asked anxiously.

"No, they have fur and wings like hands." He picked up a stick and drew a crude picture of a bat in the dirt.

"A demon!" exclaimed another man, making the sign of the cross for protection.

Some of the men scoffed, but a number of them looked around at the trees. They had to break down camp then, but, as they started to walk through the jungle, some of the men who'd been listening walked with Felipe.

"How do you keep them from coming after you?" they asked.

"I do not know," said Felipe, and then he realized this was something that might actually help someone. He added, "The people in the temple handle that. I was never a religious."

Two nights later, a man stabbed a companion of his in the dark thinking he was a night-flying demon. Both he and Felipe might have gotten in serious trouble except that two of the horses had new round wounds on their backs, and they had not made any noise. "Yes," said Felipe, "that is the way it is. No one feels the nightflyers bite them."

Brother Valverde questioned Felipe about the nightflyers to find out if they were ordinary animals or agents of the Devil, but Felipe had decided it was better if the Spanish were scared of the unknown than if he told them anything. He would not answer except to say, "I do not know anything about it. I never studied them. You would have to ask the priests and elders."

Eventually, Brother Valverde left him alone. The men, though, kept coming over to ask if he thought this or that ceremony or device would help keep the flyers away. Some of the devices were so cumbersome to make or maintain that Felipe wanted to say that yes, that was it, except he knew that they would soon come to Recognition. He did not want to say anything Macaw or the other people of his city might deny.

After many weeks, the scouts reported that there was water just beyond the trees in front of them, as though they had come to the end of the land. Francisco Pizarro took Felipe and some of the captains with him to figure out where they were and what they should do next.

Felipe could feel his heart beat faster as he stood among the last of the trees on the earth above the wide water. Only Captain Mena stood in front of him on mangrove roots.

"This is where I come from," Felipe said. "This is the Gulf of the Fieldguardian's Shrine in front of us. Just beyond the horizon, there, is Recognition, with the Inca fortress. To our left is the island of the traders." He would not translate Highland Island for the Spanish. Francisco Pizarro, particularly, could not be expected to understand the Inca sense of humor. "I have heard it said that everyone who goes to the traders' island is given much food and drink."

"A good place to rest up?" asked Francisco Pizarro.

"I have never been there," said Felipe. "It may be swampy."

Francisco Pizarro smiled, and a couple of the other men chuckled. This was humor the Spanish understood or thought they did. "Well enough," said Francisco Pizarro, and Felipe knew that whatever debates there might be, it was settled. They would go to Highland Island, and, whoever killed whoever of either group, Felipe did not care.

14

SECOND THROUGH FOURTH YEAR OF
EXEMPLARY ROYAL HAPPINESS'S REIGN
HARVEST SONG THROUGH WATER FESTIVAL MONTH

In actual history, when Exemplary Fortune refused to travel
south to Navel, Cable sent armies marching north to defeat him
and his supporters.

The match between Great Completion and the two forts took
place twenty days after the end of harvest. Tamed Ocelot had
suggested the form of the competition. To make up for the advantage this would give the turn-warriors of Great Completion, Exemplary Fortune deprived the team of one of its best fighters by
naming himself referee. The turn-warriors from Eagle View Fort
and Narrows Fort marched into the capital the afternoon before
with their wives. They all waved bright banners in tribal colors
that the women had made for the occasion. The people of Great
Completion lined the streets to welcome them and to help set up
tents. They also offered enough hospitality to immobilize the warriors for days if they chose to accept. The women from the forts
acted as a buffer, teasing both their men and the people from the
capital about all the good food. The men ate and drank enough to
be courteous and went to bed early.

Morning dawned clear and cool, an advantage for the highland
Incas, Pollens, and Tens who were used to cooler weather. Since all
the teams were mixed, however, this should favor no particular

group. Everyone helped fold up the tents amid enough merriment to make Tamed Ocelot surly. "It is not good to joke before battle," he said, but no one except Exemplary Fortune was listening.

When the field had been cleared, the contestants went to their places, and Exemplary Fortune walked out into the middle. The captains from each side joined him, Anaconda and Shrine Tree for the forts and Black Hawk and Tamed Ocelot for Great Completion. Exemplary Fortune hefted the two rocks he had chosen, a red one for the forts and a dull gray for the capital. He said, "These are your families whom you must protect. Any team that can keep their family safely at their end of the field while capturing the family of the other team and bringing it home, wins. If the families change hands more than once, the team holding their own family the longest will win. Harming or endangering either family, such as by kicking it, will result in automatic forfeiture. All other rules are as for normal fighting practice. If the issue has not been clearly decided by then, we will break at midday."

The captains of the forts, whose forces outnumbered those of Great Completion by nearly three to one, were grinning broadly. Black Hawk grinned back, but Tamed Ocelot only looked calculating. There was, though, Exemplary Fortune thought, a pleased gleam in his eye.

Exemplary Fortune stepped back off the field. The captains carrying their stones went to their respective ends of the field. Esteemed Egg and Skein Reckoner dipped the team banners as Red Deer cried, "Now," and the contest was joined. The forts left a third of their men to guard their stone, and the rest set off downfield in a great rush, yelling as they went.

Great Completion left twenty men in a tight outward-facing square around their stone, and the remainder formed into a much-larger square facing upfield. Though they had practiced the maneuver, the forts' team was more than halfway down the field by the time the square was functional. Then they began to move, silently, except for Black Hawk's called instructions in the strange half-Humanity's Mouth, half-Spanish that everyone on the Great Completion team had come to understand. The fort's team met them and bounced off the massed shields, literally in some cases.

Anaconda, who was leading the forts' offensive forces, took his men around the steadily walking square and bounced off the much-smaller stationary square. The forts' men clearly didn't believe it, trying again and again to bring their padded and stickily painted clubs down on someone's head and striking only shields and blunted weapons. Against the tight knot of Great Completion's forces, their superior numbers were useless. Meanwhile, the capital's forces reached the men guarding the forts' stone and plowed through them like a knife through thick soup. Occasionally a skilled and determined fighter briefly checked the front line, but basically the square just kept moving, not rapidly but inexorably.

By the time Anaconda broke off his attack on the capital's home team and went to rescue Shrine Tree, it was almost too late. His men ran down the field and bounced off the back of the square, whose men had turned to face the approaching warriors. Again they flowed around the square, and again they discovered that all sides of the square were equally impregnable.

Shrine Tree surrendered shortly before Exemplary Fortune would have called the game. The forts' team had been pushed out of the field and onto more-uneven ground, where a misstep could be dangerous. Not only that, but the forts' turn-warriors had clearly become discouraged. Some of them had already conceded, throwing down their arms or moving off the field. The contest had lasted less than an hour.

The watching crowds, mostly from Great Completion, cheered heartily, and everyone drank beer from the province's stores. The two captains from the defeated team accosted Exemplary Fortune. "Most impressive," said Shrine Tree, looking only a little glum.

"How would you like to teach us those tricks?" asked Anaconda.

"I'd be glad to," said Exemplary Fortune.

"So when do we attack the Pormoco?" asked Shrine Tree.

Exemplary Fortune shook his head. "We're not authorized."

But the question stayed with him. Conquering the Pormoco would be suicidal for him; but, say, having a kind of contest with them in their territory, as long as they didn't totally surrender to the Four Quarters' forces . . . it was a crazy idea, and one he didn't mention to anyone, but he thought about it constantly as he helped the turn-warriors of the forts learn the weird new tactics and the strange language that went with it. Though, since Tamed Ocelot was admitting to more and more knowledge of Humanity's Mouth as time went on, the terminology gradually began shedding much of its Spanish. Some of the men, particularly among the Pichunche, could or would not learn the new tactics, and Exemplary Fortune did not require them to. The tactics were, after all, nothing the empire had ordered, requested, or even knew about. Besides, as some of the holdouts said, they took the glamor out of fighting since no individual's prowess stood out. Throughout the fallow and the growing season after, small groups of turn-workers came in constantly from the whole area of the province for a tenday, and, by harvest, most of the men who did their turn as fighters were reasonably skilled in the new tactics.

At the festivities of Sun Festival, Michalongo wove up to Exemplary Fortune with a mostly empty beer tumbler in his hand and said, "You know, now that you've taught everybody better tactics than the Incas', it would be easy to kill you all and defeat the empire."

"It would present some difficult decisions, though," said Exemplary Fortune mildly. "For instance, do you kill Cui because he works for the Four Quarters or let him live because he cares for his mother?"

"That's a stupid question," slurred Michalongo.

"Maybe, but I'd still want to be very sure that I was willing to accept the damage a hundred-thousand-man army could do to the province while I was defeating them before I started anything. Just the corpses of that many people would cause a horrendous stench, attract vermin, breed disease. It would be a mess."

Michalongo looked nonplused and not nearly as drunk as he had a couple exchanges earlier. He straightened to turn away and then, at the last instant remembering to stagger, lurched away.

Michalongo, besides being his wife's grandmother's grandson, was a good fighter and popular with the young men. He clearly wanted something daring to do. Accosting the governor with plans of revolt was certainly daring enough but not a long-term plan.

Since Exemplary Fortune did not believe that fighting the Four Quarters was a wise endeavor, he needed to provide an alternative. Maybe baiting the Pormoco was not such a bad idea, after all.

After the festival, there was another contest between the forts and Great Completion. This time, since the outnumbered capital team needed all the help it could get, Exemplary Fortune named Anaconda referee and took his place on the capital's team. The contest lasted two hours before Anaconda called it, giving the forts' team the victory since Tamed Ocelot, evidently fearing the Great Completion team would lose, had started to attack some of the forts' players in apparent earnest.

Later, when Exemplary Fortune asked him about it, he said sullenly, "I did not think anyone would notice."

"The men beside you in the line certainly had to see you," Exemplary Fortune returned.

"I did not know they would say anything," said Tamed Ocelot, hunching down into his shoulders.

"It may not be the custom where you come from," said Exemplary Fortune neutrally, "but here, when we have set the rules, everyone follows them. We do not change the rules because we might lose. If we have time, and something upsets us, we appeal to the clan leader or a higher authority to change or explain the rule that bothers us."

Tamed Ocelot did not respond to that, merely compressing his lips and staring at nothing.

After the celebration of Earthly Purification, Exemplary Fortune took his whole family with him on a tour of the southern part of Completion. Even Red Deer, who was heavy with her first child, would not be left behind. Exemplary Fortune took Michalongo along as one of his assistants and Black Hawk for whatever services he could provide.

They made their slow and stately way through the province, settling disputes, listening to complaints, and talking with everyone. The children were made much of and enjoyed themselves thoroughly. Evenings in the tampus, Exemplary Fortune would sometimes ask Michalongo how he would have handled a given situation and then question him until he could give Exemplary

Fortune a firm basis for that decision. At first, Michalongo was sullen under questioning, but, as he watched Exemplary Fortune question other staff and make decisions based on their reasoning, he began to answer more readily. He had a quick heart, and his decisions became rapidly more mature. Exemplary Fortune watched with pleasure as he began to enjoy the exchanges. It was too bad he had not been able to go to the school.

They reached Narrows Fort in time for General Purification, and Exemplary Fortune performed those ceremonies at the fort. When the festival was over, he went with Black Hawk, Shrine Tree, and Michalongo to the parapets just under the top of the wooden walls of the fort and stared out into Pormoco territory.

Shrine Tree gestured in a sweeping arc at the land below. "Up until three years ago," he said, "they used to test us regularly. Now, a couple times a year they parade out into the plain below, out of missile range, of course, to yell at us and wave their weapons. We occasionally sortie out to cut the brush so they won't have places to hide. Otherwise, we grow corn and beans."

"They sound like good fighters," said Exemplary Fortune.

"Not as good as Tamed Ocelot," said Black Hawk significantly.

"I admit I'm tempted," said Exemplary Fortune, "but we are not authorized. I have had to lecture Tamed Ocelot on following the rules, and I'd hate to provide him with a bad example."

"I think your rules make you weak," said Michalongo.

Shrine Tree stiffened, but Exemplary Fortune said mildly, "We barely have enough personnel to keep the people of this province well fed, housed, and happy. Certainly there are not enough people here to administer another two hundred square miles. The epidemic hit the whole empire hard. Undoubtedly, the Unique Inca is also short of people. Even if I were a flagrant rule-breaker, I do not know enough to decide that the Pormoco should be conquered."

The other two frowned, looking downslope with dashed hopes, but Michalongo had been watching Exemplary Fortune closely, and his eyes lit. "Then what is your plan?"

"I do not have a plan. I have an idea, probably a stupid idea. . . ." Exemplary Fortune paused. He had made this opportunity, but his was a dangerous and undoubtedly idiotic plan. It would probably get him killed. This was his last chance to back out without nasty repercussions. "I have been thinking: We have tested our skill in Spanish tactics for two years now. We already know how the mock battle will come out next year, and so, particularly for those of us from Great Completion, it is not as much fun. But, if we were to play our game with the Pormoco, we would have a real exploration of our skills again."

They all frowned at him in thought and some bemusement.

Black Hawk asked, "Don't you think it might be just a little difficult to get the Pormoco to follow our rules?"

Exemplary Fortune dismissed that difficulty with a shrug of his shoulders. "A minor problem. I believe that, even if they fight by entirely different rules, if we keep to our squares, we can march out a few miles, observe practice rules, stay overnight, and march back with no casualties."

Shrine Tree, too, was regarding Exemplary Fortune with skepticism. "If that is a minor problem, then what, please, is the major?"

"Michalongo?" prompted Exemplary Fortune.

"Our people," said Michalongo without hesitation. "Many in the province, once in enemy territory, would want to make any skirmish into a real war. The Pormoco have raided this province, and all of us Pichunche know of clan members or friends who have died at their hands. It would be difficult to hold back."

"And yet," said Exemplary Fortune, "if we cannot follow orders in a situation that resembles battle, then all our discipline on the practice field is worth nothing."

"That is true," said Michalongo.

Exemplary Fortune left the discussion there. Michalongo knew very well the challenge that had been made, and, since in later discussions he showed that he understood Exemplary Fortune's arguments, Exemplary Fortune trusted him to give an honest report to his friends.

Red Deer had her child at the beginning of Corpse Procession, a new life to honor the ancestors and, in time, hopefully to become an honored ancestor herself.

During Majestic Festival, Michalongo invited Exemplary Fortune to a conference with a number of other young Pichunche. They questioned Exemplary Fortune thoroughly about his plan. In the end, their feelings were summed up by a young man who said, "If we do this, we will make the Pormoco more upset than if we decided to conquer them. We will show that we do not regard them highly enough to make war on. I think we should play our game with them."

And so Exemplary Fortune was committed. No one in the province commented on how flimsy his division was between invading Pormoco territory and going there for a "game" that would, if successful, undoubtedly result in injury to a number of them. All the turn-warriors who decided to participate—Exemplary Fortune refused to designate this madness a duty—spent the rest of the fallow season practicing with renewed vigor.

The pass's reopening had Exemplary Fortune more worried than usual with fears that another inspector would come over the mountains and find out what was happening, but, as Majestic Quinoa had promised, no one came. Of course, sooner or later an inspector would come, and, assuming success, there would be no way to stop some farmer-warrior from boasting of his exploits. Well, it would be one way to get the Unique Inca Exemplary Royal Happiness to pay attention to the superior Spanish fighting skills, even if over his dead body. He was enjoying this too much, Exemplary Fortune thought. It was a way to keep down the ambition that ate at his heart sometimes when he had nothing else to do—or maybe it was a way to satisfy it. Certainly starting a fight with neighboring tribes was not a governor's duty.

The winter was drier than usual, and, without any irrigation canals off the rivers, the corn got a slow start. An impressive thunderstorm gave them the moisture the winter had lacked and also flattened the young corn plants. As the plants righted themselves, Exemplary Fortune, his conscience pricking him, went to the temple to ask Potato Flower for an augury of the coming exercise. If the omens were bad, he would call the event off no matter what the young men of the province would think of him. The Sun gave an ambiguous reading, not quite bad enough to justify stopping the game. Potato Flower suggested they ask Lakefoam to intercede with the Sun.

Exemplary Fortune sighed. "I had hoped for a clear answer. Very well, ask."

Potato Flower cut open another cui, and this time the omen was excellent.

"Are you sure?" Exemplary Fortune asked.

Potato Flower grinned at him. "Do you want me to try again to find out if some god will give a negative answer?"

Exemplary Fortune was tempted to say yes, but a negative answer now would hardly make things more lucid. He had to be satisfied that the Sun was not particularly happy with his idea, while Lakefoam promised full support and success. Odd, or maybe not. The Sun was the empire's and the Unique Inca's sponsor, and this was not something the current Unique Inca would approve of. Lakefoam, though, was the one who had given each people their special characteristics, and, if the Incas were made to rule others, he should approve of anything that would further that goal. Exemplary Fortune had never before thought of the empire as limiting the Incas. It was this province, he decided; living in Completion gave one all sorts of peculiar ideas.

Having given the responsibility for the planned game over to Lakefoam and the Sun, Exemplary Fortune was able to relax. Only his father's random nighttime visits disturbed his equilibrium. Maybe he should appeal his father to Lakefoam, too, but he did not. He knew his father would be deeply offended by the idea, particularly since it was clear he felt he had something vital to communicate.

Beautiful Orchid complained only half in jest that, with all the young men practicing battle formations, there were not enough turn-workers to maintain the roads and build larger tampus. Michalongo willingly became one of Exemplary Fortune's assistants. Almost palpably, Exemplary Fortune could feel himself settling into the province—as the local idiom would have it, putting down roots.

Harvest came, and, before it was over, some of the younger men began asking when they were going into Pormoco territory. "We will have a month of practice after harvest. Then Black Hawk will decide if we are ready," he told them.

They all practiced assiduously, and, by a month after harvest, the young men were fully ready. Beautiful Orchid had gotten the necessary supplies to Narrows Fort. It remained only for Exemplary Fortune to send out messengers to Eagleview Fort. Potato Flower performed the auguries, which were ambiguous, and interpreted them to mean that they must persevere with order and diligence, which was indeed what the Sun would say.

A large portion of the young people of the province along with their captains gathered in the lands on the Four Quarters' side of the Narrows Fort. They camped for the night, but the men, unaccustomed to facing a real enemy, did not sleep much. They all ate a light breakfast, and Exemplary Fortune gave a sententious speech that could have been boiled down to "Don't forget what you are doing." He was, unfortunately, only too good at following his own advice. He knew perfectly well what they were doing and wished, with a large part of his heart, that he didn't.

They marched through the fort in good order and formed themselves into four large squares on the other side. They marched slowly but steadily to the edge of the area that Shrine Tree's men had cleared. There they began reforming into one square with spearmen four deep around the perimeter and slingsmen wielding pepperball missiles in the middle.

As they began rearranging men, Pormoco ran screaming from the trees. "Outthrust spears," yelled Exemplary Fortune, and, without any hesitation or wavering, the front line went to one knee, their spears leveling themselves at the oncoming warriors as though the two actions were one. "Twotree's men set slings, Boldo's men set slings, Twotree's men throw stones." It all went as they had practiced, right down to the vast majority of the pepperballs bouncing off of the Pormocos' shields. As rehearsed, Black Hawk took control of the unengaged sides of the square. Shrine Tree moved men as necessary to keep the square intact while Anaconda kept supplies properly distributed.

The Pormoco also played their assigned role. They did not, except for a few, so forget themselves as to throw themselves against the massed dull spears of their opponents. Instead, as they reached the square, they ran around it, seeking an opening or a vulnerable backside. They didn't find one. So they threw stones of their own instead, which had to be shielded against, thus depriving the square of much of its ability to move or throw missiles of its own. Against a more numerous or better-armed opponent, that could have been a serious problem. Here it was mainly a nuisance. The few men who were hit were generally able to move from their position in relatively good order, and the one time Exemplary Fortune saw someone knocked unconscious, the men around him shifted their spears so quickly that the Pormocos trying to take advantage of the gap impaled themselves on those spears. They were dragged away by their companions to recover their breath.

The worst injury the Completion troops suffered happened when a turn-warrior so forgot himself that he ran forward alone into the Pormocos' army. The men around him filled in as they had been trained, and Exemplary Fortune sent the square slowly forward to rescue the man. The man managed to back slightly before the Pormocos clubbed him to the ground. When the square started to move, the Pormocos abandoned him and began their again-vain search for an opening. Stepping over a downed man was something they had evidently not practiced enough. Some of the men stepped on him, nearly falling over themselves and undoubtedly doing him further injury, but they did get him back inside the square.

Less than an hour later the Pormocos pulled back just beyond sling range. Exemplary Fortune told the men to stop firing. The Pormoco stayed just out of range long enough for some of the turn-warriors to get worried, wondering what they were plotting. "Don't defeat yourselves," Exemplary Fortune warned them. Telling the turn-warriors to stay calm helped Exemplary Fortune quash his own fantasy that the Pormoco would surrender completely to the Four Quarters and ask to join the empire, a request that Exemplary Fortune would have to duly pass on to the Unique Inca. They rotated men from the front ranks to reserve and passed out a ration of water.

Exemplary Fortune talked to the healers about their patients. The man the Pormoco had clubbed to the ground was still alive, but they would not yet give a prognosis.

Having done everything possible to refresh his warriors, Exemplary Fortune was fighting down a nearly overwhelming need to jitter aimlessly when an individual stepped out of the Pormoco ranks and, moving to the edge of sling range, carefully set his weapons on the ground. He took two more steps toward the square and stopped.

Exemplary Fortune breathed a hopefully inaudible sigh of relief. He gave command to Black Hawk and made a narrow space for himself through the wall of the square. Once past the end of the spears he too put down his weapons and walked toward his opposite. The man stepped another few paces toward him, and they met at a spot within slingshot range of both groups but out of hearing if they spoke quietly.

"You use blunted spears and soft missiles," said the Pormoco representatives without any preliminary.

"We do," acknowledged Exemplary Fortune.

"Is this meant as an insult?" the Pormoco asked.

"Not at all," said Exemplary Fortune. "All those in the Four Quarters who have met the Pormoco know they are excellent fighters. This is a new method of fighting. We practiced it in competitions with ourselves, and it seemed to work very well, but we wanted to find out if it would work as well against someone who was seriously trying to kill us. We blunt our spears because we do not wish to hurt you but rather to test our tactics."

The man digested this in silence for a time. "Do all in the Four Quarters learn these tactics?"

"Not so far," Exemplary Fortune admitted. "We have with us a man from a distant kingdom called Castile who has taught us these tactics and maneuvers."

"Will he teach the Pormoco as well?" There was a glint in the Pormoco's eye that said he already knew the answer, as indeed he should.

Exemplary Fortune found the correct answer rising to his lips automatically and without a tremor. "I will ask him once the Pormoco have joined the Four Quarters."

"Well then," returned the other, "we will wait."

"As you wish," said Exemplary Fortune, trying not to show his relief.

"Does Castile seek alliance with the Four Quarters?" the representative asked next.

"It does not."

"Perhaps then," the man asked more hopefully, "it seeks to conquer the Incas?"

"Not so far. From what I have observed, I believe that once they start conquering, they will not stop at any boundary."

"You talk of one person. One person is not the true measure of a tribe. Even among the Pormoco, besides brave warriors, we have a few who, with a spear, are more of a danger to themselves than deer or an enemy."

"This is also true with us," said Exemplary Fortune. He wondered if Pormoco etiquette demanded that he take the self-deprecation another step and decided he didn't want to. "It is not just his warriors' skills that make me believe most of the tribe of the man I know must be skilled but crazed warriors. He believes that worthwhile people do not till the soil and is ashamed of himself when he does. In Castile, he says, all the important people would kill themselves rather than farm."

"Then how do they eat?"

"I believe they battle other tribes to steal their food."

The other man considered this for several heartbeats. "They must indeed be good warriors."

"He says all our weapons are inferior. You have seen the tactics he has taught us."

"Fighting them would prove a warrior's courage."

"This is true."

"If they attack the Four Quarters, you may ask the Pormoco for help, and we will send our best warriors to help you."

"Thank you," said Exemplary Fortune. "I do not know if I will be able to act on your offer when the time comes, but, if I can, be sure that you will fight alongside us."

"I am Far-Spear," said the Pormoco.

"And I am Exemplary Fortune."

"A good name," said Far-Spear. "I have a request of you, Exemplary Fortune."

"And what is that?" Exemplary Fortune did not say his name lest it bind him to some agreement.

"I ask you and your men to go back to the Four Quarters. I know this will not bind you or your people in any future meeting or battle, but, for today, we have seen enough of you."

"I will honor your request, Far-Spear; today we will go home."

"Thank you," said Far-Spear. He turned to walk back to the warriors of his people, and Exemplary Fortune did the same.

The victory over the Pormoco was, as Exemplary Fortune had fore-known, the biggest source of tale-telling and wonder to come to Completion since the province's inception. Everyone crowded around those who had fought in the "game," asking to hear again and again what had happened. It helped to foster a unified spirit among the people of Completion, but it still made Exemplary Fortune extremely apprehensive. He should compose a report, but even a friendly Unique Inca would be likely to regard an excursion into outside territory without permission or provocation as treason. Cable, who was evidently looking for an excuse to overturn his earlier decision to let Exemplary Fortune live, would be much less likely to even listen to Exemplary Fortune's explanation. And yet, the information gained was something the Unique Inca should know.

Obviously, Exemplary Fortune could not carry the news, but the report's bearer should not be a simple messenger either. Rather it should be someone with military experience who could defend and explain their actions as necessary, someone moreover who had spent time in Navel and had some chance of dealing with the politics there. That narrowed the choice to Anaconda and Shrine Tree. For each of them he knew both their tribes and clan affiliations; but, since he had no idea who the Unique Inca's trusted advisors were, the information did him little good. He would have to trust instead his own evaluation of the men's intelligence and guile. He called Anaconda to Great Completion.

Anaconda came into his presence with a smile on his face. After they each drank a little beer, he asked, "So, what is your plan now?"

"Unfinished business," said Exemplary Fortune.

Anaconda took another swallow of his beer and then said, "Your arguments against conquering the Pormocos were quite cogent. In fact . . ." He shifted position slightly. "Has the Unique Inca expressed displeasure with our, ah, training exercise?"

"Not yet," said Exemplary Fortune. "In my enthusiasm for the project I deafened myself to some of the future consequences. Specifically, the Unique Inca needs to know the great tactical advantage the Spanish would have in any battle, but he is also likely to be upset that we did not tell him about our excursion into Pormoco territory beforehand. I believe a single messenger with experience in Navel's politics and a certain ability to dissemble when necessary has the greatest chance to give him the information without incurring his wrath."

"Just how upset is he likely to be?" Anaconda asked warily.

"My advice is, protect the province first, yourself second, and be ready to sacrifice me to achieve either of those goals."

Anaconda regarded Exemplary Fortune for a time. "Just how thoroughly did you think this out beforehand?"

"Some. It was an overwhelming compulsion."

"God-sent?"

"Most likely. Not the Sun, though." And the Sun was the important god in matters affecting the Four Quarters.

"Lakefoam?"

"Lakefoam gave an excellent omen for the proceeding." But it might very well have been his waka father who had inspired him.

Anaconda took another swallow of beer. "How soon do I start?"

"You will be Completion's messenger with the census data and tribute for Majestic Festival. While in Navel, you will make an opportunity to talk with the Unique Inca's courtiers or perhaps request an audience with Exemplary Royal Happiness himself concerning what we have learned about Spanish tactics. I trust your heart. Come to Great Completion two tendays before Corpse Procession, and we will give you the census information."

Anaconda didn't say anything for quite a while, staring pensively at his beer. Finally, he looked up and, with a twisted smile, said, "I figured you had something adventurous planned, but I didn't realize that you intended anything so final. I should have thought beforehand."

Exemplary Fortune shook his head. "That was my responsibility." And he talked of other things.

Planting season came, and the pass reopened. Again there was no Inca inspector. One last worry—that Cable would find out before he sent his messenger and blame him doubly—gone. The corn in the fields sprouted, turning the earth green when, just as Anaconda was making preparations to leave for Navel in the morning, a relay-messenger came, not over the pass, but from due north across the Fortunate Soul Desert. That was the shortest route, but difficult enough that it was used only for urgent messages.

Exemplary Fortune invited Anaconda into the governor's office to hear the message. The message was simple. "The Unique Inca Exemplary Royal Happiness summons Exemplary Fortune to his presence in Navel."

Exemplary Fortune's first half-guilty reaction was one of relief. Cable still might not listen to him, but at least he would not have to send someone else to possible death. Further, since there had not been time for the Unique Inca to receive word of Exemplary Fortune's unauthorized excursion into Pormoco territory, the Spanish must have come. His quasi-invasion had been justified.

He turned to Anaconda. "I will deliver our message to the Unique Inca in person. But I would still like you to deliver the tribute."

"They've come, haven't they?" Anaconda returned.

"It does seem so," said Exemplary Fortune. His immediate relief had already been replaced with a sense of urgency, a need to be moving, a hope that he had not already waited too long.

But it was late afternoon, too late to get over the Warbler Hills before dark. Exemplary Fortune went to the temple and sat before the Sun's image, but the Sun did not seem to want to give him strength for the journey, making him feel extremely uncomfortable instead. So, after a short time, he went to the riverbank to commune with flowing water and therefore Lakefoam. He didn't say anything, asking silently for guidance. In Lakefoam's presence, he could feel peace slowly infuse his heart. After a while, he got up and walked back to the governor's compound.

At the compound, Michalongo was waiting impatiently in the courtyard. "Take me with you," he said without preamble as Exemplary Fortune walked in.

Exemplary Fortune smiled at him. "Come inside with me."

After they had settled themselves comfortably on the floor of the main office, Exemplary Fortune said, "Tell me what makes the peace of this province."

"You," said Michalongo, "my grandmother . . ." He trailed off. "And?"

"And me," Michalongo admitted unhappily.

"Staying in Completion may well not be as dull as you think," said Exemplary Fortune. "Either, as I believe, the Spanish have invaded the Four Quarters, and we will soon need all our fighting skills and men, or else the Unique Inca has somehow decided I am a traitor, and you will have to spend the next months deciding exactly what you plan to do next."

Michalongo regarded him. "You would go even if you knew the Unique Inca planned to kill you as soon as you arrived, wouldn't you?"

"I would."

"I will think about it."

"Yes, you are one of those who thinks." Once Exemplary Fortune left, Michalongo would have rethought whether he wanted to continue to actively support the Four Quarters in any case; but now, whenever he thought about the empire, he would think of Exemplary Fortune. Whatever he felt about the empire, he had bound himself to Exemplary Fortune. "Now I need to talk with Cui."

Michalongo pursed his lips, and, instead of going to summon Cui, sat in silence for a time. Finally he said, "He is not as inoffensive as he looks."

"That is true."

"I think maybe you prefer people who hide their true natures."

"I will miss you," said Exemplary Fortune, "but I am going to a place where I must be very humble. You are not good at that. Your cockiness is not a flaw because it makes you strong, but I cannot take you with me."

Michalongo opened his mouth as though he would say something more, then closed it again without speaking. He left.

After telling Cui that they would leave together just after sunrise, Exemplary Fortune sent messages to the forts that he had been summoned to Navel. He thought for a time about what else he should say to Shrine Tree, but decided finally there was nothing else to say. Beautiful Orchid would handle any questions.

He spent the rest of the evening at home. His wives looked at each other, exchanging messages with their eyes, and then Red Deer asked to come with him. She was a good choice, not an Inca or honorary Inca and so no possible threat to anyone, long limbed and a strong traveler. Her child had accepted Grasshopper as her main caretaker. Chatterer wanted to come too, but he understood when Exemplary Fortune said his legs were too short. He would not understand, though, why Exemplary Fortune refused to say when they would see each other again.

"You must come back. She has to come back for her baby's hair cutting," he said.

"We will try," said Red Deer.

Chatterer stared at her and said nothing more.

They seemed to spend a large part of their life saying good-by, Exemplary Fortune thought. It was the pattern his life made, and there seemed to be nothing he could do about it.

He slept well, got up before dawn, took a quick bath with Red Deer in the river, put on a plain tunic, and went with her to the plaza, where Cui was already waiting.

As he walked onto the plaza, another figure stepped out of the shadows. "You," said Tamed Ocelot.

Exemplary Fortune's heart beat faster, but he knew that if Tamed Ocelot wanted to kill him, he would already be dead. There seemed no adequate response to that one-word statement, so Exemplary Fortune waited silently.

"You have done this to me," said Tamed Ocelot. "You put me in these clothes, this stupid town. You made me tell you how to fight."

"I did all that," Exemplary Fortune agreed, "as my father asked me."

"Your father is a ghost," Tamed Ocelot retorted. "He is not some demon who knows everything. He is already in the torment-place." Tamed Ocelot was talking loudly enough to wake people in nearby houses. Now he took a step closer to Exemplary Fortune, close enough that Exemplary Fortune had to fight an impulse to step back. "You gave me that woman. You made me . . ." But here Tamed Ocelot ran out of words and stopped, spluttering, for a moment. "Now you are going to get killed, and you leave me here."

"I could take you with me." It would probably not make the Unique Inca that much more suspicious of him and might actually be useful.

"No," howled Tamed Ocelot. "I like that woman, I like her family, Black Hawk, the stupid *peon* warriors. I like everybody. You have done this to me." Tamed Ocelot struggled with himself another bit of time. "I will not go back, but you, beware of the *caballos*. They will kill you."

"What is a *caballo?*" Exemplary Fortune asked. From habit perhaps, he tried to keep all eagerness out of his voice, but his heart focused on Tamed Ocelot.

"It is like a llama but very big and deadly. Their feet are sharp with metal plates, and, if they rear up and then come down on you, if they step on you, they will kill you. They will kill you all."

"Thank you for your information," said Exemplary Fortune with all sincerity. "I will remember."

"Stupid *indio,*" said Tamed Ocelot.

Exemplary Fortune grinned, relief at Tamed Ocelot's help and humor at his words mingled in that smile. "I will miss you. I need someone to remind me of my failings from time to time." He paused, and then said seriously. "I will miss you. We have learned much from each other."

Tamed Ocelot merely shook his head and muttered something unintelligible.

Exemplary Fortune turned to Cui and Red Deer. "Come, we must go." He gave Tamed Ocelot a half-bow, then the three of them ran out of the plaza together.

As they ran into the woods, the Sun brightened the sky behind the commanding eastern mountains. Exemplary Fortune put all thoughts of anything except running out of his heart. They should make fifty miles this day, and fifty the next. In the Fortunate Soul Desert, they would run through the dark and so make better time, but, on the other side of the desert, they would have to rest and so gain no time on the journey. It was good that they would travel as hard as they could because Exemplary Fortune's heart said that however fast they traveled, it would not be fast enough. It would take disaster to make Cable call him to Navel, and they would be at least a month on the road no matter how fast they ran. He had to know what the Spanish were doing, what the empire was doing, but for a month he would be almost too tired to care. They ran.

15

In actual history, though Incense appeared tranquil to the Spanish, the whole Inca Empire was rent by civil war by the time Francisco Pizarro returned to the Four Quarters.

It took several days for the Spanish with their cannon and the horses and their constant bickering to walk east to the point where Highland Island came closest to the mainland. By the time they stepped out onto the one open beaten-down patch of earth along the water, rafts were already sailing out to meet them. The Highland Islanders had clearly had spies watching them as they traveled near their land. The Spanish seemed to think the same way, and they eyed the Islanders with suspicion.

The Islanders wore flowers in their scarlet-and-cream headbands and offered the Spanish flowers as well. The Spanish looked at the flowers as though they must be poisonous. Felipe, though, stepped forward to take a flower and put it in his own hair. After that, a few of the Spanish took flowers to hand to their girlfriends. The Highland Islanders smiled ingratiatingly and, in broken Humanity's Mouth, asked everyone to come visit their beautiful island. Felipe translated the invitation as accurately as he could. The Islanders listened to his translation and smiled again. As they saw how closely everyone attended to Felipe's words, their own speech became much less broken.

Now that he was actually meeting the smiling Islanders Felipe had promised, Francisco Pizarro was clearly uneasy. Still, he was the one who had backed the idea of using Highland Island as a place to rest and reconnoiter before starting the conquest of "Peru," and he had little choice but to accept the invitation. When the flowers proved harmless, most of the other Spanish relaxed, and some of them grinned back at the smiling Islanders. Now they seemed to think that the Islanders had watched the Spaniards only so they could entertain their guests properly. They were more than ready to accept the promised hospitality. Francisco Pizarro growled at them to keep their swords loose in their scabbards.

Felipe told the Islanders that their leader was upset because his men were not properly dressed or otherwise prepared for them. He felt very odd. He did not know what would happen. He would translate suitably for each group and let whatever their rotten hearts caused happen. The resulting fight might not kill all of the Spanish or even most of them, but some of them would surely die.

Francisco Pizarro waved Captain Mena onto the first set of rafts. The captain led a third of the men aboard, keeping a watchful alertness. Greek complained that his cannon should go first in case of trouble, but Francisco Pizarro said that he did not want the cannon to go to the island until there were enough people to guard it. Felipe had not thought that the Highland Islanders might capture the cannon, and he did not know how to suggest it to them now. Besides, with a cannon, the Islanders might be as big a threat as the Spanish. He did not know if he wanted them to know the cannon was a weapon.

The horsemen had climbed off their mounts, and Francisco Pizarro said they would go next. Some of the horsemen put blindfolds across their anxious animals' eyes before they led them onto the rafts. The Islanders looked sidelong at one of the horses when it defecated onto a raft right after it climbed on, then they almost visibly shrugged and looked away. Greek, grumbling, went with the last group. When the Islanders asked what the long cylinder was, Felipe told them it was a lightning-like noisemaker. That was not a lie; and, if they thought carefully about his words, they would certainly be cautious around the device. Nothing Felipe had told either group so far was a total lie, and, as long as he could, Felipe would continue to tell at least partial truths.

Once on the island, the Highland Islanders showed the Spanish neat log houses where they would stay. The houses all had bright flowers growing up the walls, but the Spanish barely even looked at them. Felipe's throat constricted, though, as he recognized heliotropes, passion flowers, yellow oleander, fuchsias, and others that also grew in Recognition's gardens. And then he thought again. He knew fuchsias were sometimes used as a drug and so was yellow oleander. He had been warned that yellow oleander was poisonous. He wondered if the Islanders were planning to poison them after all.

The Islanders had built large fires in an irregularly shaped plaza among the houses. The Island women cooked soup and roast fish for the Spanish. The Islanders fed everyone fruits like pineapple, and passion fruit. Felipe ate freely. If he died from the food, many of the Spanish would die too, and, if he acted suspicious, others might refuse to eat, too. Besides, if Felipe was one of the only survivors, probably either the surviving Spanish or the Islanders would kill him anyway. The food all tasted very good, and, at least the first night, no one got sick.

The next morning, the Islanders offered everyone new clothes and garlands of flowers. The Spanish refused the clothes, but many accepted the flowers. Only Francisco Pizarro and a few of the other men who had been in Panama for a long time kept their stiff manner as the Islanders plied them with food, drink, and bright flowers. The others relaxed and let the Highland Islanders tend their every whim.

As the days went by, some of the men began to talk about settling on the Island, but most of them felt there was not enough gold, and the weather was too hot and humid. All agreed, though, that the natives were very friendly.

Felipe walked among the houses of the Highland Islanders and tried to guess where they stored their weapons. He noticed how carefully they watched fighting practices. They clearly thought the Spanish armor and swords were a delightful innovation, though they were careful not to show their interest openly.

After the army had been on the island for nearly a month, two more Spanish ships rounded the cape to the west of the Island. As before, the men went down to the coast to yell and fire off the arquebuses so the ships would notice them. Francisco Pizarro watched the ships come in with unfeeling eyes. Only when the first boat came ashore did his eyes light with a small measure of triumph. Since Francisco Pizarro had to ask who was aboard, it was not because he knew the men on the boat. Most likely, it was because he didn't know them, because they were not Diego Almagro. The longer Diego Almagro was not part of the expedition, the less claim he would have to honors and gold.

There were about a hundred men on these ships, too many for Felipe's heart's peace. Most of them were on foot, but their leader was lowered over the side of a ship already on his horse, and he rode ostentatiously onto shore. He was a small man, and even Felipe could see that he rode very well. Francisco Pizarro greeted him with a smile and a warm "Hernando de Soto." Sebastian de Benalcazar compressed his lips and turned away to talk with some of the other men. Greek greeted everyone, especially the arquebusiers, with great enthusiasm as was his way always.

Later, when Felipe asked Greek anxiously what was between Hernando de Soto and Sebastian de Benalcazar, Greek laughed and said, "The Spanish are always like that. They think it is a good thing to have someone you are upset with. It keeps the blood flowing. Myself, I think it is no fun. Do not worry. When the time to fight comes, they will fight together."

Felipe thanked him and went to the meetings Francisco Pizarro had in the house where he was staying. Felipe stayed very quiet and poured drinks when none of the Islanders were around. He didn't learn much because everyone was trying to be polite with everyone else, but there were covert nasty looks between all the leaders. Maybe it was as Greek said. They all wanted someone to be upset with.

When Francisco Pizarro was alone with his brothers, he complained about how popular Hernando de Soto was becoming. "We will send him out in front," said Hernando Pizarro, grinning to show his teeth. "He will like that."

Francisco Pizarro nodded. "He is too eager. Maybe someday he will get lost from the main party."

Hernando laughed.

It was another month before Francisco Pizarro had Felipe tell the Highland Islanders that they were ready to leave. The Islanders all expressed great sorrow and asked them to stay longer. Francisco Pizarro said that they were leaving immediately, which Felipe translated with flowery regrets. The Islanders said, very well, they would raft them to Recognition's harbor.

"We are not going to Recognition," said Francisco Pizarro, "just to the far shore of the river."

For the first time, Felipe saw the Highland Islanders look honestly surprised. "It is all jungle and desert to Recognition," they said, "a barren waste. We would not treat our guests so unkindly."

Francisco Pizarro drew himself up. "That is where we will go."

"Oh, so sad," said the Islanders, "but we will do as you wish. For the rest of today and all tomorrow, we will gather our rafts together, and, then, the day after tomorrow, we will take you across."

Felipe did not really understand why Francisco Pizarro did not want to go directly to Recognition, but he understood why the Highland Islanders wanted to take them in that direction. The strait between Highland Island and the mainland was narrowest on the north. If the rafts dumped their passengers into the water there, it might be possible for some of the Spanish to swim to shore; but, if they were dumped into the water halfway between Highland Island and Recognition, they would surely drown before they reached either shore.

All that day and the next, while some of the Islanders busied themselves moving logs and rafts around, others plied the Spanish with beer. Many of the Spanish got roaring drunk, but Francisco Pizarro and the other captains made sure at least two-thirds of the Spanish were always sober. Once, after Francisco Pizarro had once again refused a drink, Felipe saw an Islander so forget himself as to look disgusted.

By the third day, many of the Spanish who were not still drunk were hungover and surly. The Islanders were very polite indeed as they urged the best horsemen onto the first group of rafts. "Please, we worry about these animals. They look so anxious when they are on the water. We do not want them to be hurt."

Hernando de Soto and others of the horsemen willingly climbed on the first rafts. Francisco Pizarro also sent about a third of the foot soldiers and two of the king's men. The rafts were about two-thirds of the way to the other shore when the men on them starting yelling. The Islanders still ashore, coming from around the sides of their houses, suddenly attacked the Spaniards still on the island with swords and clubs. The Spanish were not totally unprepared. Like Francisco Pizarro, many of them expected to be attacked at any time. The Islanders smashed several solitary men to the ground before the rest of the Spanish, yelling battle cries, were able to pull out their swords and run for their attackers. By that time a few of the Islanders had steel swords, and, when the two groups met, Spaniard as well as Islander fell.

The Islanders had attacked in two groups, one coming from the nearest houses, and one, with a longer way to run, headed for the remaining horsemen standing by the shore. Like the Spanish, they evidently assumed anything they didn't understand was a weapon.

Greek, swearing, began calling for people to help him turn the cannon. Felipe ran to him. "Don't lose your head this time, boy," Greek admonished.

Felipe had actually been planning to help, but, with Greek's words, he realized he couldn't. If the Spanish survived this fight, their next battle would be against his own people, and he could not have any fighting skills then. He fumbled and got in the way. Behind him, the noise of people yelling orders and screaming in pain constantly startled him. It was not hard to constantly twist and duck as he waited for somebody's sword or club to hit him in the back. Greek finally yelled at him to get back.

He stepped away from Greek and the cannon and looked around to see what else he could do. He couldn't really see anything. Lots of people were running, hitting each other with weapons, or lying sprawled on the ground, but there didn't seem to be any pattern to it, no place he could put himself where he would make the action even more confused. He turned toward the horses. About a third of the horsemen still ashore had gotten onto their mounts and were slashing at the Islanders who had attacked them and making it easier for the rest to mount up, but none of them were riding after the Islanders yet. The horses were all dancing around and snorting. Now, they even looked dangerous, as though they would attack anything.

Felipe finally walked over to one of the Spaniards lying on the ground who was still trying to move. He had meant to stab him with his knife or something, but, when he knelt down beside the man, the man looked up at him and said, "I need a drink." There was a trickle of blood coming from the man's mouth and a long gash across his middle where his leather armor had been cut through. Felipe could not see under the armor, but there was a growing puddle of blood on the ground next to the cut. The way the Spanish did medicine, Felipe did not think a drink would do the man any good. Nevertheless, he said, "I will bring you some water." But, when he made to stand up, the man grabbed at his arm and said, "Don't go." Felipe sat down next to him and let him take his hand.

"All I wanted," said the man, "was *dinero* for my family. They said the streets were paved with gold. They said anybody could get rich. . . ."

At the shoreline, Hernando de Soto, his armor running rivulets, rode his horse out of the water. Two other men hanging onto his horse's tail staggered out of the water behind him. When the two men who were hanging on reached shore, they let go of the horse, staggered a few feet up the shore, and collapsed in a heap. Hernando de Soto looked around at the scene on shore, looked back into the water as three other horsemen struggled out onto land. Drawing his sword, he ordered, "Follow me," and rode up toward the town.

Felipe cringed a little, afraid he would be run down. The man holding his hand did not seem to notice. In fact, he now seemed to think Felipe was one of his relatives. "You have to make sure everyone's taken care of," he said. "Don't forget Dolores, she . . ." Then he coughed a little and could not catch his breath for a time.

The horsemen rode past them, kicking up mud, which splattered against Felipe's clothes. One splatter hit the man's face, and Felipe wiped it off.

The man recovered his breath enough to say, "You will take care of it, won't you?"

"I will do the best I can," said Felipe, which meant, of course, nothing at all, but it seemed to make the man feel better. The man closed his eyes with a little sigh, and the next time his eyes opened, his will was not in them. Without letting go of his hand, Felipe asked quietly, "So why did you have to come here to die? You could have died better at home." Then he put the man's hand on his chest and looked for someone else to sit with. It was, really, a stupid thing to do, but it was better than being anxious and worried with nothing to do. None of the sprawled bodies closest to him were moving at all.

Hernando de Soto was at the end of the village with the other horsemen who had ridden out of the water, and they were hacking at the Islanders. They had ridden past the footmen, and there were few enough of them that the Islanders could get behind them and hit at them from the rear. But the other horsemen had almost all mounted up and were getting ready to ride over their attackers. It looked like the Spanish were going to win again.

Felipe turned back toward the shore. Greek had his cannon turned around and was loading it up. The two men who had followed Hernando de Soto ashore were sitting head down next to each other. He walked over to them. "Can I help you?" he asked.

They looked up at him dully. "Where are they?" one asked hoarsely.

"There and there," said Felipe pointing with his finger the way the Spanish did.

"Blasphemous *indios* bastards," said the man, but the words sounded dutiful, like he thought it was something he should say.

"We need dry clothes," said the other.

"Yeah," agreed the first.

"I will try to find you some," said Felipe.

The first man laughed and then coughed. "All my clothes are at the bottom of the sea, river, whatever."

"Oh," said Felipe. He kept forgetting that, among the Spanish, it did not matter if somebody really needed something or not. If they did not have the proper *dinero,* they would not get it. He thought for a bit. "Do you want me to get Francisco Pizarro or one of the king's men?"

"Forget it, kid," said the second man not unkindly.

"Just bring us an infidel to kill," suggested the first.

"I do not know how to do that," said Felipe, unsure whether or not the man was joking.

Not too far away, Greek was cursing loudly at the Spaniards who were between him and the Islanders. Felipe fought the impulse to go help him. And then Greek stopped cursing. Felipe turned in time to see him light the fuse cord. One group of Islanders was milling in confusion at the other end of town while all the Spaniards had vanished between the houses. The Islanders finally turned together and began to retreat just before the cannon roared deafeningly and threw out a swarm of pebbles. As Greek had promised, the tiny stones tore into the whole mass of Islanders, cutting them into a ruin of corpses. The Spanish ran back out from between the houses, and the Islanders who could still move ran away as fast as possible. Hernando de Soto and his men followed, cutting them down as they ran. The other group of Islanders also broke and ran, with the second group of horsemen riding after them. It was clear that the battle was over.

Greek called Felipe over to him. "What did I tell you? A cannon may not shoot many times in a battle, but many times it does not have to." He laughed at his own witticism.

Felipe looked around the village. "There are a lot of dead people," he said cautiously.

"That is war," said Greek. "You are a good Christian, but you are not a warrior." He shook his head.

Felipe did not say anything. One thing he certainly was not was a Christian. And, if any one person had caused the deaths of all those who had died in this battle, it was he. Sometimes he wondered if Greek saw anything except what he wanted to see, but it seemed to work for him. Felipe knew better. It bothered him that he didn't really feel upset or anything.

While Brother Valverde went among the dead and badly injured, making them acceptable wakas, the other Spanish chased down and killed all the Islanders they could find until Hernando Pizarro, of all people, said they should capture a few alive to raft them to shore. "And this time," he said, "we put ropes around their necks and watch every move they make."

Eventually, they found five Islanders who had not either been killed or escaped. They stripped them of their weapons and most of their clothes and had Felipe tell them that, unless they did exactly what they were told, they would die. As usual, the Islanders agreed to do anything the Spanish asked.

Together the Spanish and the Islanders tore apart a few of the Islander houses, and the Spanish relashed the logs into rafts. It was late afternoon before the new rafts were ready. Probably the Spanish would have waited another day to cross to the mainland, except that many of those who had been on the Islanders' rafts when they disintegrated had made it to the far shore. Since they were without weapons or other supplies, the Spanish did not want to leave them alone overnight. Felipe thought that was too bad. If the Spanish stayed on Highland Island another night, the Islanders might well find a way to regroup and kill more of them.

Just before they left the island, Felipe went into two of the intact Islander houses, stirred up the household fires, and built a wood bridge from the fires to the walls. No one noticed.

This time the crossing on the Spanish-built rafts was without incident. The Islanders did everything the Spanish asked without tricks or protest. When they got to the other side, the Islanders helped the Spanish take one of the rafts apart for the night's firewood. Then the Spanish strangled the Islanders with the ropes around their necks. The Islanders almost seemed to expect it. The Islanders and the Spanish seemed to think alike, which made them well-matched opponents. Still, Felipe wished he had told the Islanders they were going to die.

As the sky darkened over the water behind them, Felipe saw that not two but three Islander houses were burning. He had thought maybe only one house would catch, but maybe some Spaniard had decided to burn some Islander's house, or an untended fire had spread from its hearth on its own. In the dark, the fires were very bright, and, as they spread to the wet wood on the outside of the houses, they sent up a great cloud of smoke. The smoke cloud was big enough that people should have no trouble seeing it in Recognition. He had done what he could to warn his people; the rest was up to the Incas.

16

FOURTH AND FIFTH YEARS OF
EXEMPLARY ROYAL HAPPINESS'S REIGN
CORPSE PROCESSION THROUGH GREAT RIPENING MONTH

In actual history, Exemplary Fortune's commanders—Thorniest, Shrewdness, Stone Eye, and all the rest—easily defeated Cable's commanders in battle. They slowly fought their way south into the heart of the empire.

Exemplary Fortune, Cui, and Red Deer jogged into Behindari hot, sweaty, and caked with a thin layer of dust from the surrounding desert. Cui and Red Deer were breathing heavily, and Exemplary Fortune himself felt slightly out of breath as though he had a touch of altitude sickness, odd since Behindari was lower than Kitu Dove or Navel, not to mention the true highlands.

"A bath," promised Exemplary Fortune, "the tampu should have a bath."

The others nodded but didn't say anything. Cui looked as though he were ready to fall over. Exemplary Fortune slowed his pace to a walk as they went through the town to the tampu. As they walked into the tampu, a young man hailed Exemplary Fortune by name. The young man's short hair and large gold earrings proclaimed him an Inca, and he wore the yellow headband of a prince. He grinned as Exemplary Fortune studied him, trying to figure out which of his brothers he was.

That face had been much younger last time Exemplary Fortune

had seen it. Yes. His name had been . . . but that was his childhood name. "Happy Speaker," said Exemplary Fortune finally. "You have become a man since I last saw you."

"The Unique Inca said you wouldn't recognize me," said Happy Speaker, sounding disappointed.

"How can I forget a brother who decided a llama was a stool?" Exemplary Fortune asked, relating one of the few vivid memories he had of the young man before him. "You not only made an impression on that llama, you made an impression on me."

"It was a childish stunt."

"I enjoyed it," said Exemplary Fortune, studying Happy Speaker covertly. The last time he had seen Happy Speaker had been just before he left for school seven years earlier as a partially formed child. At that time, he had been charming but perhaps overeager to let others make his decisions for him.

Happy Speaker shrugged uncomfortably. Maybe he had been reminded of the llama incident too many times. Then, assuming a messenger's pose, he said, "The place of your meeting with the Unique Inca Exemplary Royal Happiness has been changed. You will now meet him in Great Granary." He smiled. "That's it. I guess you know the rest."

Exemplary Fortune did not know the rest, did not know anything at all that might be relevant to the Unique Inca's summons. "What have the Spanish done?" he asked anxiously.

"The Beards?" Happy Speaker hazarded, miming with a hand. When Exemplary Fortune agreed, he shrugged. "For the past few months, I've been with Whence Reckoning in Sundried. The day after we got back to the Unique Inca—he had already started for Great Granary—he told me to deliver that message to you. I think the Beards have landed in the north somewhere. I'll be traveling with you to rejoin Cable . . . ah, Exemplary Royal Happiness."

Happy Speaker delivered this information, or rather lack of information, with a naive gusto. He did not change his tone or indicate in any way that he knew Whence Reckoning's name might upset Exemplary Fortune. Whence Reckoning had assiduously avoided Exemplary Fortune on his journey into exile, as though his

very glance carried political suicide. If Exemplary Fortune understood Whence Reckoning's character properly, he would do everything possible to make sure Exemplary Fortune would never be in
a position to retaliate for that snubbing. Any other Inca would have
said his name in a way to indicate either sympathy or threat, but
Happy Speaker seemed oblivious.

Exemplary Fortune, Red Deer, and Cui bathed while Happy
Speaker went to start the messenger relay back to the Unique Inca.

"We'll have coca leaves against altitude sickness tomorrow,"
Exemplary Fortune promised Red Deer and Cui as he washed the
grime off his body.

"Is it all uphill from here?" Red Deer asked. She was slouched
down in the tepid water the tampu-keepers had provided, so only
her head stuck out.

"It is."

"How much higher do we go?" Cui asked, similarly immersed.
There was only a hint of plaintiveness in his tone, but, for Cui, this
was more significant than a vigorous complaint by others.

Exemplary Fortune had, foolishly, not thought about the problems of taking lowlanders into the highlands. "We are only a little
over seven thousand feet above the Great Lake here. Short stretches
of the route we must travel are eight thousand feet higher."

Cui turned slightly green, and Red Deer slid a little farther
into the water so that it sloshed against her lips.

"If you wish," said Exemplary Fortune, thinking as he spoke,
"we could stay here for three days to get accustomed to the altitude." Behindari was six days from Navel at the speed they had
been traveling. Great Granary was six or seven days farther, which
meant that the seventeen-day allowance for bad weather or accident
they had originally had was down to a tenday.

"Will that help?" Cui asked.

"Probably."

"And then we go higher," Red Deer said. Her tone was almost
too calm.

"Yes."

Cui and Red Deer looked at each other.

"We could try to travel tomorrow," said Cui tentatively.

Red Deer nodded. "Then, if we do have to rest, at least we will be closer to the right altitude."

Exemplary Fortune regarded them. Pushing ahead would not necessarily get them to the Unique Inca any faster, but they were right, they had to reach to a higher altitude to adjust properly. Unfortunately tomorrow's travel, even if they ran the whole day, would not get them into true highlands. Hopefully, it would be high enough. "Okay then, tomorrow we go up."

Cui pulled himself out of the tub, turning away from them so as not to expose his genitals to Red Deer. Traveling together as intimately as they had been required a certain delicacy that Cui had proved himself good at.

As Cui dressed, Exemplary Fortune pulled himself out of the tub and began drying himself off. As he dried himself, he thought about the situation he had walked into. Cable had surmised that Exemplary Fortune would not recognize Happy Speaker and so had underestimated him, but not by much. Exemplary Fortune had not thought to ask Majestic Quinoa about the brothers he had known only as children. The Unique Inca's implied warning that Exemplary Fortune did not know enough to meddle in the Four Quarters' politics was valid.

Headband and Slinger—he did not even know Slinger's adult name—both would be nearly eighteen now, and both were children of Young Majesty and a sister-wife. If they had any character at all, they would soon be political forces to reckon with. Whence Happiness, Headband's mother and Young Majesty's queen, had briefly been the Unique Inca's mother when her son Bright Rainbow was fringed. She, like many of Young Majesty's wives and other Incas, had ambitions. Or had Exemplary Royal Happiness so consolidated his power that no one was thinking those thoughts anymore? Exemplary Fortune did not know.

In a real sense he did not even know the Unique Inca. He still thought of Cable as a petulant child. Whatever he had become, he was no longer a child. Exemplary Fortune would have to discipline himself to accept Cable's reign unreservedly. Winning Cable's—the Unique Inca's—trust would probably not be easy.

That evening the four of them sacrificed to the mountains they were entering and especially the volcano, Risk, which towered over the town and had once destroyed it, killing all the original inhabitants. The people who now lived in Behindari were all descendents of colonists. The name of the town gave their ethnic origin, saying "behind" in both Humanity's Mouth and Aymara. The mountain gave them a mixed omen, promising they would reach their destination but without speed or comfort.

The next day, everyone started at a brisk walk, but, by midmorning, Cui had to stop for a break, sitting by the road with his head down breathing heavily. Red Deer sank down next to him in similar distress. Even for Exemplary Fortune the upland air had become cold and unforgiving. The coca, which normally kept altitude sickness at bay, gave little relief.

They traveled the rest of the day at slow walk, which got them to the next tampu by midafternoon. This was the pace of the Unique Inca's court. It was not the pace to get them to Exemplary Royal Happiness by Majestic Festival or during the festival or even during that month. They needed acclimatization. The four of them stayed at the small tampu for three days. The first day Exemplary Fortune was glad to rest, but, by the third day, he was walking restlessly through the small town around the tampu.

Happy Speaker went with him, and, as they walked, they talked about what Happy Speaker had absorbed of the current government. Most high administrative positions were filled by the same people who had filled them under Young Majesty, but Royal Reckoning, who had inspired Exemplary Fortune's homesickness at his trial, though still a courtier, was no longer Cable's chief advisor. That position had been taken over by Excellent Royalty, another of Young Majesty's advisors and his brother.

The commander of the Lynx Quarter was also new, someone Exemplary Fortune knew all too well, Magnanimous Strength, the former governor of Granary. He had won the game he had played and was, as far as Exemplary Fortune was concerned, in a dangerously powerful position. His duties would keep him from the army, but, sooner or later, they would meet again; and, when they did, Magnanimous Strength would still be the one in a position of power. Exemplary Fortune's only advantage would be that this time he would know what he faced.

Happy Speaker's view of Navel's politics was oddly free of interpretation, not, it seemed, from guile, but from a rather astonishing naivete. He saw events, but he did not think about them. His view of the war at the far edge of Sundried was more thoughtful, at least regarding battle tactics and the relative advantages of the empire and the Colddungs, who were still testing the empire's border. It would probably be easier, Exemplary Fortune thought, if the Four Quarters just conquered the area beyond Sundried rather than engaging in this interminable skirmishing. Happy Speaker did not offer any such overall strategy, nor, from his account, was it possible to decide whether the Unique Inca had any overall plan.

It was odd, Exemplary Fortune thought, that he had felt out of control in Completion. There he had gained the support of the people with knowledge and power so that he had known exactly what to do in each situation. He had also known the limits of his authority. Here he knew nothing and no one. He wished for one despairing moment that he had not brought the others with him, his position seemed so hopeless. But that was why he had brought them, to be his eyes and ears in places he could not reasonably or safely go. He simply had not realized before how little he knew. He had, after all, spent most of his life at court—but not the court he was traveling to.

The next day, the group again headed up into the mountains. This time Cui did not slow until nearly noon, and Red Deer, who had evidently decided she would keep going as long as he did, kept pace. They both refused to stop, even at noon, for more than a short break. They still could not run. The group traveled two tampus worth of distance that day, about half their speed before they started into the mountains. The next few days, as they ascended into the highlands, were equally slow. To his annoyance, Exemplary Fortune's hands, feet, and lips all swelled slightly. Exemplary Fortune called a break whenever Cui or Red Deer started to stagger, and the two always sank to the ground as though they would never get up. By evening, they stumbled as they walked no matter how many stops Exemplary Fortune called.

The group did not run or even jog; it toddled at a baby's pace. Every hour or two, the four would take a break, sitting by the side of the road, two exhausted figures, Exemplary Fortune, who fretted at their pace, and Happy Speaker, who was annoyingly blithe. As they rested, Happy Speaker practiced lilting tunes on a flute he had made. He did not seem the least bit bothered by their slow pace or worried about Cui or Red Deer. He apparently did not care what the Unique Inca Exemplary Royal Happiness might think of their tardiness. There were times when Happy Speaker's unfailing good humor made Exemplary Fortune want to strangle him. Perhaps he had been spending too much time with Tamed Ocelot.

Once the group reached the Majestic Road, it slowly increased its pace. The lowlanders began to adjust to the heights, and the undulating terrain went down as often as it went up. They finally reached Great Granary two days after the close of Majestic Festival's celebration, exhausted and sweaty late one afternoon.

A ten-group of guards was watching the southern entrance into the city as they walked in. Their leader and Exemplary Fortune recognized each other immediately. He was the fifty-captain who had taken Exemplary Fortune in bonds to Navel. Exemplary Fortune nodded civilly to him as he stepped forward to say, "I am to welcome you to Great Granary. Happy Speaker, your task is complete." That incurious young man nodded and left. "Exemplary Fortune, you," the captain hesitated a beat, "and your companions are to come with me."

The thirteen of them did not say anything to each other as they walked through the quiet streets of the city, its people resting after the festival. Exemplary Fortune was too tired to do much beyond contemplate a bath, food, and bed. He was not pleased when their guide turned away from the tampu and toward the Unique Inca's local compound. It might be a sign of goodwill if he were housed in the compound, but he was too tired and grubby to want to deal with sliding into the Unique Inca's court even at that low level. His heart beat faster as other, less pleasant possibilities occured to him. Cable could have lured him here simply to kill him. As an unwitting messenger, Happy Speaker would be ideal, and sending an escort whose captain had known Exemplary Fortune only as a prisoner was not a hopeful sign either.

His second-worst fear was realized when the captain stopped at the entrance to a storeroom that held the packets everyone must carry when being introduced to the Unique Inca's court. Exemplary Fortune was given a bag that was light enough to be a largely ceremonial burden while Cui and Red Deer were given more substantial weights in line with their lesser status. Exemplary Fortune tried to gather his wits in the short time it took the captain to cross the courtyard and announce him to a room filled with Incas and honorary Incas, the Unique Inca himself sitting at the far side of the room.

Exemplary Fortune advanced into the room, his burden properly on his back. He bowed low, giving Cable the ceremonial kiss with his free hand. This was, in fact, the first proper obeisance he had ever given Exemplary Royal Happiness, since a bow with one's hands tied could hardly count as proper. When he looked up, Exemplary Hawk, standing two places to the Unique Inca's left, nodded him to an empty spot in the first row of those sitting on the bright, patterned rugs. Exemplary Fortune sat down on the rug indicated, while Cui and Red Deer squeezed in behind him.

Exemplary Fortune tried to gather with his eyes the positions of everyone in the room, trying to evaluate who was in favor and who was not. He was singularly unsuited for this task. In Young Majesty's court, his place had always, even as a young child, been at his father's side. He had disdained the maneuverings of others for royal favor or for his favor because he was close to the emperor. It would be very difficult to match those who had been scheming since they were weaned.

"You have been quick," the Unique Inca said. "We are pleased."

"My lord, I seek only to do your will," Exemplary Fortune replied.

Cable had grown into his position. His face was calm and composed, though his mouth had hardened, and its edges turned down. Something in his eyes said he had indeed become a god, even if an unhappy one. He nodded to Excellent Royalty on his right, who asked, "Do you have information we should learn about the Beards who came to Recognition four years ago?"

"Indeed I have," said Exemplary Fortune.

"Tell us."

"The Beard who has lived with me these past four years knows about nothing but fighting. He believes those who work the land are inferior. He believes all the gods except the Spanish—Beard—ones are rotten and that all humanity must eventually learn to worship Beard gods. His desire for gold is totally irrational, unmotivated by any pleasure in its beauty or any other feeling that I understand.

"None of his other traits would be as frightening were it not for his excellence in combat. He is unsurpassed in all forms of hand-to-hand fighting." Cable and his court already knew something about that, but he had to reinforce this beyond hope of quibbling. "Because knowing his fighting capabilities is so important, I had him practice with the turn-warriors as he wished. He beat them all. He beat me. He beat the province's military trainer. He beat any three or four who were sent against him, even me and the provincial trainer. No one and no stratagems could stand against him.

"But he complained. He complained that our swords were dull and too easily broken. He complained that our tactics stank. I did not know how to make a Beard sword to discover if it was indeed superior to ours, but I could let him teach his tactics to the turn-workers of Great Completion. And so I did."

Cable's face grew very still, Excellent Royalty raised his eyes to the room's guards, and there was a general uneasy silence at that remark. This they had not expected. He had their attention.

"Not all the turn-workers of Great Completion learned Beard tactics, but many did. After a winter of training, we met the warriors of Completion's two forts, who outnumbered us by three to one. We defeated them in one hour. The next year, after the forts had been trained in Beard tactics, we did much worse, and, when the Beard fouled a fort player, the forts' team was declared the winner. The Beard tactics were clearly the deciding factor.

"But I was not satisfied. All our fights had used practice rules.

There might be some flaw in Beard tactics that would only show itself against an opponent who did not follow those rules. And so, the next year, I had Completion's warriors take their blunted practice spears into Pormoco territory to learn if we could hold out against a determined enemy. After less than three hours of throwing themselves against our solid wall of fighters, the Pormoco sent a leader to ask if we mocked them. When I said no, he asked us to go home, which we did. In those three hours of concentrated attack by an enemy at least six times our size, only one man received serious injury, a young man who broke our pattern. The rest of us were never in any danger, and, had the Pormoco force been twice as large, the result clearly would have been the same."

There was a murmur throughout the room at this confession, but neither the Unique Inca nor his chief advisor moved.

"Weapons and tactics I know about, but, just before I left Completion, the Spaniard told me to beware of an animal he called a *cáballo,* which, he says, is something like a llama but much bigger and with sharp metal feet. He says they will kill us all.

"Spanish tactics give an advantage of about ten to one over those we are used to. If their weapons and the *caballo* each give a similar advantage, it is likely that a single Spanish warrior could do as much damage as a thousand of ours. I believe that the Spanish are the worst threat ever to face the Four Quarters."

There was absolute silence in the room as Exemplary Fortune finished talking. He discovered that he was shaking. He had put all of himself into that speech, and what happened to him and the empire would depend on how the Unique Inca responded.

The Unique Inca regarded him for some time before saying, "I do not remember your report about the excursion into Pormoco territory."

"I had intended that report to be part of this year's tribute. When I was summoned to your presence, it seemed a perfect personal offering. I did not realize I would be too late to make this a Majestic Festival offering. I apologize."

The Unique Inca regarded him a while longer before again turning to Excellent Royalty. Excellent Royalty said, "You seem to trust a great deal that this Beard who has been with you is typical of his tribe. What evidence leads you to this conclusion?"

I'm too tired for this, Exemplary Fortune thought, but he had no choice, and he had thought about the question beforehand. He wished, though, that Excellent Royalty did not sound quite so skeptical. "Two things: His own, originally unquestioned, belief that his way was always right. He did not even consider that alternative ways of functioning might be anything but barbaric and illogical. Second, he was left by his fellows in an unknown but apparently friendly land. Either he was someone they wished to get rid of as a miscreant, and they did not warn us, or he was someone they regarded as a true representative." He was too tired to think of the logical arguments against the first possibility, which had been obvious earlier, but Ginez's new name was still in his mind. With a silent apology to the man, he spoke that name. "Partridge believed he was someone who should be obeyed."

At Partridge's name, the Unique Inca's eyes grew wary, and Exemplary Fortune wondered what he had stirred up. But no one said anything about Partridge. Instead, Excellent Royalty continued to question him about Tamed Ocelot, asking questions designed to shake his assertion of the Beards' fighting prowess, asking for examples, specific tactics, signs that Tamed Ocelot's madnesses were such that a culture could not survive if they were common to all.

Exemplary Fortune could answer all the questions, but his replies grew steadily less polished, and, perhaps, less convincing. He was also too tired to hear any traps that might exist in Excellent Royalty's words.

At last the Unique Inca waved his hand. "This will not settle anything. Exemplary Fortune, you have said that you believe the Beards are great tacticians. How long will it take you to teach selected members of my court these tactics?"

Exemplary Fortune hesitated, torn between his need to convince Cable as quickly as possible of the imminent Spanish threat and his memory of how hard it had been for Tamed Ocelot to convince them that the Spanish tactics would actually work. "At least a month and a half for the basics. The tactics are strange at first and difficult to accept."

"How soon will you be ready to start teaching?"

"Tomorrow morning."

The Unique Inca regarded him again. "We will watch your progress with interest. You must be tired from your long journey. Go, rest yourself."

Exemplary Fortune was indeed tired, too tired to argue that he wanted to stay to learn more about the Spanish threat. He had, in fact, learned nothing. But he could not assert himself. The Unique Inca had given him a small space in which to move, and he had to prove himself there. He made the proper obsequious gestures and left.

The next morning Exemplary Fortune woke in a room in the Great Granary palace, like many rooms in many emperor's palaces throughout the empire. It felt at once very familiar and very strange, like waking up in one's bed and discovering that strangers had moved into the family compound during the night. He reached out a hand to touch the stone wall next to him and ran his fingers along the smooth, closely fitted join between one stone and the next. The exquisite stonework filled him with homesickness and a vague disquiet. He threw off his covers. Red Deer stirred as he sat up, and they dressed together.

Outside in the courtyard was someone Exemplary Fortune had not expected to see. "Partridge," he said happily. He was delighted to see someone he knew. Only his second thought made him wonder if Partridge would be as glad to see him. Perhaps Exemplary Fortune's presence would be only a bitter reminder of his unhappy first days in the Four Quarters.

Partridge was wearing the copper earrings and pale blue headband of the Copper tribe. He looked much more relaxed and sure of himself than when Exemplary Fortune had last seen him. He smiled in his turn. "Exemplary Fortune, it is good to see you again." His smile and his words both seemed sincere. His speech was only slightly accented.

"As it is good to see you. The Copper garb and earrings are very attractive on you."

Partridge ducked his head shyly. "At first, I was trained as a courtier, but it was hard for me to learn everything I needed to know. An omen of the Sun said I should be adopted by my wife's tribe. Among the Coppers, I discovered a talent for fighting. I am a better warrior than a courtier." He raised his right hand to his ear. "Also, my earlobes have not torn as some people said they would." Then he laughed. "Excuse me, I am to take you and your wife to breakfast. She will meet women there she can work with. Afterwards, I will take you and Cui to the courtyard where you are to teach."

"Ah, yes," said Exemplary Fortune. "This is Red Deer. I was so tired that I don't believe I introduced anyone last night."

"You didn't," said Red Deer. "I was tired too and welcomed the wait."

Partridge laughed again, but, over breakfast with Exemplary Fortune and Cui, he became somber. "Exemplary Royal Happiness brought me back from Sundried so I could tell him about the Beards, but I do not know enough to make him happy," he said with some of the anxiety Exemplary Fortune remembered.

"What have you told him?" Exemplary Fortune asked.

"I have told him that the Beards plan to conquer the Four Quarters, but I cannot tell him when or how. Because I know so little, I do not think he believes me. I wish I were back on the battlefields. I know what to do there."

"I can talk to the Unique Inca about some of the Beards' tactics," said Exemplary Fortune. "Maybe you could tell him about their weapons."

Partridge smiled sadly. "Their swords are very sharp and do not break easily. While I was in Castile, I never saw a battle. I was not supposed to be a fighter. I was not among the most respected people." He ducked his head. "I do not like saying that."

Yes, that would be an issue, especially among those who wanted the Beards to be innocent traders and would therefore malign anyone who tried to say they were dangerous. "Do you know about *caballos*?" Exemplary Fortune asked.

Partridge looked surprised. "I have never . . ." he hesitated as though looking for a word, the first time he had done that this day ". . . sat atop one while it was moving."

"Is this how they are used?" Exemplary Fortune asked.

"Yes."

"Can someone use a sword while sitting on one?"

Partridge closed his eyes and thought for a heartbeat. "Yes."

"How high is a person sitting on a *caballo*?"

Partridge looked around at the other people eating and then stood. He raised a hand over his head. "A person's shoulder would be about here," he said. He sat down again.

"So a person sits on a living seat that will go wherever he wants, and he can cut down at standing people," said Exemplary Fortune.

"Yes," said Partridge again.

"I would think that would give them quite an advantage."

"It does."

"This is something Exemplary Royal Happiness should know."

"You are right," said Partridge unhappily. "I will have to ask for an audience."

"It may be that he will summon you himself. I mentioned *caballos* to him."

"That would be easier," said Partridge, and then more happily, "but come, let me show you the courtyard where you will teach."

For the next few days, Exemplary Fortune and Cui gave lessons to twenty of the Unique Inca's men, among them six captains that Exemplary Royal Happiness had specifically ordered to study under Exemplary Fortune and fourteen volunteers. Among the volunteers was the captain who had taken Exemplary Fortune to Navel as a prisoner. His name was Inca Garden, and he was one of Exemplary Fortune's most apt pupils because he actually believed that the cumbersome-feeling moves and arrangements would one day improve his fighting ability. Meeting Tamed Ocelot tended to have that effect on people.

Most of the volunteers, though, were only moderately interested in the moves or the Beards and came to practice because they thought it might improve their standing with the Unique Inca. Unfortunately, those who thought associating with Exemplary Fortune would improve their lot were neither among the smartest of

Exemplary Royal Happiness's courtiers nor his best warriors. Still, they were at least as skilled as the turn-workers Tamed Ocelot had had to work with. If Exemplary Fortune could somehow simulate Tamed Ocelot's edged fierceness, he might get more out of them, or, then again, they might all quit.

For his part, Exemplary Fortune had forgotten how consistently the empire's warriors focused their attack on their opponents' heads. It now looked odd, and he could hear Tamed Ocelot's nasty comments about how easy the students would be to bring down. In spite of that, Exemplary Fortune decided to ignore where their clubs hit at first and instead concentrate on having them move together and support each other's attacks.

The second day, Cable invited Cui to dinner, which Cui accepted with equanimity. Afterward, Cui reported that the Unique Inca had asked not only about the Beards but also about Exemplary Fortune. "He wanted to find out if I would say anything bad about you," he said with a sly grin.

"And?" Exemplary Fortune prompted.

"I told him that, when you were deprived of your wives for more than a month, you became positively surly."

"Now that," said Red Deer, "is unfair. If the Unique Inca takes my husband away, I will likewise become sullen. The whole camp will have to endure my outrage. You did not think of your fellows."

"If the Unique Inca asks me again," said Cui gravely, "I will be sure to tell him that my first comments were less than half the story."

Exemplary Fortune smiled and hoped their implicit optimism was justified.

Red Deer spent her days with the women of the Unique Inca's court, eagerly learning all they would teach her about logistics, cooking, and politics. She was well on her way to making friends, to fitting into court life.

Exemplary Fortune, contrariwise, felt even more alienated than he had expected. Even though he had known many of Exemplary Royal Happiness's staff only four years ago as Young Majesty's courtiers, they were all strange to him. They had different interests, a different lord than they had had before. Their motives were strange to him and his to them. He could no longer provide them an automatic audience with the Unique Inca if he chose. But that was perhaps too cynical. Everyone had a great deal of work to do. Or perhaps not cynical enough. Some who had sought his company in Young Majesty's court now looked away when he walked by and even moved away from him, as though he had some contagion that would infect them if they were too friendly.

He sometimes felt as though Red Deer, Cui, and Partridge were the only ones who were willing to talk with him when they weren't required to, but that wasn't quite true. Splinter, now a ten thousand–captain, greeted him cordially when their duties intersected, which was rarely.

Inca Garden, now one of Cable's trusted courtiers, also talked with him much more than was required by the lessons. Though Exemplary Fortune suspected the Unique Inca had told him to draw Exemplary Fortune out, Inca Garden seemed honestly interested in Exemplary Fortune's opinions. He was the one who, on the third day, in a midday break from fighting practice, told Exemplary Fortune how the Beards had come to the Four Quarters. Two hundred and seven people of whom 163 had beards had walked into Incense from the jungle to the north and had since settled into the tampu there as though they intended to stay forever.

"What has everyone wondering, though," Inca Garden said, "is the message we received the morning of the day you arrived. Another thirty-six Beards got off another boat and joined those already in town. Most think the number is too small to mean anything."

"They could have had the order to attack," said Exemplary Fortune. "Did they unload any supplies?"

Inca Garden shook his head. "All the message said was men and twelve llama-like animals."

"We need to capture one of these animals."

"That is not our decision to make," said Inca Garden without any reproach in his voice.

"That is true." Exemplary Fortune fought down an impulse to get up and pace. "Forgive me. My father did not give me lessons in being subordinate."

"That is what I had heard," said Inca Garden gravely. Then suddenly they were grinning at each other. Somewhat diffidently, Inca Garden said, "It took me a while to realize that you really hadn't provoked the Beard. I heard about the man he killed in Navel, and every time the story was different. There are still a few who believe you tried to incite him to kill Cable."

Exemplary Fortune grimaced, but there wasn't anything he could do about the rumor except practice humility and not kill Cable. The second would be much easier than the first.

"Partridge has convinced a fair number of people that his version of what happened is true, partly because it was seen in such ignorance," Inca Garden said after a time. "His gentle manner has even convinced a few that you must have a quiet heart."

"Do you think I am a danger to Partridge?" Exemplary Fortune asked. It was something he had worried about off and on since he arrived.

"Probably not. Since everyone knows you were his teacher, most do not hold his defense of you against him even when they do not believe it."

"He seems to feel that the Unique Inca is upset with him."

"Disappointed. Cable had hoped Partridge would give him definite information about the Beards. He does not enjoy having to rely on you."

"I do understand that," said Exemplary Fortune. "I would want as many informants as possible myself were I in his position." And then, as his students began drifting back onto the practice field, he said, "Thank you for your information. I've been gone so long and so far away from the Four Quarters' center that I feel almost totally ignorant."

"It is good you know that," said Inca Garden. "Many felt you would be dangerously arrogant once you returned to court. You do have a following."

A following. No one here had mentioned Shrewdness, Thorniest, Flowerbud, or anyone else in the northern army, and he had not dared to ask. "Not here," he said, and then, hearing in those words an ambition he would not admit, he added, "My first loyalty has always been to the Four Quarters. There may have been times when I had overly grand ambitions, but, while the Beards are undefeated anywhere near our borders, my love for the empire will not let me stir up political turmoil." He gave a wry grin. "Maybe, in a hundred years, when we have defeated the Beards on their home territory, Exemplary Royal Happiness's grandson will have trouble with my waka. Until then—," he shrugged "—you can tell the Unique Inca he doesn't have to worry about me."

"I do not think Cable believes the Beards are a hundred-year threat," said Inca Garden.

"That is the problem," said Exemplary Fortune. "Most people don't." He got up to begin the afternoon lesson.

An hour after practice started, a young man came running up to the practice field. "The Unique Inca wants you," he said somewhat breathlessly to Exemplary Fortune. That had been Cable's previous message, and the meaning of this one was undoubtedly the same: the Beards had done something. Stinking, he needed more time. "Take over," he said to Cui and ran.

The Unique Inca's audience room was in turmoil, people talking loudly and fast as though they were frightened, interrupting each other. No one seemed to be in control.

The Unique Inca was staring fixedly at the doorway, and so he was almost the first one to see Exemplary Fortune. "Exemplary Fortune," he said, not loudly, but cutting through the babble like a knife.

Exemplary Fortune stepped into a completely silent room. He gave the formal kiss and walked to within paces of the Unique Inca's seat. "My lord, I come at your bidding."

Cable lifted a quipu he'd been fingering from his lap. "We have just received a message from Reckoning Sadness, who was sent with five hundred warriors to reinforce Incense's troops. They arrived too late. According to the message, all Incense's defenders have been killed by the Beards. The quipu gives no details." He held the knotted cords out as though Exemplary Fortune could find hidden messages in them.

Exemplary Fortune took the necessary four steps to take the quipu from Cable's fingers. The quipu gave numbers: 487 warriors;

487 dead. No dead enemies. He ran the quipu through his fingers, and then looked up at Cable.

"You are the only one who came close to predicting this," said the Unique Inca. "I must regard your words more seriously now. What do you recommend?"

Exemplary Fortune seated himself about two paces away from and facing the Unique Inca. He looked at Excellent Royalty on the Unique Inca's right. "In a battle with troops of similar skills, how great would the odds have to be in your favor before you would expect your troops to take no casualties?"

"We do not know that the Beards expected no casualties," Excellent Royalty protested.

"That is true," said Exemplary Fortune. "We also have no evidence that they wouldn't have escaped unscathed from forces two or ten times as large. The quipu says battle rather than ambush. That is all we know. Our estimates will necessarily be crude."

"Even against overwhelming odds," said Excellent Royalty, "a boy with a sling may get lucky—"

"At least a hundred to one," interrupted Inca Fox, standing at Excellent Royalty's right. Excellent Royalty and he exchanged an unfriendly look.

That was not what Exemplary Fortune wanted either, to stir up dissension among the Unique Inca's advisors. Maybe he was doing this all wrong. "Very well," he said. "Let us take that as a starting point. I have been told there were two hundred Beards. So we should gather an army of at least twenty thousand. My personal recommendation is fifty thousand. That gives us reserves in case the Beards receive reinforcements before we meet them.

"We also need more information about them. Putting one or two spies in their camp would be ideal, but, if we can't do that, we at least need to have scouts follow them through the jungle.

"We need to be closer to where they are." Exemplary Fortune paused, wondering how many recommendations he could give before the Unique Inca would balk.

"Do you have any idea where they are headed?" Cable asked.

Exemplary Fortune closed his eyes, listening to his heart. "Recognition," he said finally. "They left two of their men there four years ago. They will return to find out what their spies have learned." And discover that neither was there. How would Tamed Ocelot react if he found them missing? If his words were any indication, he'd massacre the whole city for the disappointment.

"So you think we should go to Recognition?" the Unique Inca asked.

"I think an army should go to Recognition," said Exemplary Fortune. "So much of what I have recommended is based on probabilities that I would not risk the Unique Inca and his court on them. Perhaps I have been too conservative, and a smaller army could utterly destroy the Beard force. Perhaps they can destroy a force of fifty thousand as easily as a force of four hundred and ninety. If the Four Quarters loses fifty thousand warriors, it will survive; but, if it loses the Unique Inca and his entire court in battle, it may not. The Beards may even believe we will know where they are going and have reinforcements meet them in or just before Recognition. Recognition could be a trap."

"Then what exactly is your proposal?" Cable asked.

"I propose that the court should move north, but no closer to Recognition than Heads-of-Corn. Meanwhile, a fifty-thousand-warrior army should be assembled and moved as quickly as possible to Recognition to defend or, if the Beards are moving swiftly, retake the city. If at all possible, the army should be in direct contact with whatever spies we can insinuate into the Beard force."

"Who should lead this army?" Cable asked, his voice full of mistrust.

Exemplary Fortune's heart beat faster. He had faced this Unique Inca's suspicion before. That time he had survived, but he did not believe Cable would send him into exile again. He spread his hands. "I am not qualified to make that decision. I no longer know who the Four Quarters' best commanders are. I can advise you about the Beards, not about the empire." That was not only the politically safe answer, it also happened be true. Thorniest was the empire's best commander against unexpected strategies; but, as far as the Unique Inca's court was concerned, he apparently didn't exist.

Cable nodded. He turned to Excellent Royalty. "Have the appropriate messages sent to Reckoning Sadness and to the cities on the Road. We start north tomorrow. Inca Fox, you will organize the army. Exemplary Fortune, you will continue to teach Beard tactics."

It was a clear dismissal. Exemplary Fortune bit back the remaining words he wanted to say, got up, and, bowing low, left the room. Cable had made his role clear. He would be the Unique Inca's expert on Beards, called in whenever his other advisors could not deal with whatever the Beards had done. He was a panic stopper, not a true advisor. As such, he should do well. If the Unique Inca and his advisors did not change their attitude, Exemplary Fortune expected disaster and so would not panic no matter what the Beards did, but this role was not what he wanted. He wanted more information. He wanted to be able to create a plan that would upset the Beards as much as the Beards were upsetting the Unique Inca's court, as much as he apparently upset the Unique Inca.

He tried to tell himself it was all right, that, as one of the few people in the empire who knew Spanish tactics, his role should be that of teacher. But there was so much more that had to be done. Enough, he told his restless heart; he had done what he could. The rest had to be the Unique Inca's problem. He went back to the practice field to teach his unbelieving pupils.

For the next tenday, the Unique Inca's court moved from tampu to tampu north through the heart of the empire in a slow-motion reversal of Exemplary Fortune's journey of four years before. It was even the same season, and crops flecked the fields with green while the rains came down lightly and then more heavily as the days went on. Inca Fox assembled an army of local tribes while messengers ran ahead ordering supplies redistributed to provide for the army and the Unique Inca's court.

Exemplary Fortune again began having nightmares of death and destruction, his children, wives, mother, Partridge, Cui, everyone who relied on him being cut down in flight while the Unique Inca watched in openmouthed incomprehension. When Exemplary Fortune moved to help, he found his hands and feet bound. Sometimes his father watched, shaking his head sadly or offering unintelligible advice.

On the eleventh day, Exemplary Fortune was again summoned to the Unique Inca's presence. His troops were not ready was his first thought. But that was unreasonable. Twenty men would not make a significant difference. And that was only part of the problem.

This time, the Unique Inca's office was a moving space on the Majestic Road defined by lower-level courtiers carrying umbrellas. The rules were the same, though, and Exemplary Fortune bowed, blowing a kiss as he entered. The same courtiers flanked Cable. Excellent Royalty had his own litter. The gold of Cable's litter gleamed wetly as he greeted Exemplary Fortune. Then he said to a young man Exemplary Fortune had not seen before, "Ichu Grass, now give us your report."

Ichu Grass bowed his head. "My lord, I was with the forces Reckoning Sadness gathered to relieve the forces of Incense." He took a deep breath. "We marched into Incense in early afternoon. The fields outside, there were bodies in the fields. Young and middle-aged men. We could hear no sounds of battle. As we marched into the city, there were more and more dead, some with grievous wounds like none that we had seen before. As we approached the plaza, in some places the streets were so thickly strewn with bodies it was hard to find a place to step. The bodies were cold like those who have been dead for many hours, and there were flies and other insects crawling on them. They had not been moved from where they had fallen. Because we still heard no sound of battle, Reckoning Sadness called out to ask if anyone were still alive. An old woman came out of a house. 'Help us,' she said, 'we have given hospitality to those with foul hearts, and they have killed us all.' That is what she said, but it was not quite true."

As Exemplary Fortune walked slowly through the rain listening to Ichu Grass tell the story of the massacre, he thought he had been wrong to believe the Beards would slaughter people only for cause. He had forgotten how long and how hard Tamed Ocelot's civilizing had been. His lips tightened with anger.

He watched the Unique Inca and his court to see how they

reacted to the story. They all listened openmouthed with shock. Perhaps they would take the Beard threat more seriously now.

"They made the tampu-keepers feed them," Ichu Grass said, "and stayed in the tampu for the night as though they had done nothing wrong. In the morning they went away south into the jungle.

"We came that afternoon. There were only a very few men of fighting age left in the whole city. Most were crippled. Three had run away and hidden successfully. The Beards also killed a number of women, protesting Mothers, women trying to defend their homes, some apparently at random. They also killed some older men, even a few children. As one of the women said, they had not even enough left to tend the dead.

"The men who had been killed by the beasts had horrible wounds as though the beasts had feet like knives, as though a huge weight had landed on them. When I left, Reckoning Sadness's other warriors were busy preparing the dead. The people have asked for a cleansing ceremony to wipe out the foulness. The town will also need new husbands for the surviving women. All this Reckoning Sadness ordered me to make known to you."

As Ichu Grass finished his narration, there was a great sigh through the Unique Inca's court. Even the Finger tribesmen bearing Cable's litter took a deep breath as though they had not done so for some time.

The Unique Inca sat with his head down for a time as his bearers carried him ever closer to the Beard army. When he raised his eyes, his gaze sought out Exemplary Fortune. "Again, you seem to have predicted this. You seem to understand the Beards well. And again I ask, what is your recommendation?"

"May I ask a few questions first?"

The Unique Inca inclined his head in permission.

"From what you have said," Exemplary Fortune said to Ichu Grass, "the Beards were able to talk with the people of Incense. Did the Beards know Humanity's Mouth, or did they have interpreters?"

"They had interpreters," said Ichu Grass without hesitation. "The tampu-keepers said two young men without beards translated for them, and one of the Beards was trying to learn Humanity's Mouth, though he wasn't yet proficient."

"Were the interpreters free or confined?"

"Nobody said anything about them being confined."

"Besides the beasts, did the Beards have any other strange animals or devices?"

Ichu Grass thought a bit. "The survivors mentioned several devices. The swords the Beards carried were very sharp and gleamed like water in the midday sun. They had a long heavy tube on a platform—I didn't understand very well—but it required many men to pull the tube and platform together. No one said anything about it doing anything, but it was big enough that several people mentioned it. Maybe it was their waka."

Still not enough information. Exemplary Fortune looked at Cable. "Since we do not have any likely spies in the Beard camp, my recommendations remain basically unchanged. We need, as quickly as possible, to find out any and all information about the Beards and wipe them out as a fighting force.

"My one new thought is about these beasts of theirs. They sound far more deadly than I would have believed possible. It sounds as though we need to know more about them before we send a full-scale army against the Beards. But we are still more than a month away from Recognition. If they move quickly, it may be impossible for us to get the information we need before they reach that city. My heart is torn. To send an army, even a small army, to be slaughtered is unconscionable; and yet, if we take time to gather information first, they may well occupy Recognition." If Macaw were still chief, Exemplary Fortune would bet his canniness against the Beards; but, if he said that, he might well make Cable suspicious of Macaw and less likely to accept any plan using him. "Who is Recognition's chief?"

At Cable's glance, a courtier answered, "Macaw."

"I have only met him once," said Exemplary Fortune to the courtier. "Is he the type of man who could turn his city's occupation against the invaders—?"

"No," interrupted Cable. "We will not sacrifice one of our cities to the Beards." He glared at Exemplary Fortune.

"Forgive me," said Exemplary Fortune. "I see only bad choices. I was exploring one of them."

"That choice is unacceptable," said Cable stiffly.

"Understood," said Exemplary Fortune, "but, given that we do not know how fast these Beards can travel when they wish to hurry, I do believe we should warn Macaw that there is an invasion force headed toward his city."

"We will take it under advisement," said Cable. "You are dismissed."

Exemplary Fortune bowed again and jogged to his place near the beginning of the line where the lesser types walked.

"What was it?" Cui asked, and everyone on either side of them leaned in to hear the news.

"More information about how the Beards devastated Incense. Unfortunately, the *caballos* appear to be even more dangerous than I had expected." For the benefit of his listeners, he gave a full account of the massacre.

After walking in silence for a time, Cui asked, "Do you think Tamed Ocelot's tactics will defeat these animals?"

"I think we're missing information," said Exemplary Fortune. "The Beards must have a way to defend against *caballos,* but Tamed Ocelot taught us tactics to fight against warriors on foot." If they couldn't get information from the Beards' army, they should try to get it from Tamed Ocelot, but Tamed Ocelot was tendays away. Besides, given the way Cable reacted whenever he said anything, to mention Tamed Ocelot's name might well condemn him to death.

He needed a personal interpreter. Someone to explain to Cable that, however uncouth or arrogant or whatever it was that bothered the Unique Inca, he was really a gentle person, full of goodwill for the empire and its Unique Inca. Partridge did some of that, but Partridge was too timid to be a good defender. And Cable's chief advisors seemed to be defaming him. Exemplary Fortune had the feeling Excellent Royalty would much rather he were dead. Cable himself might even be a moderate. Exemplary Fortune's supporters were all elsewhere, unmentioned and unmentionable.

That evening at the night's tampu, Inca Fox stopped for a time to watch Exemplary Fortune's fighting practice. The next morning he left with his army for Recognition, moving faster than the emperor's court with all its functionaries could manage. Still, Cable did start moving more quickly, traveling two tampus' worth of distance a day instead of one whenever possible.

Exemplary Fortune had mixed feelings about their new pace. It brought them closer to the Beards so that they could learn their doings and tactics more quickly—though Inca Garden said Cable had not yet sent out spies to watch them as they traveled—but it gave him less time for practice just when some of the men were beginning to show signs of understanding what he wanted, and he was dreadfully afraid that Cable planned to go all the way to Recognition—because Exemplary Fortune had recommended against it, if for no other reason. They did not have nearly enough information to risk the Unique Inca against the Beards.

Information was constantly flowing into and out of the Unique Inca's court, but Exemplary Fortune heard little of it. Inca Garden and Partridge both gave him tidbits, though Partridge tended to talk mostly of court personalities, which, given the circumstances, often made Exemplary Fortune impatient. Cui and Red Deer picked up some of the daily chitchat, again mostly information about court personalities. Exemplary Fortune had to keep reminding himself that, though this would not save the Four Quarters, it could keep him alive.

One piece of information caused such a stir that even Exemplary Fortune heard. A messenger, sent to the World Animator's oracle before the court had learned of the slaughter at Incense, came back with the report that the World Animator said the Beards were peaceful travelers who would cause the Four Quarters no harm. Thankfully, Cable did not summon Exemplary Fortune to comment on the prophecy. Inca Garden said the courtiers who dared venture an opinion on the oracle divided into two groups. Some said the slaughter at Incense must have been some kind of mistake, while a few held that the Beards came from a land so far away it was beyond the ken of even the World Animator. The news cast a pall of uncertainty over the court. Nearly every night, the Unique Inca would go into the local Sun temple to have omens taken.

Exemplary Royal Happiness stopped only the minimum four days for Little Ripening's festival and then traveled on. It took all four days for Exemplary Fortune to get his trainees back to the level they had been at before the Unique Inca had started traveling so fast. When they moved on again, it took all his self-control not to vent his frustration.

The Unique Inca's court reached Heads-of-Corn in time for the festival of Great Ripening and spread out above the town in bright tents. Cable, though, wanted to be closer to Recognition and, as soon as the festival was over, had an encampment erected on a rough promontory on the edge of the cliffs as close to Recognition as possible. The site, according to Cui, was above a stream that carried water only in the rainy season. It was also twenty miles from the city, half a day at a fast walk and much too close for Exemplary Fortune's peace of mind. But he had made his position clear. He could do no more. He drilled his twenty, trying to get them proficient enough for a practice battle before Cable moved again and fretted.

Five days after the end of the festival, Cable moved the entire court onto the desert promontory. It was at the edge of the coastal desert, and therefore dusty and almost unbearably hot.

The first night there, Cable invited Exemplary Fortune to dinner. He did not invite Red Deer, as might be expected, so Exemplary Fortune was a little suprised to find Cable's queen at the meal. But Fecund Dove was a quiet woman who Red Deer said never spoke in council. If Cable wanted to isolate Exemplary Fortune in any disagreement, Fecund Dove would not likely upset his plans. The fourth member of the party was Excellent Royalty, whose opinions Exemplary Fortune had heard too often. Cable appeared to have chosen his guests in a manner designed to produce indigestion.

The Unique Inca kept up a light patter throughout dinner while Exemplary Fortune and Excellent Royalty eyed each other warily. The queen tried to keep the conversation going, and, for her sake at least, Exemplary Fortune tried occasionally to insert some pleasantly neutral comment; but, all too often, he and Excellent Royalty would choose the same observation to remark on, and, each falling silent as the other started to speak, the group would relapse into silence. Only Cable seemed to be enjoying himself. After dinner, the queen, who was visibly pregnant, pleaded exhaustion and was excused.

Cable looked at his two remaining guests with satisfaction. "I wanted you here together because you agree about a decision I need to make immediately. Both of you think I should stay out of harm's way, in Navel perhaps, during the coming battle with the Beards. Both of you say we cannot afford to risk the Unique Inca at this time. Neither of you mention that our fathers spent most of their lives in battle. Neither Young Majesty nor Royal Reckoning Inca allowed their advisors to keep them hundreds of miles from the cities and fields where the empire's fate would be decided. Tell me now, why should I be the only one thus sequestered?"

Excellent Royalty was staring at his beer tumbler. Exemplary Fortune had the strong feeling that he and Cable had already had this discussion at least once. He wished he and Excellent Royalty had talked earlier, but Cable knew they hadn't, and so now he could play them off against each other.

"This is not the same kind of war," said Exemplary Fortune. "When our father and grandfather fought, they chose the battleground and the time. They went looking for people to conquer. The Beards have come looking for us. If the Glowings or the Chimu had not been added to the empire for another twenty years, it would have been unfortunate, but it would not have been a tragedy. If I am right, and the Beards seek to strike at the heart of the Four Quarters, then they may know enough by now to strike at your majestic person. For us to lose our Unique Inca during an invasion we do not know how to counter could well destroy us."

Cable eyed him for a time, not saying anything. Then he turned to Excellent Royalty. "Have you anything to add?"

"Only what I said before," replied Excellent Royalty. His voice held so much restraint that it hurt.

Cable turned to Exemplary Fortune. "He thinks I am still a child to be protected from all danger or chance of making a wrong decision."

Excellent Royalty's jaw worked, but he didn't say anything.

"I am not sure what you think of me," Cable continued to

Exemplary Fortune. "Since you may not have heard, four days ago Inca Fox reported columns of smoke from near the northern end of Highland Island. The islanders have not told us what happened—a lightning strike perhaps." Cable's voice was full of casual irony. "Tomorrow morning, I am going down to Recognition to lead a scouting party along the coast to see what we can find. Since you seem to know so much about these Beards, I'd like you with me in case we encounter any."

Four days, four days was exactly the time it would take a force to walk down the coast across from the northern end of Highland Island to Recognition. Exemplary Fortune had the strong feeling Cable was counting on that. "Where are Inca Fox's forces?"

"In Recognition," said Cable, as though it didn't matter. Then he added, as though it were a concession to Exemplary Fortune, "They have decided invasion forces are on the way."

With a fifty-thousand-man army in and around Recognition, and the five thousand men of the Unique Inca's court on the hills, Cable probably foreheard the Beards' puny forces trapped and destroyed in an action that would bring him fame and glory. Exemplary Fortune said, "I do not yet know how to defeat the Beards—"

"Then we may have to learn quickly," interrupted Cable.

"I will go with you and help you to the best of my ability," Exemplary Fortune started again. But that was not the right response either. It accepted too many of Cable's assumptions.

"I also will go with you," said Excellent Royalty.

"You have told me that you retired from fighting years ago," Cable said.

"My place is at your side," said Excellent Royalty.

"Not always," said Cable. His eyes were hooded, indecipherable.

"My lord, I beg of you—"

"I have spoken," said Cable, looking down at his beer. The calm in his voice was eerily disquieting.

Exemplary Fortune decided to try one more time. "My lord, if you wish to kill yourself, you have certain responsibilities—"

"That is not what I said," Cable retorted angrily. He started to get up, then thought the better of it and settled back down. "Excellent Royalty, tell him the results of the divinations."

Excellent Royalty sighed.

"Tell him," Cable insisted.

"All of the sacrifices we have done on the way here have suggested an ambiguous future for the Four Quarters. Some—"

"All," interrupted Cable again.

"—have suggested that the empire's future may be better if the Unique Inca himself leads the armies into battle."

But this was not the way to begin someone's military experience. Maybe Cable had led armies while Exemplary Fortune was in Completion, but he doubted it. He looked at Excellent Royalty, who was again staring at his beer. Obviously the man had given Cable all the arguments against this course of action that he could think of.

The Unique Inca was watching Exemplary Fortune appraisingly, waiting for his response. Why are you doing this? Exemplary Fortune wanted to ask. But, as the question formed in his heart, it answered itself. Unlike many of his brothers, Cable had never been in battle. Exemplary Fortune had always been a better fighter than he, and so were others Cable had to test himself against regularly.

Probably he had started this whole excursion to prove himself to his brothers. Though his brothers might defeat savage tribes on the edge of the Four Quarters, only the Unique Inca would settle the disposition of these strangers from unknown lands. Now that the Beards had proven themselves to be enemies of waka brutality, it would be the Unique Inca's duty and glory to bring peace back to the empire. Perhaps Cable even welcomed Exemplary Fortune's tales of the Beards' deadliness; for, if he could defeat Exemplary Fortune's superwarriors, his actions would rival World Reverser's defeat of the Ten tribe. But, if Cable reasoned thus, it might not be his brothers he sought to convince of his legitimacy but himself.

If Cable sought to prove himself to his brothers, his actions made political sense. Militarily, though, whatever his motives, his course of action was nearly insane. Cable had been working on this plan for months. No one was going to change his heart now. Exemplary Fortune took a deep breath. "My apologies. May I make one suggestion?"

"As you wish."

"Before the battle make it very clear who will lead the army if you can no longer command."

"You," said Cable simply.

Excellent Royalty stared at Cable as though he had suddenly and completely lost his reason.

There was a brief surge of joy in Exemplary Fortune's heart, and then an overwhelming dread. With no more introduction than that, he had very little chance of successfully doing anything. He swallowed. "Be sure that is clear to all the captains and to Inca Fox."

Cable turned to Excellent Royalty. "Make sure of it."

Excellent Royalty said cautiously, "As always, my desire is only to do your will—"

"Good," said Cable, cutting off whatever caveats Excellent Royalty would have added. He looked at each of them. "You have your duties."

Exemplary Fortune stood and made his farewells. Excellent Royalty followed him out the door of the tent. They stared at each other for a brief time, and then, as if by mutual agreement, turned each to go his own way. The dusty air was hot, and the wind seemed to blow their thoughts away before they could be uttered.

All that evening, Exemplary Fortune went to each of the captains who would be going down to the desert with the Unique Inca, talking with them briefly about the orders they had been given for the morning and, most importantly, their attitude toward the coming action. Most of them regarded the Beards with irate contempt. "Their hearts are rotten," said Alder Tree scornfully, the first man he talked to. "First they destroy one of our towns, and then they come with their three hundred men against us."

"Three hundred?" Exemplary Fortune asked, startled from his agenda.

Alder Tree nearly smirked. "Two of their boats were seen off Highland Island about a month ago. Weren't you told?"

"No, I wasn't," said Exemplary Fortune. "Most people do not seem to regard it as important whether the Beards have two hundred men or three. We are confident that, whatever their superiority in tactics or weapons, our numbers will overrun them. We do not stop to consider that they may have invaded with so few men precisely to lull us into this smug certitude." He paused long enough to let that sink in, but not long enough for Alder Tree to reply, and then said, "I ask only one question of you: if things do not go as you expect, will your men hold, or will they panic at the unexpectedness?"

That was the question he asked all evening long. He did not ask the captains if they would panic, he asked if their men would panic. Only some of the captains considered the question, but all of them, whatever their reaction, had had it put into their hearts that tomorrow's endeavor might go wrong. They also knew that he took seriously his charge to command if necessary. That was all he could do on such short notice and without any authority of his own until everything fell apart.

Exemplary Fortune decided not to take Cui with him. It would be a comfort to have someone he could depend on; but, if the battle went against them, he could not use Cui to relay commands or to command units who had lost their captains because he was not well enough known.

Inca Garden came to visit him about the time everyone was settling down for bed. He sat next to Exemplary Fortune outside the tent Exemplary Fortune shared with Red Deer and several low-level couples and said quietly, "You are certainly stirring up a fuss."

"I see that as my function," Exemplary Fortune replied. "Everyone else plans for a quick and easy victory, and I plan for what happens if everyone else is wrong."

"Inca Fox has the number of men you requested."

Exemplary Fortune shrugged. "We may win. That is certainly one possibility, but I cannot reckon it a surety the way everyone else does."

"Frankly," said Inca Garden, "I predict our greatest problem will be finding the Beards once they see us."

"May it be so," said Exemplary Fortune.

Inca Garden regarded him. "That will not accomplish our purpose of destroying them."

Exemplary Fortune shrugged. "If the Beards are hunted fugitives in our land, sooner or later we will track them down. I am not worried about that."

Inca Garden shifted position slightly. "There may be one possibility you have not thought of. I do not know if I should tell you this or not, but the Unique Inca regards tomorrow's venture partly as a test of your trustworthiness. If the Beards are as easily defeated as many expect, you yourself may be at risk."

"I am not surprised," said Exemplary Fortune. "It does not change my understanding of the Beards. I do not plan beyond tomorrow."

"I did not believe it would be otherwise," said Inca Garden, "but I did want to tell you."

"May it go well with us tomorrow," said Exemplary Fortune.

"May it go well," Inca Garden echoed. He stood and walked into the darkness.

Exemplary Fortune's last task of the evening was to talk with Red Deer and Cui about how to prevent panic and help the evacuation should the Beards appear to be in danger of penetrating this far. Then he went to bed. Sleep, with or without his father's warnings, was always the last task before battle.

17

SIXTEENTH YEAR OF KING CARLOS'S REIGN
FEBRUARY 1532

In actual history, Recognition had been ravaged before the Spanish returned. While the Incas were distracted by their civil war, the Highland Islanders pillaged the city and razed many of its buildings.

The Highland Islanders had set the Spanish down in the middle of a stinking swamp. It was almost nightfall when they reached land, and, since the Spanish killed the Islanders before they could guide them to a better campsite, it was up to Felipe to lead the way. Everyone knew this was his home ground. The terrain was simple, and Francisco Pizarro, among others, would figure it out if Felipe tried to lead them astray, so he simply led them straight away from the water. "Come," he said, "this is the fastest way to solid land." It felt like power to lead the Spanish in this manner, but that power was an illusion. He could take them only in the direction they wanted to go.

By the time the army reached solid ground, the night was fully dark, and, under the jungle's trees, not even the stars and moon could be seen. The Spanish looked around fearfully for unseen dangers. "Are there any villages here?" Francisco Pizarro asked.

"No one lives here," Felipe said, and then, because the Spanish did not treat their dead well, he added, "This is a land of the lost dead." After he said that, he bit his lip. He had promised himself that he would not say anything the speakers and elders in Recognition might contradict, and yet he just had. His heart was in too much turmoil. He did not act like he was frightened or upset because he couldn't, but he could no longer be sure what he might say or do.

"Whose dead?" Francisco Pizarro asked.

"I do not know," Felipe said. "That is just what I heard." He did not want to say anything else at all. He was worried about what he might blurt out. But he knew what he had been thinking when he started talking about the dead. He had been thinking of his family and friends in Recognition. He had seen the Spanish strike down the people of Incense, who had not tried to hurt them, and the Highland Islanders, who had. He could not make the Spanish turn around and go somewhere else, and the Highland Islanders had not killed enough of them.

He did not really even believe the Incas could stop Francisco Pizarro's army. They had run down the Inca captain so easily in Incense. Probably all his efforts to warn the Incas that the Spanish were coming would only mean that more people got killed.

He wished suddenly that Little Francisco was with him. Little Francisco would be even more frightened and helpless than Felipe. Felipe could take care of him and act strong. Maybe together they could even think of something that might stop the Spanish from overrunning the world.

Francisco Pizarro did not say anything to Felipe's words about the dead, but some of the men began starting at any sound outside of camp. A few even exclaimed when a boat-billed heron flew by with its low croaking cry. They had seen and heard these birds all the way down the coast and even hunted them once in a while, but now they thought it might be another night-flying demon like the bloodsuckers Felipe had also known about. It took a long time for the camp to get to sleep.

After the camp quieted, Felipe lay in the dark listening for sounds of home that he might recognize. After he fell asleep, he thought he saw his family sitting quietly at home, resting after their day's efforts and talking to each other. When he tried to say something to them, to warn them, he woke back in the Spanish camp. He thought then about stealing away into the darkness to make his vision real, but Francisco Pizarro and the other men would know where he had gone. In the morning or even earlier, they would send Hernando de Soto and the other horsemen after him. Even if the men could not ride their horses until they reached the edge of the trees, they would still catch him before he reached Recognition.

Besides, he had done one thing that had actually helped a little. If he had not been with the Spanish army, they might have stayed on the mainland and so avoided the Highland Islanders. He had killed fourteen of the Spanish with his words. If he stayed with them, he might be able to kill still more. He did not know where the Incas were, if he could contact them, if they would even believe what he told them. He only knew this one thing: if he stayed with the Spanish, there was a very small chance that he might be able to stop them somehow; but, if he left, they would certainly ride him down and kill him.

Something else nagged at his heart that did not let him go back to sleep again, but he was not sure what it was until he went back over everyone's actions all the way back to when they had first reached the Gulf of the Fieldguardians' Shrine. And then he wondered why none of the Spanish had blamed him when the Highland Islanders had attacked them. Somehow, he had convinced the Spanish that he was harmless or at least not capable of guile. Maybe they did not understand how someone could want both sides in a battle to lose. Maybe they understood fighting only when it used weapons or hitting or loud angry words.

They had all seen how clumsy he was when he tried to help with the cannon, and they knew Greek and he were friends. Maybe they thought that because he could not use weapons, he could not fight. Maybe because he had eaten the Islanders' food and decorated himself with their flowers more eagerly than anyone else, they believed he must have truly trusted the Islanders' hospitality. Whatever the Spanish believed in whatever combination, it gave him a little more space than he had thought he had to try to stop them. He did not know what he could do, what he might have to do;

but, if there was anything he could do to help the Incas and his people, he would.

In the morning, a number of the men who had been dumped into the water by the Highland Islanders were sick. Some of the Spanish wanted to stay where they were until the men were well, but their camp had no water except for the salty, muddy water from the marsh. Everyone knew Recognition was only a few days away, and Francisco Pizarro had little trouble convincing the men to make stretchers for the sickest and set out.

All that day and the next, they traveled along the edge of swamp with jungle on their right. Francisco Pizarro asked Felipe over and over again how his city was laid out, where the river came into it, and how many soldiers were in the Inca fort. These were all things Felipe wanted desperately to lie about, but he did not know how. He did not know what kinds of confusions would hurt the Spanish as they invaded the city. Would it be better to tell the Spanish there were more soldiers in the fort so they might be afraid, or fewer so they would not take the Inca defenders seriously? Also and always, he knew that, if the Spanish did make it into the city, and he had lied, they would never trust him again. They might even kill him. Felipe did not know if his possible murder should be important to him or not, but he did worry about it.

On the third day, the jungle began to thin a little, and on the fourth day, shortly after noon, they broke out into the open. The dusty air with the tang of the salt sea in it smelled achingly familiar to Felipe, and his eyes stung, and his throat grew thick. The army he was with had come to kill his family and friends. He did not know how to stop them. He did not know what the Incas were doing or where they were. He did not even know if anyone knew the Spanish were coming. If the Incas knew an army was headed toward them, why hadn't any of the Spanish seen their scouts? Maybe Young Majesty was still in Kitu Dove or Navel. Maybe the Incas weren't trying to protect his people after all.

All that afternoon, whenever the Spanish force climbed up small rises, they could see the top of the Inca fortress's walls ahead of them. Francisco Pizarro had a satisfied look in his eyes, and all the men were very alert. The women from Panama stayed in the very center of the group and carried their children. One of the men who had been sick died, but, except for his partner, none of the Spanish really seemed to care. They were much more cheered by the sight of the city ahead of them than saddened by the death of their companion. It was the Spanish way always.

They camped that evening on a bend in the Littlecorn River about half-a-day's march from his hometown. All that evening as Felipe helped set up camp and make dinner, he could hear the seedeaters singing their beautiful song from the grasses between the swampy shore and the desert. His heart ached with the music, and once, when he caught sight of the black-headed bird with white stripes on its wings, he almost called out to it. But he knew it would not carry his message or tell him anything he needed to know. Neither he nor the Spanish sentries saw anybody outside of camp, whether Inca, Matron, or Highland Islander.

In the morning, as they prepared to break up camp and march into Recognition, scouts reported that a huge army with tens of thousands of men in it was between the Spaniards and the city. Felipe lowered his head so no one would see his relief. The Incas were ready for them after all. The Spanish all looked at each other uneasily. Felipe could tell that the men were worried. Some of them muttered that it was time to retreat.

Francisco Pizarro, though, looked completely calm, like he was happier facing tens of thousands of the enemy than he would have been marching on with no enemies in front of them. He did not say anything to the worriers. Instead, he turned to Hernando de Soto, who was looking thoughtful, and said, "See if you can find us a route upriver around the Inca army."

Hernando de Soto smiled slightly and nodded. He gathered four more of the best horsemen, and they all climbed on their horses and rode east. Everyone else packed up camp, made sure their weapons were ready, and waited. To the men who insisted that they should go back into the jungle, Francisco Pizarro said, "Where should we go? Do we go back to the hospitality of the Highland Islanders? Do we go back to Incense, where there is no more gold? Or maybe you want to wander around in the jungle until you die of hunger?"

To this, the men had no reply.

In just over an hour Hernando de Soto and his small band came galloping back. Hernando de Soto was grinning as he pulled up in front of them. "There is another force coming from the east. It is much smaller than the army outside the city, maybe two thousand men. Even over the slopes, the men are carrying someone in a golden litter like the Highland Islanders say the Inca king rides in. If we move quickly, we should be able to cut them off before they can join with the main force."

Francisco Pizarro smiled thinly. "Take all the horsemen. Capture the man on the litter alive. The rest of us will guard your rear against the larger army."

But they did not know the person in the litter was the Unique Inca, Felipe told himself. Maybe it was . . . but Felipe could not think who else it might be. Macaw did not travel in a litter. Felipe had heard that the Taciturn chief traveled in a litter, but he had never seen him except on the Spanish ship. Besides, if that chief had traveled to Recognition, surely he would be with the Unique Inca.

Even as Francisco Pizarro and Hernando de Soto spoke, the rest of the horsemen began to climb onto their already-saddled mounts, and the footmen to form into marching companies. Getting ready to fight was the one thing the Spanish could do without a lot of extra fuss and bother. As soon as the horsemen were mounted up, Hernando de Soto turned and led them east.

Francisco Pizarro followed immediately along with all the other men who were fit to fight. Felipe was left behind with the sick, the women, children, and the few others that the Spanish regarded as ragged people rather than Spanish. Maybe, somehow, the Inca army could defeat Francisco Pizarro and his army, but he had seen how the horses had destroyed the men of Incense. If the Unique Inca had only two thousand men with him, it would not be enough.

Felipe could not outrun the horses as they galloped toward the Unique Inca. Instead, he stared helplessly east toward the mountains. Go back, he willed Young Majesty and his forces silently. Go back.

18

FIFTH YEAR OF EXEMPLARY ROYAL HAPPINESS'S REIGN
GREAT RIPENING MONTH

In actual history, as Exemplary Fortune's troops approached the heart of the Four Quarters, Cable decided to lead his troops into battle himself. They were defeated. Cable himself was captured and later executed at Exemplary Fortune's command.

The Unique Inca's camp began stirring before dawn. Exemplary Fortune found himself half-hoping Cable would break his leg or do something else equally incapacitating. It was a stupid wish. Temporarily crippling the Unique Inca would neither give him the self-confidence he needed to rule nor get rid of the Beards.

Exemplary Fortune prayed with the others at the Sun's rising over the mountains, but he also put in a silent prayer afterward to Lakefoam, who seemed far more friendly toward him personally.

As they prepared to move out, Exemplary Fortune stood to the left of the Unique Inca. Everyone kept throwing him quick covert glances as if to ask how he'd got there. Cable ignored him, talking to Whence Reckoning and Exemplary Hawk, who were on his right.

The Unique Inca's troops took the only path down the west side of the hill, too narrow and steep for the Fingers to carry the Unique Inca in his litter. Cable walked, and the Fingers followed the party, taking their time maneuvering the golden litter around the turns on the narrow path with shattered rock faces above and steep drops below. The Unique Inca was in a good mood, scanning the land to the west for a formation of three hundred men, happily accepting Whence Reckoning's guesses as to where the Beards were hiding.

The two thousand men with the Unique Inca were not hiding. Coming down the hill in a long thin trickle, they could be seen to the horizon. No one except Exemplary Fortune worried about that. They wanted the Beards to find them.

By the time Cable reached the bottom of the hill, the other men had already formed up again, ready to move out. They waited in the shadow of the hill in the loose sand and stone for the Fingers to finish maneuvering the Inca's litter down the winding path. It would, thought Exemplary Fortune, be an easy place to get pinned by a superior force, but no one was thinking about that either. As the Fingers maneuvered the litter down the last slopes, a messenger with a baton in Inca Fox's colors came running up to them.

He made obeisance to the Unique Inca and reported, "The Beards are camped about eighteen miles downstream on a small bend in the Littlecorn River. They can't be counted without the scouts revealing themselves. Inca Fox is marching toward their camp."

Cable compressed his lips in annoyance and then relaxed again. "Good, we will meet him there." He sent a messenger of his own to Inca Fox, assuming, as Inca Fox evidently had, that the Beards either would not have scouts out or that the messenger would be able to evade them.

Exemplary Fortune kept his face very still. Any worry he showed would count against him. He could not act, not yet, not until everything fell apart, as it probably would. The Unique Inca and his men were too confident. Whence Reckoning, for one, should know that war was not a festival.

As the Fingers caught up with them, they set out. Within a half hour, they saw a small dust cloud, maybe ten men's worth, headed toward them. Before it got close enough for them to see its exact composition, it turned and went back the way it had come, toward the Beards' camp.

"They run from us," exalted Cable.

"Those were scouts," Exemplary Fortune corrected, unable to keep silent any longer.

"I must agree," said Whence Reckoning. "They have gone to tell the others we are here."

The Unique Inca compressed his lips and didn't say anything for a while. Exemplary Fortune kept his own mouth clamped shut with an effort. He already knew that nothing he said or did would change Cable's actions. Even if Whence Reckoning and all his other trusted advisors told the Unique Inca to go back up the cliffs, he would likely not do it.

They traveled for another two hours across the hot dusty desert alone without intelligence from dust or messengers. Not even condors flew overhead. Then the dust cloud reappeared, considerably larger this time. It grew in size with incredible speed, as though the men in it were running impossibly fast.

"Have the men ready their slings," Exemplary Fortune said to Cable, who was watching the spectacle with openmouthed fascination.

Cable shut his mouth, glanced at Exemplary Fortune, and then looked back at the dust cloud. "Ready slings," he ordered.

The dust cloud resolved itself into men up in the air atop something. There were not very many of them, no more than fifty, but they did not show any hesitation or other signs that would indicate they were unsure of their purpose.

Inca warriors ran forward, yelling and swinging their slings around their heads as the shadows under the Beards formed themselves into giant long-legged beasts that moved like an avalanche—fast and in a constant pattern. The Beards' heads were covered with a shiny something that had to be the Beards' hard metal. The first barrage of sling stones flew away with no visible effect.

"Go for their eyes," Exemplary Fortune found himself yelling, "go for their eyes." Even he did not even know whether he meant those of the animals or the men.

At the next barrage one of the front Beards reeled as though ready to fall, and two of his companions slowed their own beasts to stay with him. By then the rest of the Beards had met the Unique

Inca's fastest runners. The Beards wielded bright shining swords and, leaning down, began slashing into the Incas with the ease of farmers harvesting grain. They did not even seem to notice when Inca clubs and swords, reaching up, hit their legs or the beasts' sides. They slowed, but they did not stop, moving steadily through the men running at them, leaving bodies strewn behind them. They yelled as the Incas did. Their beasts reared up to smash the Inca warriors to the ground, their long teeth flashing like the Beards' metal in the sunlight. Some Incas hurled another round of stones, but many, like Exemplary Fortune, drew clubs or swords.

"Exemplary Fortune?" said Cable. His voice was filled with wonder rather than fear.

"Back, a slow retreat. Keep hitting them." The Beards were carving a bloody trail that reached directly for the Unique Inca. So far new warriors stepped into their path as soon as their companions were cut down, but no Beard had fallen since they had had to counter only handheld weapons.

As Cable relayed his orders, Exemplary Fortune resheathed his sword and got his sling ready again. Even with his companions between, the Beards were high enough to be easy targets.

As the Incas turned to retreat, the Spanish moved in on them and, moving several times faster than the walkers could, slashed them down even more readily, or else ignored them altogether. They moved ever more quickly toward the Unique Inca. A few of the less experienced Incas began to panic as the Beards made their inexorable way through the army, opening yet more room for the beasts. They could not retreat without allowing the Beards their chance at the Unique Inca. They could not retreat.

"Cancel that order. Stand fast. Use slings." Exemplary Fortune was using his command voice, for there was no time to relay orders. In any case, Cable repeated his commands as soon as he said them.

It worked after a fashion. The Beards' advance on the Unique Inca was halted, but they did not retreat. In the middle of the Inca forces, they were destroying men so quickly that their tiny numbers would eventually overwhelm the army. The holes that they hacked around themselves filled more and more slowly. The exultant cries of the Beards, and the moans and cries of the Inca wounded, told the whole story. The Beards swung their weapons with an ecstatic ease, and the Incas moved more and more clumsily as their hardest, highest blows merely seemed to show the Beards the proper targets to aim for.

As the Sun shortened their shadows, Exemplary Fortune could hear the fast hard breathing of men near panic all around him. They couldn't hold much longer. Another Beard slumped, and the Inca forces cheered, but that was what they were reduced to, cheering when one of the enemy went down to a hundred of theirs. Inca hands reached for the stricken Beard, but the other Beards maneuvered to get him and his beast into their ranks and protected before the Incas could pull him down.

One of the leading Beards said something to his fellows, waving in Cable's direction. We should have put someone else in the litter, Exemplary Fortune thought inanely. In any case, they could not do a substitution in the middle of battle, not without the Beards noticing and not without opening up far too much room for those stinking beasts to get through. As the Beards made their determined rush at the litter, a clump of Inca warriors gave way as the beasts came toward them. The Beards picked up speed in spite of the weapons pounding on them. They were cutting people down now only as they had to, and far too many men were giving way without being hit.

"Protect your Unique Inca, you cowards," Exemplary Fortune yelled almost without being aware of what he was doing.

It nearly worked. Some men actually stepped in front of the beasts, but they were too few, and the Beards had too much momentum. As the Beards closed in on the Inca's litter, Exemplary Fortune and other of the commanders stepped between the litter and the ravening beasts towering over them. As a beast made to trample him, Exemplary Fortune aimed upward with his sword for the beast's head and hit something solid, but the beast's warrior merely leaned forward swinging his sword. Exemplary Fortune ducked low, using his sword as a shield, hoping at least to deflect the blow upward. The sword checked, and then something hard hit him on the head. He went down, trying to roll away from the beast's feet. He shook his head to clear it. He could not see out of his right eye. He rubbed his hand across his forehead, and it came away bloody. He should already have been trampled. Shakily, he pulled himself to his feet. He didn't have time to be injured.

New warriors in empire garb pushed up against the Beards and their beasts, stopping their advance. The Unique Inca's litter was down at an angle, canted against the bodies of its bearers along one side. Cable was on the ground, sitting up and looking dazed. The Beards, hacking fiercely at the newcomers, seemed unsure of whom they were headed toward. Exemplary Fortune backed slightly, ducking to avoid swinging weapons.

"You, you, you, you, you, and you," he picked six strong-looking uninjured men without the wild panicked eyes that so many had. "Pick him up, and get him out of here. Head for the hill . . . as though the bunch of you are running away. Don't let them see it's Cable if you can help it. Go now."

One of them scooped the Inca up in his arms, and three of the others formed a wedge to get them through the packed troops around the Beards. The new warriors were actually trying to get closer to the Beards and their awful animals.

"Who's your commander?" Exemplary Fortune demanded of one the newcomers.

"Inca Fox," the man replied.

"Where?"

The man pointed, and Exemplary Fortune went that way against the flow of soldiers moving in. He said, "Excuse me" constantly to show he wasn't running away.

Inca Fox was probably only twenty feet away, but it seemed to take an immeasurably long time to get there. "Where's Cable?" was his demand-greeting.

"Not here. I sent him back toward the hill without his litter. We can retreat now," Exemplary Fortune said.

"Retreat? There's only forty of them."

"Have you seen any go down since your men arrived? We can discuss it on the way back."

Inca Fox's eyes raked Exemplary Fortune, taking in his injuries and general dishevelment. He nodded and gave the necessary orders.

"How many men do you have here?" Exemplary Fortune asked.

"Twenty thousand. Twenty thousand here, twenty thousand against the foot soldiers, ten thousand outside the city."

Twenty thousand should be enough to get them back to the hill, and then what? Exemplary Fortune had no idea what would stop the beasts. Standing with their back to the hill, they could hold them off longer than otherwise; but, unless someone found a way to turn the beasts back, they were dead. A few hours ago, it would have seemed impossible that forty men could overrun the whole empire, but he was no longer sure. They just kept killing people. As the army retreated slowly toward the hill, Exemplary Fortune watched Inca Fox's surety melt away like frost in the hot desert sun.

The Beards sat totally surrounded by a mass of enemy warriors and moved with a terrifying confidence. They reached out to slash, and men died. Whatever tricks, whatever weapons those men tried against them seemed to have no effect at all.

"Use slings," Exemplary Fortune told Inca Fox, and they actually brought one man off his beast with a well-placed stone.

He fell into the empire's men, who started clubbing at him. The other Beards, moving quickly, soon surrounded their fallen comrade with enough bodies that those in the middle were able to get down off their beasts. It was bitter that the Beards, who were so few, had men to spare to rescue one fallen warrior while the Inca's forces were leaving hundreds to rot on the ground. As though dropping one man were a signal, the Beards began to back out of the Four Quarters' army. The army parted to let them go, and, as soon as they were beyond the farthest ranks, some warriors dropped weapons and ran toward the hill.

"Keep your weapons," Exemplary Fortune yelled.

Between them, he, Inca Fox, and some of the captains were able to keep the core of the army from running, but the whole army was very close to total panic. It would not help. The beasts, even from a distance, could run them down. Exemplary Fortune began going from warrior to warrior trying to talk some heart into them. It was not easy. They all knew that if the Beards came back, there would be nothing they could do to stop them from killing everyone. All he could say was "Try for a good death, one that you will not be ashamed of when you meet your ancestors in the underworld." It seemed to help.

And the Beards' beastmen did come back. The Inca army was almost to the hill, but the path up was clogged with those who had totally panicked, who had lost all sense of anything except for the need to get away. They had not even the sense anymore to stay on the path and not walk over those above them. So they kept knocking each other back to the desert floor, sometimes battered and broken. It was no longer possible to talk to them. For some of the men still functioning their bad example seemed to be a steadying influence. But others it brought closer to the edge of breakdown.

"Hold steady," Inca Fox yelled as the Beards bore down on them again, but Exemplary Fortune could feel that it wasn't going to work this time. They had been pushed too hard.

Then someone new was among them. A messenger. "Get them to the bottom of the hill," said the messenger. "Excellent Royalty's got some stones up top to throw down on them."

It was an excellent idea. Exemplary Fortune did not know if it would work or not, but at this point that hardly mattered. As word spread of something they could actually do, the men's eyes and motions steadied. They began once again to move with surety and purpose.

Inca Fox gave the army commands to retreat directly to the bottom of the cliff and then begin moving along it to the east. The beastmen followed the ever-retreating army without hesitation, slashing as they came. Their eyes were wild with victory and death.

The dreadful beasts would not step on the loose rock at the bottom of the hill, but otherwise the Beards did not seem even to notice that the cliff was there. They should be close enough. They had better be close enough. There was a heartstopping moment when the beastmen were in range and nothing fell on them, and then a large rock landed in their midst, smashing one beast and its man to the ground. Another rock followed, knocking a man off his beast. The small man who had been leading the Beards all day raised his arm and pointed back toward the coast. Another rock landed in their midst as they began their retreat, and everyone cheered.

Inca Fox and Exemplary Fortune looked at each other, and Exemplary Fortune managed a smile. "You look as though you could use a healer," said Inca Fox.

Exemplary Fortune nodded. He was suddenly too tired to talk, almost to stand up.

Inca Fox got the path cleared. It was not a pleasant task, with the bodies and the panicked. As soon as the path was clear, Inca Fox insisted that Exemplary Fortune be one of the first up. Two of Inca Fox's warriors helped him, and, as they approached the top, he was leaning on them heavily.

Excellent Royalty met him there. "He's been asking for you," he said, and led Exemplary Fortune, still leaning on Inca Fox's men, to the Unique Inca's tent.

Inside, the tent was very quiet, Cable an unmoving form beneath a blanket with healers on either side of him. His eyes were closed, and his skin had an unnatural grayish tinge. Exemplary Fortune sat down beside him. "Brother," he said. It was not what he would have said if he had thought first, but it felt right somehow.

Cable's eyes opened. They did not focus immediately, and Exemplary Fortune could almost see the act of will that let the Unique Inca see him. "Exemplary Fortune," said Cable in a voice that was barely a whisper. He paused to regather his strength. His eyes held Exemplary Fortune in an almost physical grip, as though he could communicate with sight alone. "You are the Unique Inca."

That was not what Exemplary Fortune had expected. "Broth . . ." he started again almost in protest, and then realized that was not what Cable needed. He took a deep breath to work the shock off and wet his lips. "I hear and obey." It seemed he should say or do something more, but he did not know what.

Cable's eyes drifted away from him, and then sharpened again on those on the other side of the bed. "Excellent . . ." but he could not say the full name in one try.

"I hear and obey," said Excellent Royalty. His voice was thick with as-yet-unshed tears.

"Shrewd . . ." said Cable.

Shrewd Reckoner, Cable's Divine Speaker, made a little protest noise. His face held a look of total disbelief, and it was several breaths' worth of time before he could get out the words "I hear and obey."

I'm going to have trouble with that one, thought Exemplary Fortune, shocking himself at the ease with which he accepted his new status.

Cable's eyes slid shut. A healer daubed at the corner of his mouth, and the cloth came away bloody. Another healer came over to Exemplary Fortune and, with the help of Inca Fox's men, got him to standing. He could barely move his feet, but he would not be carried out, not into the sight of men who needed to be reassured that the Four Quarters was still intact.

Excellent Royalty followed them out of the tent. "Are you all right?" he asked anxiously.

Exemplary Fortune did not want to feel how badly damaged his body might be right now. "I hope so." He paused briefly, his thoughts refusing to let him rest. The Incas in Navel had to know of Exemplary Royal Happiness's decision as soon as possible so that, hearing of his death, they would not decide on a new Unique Inca before Exemplary Fortune had a chance to present his case. "Send a messenger relay with the Unique Inca's decision immediately. The rocks were an excellent idea. They saved us."

Excellent Royalty nodded. "I will do whatever you command."

That was not the formal response; that was a pledge of allegiance. Exemplary Fortune gave him a half-nod of acknowledgement. If Excellent Royalty would follow him willingly, then there was hope.

The healers pulled him away before he could think of the other things he needed to say. They took him to a nearby tent, where they lowered him onto a bed, stripped off his clothes, and fed him herb soup as they washed his wounds. He fell asleep while they were cleaning his hands. When he awoke, there would be a world to save, but for now he had to rest, gathering strength for the coming test.

AFTERWORD

The Incas say that they were created to rule all the tribes. It happened this way.

At the southern end of Lake Titicaca, Lakefoam and his assistants sculpted stone models of each tribe and painted them in their tribal colors, delineating their headbands, hair styles, and clothing. They gave each tribe the language it would speak, the songs and dances the tribe would perform, and the crops it would grow. Finally, they endowed each tribe with its name. Then Lakefoam buried the tribal models in the dark fertile earth, where they waited until He was ready to call them forth again.

From Lake Titicaca, Lakefoam and his assistants traveled north, calling forth each tribe from the mountain, spring, cave, tree, rock, or lake that would be its sacred ancestral home. One of Lakefoam's assistants walked along the coast of the Great Lake, and one walked at the edge of the eastern jungles. Lakefoam Himself walked through the mountain valleys. "O peoples and tribes," they called, naming each tribe as they spoke, "hear and obey the command of Lakefoam, who orders you to come out, multiply, and bring fertility to the Earth."

Now, when Lakefoam had made the models of the eight who would be the ancestral Incas, the Sun Himself had put a gold staff into Majestic Headband's right hand or, some say, Mother Chosen's hand. This was the Sun's sign that these were His chosen children and that He had ordained them to rule all the other tribes.

When Lakefoam called the Incas' ancestors from the cave at Origin Tampu, they carried the Sun's staff with them as they emerged into the world. The eight walked north from their origin cave looking for the valley that the Sun had ordained for them. When they reached each valley, the ancestral Incas would throw the gold staff into the soil, but, in the first valleys they came to, the soil was thin and the staff did not sink in to fertilize the Earth. None of these valleys would be the Incas' heartland.

Finally, after many adventures, the eight came to Navel Valley. This time, when they threw the gold staff into the soil, it sank completely into the rich black fertile earth. This was the valley promised them by the Sun. Navel Valley had abundant soil, life-giving streams, and a climate that promised bountiful corn crops. It would be a rich home from which to spread out and teach all the tribes to share the benefits of each other's knowledge and skills.

Archeologists say that, in the time after the fall of the Wari and Tiwanaku Empires, the whole of the Andes became one seething mass of warring tribes and clans. Mountains and hilltops sprouted walled fortresses. Some fortresses were surrounded by as many as seven or even nine defensive walls, so that if one wall were breached by a besieging enemy, the fortress's people could retreat into their next refuge.

Only in Navel valley and the surrounding area, from Ollantay-tambo in Spider Plain Valley thirty miles north of Navel through Paruro fifty miles south, was the land free of defensive walls and hilltop strongholds. Here, where the Incas first established their hegemony, settlements were built because they were on the easiest route from one place to another, and they were built without walls. Undefended hamlets of only a few dwellings were built close to fertile cropland or good grazing for llamas.

When the Incas began to spread out from Navel and bring other tribes into their growing empire, they made each tribe and clan abandon its hilltop fortresses. The Incas promised that, as long as the empire lasted, each tribe would be valued for its own par-ticular genius. They promised there would be peace and prosperity for everyone throughout the Four Quarters.

•   •   •

When the last Unique Inca was killed, his body was buried in the earth, somewhere near Navel. Today, the Andean people say that, down in the dark fertile earth, his body is growing a new head. They say that, when his head is fully regrown, he will come out of the earth to reestablish the Inca empire. They say that the world will be turned upside down again, as in the days of World Reverser. Who can say this will not happen?